# Keep My Secrets

# Keep My Secrets

Elena Wilkes

hera

First published in the United Kingdom in 2021 by

Hera Books
28b Cricketfield Road
London, E5 8NS
United Kingdom



A CIP catalogue record for this book is available from the British Library.

Print ISBN 978 1 80032 611 8
Ebook ISBN 978 1 912973 57 6



Look for more great books at www.herabooks.com

Printed and bound in Great Britain by Clays Ltd, Elcograf S.p.A.

1

# *Prologue*

## *Then*

The girl knows she's going to die.

She drags herself back on her elbows, the gritty boards digging into the soft skin of her forearms as her heels struggle to find purchase. There's the jangle of a belt buckle in the darkness and the canal boat pitches gently with the swell. Her terror ratchets higher.

*Please no.*

*Stop.*

Her eyes widen as her breath wheezes in her lungs.

*No.*

'You don't want to do this. You know you don't.'

But death is closing in and she wants to survive, no matter what.

'You can do whatever you want, I promise I won't say anything.'

Tiny sparks flash and burn in front of her eyes. She touches her temple where she hit her head. Her fingers drift to the place on her throat where the red weal burns.

*It's not far to the bank. If she shows she's totally compliant, then…*

She shuffles back on her bottom, levering herself up onto the boat side and glances out at the black water. Her eyes search that dark, undulating emptiness. She longs for the lights of the town, to be back at that party again, to see people.

*It was safe there; you should have stayed.*

But it's not safe here.

There's a rustle out there and the boat rocks – the hands on her pause. *Someone's there? Her rescue?*

Everything freezes. She snatches round and takes her chance. *Now!* There's a scramble towards the side, but her knee catches on something hard and she lurches sideways, the bank, so close, her hands reaching out, her arms flailing, meeting—

Skin.

Warmth.

Strength.

Someone's here. *Thank god.* Someone whose grip is tight and can save her.

*Thank god you're here.*

They won't let anything bad happen, she's sure of that. She can trust them: they'll stop all this. But these hands move in a way she's not expecting – they loosen and grip again, towards her shoulder this time. Aggressive. She's shoved hard, the power of the blow knocking her backwards, and her ankle twists in a shock of pain. She loses her balance, toppling awkwardly, grasping out but falling – her hip cracking on the side of the boat. The sudden shock and plunge of water punches into her mouth and eyes. She breathes in only water; it fills and chokes and squeezes her lungs until all she can hear is the banging echo of escaping bubbles skimming past her face.

The pain in her head clamps down, vice-like. It's unbearable: a pressure beyond pressure, an agony that grows and grows until she thinks her skull might burst. She gropes wildly, lungs burning, her hands reaching up out of the water to grab the hands that are holding her down. She fights, her mouth just breaking the surface to furiously suck at the air. Her eyes are wide open, popping with terror and the sheer will to survive.

'… *No… Please!…*'

The two faces hang above her like a pair of pale balloons, bobbing with effort. The moonlight picks out their mouths set with determination, the flare of their nostrils, but their eyes tell her what she already knows. They want her dead.

The stars above her head pulse dully with the beating of her heart that gets smaller and smaller. Her hair whispers across her face as her hand trails out in the water. The faces gaze down blankly, their images reflected, one to the other, knowing, from this moment on, and for eternity, the three of them are bound together forever.

# Chapter One

*Now*

Frankie walks quickly towards her car from the children's care home. It's still raining hard and the wind is getting up. The only sounds are the echo of her footsteps on the black tarmac; it's so dark she can't see her own feet moving.

Over in the distance, the bulky outline of Caer Caradoc and the trail of the Long Mynd hills sit blackly against the darkening skyline of the Welsh border. Tucking her chin closer into her jacket, she blips the immobiliser. It flashes a reassuring orange into the ghost outline of the hedges as she drops her case into the back.

There are no streetlamps this far out of town. Slipping into the driver's seat, she fumbles a little for the ignition as the engine turns over. The squeal of the wipers startles her and sets her heart racing. She finds her hands are shaking.

*I'm not scared*, she tells herself. *It's just the adrenaline from all that earlier bravado*.

*You've done good today, Frankie.* She presses her lips together in determination. *Concentrate on that.*

Taking a deep breath, she begins to pull away. The road is quiet as her car picks up speed.

*Come on, get a grip, Frankie. Thirty minutes and you'll be home.*

It's Friday, well after going home time and the road is eerily dark. Her car headlights leap awkwardly, illuminating only a small stretch of the black tunnel ahead.

Letting the air slowly out of her lungs, she tries to relax her shoulders from up around her ears and she glances warily into the rear-view mirror. No one would believe this was the same woman who'd been trying to talk a teenager from a roof just half an hour ago. She wavers a smile at the memory. She doesn't think that getting up on a line of ridge tiles in the pouring rain is high priority on her regional manager's job description, but that's precisely what she did.

She closes her eyes briefly. *See? Think about the good stuff and block everything else out.*

The radio fizzes and floats in and out of its station and her eyes sweep again and again into the shadows in the hedgerows. She concentrates hard on the shining road in front of her. But her eyes keep flitting back.

*This isn't working.*

There's something about being in the car at night: that feeling of not really being alone. She keeps thinking that there's something else in here with her—

Her eyes flick up to the mirror.

That back headrest is just a headrest. She's fully aware of that. It's not a man sitting with his head bowed. *Don't be ridiculous Frankie Turner, you're thirty-three years old, not three.*

But her three-year-old self knows that if she keeps watching she'll glimpse a movement, a darkness that will slowly detach itself, and if she keeps listening she'll detect the quiet draw and pull of someone breathing.

*No.*

*Stop it.*

There's no one there. You know there's not. She chews her lip. *You know this because you deliberately checked the back seat.*

The rain is beginning to slant in fine shards through the beam of headlights, the skeins twisting down the windscreen, forcing the wipers to dash pointlessly back and forth. She grimaces, screwing up her eyes, trying to peer through the pouring streams.

*Home soon, home soon, home soon...*

*What's with all this front, Frankie?* her head says. *Who are you trying to kid? Just look at you – Look at you in your fancy Range Rover, desperate to get back to your nice upmarket husband and your upmarket country cottage. You're such a fraud, you know that? Drive as fast as you like Frankie-girl, the past is coming up right behind you.*

She swallows and stares hard into the lashing water. All she has to do right now is stay in control and not get spooked. It's not difficult; she's been doing it long enough. All she needs to do is stay in control of the car... Of herself... Of her life.

The radio station suddenly clears and she grips the wheel tighter. *Come on Frankie, you've got this.* She hesitantly begins to hum along. She likes this song: it's 'Where is the Love?' by The Black Eyed Peas. She even knows some of the words.

That's better.

She smiles.

The radio fizzes and crackles. She goes to adjust the scan button, but it drops into silence.

There's a sudden flash.

The interior of the car lights up. She squints and takes a glance in the mirror. There's nothing but the searing dazzle of headlights behind. She dips the mirror and checks again. All she can see is a maddening white light and a ghost-like blur bobbing in her sightline. The tension in her gut mounts.

*Keep a hold now. Keep it steady.*

The lights rear up again like a charging beast. It's getting closer now: too close. The blazing flash patterns and strobes across the dashboard, momentarily blinding her. Her right thigh begins to shake, trying to hold the accelerator steady. She daren't brake. The road twists and bends in the bouncing arc of headlights as she desperately tries to concentrate, leaning into the windscreen and blinking like crazy. The familiar road is suddenly dangerous and unfamiliar. *Christ…*

Acute curves come up where there were none before, making her grip the wheel. She clicks the mirror up and snatches a glimpse of the car behind. There's a black figure, silhouetted in the driver's seat. A tiny knot forms in the base of her stomach. She hovers from brake to gas, not speeding up, not slowing down, and tries to breathe as the panic rises.

*He's too close… Far too close… Any second, any second now…*

A phosphorescent light floods the whole space. Each pulsing second ticks by; she can almost hear each one counting down before she'll feel the juddering tap and thud of the car touching her back bumper. There are trees and ditches on either side of the road and then just blackness going on and on, empty fields full of nothing and no one. If he runs her off the road… If she's trapped in this car…

Suddenly with one brilliant flash and a roar, the car pulls past. She glances quickly across. There's just a dark shadow whizzing by as the taillights flare red into the darkness. He guns away, disappearing round the bend into the black cavernous road and she finally manages to calm down, her stomach unfolding rapidly, the sudden relief quivering through her arms and legs. *Not him then, it wasn't him, just someone being stupid, that's all.* That. Is. All.

Dropping her speed to thirty, she attempts to collect herself as the Black Eyed Peas carry on singing and everything feels ordinary again. She tries to hum along, but knows that this time it won't work. Nothing's working. He wants her to know he's out there.

Every few days odd things have been happening. Whispered phone calls dropping into silence; a bouquet of flowers arriving on her work desk with no card; notes left under her windscreen wiper or propped against the front door, waiting for her. She's terrified Alex will find them. Every time she leaves the house or gets in the car, she finds her eyes flitting – looking, checking – because she knows that it could be today, or tonight, or in the early hours that she'll open her eyes to find he's taken it one step closer; it won't be a note or a call this time – it'll be a figure standing over her, staring down. She knows it's only a matter of time. And time is running out.

She swallows.

She knows he's circling. Because three days ago, she was followed.

He couldn't have known where she'd be and what time.

*Unless he was watching the house.*

The thought of it sends her almost hysterical.

*That was the whole point of moving here.*

When Alex had suggested a village in the Welsh Marches she'd jumped at the chance. He was stunned.

'Are you sure? You know it's a different way of living, don't you?' he'd laughed. 'You won't be able to move an inch without them noticing.'

But all the time she'd been thinking 'Yes, nothing gets past them, he'll *never* slip past them.'

But it seems he had.

She'd felt stupidly safe that day. She'd been at a conference in Ludlow with Diane, her boss. Diane had arranged to pick her up and drop her off, but by the time they got back, the unmarked country lanes around Church Stretton had become too complicated even for the GPS.

'Just drop me here, Di. It's fine. It'll save you from meeting any late-night tractors coming the other way.'

Diane looked supremely grateful to be heading back toward the main road and proper street lights at last. They'd said their goodbyes and she'd got out of the car not giving it a second thought.

It wasn't like it was far: a few minutes, that's all. There was a cut-through between the cottages that brought her practically opposite her front door. It was lit at both ends and she'd walked through there a hundred times; just five strides of darkness right in the middle, that was all, and then—

That was exactly where he'd been standing.

She instantly knew it had to be him. Her eyes locked and her feet automatically slowed. He didn't move. There he was: a black silhouette, caught in the moonlight. The alleyway was narrow, the pausing strike and scuff of her heels and her slightly laboured breath were the only sounds.

And then he started coming towards her.

She took a step back. She couldn't see his face. She could run, but he could catch her easily. The adrenaline surged – she was trapped and terrified, her mind whirled – but then he stopped suddenly and put his hand on the wall, before turning and walking away.

Nothing would work: her legs were wobbling and her heart was thudding painfully as she fumbled in her bag to find her phone.

'Alex? Alex, can you come outside?' She could hardly get the words out.

'Outside?' He sounded slightly anxious. 'Where are you?'

'Can you come outside and meet me? Diane's just dropped me off…' The words tumbled. 'It's a bit dark… I've come down the alleyway and I haven't got a torch.'

She heard his worried exhalation of breath. 'What the hell did you come that way for? Hang on. I'll be there in a sec.'

He'd hung up and in less than a minute, she saw the reassuring swing of a light coming towards her. She nearly ran to meet him, her legs barely holding her, containing her shivering and attempting to smile.

'You alright?' He put his arm around her, frowning. 'Has something happened?'

'I thought there was—'

'Was what?' He was sharp and protective. She bit the words back. *Why the hell had she said that?*

'I only said "thought". It was nothing. Just shadows. I was being daft. And why do I ever put these heels on?' She tutted, clinging onto his arm and pretended to be checking out the sole of her shoe allowing her to turn her face away. She'd panicked. *Alex couldn't ever know*. Her fingers skimmed the wall for balance. *He'd put his hand there – there on that wall*. A shiver went through her.

'I forgot I can't walk down this path in these. Complete madness.'

He'd laughed, made fun of her, allowing her to change the subject; she was aware the whole time of the scene playing over and over in her mind, joining all the other incidents: the calls, the flowers, the letters. He'd shown himself. He'd come out of the shadows. He was getting closer and more daring. *Jesus.*

The Black Eyed Peas have morphed into Lady Gaga as the finger signpost towards her village comes into view. The familiar fields line her road, guiding her home. It's comforting and utterly familiar – the lit cottage windows on either side, the shapes of cars and hedges parked out front – and then the heartening sight of her house. A tremble of relief instantly runs through her.

*All she has to do is get from the car, up the path, to the doorway – It's just a matter of a minute, two at the most. Then she'll be safe. Totally safe.*

Pulling onto the driveway, she forces herself to compartmentalise every thought and anxiety and put it away, at least for now, setting her face into a bland happy-to-be-home mask. *Alex must not know*. Killing the engine, she starts to count the seconds she knows it will take, gathering her briefcase from the back and then finding her keys from her bag and zipping it firmly back up. She focusses on steadying herself, fixing her face. She glances down, suddenly seeing that her clothes are beyond filthy; there are stripes of black across the front of her thighs and down her jacket.

Slotting her key in the lock, she pushes the door quietly open. The house feels empty.

'Hiya?' she calls out tentatively.

'I'm in here.'

She can tell by his voice that Alex is not happy but at least he's trying. As she treads down the backs of her sneakers and eases them off, the hallway light shows her just how filthy she is.

'Jesus! What's happened to you?' He is standing in the doorway looking her up and down.

'Ah...' She peels off her jacket. 'Yes, well... Thank god I was wearing flats this time. It's a bit of a story.'

'It looks like it.'

'I talked a girl down off a roof.'

'Jesus Christ, Frankie.'

'I climbed a ladder to get up there.'

His jaw drops in shock. She thinks for a moment that he might be angry but then he laughs, his whole face crumpling as he shakes his head. He's got such a lovely laugh; it's such a shame that she doesn't hear it so much these days.

He raises an eyebrow in amusement. 'Off a roof, eh?'

'Yeah. She was threatening to jump.' She dumps her bag down. Her hands look as though she's been changing car oil.

'Jump?' he frowns. 'Jeeze. She must have been in a state.'

'Yeah, I was scared the emergency services wouldn't get there in time. I happened to be around when it all kicked off.'

'You already know this girl?'

'Keeley? A bit. She's only been a resident for a couple of days, but I've seen her file so I know what she's been through. I've seen how quickly emotions can change if you don't get a handle on them... And anyway, she said she was armed—'

'Armed? For Christ's sa—'

'—with a potato peeler.' She gives him a wry look. 'Can you imagine? That's what I'm saying. There she was, sitting on a roof in the pouring rain with a vegetable scraper. It kind of sums up her pitiful life. She needed someone who really understood what she was going through.'

'And why does it always have to be you who gets these kids?' Alex looks annoyed but his eyes are soft.

'You know why. I was that girl, once upon a time.'

Alex leans forward and kisses her forehead. 'But you're not now. Look, why don't you go into the laundry and strip off in there while I run you a bath. You look absolutely shattered.' He moves past her, squeezing her hand briefly as he bounds up the stairs. The sudden touch shocks her. It feels like forever since he's spontaneously shown her any kind of affection at all.

'Yep, great idea.' She pads through the kitchen, knowing that her wet socks are leaving smears across the stone tiled floor. She instantly feels guilty about the mess and tries to tiptoe the rest of the way, but it doesn't make a lot of difference. Overhead, there's the sudden drumming of water into the bathtub as she begins to peel off the layers. Her guilt worsens as the slow-drifting scent of some kind of casserole twitches her nostrils and she peeps into the Rayburn where she sees a banana cake, her favourite, just beginning to rise. Her heart crumples just a little; *god, Alex*. Good, decent, kind, Alex, who's been through so much stress recently and yet he still tries, in all these little ways, to show how much he values her. How she wishes she could make him see the same value in himself.

'You coming up?' His voice echoes from the top of the stairs as she listens to the creak of him moving from the bathroom to their bedroom. 'This bath will be ready in a few minutes. I've put some bubble stuff in it.'

Her heart wavers just a touch. 'Lovely! Right. Perfect!' She tries to keep her tone light and grateful, but his words have sent her antennae twitching.

'Come on! Don't let it get cold!'

She takes a quick inward breath as she sneaks quickly across the kitchen in her bra and knickers and makes her way up the stairs. Not only has he run her a steaming scented bath, but he's also laid out her snuggly dressing gown and socks on the chair. He's trying to make things normal and right between them; she can see that. Perhaps tonight will be different. Perhaps tonight he'll try to be the old Alex she used to know, and they can sit down together, eat a meal, relax.

'I'll get the bottle of red I opened earlier, shall I? And bring up a couple of glasses.'

He disappears, leaving her to strip off, pin up her hair, and sink gratefully into the crackling bubbles. Lying back, she lets the water cluck into her ears, staring up to watch the condensation billow around the light fitting. The kinks of tension ease a little in her neck. She loves this room, this echoing space with its long, slanted ceiling, sash windows and a white turn-of-the-century fireplace with beautiful Art Nouveau tiles. This is the one room in the house where she can truly relax. She closes her eyes, trying not to dwell on what's happening downstairs, but she knows he's taking too long. Her stomach contracts. He'll be down there now, going through her bag. She knows it. She deliberately left it zipped at the foot of the stairs. He'll try to memorise its position, before rifling through the splay of jumbled contents, picking her phone up and trawling through the calls and checking the numbers. Then he'll work his way to the clothes on the laundry floor, going through the pockets, one by one. He won't know what he's looking for: some telling shop receipt perhaps, a suspect serviette from a café he doesn't recognise, some tiny inconsequential thing that he'll find to build a whole story around. He's even searched through the files on her computer, her Twitter account, her Insta, her WhatsApp.

Alex thinks she's having an affair.

She presses her lips together. Her irritation mixes with her guilt as it seeps quietly into the bathwater. She knows, because she's been monitoring him. She's set little traps: the event viewer on her PC to note the times he logs on, the strategically placed bits of paper in her handbag, the single strands of hair across the cover of her phone that have disappeared when she comes to use it. She knows it all, but if he ever found out about the flowers and the notes... A squall of dread clutches at her insides. She'd never explain. He'd never understand.

'Dinner smells wonderful.' She sets her face, gazing up at him appreciatively as he appears in her sightline clutching two wine glasses and an open wine bottle in the crook of his arm. He pours, handing one to her, and then settles himself on the wicker laundry basket.

She takes a sip. It slides thick and fruity across her tongue. 'God, that's good...'

'Frankie.'

She turns to find he's studying her. She wonders if he's going to tell her that he's been prying.

'I would never try and stop you doing something you wanted to do, you know that.'

'Okay.'

'But you really can't keep pulling these kinds of stunts.'

*No, clearly not.*

He leans forward cradling his glass, elbows on his knees. The chair creaks comfortingly. His eyes are full of genuine concern. 'Look, I understood it when you were working as a care worker with volatile kids on a day-to-day basis – even when you became a manager, I knew there'd be the occasional bump and bruise. But with this new job I was hoping you might just sit in endless boardroom meetings talking policy nonsense and analysing tick-box data.'

'Yeah, well, that's the thing.' Frankie tries to sound light-hearted. 'I'm not really a policy-and-tick-box-data kind of person, am I? We both know that.' She grins and takes another sip. *All this half-truth and pretence. Oh, how wonderful it would be to come clean.*

'But you can't carry on doing these things, you know that, Frankie. You'll come unstuck sooner or later.'

*If only he realised how close to the truth that was.*

'Yep, I know. But these kids are individuals, Alex. Keeley isn't a "case" or a name on a file to me. She's a real person. I *know* what she's going through. I know what that life is like.' She looks into his eyes.

'That was then, this is now.'

'Thanks to you.'

'But not anymore, we both know that.'

She knows what he's referring to. The failing business feels acutely personal.

'It will get better. All things pass.'

'As long as you don't pass on me.' He smiles but there's real pain there.

At that moment she doesn't care about the snooping and the prying. She only cares that his terrible gnawing, checking, compulsion comes to an end. She can see what it's doing to him and it's awful to watch.

*How easy it would be right now to tell him what's going on. How easy – And how totally selfish.*

'So that's why I thought I'd cook something special. I want us to relax over some food and good wine and chat about it all.'

'Yes, let's make a plan; let's take back some control. Let's make some decisions about the future – our future.'

She smiles but feels a twitch of uncertainty as he suddenly stands.

'Hold that thought, I'll be back in a sec, I just have to stir the casserole.' He makes a move to the door but then pauses. 'I'm very proud of you, Frankie. You do know that, don't you?'

She goes to speak but he interrupts her.

'Hold that thought, too,' he lifts a finger.

He's excited, but it feels brittle. 'I want dinner to be perfect tonight… I've got so many ideas to talk to you about.'

He dips and plants a kiss on her wet forehead. 'I've made your favourite pudding.'

'I know. I peeked. You're *seriously* lovely.'

He winks. 'Yeah. I have my moments.' And he pulls the door closed behind him.

The tap plinks into the sudden quiet. A gust of wind sends a scutter of rain and leaves across the Velux window on the landing. She sinks back into the heat of the water and nestles the wineglass against her cheek. She takes a deep breath.

The business will go under completely; it's gut-wrenchingly obvious. Every which way he's turned, the doors have closed in his face. The orders dwindled away, and his self-esteem went with them. She was pleased when he said he'd do voluntary work, but it's only served to make it ten times worse. Now he's there every day with the ex-offenders, the homeless, and the dispossessed. She lets the air out slowly. The whole bloody framework of his life has crumbled. He feels the loss as keenly as a razor cut.

'You can't imagine what it's like,' he keeps telling her. 'It's the loss of the family name that really gets to me. We go back generations. My father is an MP, my grandfather was massively successful as a landowner and businessman. There are baronets and peers right the way through my ancestry. We're practically feudal… We're not just a name, we're a clan.'

She does understand but she sees the millstone of it too. This whole torturous lead weight of 'McKenzie,' synonymous with handcrafted furniture. It's the enormous guilt that he, grandson of the great Dafydd McKenzie and of all those Scottish and Welsh 'B' list McKenzie aristocrats, *he*, Alex McKenzie, will be the one who'll have caused the family firm to fail. His two sisters do nothing. They're more than happy to stand back and watch his downward spiral with pursed lips and folded arms and an appalling kind of glee that their big brother is turning out to be what their father had always suspected: a soft-hearted incompetent nerd, devoid of manly backbone, a weak-charactered sop who had married far beneath him just to bolster his failing ego. Frankie had hated them on sight.

'Oh my goodness! Where on earth did you find her?' His sister Marianne had smirked. That just about summed Marianne up.

Alex had 'found' her crying on a park bench. He'd tried to cheer her up by buying them both a cup of tea and piece of chocolate cake from Starbucks and had sat chatting to her about the squirrels. He'd told her how they deceive other squirrels by pretending to bury their food in one place while the real stash was put somewhere safe.

She smiles at the memory.

'That's what going to school gives you.' She'd tried to wipe her eyes with the heel of her hand.

'Actually...' He'd handed her a tissue, tapping his foot amongst the litter at their feet. 'That's what reading "Fabulous Facts" on the back of crisp packets gives you.'

And she'd stopped crying and burst out laughing. No one in his family ever understood that about him: Alex didn't care where people came from, they were just people who sometimes just needed a bit of kindness. She listens to him now in the hallway, and she closes her eyes. How she'd love to reach back through the years and find that boy he used to be: that almost shy self-belief he had, that he would prove his family wrong, that he would never be the failure they all said he'd be. But she doesn't know where the boy has gone. His replacement is a man who is fragile, watchful, and wired tight.

'This came.'

She leaps up, sloshing her wine. 'Jesus, Alex!' She puts her fist on her thumping heart.

'Sorry.'

Something in his voice makes her look up at his face. He's standing there trying to look unconcerned and holding a parcel. It's a crumpled looking jiffy bag with her name in black felt tip scrawled across the front. Her throat constricts momentarily. She tries desperately not to swallow.

'I'll leave it here.' He props it on the windowsill and picks up his wine glass. 'I always like to see stuff addressed to Frankie Turner.' His tone is over-bright. 'It's good you kept your own name. Maybe I should've taken your name instead of keeping my own, what do you think?'

She should reply but can't find her voice.

'Are you expecting something nice?' He glosses over her silence. 'You should, you know. You should treat yourself to nice things.'

She clears her throat. Her fear feels shrill and acute.

'Oh, it's probably just something from eBay,' she manages. 'Yes… actually, I remember now. I bought a silk scarf. I'd forgotten all about it.' The thudding pulse in her neck moves into her jaw.

'It's just I thought I recognised the writing.'

'Yeah, probably. I've ordered from that seller before. She sells some nice stuff…' She's horrified at herself, how the lies slip out so easily.

He glances down and smiles. 'Ah. Right. You see, you don't get anything past me these days. Not now I'm a real homemaker and house-husband.'

He's trying to sound upbeat but the whole atmosphere in the room has changed. Her eye keeps sliding back to the thing that's sitting there on the sill. She knows the writing too. Her lungs feel like thin paper bags.

'Dinner will be on the table in ten. Will that give you enough time to drag yourself out of that bath, do you think?'

'I'll be there!' Her voice sounds tinny and false. He doesn't appear to notice as he goes over to the bag and absent-mindedly squeezes it. Her heart goes with it.

'Is it a man or a woman, this seller?'

'It's a woman. At least I think it is.' She lifts her arms to re-pin her hair that doesn't need re-pinning. The air pressure has dropped, and she realises her hands are trembling.

She's not going to query why he's asking. She wants him to just go. *Please. Leave it alone.*

He picks up the bag and turns it over.

'It's just that it's got an "X" on the seal... Like a kiss. Do women normally do that?'

She lets her hands drop into the heat of the water and turns her face to him, forcing her expression to appear calm.

'You can open it if you want, Alex. It's just a scarf.'

He looks back at her, his fingers pausing on the sealed edge. There's a heart-stopping terror that he might call her bluff, but she doesn't allow herself to blink. Her gaze is steady, open, innocent.

He drops his eyes and his face collapses. 'Shit, Frankie, I don't know what's wrong with me.' The bag slides awkwardly back onto the sill. 'I feel like I'm going mad... like, seriously mad. I'm sorry I keep doing this. I don't mean to. You've asked me to stop and I can't. I'm so sorry.'

'Alex...' She holds out a dripping hand. 'Alex,' she soothes. 'It's alright. It's okay. I would rather you tell me how you're feeling than hide it. Okay? I get it.'

He touches her fingers with his own and gives them a little squeeze.

'Whatever you've got into your head isn't real.' She tries to get him to meet her eyes. She gives his hand a little shake. 'I'm here, you're here. It's just us. Are you listening to me?'

He nods dumbly.

'Now go and check on that banana cake before I become so much of a prune we'll be having me with custard instead.'

They laugh and the pressure around them relaxes. She listens to his gentle tread as he makes his way back down the stairs. The thud in her throat sets her neck and shoulders shivering. Hauling herself slowly out of the water, she stands for a moment before shakily reaching for a towel from the rail. The wind outside has gathered strength. Behind the window blind there's the pattering shapes and shadows of trees. Her eye keeps being drawn to the parcel, sitting there, bland and innocuous. *She knows the writing.* She knows it as intimately as her own.

A tingle of fear inches across her scalp.

*She has no idea what he has in store for her, but she knows something is coming. She's always known.* It's taken him fifteen years. Fifteen years and now here he is – all her past and present and future is in this grubby yellow bag that she knows she has to open, knowing the moment she breaks the seal, she'll be undone too.

# *Chapter Two*

She pauses with one hand on the newel post at the bottom of the stairs, noticing that the zip on her bag is not as she left it. Her fingers tighten on the wood, but she knows she's not going to say a word.

The table in the kitchen is laid for dinner.

'This looks fantastic.' She tries to keep her voice upbeat while sliding into the bench seat. He's already put out a tureen of mashed potatoes and broccoli and a second bottle of wine. 'Napkins, too.' She barely recognises her own voice.

If he's aware, he's clearly not going to remark on it.

'Isn't it nice to eat at the table for once rather than on our laps?'

He deposits a huge cast iron pot onto the waiting mats and takes the lid off with an oven-gloved hand. Steam mushrooms in a cloud and she waves it away.

'That smells *dee-vine.*' She says it as though she means it, but her stomach feels sour and bloated with anxiety.

He puts down two plates and proffers the serving spoon. 'Dig in.'

She helps herself, ladling out the rich chunks of meat and gravy.

'Is that all you're having?'

She can hear the disappointment.

'I've got tons already.'

'That's hardly anything. Do you feel okay?'

'I'm just a bit knackered to be honest but it all looks fabulous.'

'Here.' He picks up the hidden spoon and dollops a whole pile of potato onto her plate. The sight of the glistening butter makes her feel queasy, but she distracts herself by picking up her wine glass and pretends to take a sip.

He sits down opposite, loading his plate and then picks up the wine bottle and refills both glasses even though they don't need filling.

'This sauce is amazing, what's in it?' She licks her lips.

'This and that… So, what did you think of your scarf?' He begins to concentrate on his food, shovelling up a whole mound of potato and meat. 'Is it what you wanted?'

'Perfect.'

She doesn't let her face register what's happening in her gut, pretending to wipe an imaginary spill from the table with her finger and then reaching again for her fork.

'What's wrong?' He pauses, mid-chew.

'Nothing's wrong.'

'So why aren't you eating?'

'Alex…' She goes to touch his hand, but he manages to drop his napkin at the same time and bends to retrieve it. She watches him, the way his hair flops across his forehead, that almost shy schoolboy expression she remembers as he pushes it back. So handsome. So lovely. She knows there's a tornado coming. Their whole relationship – this whole house of cards is standing right in its path. She has to do something, say something – but then she notices the shake in his hand.

He looks up at her expectantly. She can't do it to him.

'I wanted to say thank you for doing all this.'

He swallows with a kind of gulp and puts down his fork.

'Thank you for sticking around.'

She makes a half smile. 'Sticking around? Look, I've already sai—'

'Look, I'm not stupid. I know things haven't been easy. I know I've made things far worse between us. All my constant questioning of where you are and what you're doing... going on and on – I'm pushing us apart, I know that. That's what's made me think about our future.'

She steels herself. 'Alex—'

'No, seriously, listen—'

'I *am* being serious.'

'Yeah, but you're not listening. I want to talk to you about some ideas I've had. *Amazing* ideas.' He attempts a smile but it looks more like a grimace. Whatever's going on with him is making him agitated and intense. This doesn't look like excitement. It looks like desperation. She suddenly realises how near the surface his anxiety really is. It scares her a little.

He pauses and his shoulders jerk with tension.

'I'm sorry. I'm not explaining myself very well.' He attempts a little laugh. 'The thing is...' He spreads his palms. 'Just look at me, Frankie.' He glances into his lap and then back up at her. 'I've become an obsessive wreck. I do nothing all day, I see no one but the helpless and the vulnerable in one rundown community centre or another. We sit around on knackered chairs talking about how helpless and knackered we all are.' He musters a grin. 'I've gone from running a business to running us further and further into debt. I used to interview staff for management positions, now I'm going to Job Seekers and being interviewed by eighteen-year-olds with a couple of GCSEs in Media and Social Studies.'

'Alex.'

'Seriously, Frankie. Look at your life and look at mine. I'm going down the ladder, while you're going up it.' He shrugs. 'Literally, if today is anything to go by.'

They both manage a smile and she reaches over and touches his palm; it's cool and dry. 'I know this is just another way of putting yourself down. You have all this amazing ability, Alex, you just don't believe in yourself. You were the one who changed *my* life, remember?' She tries to sound upbeat and passionate. 'Not the other way around.'

But he only looks away.

'Come on, there would be no "ladder", as you put it, if it weren't for you. We both know that. Whatever we've built we've built together – fifty-fifty, equal partners, yes?'

But even as she says it, she knows it isn't true. Yes, it was Alex who'd encouraged her to go back into school and sit her exams and yes, it had been Alex who coached her and got her through them. They weren't fifty-fifty then. She'd been a tatty eighteen-year-old living a tatty chaotic life. He was a posh boy working in his father's business. She'd looked up to him then, admired him even, but now he'd become someone else: a man she lives with and cares for – but the "caring" for him is taking over, the "living" is less partners and more like housemates.

He won't meet her eye. He moves his hand away, picks up his wine glass and gestures at the room.

'When you think about it, it was my family—' She manages to disguise a sigh at the mention of them. '—It was my family who forced us into getting this place –

Christ, what a dump it was! Do you remember?' he chuckles.

She does. She remembers being able to look around the upstairs bedroom while standing in the kitchen.

'The hours and the nights we spent putting in that bloody floor.' Alex grins. 'The woodworm, the damp – hammering and sawing by poxy floodlight – you remember all that?'

She nods and a sadness rushes over her. They were happy then.

'Their hatred, their bloody awful behaviour, forced us all the way out here, and it made us work together, *build* something together. This house *is* us, Frankie. It's our marriage. We've moulded it and shaped it and added bits and created it together over the years. We were happy then.'

It's as though he's reading her mind. Living here was like stepping out of the real world. The tiny hamlet of Myndnor. Even the name sounded Middle-Earth. The hills sat in a brooding protective ring, the border Marches, separating one country from another: old self from new self, leaving it all behind. She gazes round at the latticed windows, the gorgeous stone floor that she'd lovingly scrubbed for hours on her hands and knees and restored to its pocked and pitted beauty.

'So would you do it all again?'

'I know you're worried.'

'You didn't answer my question.' He closes his eyes and takes a long mouthful of wine.

'We've been over and over this, Alex. None of this is important. I know we have this fabulous old rambling house, but it's stones and mortar. I want us to get back to where we were. I want you to get back to the person you were. I want you to be happy.'

'Then let's sell it.'

'What?'

'Let's pack up and go somewhere and do it all again. Deep into Wales, maybe. Somewhere with proper land and outbuildings. Think of the kids you work with. You've always said the challenge for the sixteen to eighteen-year-olds is that no one will give them a chance – well, I will, Frankie. I'll give them a roof over their head and some kind of future. I'll do that – *We* can do that. We'll talk to the local education authority and see if we can apply for grants to become a bona fide training provider. I'm qualified aren't I? I'll teach them skills: woodworking, carving, upholstery. It would be a massive change for both of us. But it would mean I can start again, properly. I could be my own person, and you could be involved in something real and meaningful, not just day after day of systems and paperwork procedures and dead-end dross.'

The glass swings back, the wine sloshing dangerously.

She opens her mouth but then changes her mind.

'Go on. You were just about to tell me I'm wrong.' He's prickly, she can tell.

'I don't see my work like that.' She keeps her voice small.

'But that's how I've heard you describe it Frankie – more than once, so why aren't you excited?'

'I was probably frustrated about something when I said it. I—'

'You're not even prepared to talk about my idea, are you? Why are you defending a job you know doesn't give those kids a proper chance?'

'I'm not defending it.'

'Yes, you are. You know you are. You're defending a rubbish system.'

She knows where this is going. The direction it always goes.

'We'd free up so much capital by selling this place and then buying in Wales, you know that. It's a no-brainer. It'd give you everything you say you've dreamt about doing – you can really change kids' lives and we can have a proper life again.'

She pauses. The pause is a mistake.

'So it's not about the kids?'

'Of course it's about the kids. It's always about the kids.'

'But it feels like something else is holding you there too.'

She watches his eyes narrow a little. 'Or should I be saying some*one*?'

'Oh, for fuck's sake, Alex!'

As soon as the words leave her lips, she instantly regrets it. His face blanches a little, and then his mouth hardens into a thin, hard line. He turns his face away.

'Don't worry. I've known it for a while now – I know what you really think of me. And do you know what? I don't blame you. I feel exactly the same.'

He lurches from aggression to victim in seconds. Drinking just makes it so much worse.

'So, go on then, tell me, what's our future then, eh? What does it look like? Give me a picture of how you see us living over the next five years, Frankie, and I'll be able to see how I slot in.'

And so it starts yet again. She listens, knowing the argument as intimately as if she's the one reciting it: a downward spiral that never goes anywhere. Soon he will move onto why they haven't talked about having children of their own. She's thirty-three. How much longer does she plan to leave it? Or does she plan to leave it forever? It is the subject they can never discuss.

She knows why.

But he doesn't.

*Christ.*

Her phone suddenly bursts into life, shrilling loudly on the counter-top where she left it. He stops talking as her eyes flit across. His own wince with rage and go dull.

'Go on then. Answer it. I know you want to.' He turns away, back to his food, banging his glass on the table and hunching his shoulders against her.

'Alex—'

'No. Go on.'

She wavers for a moment, thinking it might be about Keeley, before reaching to pick it up.

'Hello?'

'Ah. Frankie.' It's Diane.

She bites her lip, hard.

'I suspect you know what I'm going to say.'

She sighs. Now of all times. This is all she needs.

'You know I've always backed you up. I've always taken your side and argued your case. You know that, don't you?'

She knows the word 'but' is coming.

'But on this occasion, I'm afraid you've crossed the line.'

'I know.'

She looks across at Alex.

'It's out of my hands.'

'Yes.'

He's sitting staring at the wall.

'My boss's boss wants a conversation.'

Frankie can't imagine who the boss's boss might be. Someone ministerial? *She really is done for.*

'Just as a head's up, you're probably going to get a written warning this time.'

'Right.' She feels her cheeks burn with humiliation.

'Go on.'

'Go on, what?'

'Prepare me. Give me the worst of it. I'll have to hear it twenty times over from my boss, so I might as well get it from the horse's mouth first. Do I need to sit down?'

'Err... Probably.' Frankie squirms a little and clears her throat. She looks across at Alex. He's chewing, staring at the far wall. She knows by the set of his neck this is it for the night.

'Frankie?'

'Oh, yes. Sorry...'

'You told Declan to unlock the storage container and get the ladder.'

Frankie cringes at the memory. Diane is right, it was utterly, utterly reckless.

'And then what?' Diane sighs.

'I went up it.'

'I gathered that.'

'Onto the ridge tiles.'

Frankie hears Diane's sudden sharp intake of breath. 'And?'

'Mmm.' Frankie bites her lip even harder.

'I didn't catch that.'

'I told her I'd jump off the roof with her.'

'You encouraged a vulnerable teenager to jump off a roof, Frankie. Have I got that right?'

'Sort of.'

'What does "sort of" mean?'

'I said "you jump, and I jump too."'

'Dear Lord, Frankie.'

Frankie finds her lip is sore where she's chewed it so hard. Thing is, she knew she understood Keeley. She'd glanced up at that poor frightened kid, feeling the last rung of the ladder skid a little against the guttering as she levered up onto the tiles. She hoped her face wasn't betraying the sudden terror as her knee slithered sideways. There was Keeley's scowling face glaring down. She'd almost smiled: in all that glowering aggression, she saw her own teenage self: '*people hurt you*,' the expression said. That was the lesson they had both learned really well.

'Are you seriously off your nut?' Keeley's scowl burst into shocked incredulity. 'Has anyone ever told you you're off your fucking head?'

Another gust of wind had whipped across the roofline. She did have a very valid point. 'You lay a finger on me and I'll do you for assault, you mad cow! My brief will get you the sack.' But her eyes were darting uneasily. She licked her lips.

Frankie didn't answer. She jacked one knee under her and carefully began to crab-crouch her way towards the ridge tiles.

'You mad bitch!… You can't do this!…' Keeley huffed and puffed, but Frankie kept on going before she finally reached the roof edge and hauled herself up. She looked into Keeley's outraged face, studying her for a few seconds. 'You know, I think you're right.'

Keeley looked back, her mouth opening and closing.

'You really are. I think you've got the whole situation sewn up. I get the sack and then you can go back to sitting in one care home or another, doing what you've been doing for the last seven years: kicking off, smashing up, barricading yourself in bedrooms, overdosing, assaulting staff, cutting your wrists, and screaming the place down—'

'Like you'd know!'

'Well, actually I do.' Frankie put her head on one side. A blast of rain buffeted her and she gripped on tighter. 'I've been right where you are now. I mean, not this exact roof, you understand, but one very much like it. The only difference was, no one came up to sit with me. No one ever said: "whatever happens, I'm with you." If they had, things might've turned out very differently.' She paused. 'So I'm giving you something that I didn't have. I know you feel terrified and lost and you think no one is listening, but actually, I am. There's the difference, Keeley. What I'm saying to you is: you are not alone. You hear that? You are *not* alone, because I'm with you.'

Keeley could only stare at her.

'So you've got a couple of choices.' Frankie jacked her knees under her into a crouch. She wobbled a little in a gust of wind and took a quick glance at the ground. 'Are you going or are you staying?'

Keeley's mouth was slightly open. 'What d'you mean going? Going where?'

'Off the edge.'

'Eh?'

'Sorry, I thought that was what you wanted? You're right. What have I got to go back down for? No job? Humiliation? A whole raft of charges? You're absolutely right.'

Keeley looked at her in horror, her cheeks quivering. Frankie instantly made her move. Quickly placing her feet under her she took her first few steps as smoothly and as gracefully as a gymnast doing floor exercises. Only she wasn't on a floor, she was making her way along a four-inch tile, thirty feet off the ground, before calmly reaching around the chimney stack and grabbing the hand of the shocked teenager. Keeley reeled sideways teetering for a moment, but Frankie only held on tighter.

'Let me go!' she screamed.

Panting, Frankie regained her footing as the blare of a loudhailer from a police van down below bellowed through the air.

'You ready?' Frankie looked at the stunned girl. 'We're doing this, then? You and me? Let's do it. One… Two… All you have to do is say "three" and we're there. Come on Keeley! One… Two…'

Frankie pauses as she recounts the tale. There's a silence on the end of the line for a moment.

'I know it comes over as a little unorthodox, but what I was trying to do was—'

'I know what you were trying to do. You've just told me.' Diane cuts across sharply. 'But it's not like you're some rookie, is it Frankie? You know how this looks to the powers that be.'

*Maybe Alex is right. Maybe she isn't in the right job.*

'I've now got to defend your actions… If I can.'

'I'm sorry, Di.'

'*Oh, please!*' Diane guffaws. 'You're not sorry at all!'

'I am. I should have thought.'

'You did think. You made a very clear decision. Own it.'

Frankie screws up her eyes but says nothing, Diane is so right.

'You were offered this job specifically because you're not just another pale middle-class male in a suit. Which is why…' Diane halts, '… and I shall deny this part of the conversation if you repeat it… Which is why I think what you did this afternoon was extraordinary. Bloody stupid, utterly reckless, but extraordinary. Keeley believed you. You made her believe that you really cared—'

Frankie opens her eyes, feeling the tears suddenly prick. 'I do really care.'

'And the consequences are that Keeley Grainger, the spitting and screaming and swearing Keeley Grainger, sat herself down in Declan's office only an hour ago and said she was sorry.'

'She did?' Frankie blinks the tears away.

Di chuckles. 'Well, not exactly in those words, but near enough. Maybe it won't last, maybe she'll revert to her old behaviour, but all I can say is, tonight she is a changed girl and that can only be down to you.'

'Thank you.' Frankie can't think of anything else to say. She glances back at Alex, aware that his back is a brick wall of unhappiness. She can see the side of his face, his jaw working steadily but she can tell there's no pleasure in it. Diane is still talking about the possibility of a disciplinary hearing, of paperwork, of interviews and questions that have to be asked, but she's hardly hearing any of it right now.

'Di, I really appreciate—' But she doesn't have to say anything further.

'Oh god, sorry,' she cuts across her. 'I'm getting carried away here, aren't I? This is your Friday night and I'm eating into your weekend. All this work stuff can wait. Give my love to Alex and I'll see you on Monday.'

'Great. Thanks. Thanks for all the support.'

She ends the call and gently slides the phone back onto the counter and a deep flutter of satisfaction thrills through her. Alex doesn't speak. The atmosphere in the room is palpable with tension. She goes and sits and picks up her napkin.

'So?'

'It was Di.'

'Of course it was. Who else would you be so desperate to speak to?'

'Don't be like that.'

How she would love to share Diane's conversation with him. How she would love to blurt out that tonight Keeley is a 'changed girl' and somehow her actions have made a difference: that her job isn't all about protocols and paperwork – it's about seeing kids as people with potential – But she knows even a hint will just make everything much, much worse.

'You haven't been in five minutes.' He chucks his fork down with a clatter. 'You've been out of the house for twelve hours. Twelve. All I wanted was an hour of just us – one *hour* but even that's not possible.'

The final flutter of joy fades away. 'You're right, you're right,' she soothes. 'I'm sorry. I find it so difficult to switch off because it matters a lot to me, but you're ri—'

'You mean "it" matters a lot, but I don't. Or if I do, there's a queue and all those kids come first.'

He's like a sulky child now: wounded and angry and unforgiving.

'Alex, don't be like this. It's the kind of job that req—'

'But it's not though, is it Frankie? It's not a *job*. Climbing onto roofs is not a social services job. No one else would dream of doing that! You do it because you're compelled to. It's something inside you. You're driven. Even with the threat of the sack you won't stop. And one day you're going to meet someone who is just as driven and as passionate as you are, and who "gets" you. Someone who really understands who you are.'

'But that's you!'

'I thought I was that person.' He pauses and leans back, folding his arms. 'But let's get it out into the open, Frankie: you come home late, and you go out early. You're distracted and distant a lot of the time. You're evasive. I know something isn't quite right. I don't know if you're lying to me, exactly…' He looks at her, his eyes meet hers.

*Tell him*, a voice in her head instructs her. *Tell him what's been going on. It's better than torturing him like this.* But she finds her eyes automatically sliding away.

'Like doing that.' He glares at her. 'Can't you just be straight with me, Frankie? Be deathly honest. I can take it. It's far, far better than deceit.'

His face is pale: pinched raw with emotion.

She goes to speak but stops.

'*Arghh*, what's the point?' He shoves the seat back and it judders with a squeal across the floor.

'Where are you going?'

But he ignores her. She listens to the weighted tread as he makes his way up the stairs and then the shunt of their bedroom door as it opens and closes. She stares down at her plate of congealing food and his, mostly uneaten. She considers going after him but knows it will only make it worse. *What's happened to them both? How have they got here?*

She slumps at the table and rests the heels of her hands into her eye sockets. She knows exactly how they've got here. *How long do you really think you can keep all these secrets, Frankie? How long before he finds out exactly what you've done? You're deceiving the man who you swore to love and cherish. Are you pleased with yourself? Look at him; he's so fragile he's almost broken, and now you're going to be the one who snaps him in two.*

She glances over at the window. The blind is open and she finds herself unable to get up and close it. Some warning vibration outside in the blackness tells her he could be out there. The blank pane of glass sits there, dark and square. If she stands up he'll be able to see her but she won't see him. She has this terrible thought: what if he was there watching that whole performance? What if he's just waiting for the right moment to knock on the door? How long will it be before he makes himself known and her whole carefully constructed world comes tumbling down?

She can hear Alex walking across the landing; the loose board by her office door creaks violently.

She gets up from the table, switches the kitchen lights off and creeps up the stairs, listening for the sound of the electric toothbrush or the swish of the water down the drain, but it doesn't come; the bathroom is still and silent. Their bedroom door is tightly closed. When she clicks it open, she's shocked to find he's gone to bed, the mound of duvet is just a shadowy huddle.

She goes into the bathroom to clean her teeth and then gets undressed quietly and slides under the covers beside him. She knows that sleep is probably several hours away. She lies there, staring up at the ceiling, watching the weird shadows around the pendant light as the breeze from the window catches the shade. She hears the sounds of the foxes crying across the fields, all the while listening to the man beside her, knowing that he's awake too – unhappy and not knowing how to express it. She's never told him the truth, not even from the very moment they met.

Somewhere, down the hallway, that parcel is calling to her from its hiding place. She closes her eyes but it makes no difference: *he's* calling to her and she knows it.

Everything, from that day on the park bench to now, has been a fabrication: her marriage to Alex, their relationship, the last fifteen years is a sham. He's out there and he wants her and she knows it.

How can she even bring herself to think about that man? She disgusts herself. But there's a tiny part of her that remembers the tiny part of him that was good and kind and beautiful, and that's the tiny part of her that wants him, too.

## *Chapter Three*

She opens her eyes with a start and the grind in her stomach begins churning again. It's just light and the house feels strangely still. She looks across at the dented pillow. She didn't feel Alex get up and she certainly didn't hear him leave. She puts her hand out. The space beside her is hours cold.

Swinging her legs from the bed she goes over to the window and pulls open the curtains. His car's not on the drive. It's Saturday morning. He could have gone anywhere.

Pulling on yoga pants and a sweatshirt, she walks quickly along the landing to her office. Her desk sits there, clear and tidy. All the usual things for working from home are laid out: the wigwam of pens she never uses; the papers in their tray; the black screen of her PC, and her mouse lined up neatly.

Silently, she wheels the leather chair back and crouches to kneel beneath the desk. She feels with her fingertips for the back where the board has come loose. Levering it a little wider, she gingerly draws out a large, crumpled envelope, and then reaches in again for the jiffy bag. The seal opens easily and she shakes its contents out across the floor.

At first, the thing doesn't register. It lies, curled slightly, an old bit of red jersey fabric with crumpled silk flowers badly tacked along one edge. She swallows. Something from a long way back taps at her memory and her heart squeezes in a vice. The panic rises. Of course she knows what it is. She looks down at it, feeling oddly light-headed. Her mind conjures up images of flickering strobe light whirling across a ceiling, the sweep of long blonde hair, the buzz-thump of the music shivering under her ribs as she watches the girl raise her arms as she moves, sinuous and sexy, the coloured lights catching the contours of her beautiful face, the red fabric stripe against the blonde, like a deep crimson gash.

Her hand comes up to her mouth. *Oh. My. God.* It's the hairband.

She glances up at the window at the bank of uninterrupted morning sky. It's the same sky, same blue, but nothing is the same. She picks up the jiffy bag and turns it over. The postmark is an over-stamped blur. So this is it. This is the thing she was afraid of, and it's here: now. The tatty envelope sits on the floor next to her knee. She doesn't need to look at the contents; she knows what's in there. Opening the flap, she draws out one of the folded pieces of paper. She knows what's written on it; she knows what's written on them all.

> *Did you think I'd never find you?*

She can hear his voice saying the words. Her fingers flit over the next.

> *You can never run away, Frankie. You're mine. I'm yours.*

She can't read any more. Bundling the envelope back beneath the desk, she goes to grab up the notes, but there's a flash and the phone suddenly jangles into life.

Her heart ramps up, her eyes snatch to the handset on the desk where it sits, lighting up and drilling into the silence. Her hand grabs for it.

'Hello?'

She glances at the window again. Is he out there? Crouching on her haunches, she peers above the sill. The village lane is empty.

'Hello?'

An anxiety beneath her heart begins to flutter. The sky has that blank, dead look as though some sort of nerve gas has taken out every living thing.

'Who is this?'

At the end of the line there's the quiet purr of someone breathing.

'Can you please answer? Or I shall put the phone down.' She is aware of the begging shake in her voice. She thinks about saying his name, the one she hasn't said out loud for years. Her lips press together to form the sound, but she can't bring herself to utter the rest.

She hears the breathing change, the lips smacking slightly. There's a quick intake of air.

'Remember me?'

It slides like syrup.

The floorboard creaks, and her head snatches round to find Alex's dazed face staring at her from the doorway and then down at the strewn letters. Her mouth drops open and her hands begin to scrabble as if in slow motion. He steps back, dazed, as if she's struck him.

'Frankie?' His voice has an ache to it that breaks her heart. 'Frankie? What's...?'

And then he steps forward into her slow-motion world, only he's not slow, he's quick: dipping forward to scoop up one of the pieces of paper and reading the few words as his hand trembles and he drags its meaning into his brain. This is his nightmare. The thing he's dreaded; the thing that she said would never happen. She can see his whole world tumbling in all the rifts and shadows crossing his face.

'I-I can explain,' she stammers, the phone falling from her hand. 'It's not how it looks.'

'Yes. It is.' The piece of paper drops like an autumn leaf, the words tumbling through the air in front of her. He stares at it and looks up at her in agony. She knows what it says. It burned itself onto her memory from the moment she read it.

*I love you more than life and even beyond death.*

'This is exactly how it is, Frankie. This is how it's always been. I've just been scared to face it.'

'No, Alex, no!' Her hands reach out to him. 'It's not what you think.'

'It's not what I think, Frankie. It's what I see; what I *know*. It's what I've known for a long, long time.'

'None of this is true, Alex. Let me explain. Let me tell you the truth.'

But his head shakes sullenly from side to side.

'I've been so stupid.' His tone is soft and tender. 'All you had to do was tell me, that's all.' He casts a hand at the strewn paper, at her there on her knees in front of him. 'This isn't you, this isn't who you are. You didn't have to reduce yourself to this.'

His tenderness is killing her.

'Alex, listen! You honestly have no idea… You don't know what you're saying! Listen to me, please!'

'No, I'm done listening. I don't know who you are anymore. I don't know who *we* are.' He turns to leave.

'Alex!' She's up off her knees in an instant. 'Alex. Don't go.'

He pauses with one hand on the door.

'I couldn't tell you, I was scared—'

He blinks. 'Tell me what?'

Her brain stumbles and falls. He's giving her a chance: one chance. The truth feels like a foreign country where the language ties her tongue in sounds she can't make.

'I'm being followed. Stalked… A few weeks now. A man. He doesn't show himself but I know he's there. These started coming at the same time – and then that parcel yesterday.'

Alex's face stays completely still. He doesn't move. He looks at her and she looks at him.

'Give me a chance to tell you everything, Alex. That's all I'm asking. One chance.'

He pauses. His nod is almost imperceptible.

'I'll tell you all of it. I promise.'

And the fiction begins to fall from her mouth… *Drip, drip, drip…*

The truth, whatever it is, can't live here. There's no place for it. She has a life now, she has a future that she needs to keep together. And the past? The past is hers. It's a secret and private place that's full of pain and anguish and loss that she just can't face.

And with it, an almost unbearable love.

# Chapter Four

## *Then*

She'd been watching from the bedroom window, waiting for him to walk down the road. As he turned the corner, she dashed to the mirror to make sure her eyeliner was on point.

Practising a sideways glance, she gave her reflection that slide of her eyes that always made him laugh, and then smiled at the result. He didn't stand a chance.

She could hear some of the girls as they thundered down the stairs, squawking and giggling; they'd spotted him too and were running around to alert the others. She wasn't included. None of them were speaking to her, but who cared? She really couldn't give a toss.

The doorbell went and her heart went with it. She pressed an eye up against the windowpane, glimpsing the top of his dark head as her stomach did a complete three-sixty. She was glad they all hated her; she didn't need any of that lot. She had Martin now, only none of them knew it. Sixteen weeks. Sixteen weeks two days and... she looked at her watch and did a quick calculation – Five hours and eighteen minutes since they'd done the quiz night. Someone mentioned that the new volunteer was going to be there. He'd sat opposite her – God, he was clever. Cleverer than all the other staff. He'd winked at her when no none was looking, then in the break had come up behind her in the kitchen and put his hand on her back. The jolt of electricity went right up her spine and made her gasp. He'd asked her name and told her he thought she was beautiful. He'd said it just like that: all matter-of-fact. Not creepy: like it was obvious. '*You're beautiful.*'

She shivered at the memory as another cacophony of shrieking echoed up from the hallway and Jude's voice bellowed, telling them to be quiet. She closed her eyes in irritation. That lot hadn't worked out what had been going on right under their noses.

She could hear the deep boom of his voice and Jude's more measured tone. She was obviously going to tell him what had happened as part of the afternoon shift handover. So what if she'd given Natalie a slap? She'd deserved it. She shouldn't go around into other people's rooms, should she? She hadn't hit her that hard, really, but somehow she'd managed to smash through the coffee table. At the sight of blood, the others had gone wild and Nat was carted off to Chester A&E. Jude wasn't even giving him a chance to get his coat off before she started bumping her gums about how 'challenging' Frankie had been that morning. Stupid cow – like Martin would listen to anything she had to say.

'She's part of the system, Frankie,' he'd said. 'And right this moment, so are you. The system's too powerful to fight. Once you're eighteen it's different, they can't control you anymore. Then you're free. Free to be with me.'

They'd laughed and she'd kissed him. She'd go and live with him on his canal boat. That's what they'd planned. She sighed. *Eighteen*. It was nearly a whole year away. It felt like a lifetime.

Trying to quell the mounting excitement in her stomach, she stepped back, catching sight of herself in the mirror again and smoothing her hands over her hips. The weight of Martin's belt and buckle hung heavy in the loops of her jeans. It was their little way of touching each other when they were apart.

Running her fingers around the top of the belt, she had a sudden memory of his hands in exactly the same place and a quiet thrill thrummed through her stomach. He'd started sneaking into her room when he was on night-duty. Martin wasn't like anyone she'd ever met before. He'd shown her how to look at things differently: to see things as they should be seen. He didn't just see the bigger picture; he saw the whole landscape, the seas, the moon, and the stars. He saw beauty in a world of ugliness. The truth was, she'd been like a stone and he'd brought her to life. Colours looked different, the streets felt different, *she* was different. She would have jumped off a cliff if he'd asked her to.

She sighed, looking over at the door again, wondering what the hell Jude was telling him. All kinds of make-believe shit probably. Martin would be on her side though; his rules weren't other people's rules; he challenged all that. She knew his secrets. She knew his world, not just the different way he *thought* about things – but also the things he *did*. He didn't abide by authority and laws – they were for other people.

'I'm an old-fashioned revolutionary,' he'd whispered. They were cocooned under her duvet. He'd grinned and kissed the end of her nose. 'A dissenter, a disrupter of the social order.'

'What does that mean?'

'It means I'm dedicated to action, not words. I'm your modern-day Robin Hood. Fancy joining me on my quest to take from the rich and give to the poor?'

'What? How?' She'd felt scared and thrilled all at the same time.

'Night-tripping. The houses in Chester are great for it; they're plums ripe for picking,' he said enigmatically.

'Night-tripping?'

'Yeah, I'll teach you. You'll be fantastic at it. I can tell. Wanna come?'

Of course she did.

She blinked again languidly at her reflection and gave a mischievous smile. *He was so right. She was brilliant.*

It had gone quiet in the hallway. She glanced again at the door, her ears pricked with vague irritation. *So where was he?* Surely he could find some excuse to come up here. What was wrong now?

The slam of a car door sent her scurrying over to the window again. The passenger side opened, and Nat got out looking very sorry for herself, swiftly followed by Caro, one of the other staff members. The squawking downstairs started up again as she heard the front door open and all the girls began to pile out onto the drive to throw their arms around Nat in a great tide of dramatic concern. Frankie took her opportunity. Slipping out onto the landing, she made her way to the top of the stairs, swinging round the corner and literally colliding with Martin.

'Oh! There you are!'

'Shh! They're all outside.'

'I know.' She giggled as he drew her to him, wrapping his arms around her waist as he buried his face in her hair.

'Mmm… You smell wonderful. You're like chocolate and coconut and brown sugar. I could eat you,' he whispered.

She giggled again and glanced over his shoulder. A couple of the chattering girls trooped back inside, too busy to notice them. But they didn't have long.

'You okay?' He looked deep into her eyes. His were the most beautiful colour she had ever seen, hazel flecked with green, deep-set and heavy-lidded like a girl's.

'I warned you to keep your head down,' he admonished her with a smile. 'Don't get so wound up. Natalie's just a kid. Did Jude hammer you with a load of penalties?'

'Not too much. I'm good. You know me,' she grinned.

'No, you're not good,' he said softly. 'In fact, you're very, very bad. Look what you're doing to me.' He pulled a strand of hair from her cheek and then held out his hand; his fingers were trembling. 'That's you. That's the effect you have.' He let them drift down and gently touch the belt. She thought she might die with the sudden ache that shot through her. 'You're wearing it – wow! It looks great on you…'

'Shh! Careful,' she warned, peeping over his shoulder. 'Jude's only just down there.'

He grinned. 'Oh, she's fine, you know how much she likes me.'

She rolled her eyes. He'd conned Jude a treat; she let him get away with loads. He'd told her he wanted to be a social worker and so he wanted to get into voluntary work – well, he had got into it, just not quite in the way that Jude had envisaged.

'Shouldn't you be back in your room?' he suddenly said very loudly.

She sprang away as Jude's face appeared at the bottom of the stairs.

'You'll need to have a think about the consequences of your actions and how you're going to apologise for them.' He took a couple of steps away. Jude was standing staring up at them both.

'Ah, Jude,' he trotted down the stairs and drew level with her. 'Frankie was trying to sneak out of her room but I didn't think, under the circumstances, it was appropriate.'

'Absolutely not.' Jude glared at her. 'I think we could all do with a bit of time out don't you, Frankie?' She made a ridiculous 'T' sign with her fingertips pressed into the heel of her hand. 'Are you coming into the lounge for the formal de-brief, Martin?… Say, five minutes?'

'Sure,' Martin said loudly as Jude disappeared along the hallway. He glanced back and winked. 'Tonight?' he mouthed and held up both hands to signify ten o'clock.

Frankie nodded quickly and retreated back to her bedroom, her heart thudding like a mad thing. She perched on the edge of the bed, her knee jiggling, her fingers sawing impatiently as she stared at the digital clock on the bedside table.

There was the chatter of voices from down below as all the girls tried to talk over each other, desperate to put their ten cents worth in and grass her up. Frankie stared glumly at the carpet. Ten o'clock. Jesus. That was almost seven hours away. It felt like forever, although she knew that if he asked her to, she'd wait a lifetime.

–

Ten o'clock came and went.

She stood at the top of the stairs not daring to go down, straining her ears. It was the quiet after the storm. The girls loved a bit of drama and now they were satiated – for a while, at least. She paced around her room for a bit, picking things up and putting them down again. It felt as though she'd been waiting all day. He couldn't be too much longer, surely?

She went out onto the landing again. She could hear Jude's nasal whine behind a closed door somewhere. Was she keeping him talking, was that it? Then she heard two voices getting louder and the creak of the bottom stair which sent her scuttling back to her room to dive under the covers. There was a faint tap on her door and it creaked open. She could hear Jude's breath whistling down her nostrils.

'Frankie?'

'Mmm?'

'I thought I heard you moving about. How are you feeling?'

'Awright.'

'We'll have a group conference tomorrow, yes? See how we can come to an agreeable resolution. There's lots to discuss.'

God she hated all that fake-speak. Why couldn't she just say they'd sit down and talk about it? She inwardly sighed.

'Yeah. Sure.'

'The staff have gone off and everyone's in their rooms now. You haven't had any lunch or dinner. Are you hungry?'

'No. M'awright…' Then she added a muffled 'Thanks.'

Jude paused.

'So I'll be off to bed shortly then. If you need anything, you know where I am. Okay?'

'Okay.'

'Night-night.'

'Night.'

She heard the door close and pulled her head from under the covers. Shaking her hair back, she waited, listening to the sounds of Jude pottering about. Someone down the landing had got their TV on too loud. Good. That would cover any noise she made. Pushing the bedclothes back, she reached down for her sneakers and pulled them on. Then, very quietly, she went over to the window, opened it, and looked out. It had been raining. The road was quiet, just the occasional sweep of car headlights on the main road and the hiss of tyres on wet tarmac as they passed. She couldn't see Martin anywhere. The trees on either side of the street shivered in the darkness, their outlines like shadowy fingers against the carbon sky.

*Soon. Any minute now and she'd see him.*

She glanced anxiously again at the clock: ten past eleven. What if he'd got sick of waiting for Jude to go to bed? What if he'd decided to go alone tonight and something had gone wrong? What if he hadn't gone alone, and found someone else to take?... Like another girl? Her stomach plummeted. *No, he wouldn't do that. But what if—?* She stopped. A shadow beneath the streetlamp stretched languorously and lengthened. Martin appeared, his head hunched down into the collar of his black jacket, shucking the lapels up around his neck and adjusting the rucksack on his back. He glanced up and raised a hand. She waved madly back and glanced back into the room before holding up her fingers to ask for two more minutes.

Hurrying over to the bed, she pulled the pillows down into the centre of the mattress and bundled the duvet in a hump around them. Turning the light off, she made a beeline for the window, hoisting herself up with ease onto the sill and slipping quickly onto the ledge outside. She paused for a moment to pull the window almost closed behind her so that it wasn't immediately noticeable, and then looked for her usual escape route. The location of the drainpipe made it super easy, and the porch over the front door was a climber's dream. She jumped, landing like a cat, her fingers just skimming the driveway, before dashing across the road into Martin's waiting arms.

'I love watching you do that,' he chuckled, cupping her face in his warm hands and kissing her. 'You're so, so clever.'

'The clever bit is never getting caught,' she grinned. 'God, I thought she'd never go to bed! I kept thinking you'd go off without me.'

'I'll never do anything without you.' He ran his finger down her nose and playfully pinched the tip. 'Never.'

She smiled up at him. 'Where are we off to tonight, then?'

'It's all planned. Come on.'

She took a quick look back at the house. It was in complete darkness. No one knew a thing. No one ever knew. Here they were, the two of them out here again: bold, daring, extraordinary, doing good. She'd never felt more alive.

Martin took her hand and they ran together, each in time with the other, matching each other stride for stride, their lungs working in harmony. He glanced across at her and they both laughed, their breath pluming out into the wet night, their feet splashing through puddles. She felt lithe and light and sinewy and powerful – hedges whizzed past in a blur, houses jogged by like black cardboard cut-outs. She had no idea where they were headed. The streets became wider and leafier and their pace slowed. She could tell this area was minted. Trees loomed up on either side and Martin paused in the shadows, dragging her to a halt. The houses in this part of Chester were huge: great bulky shapes, with massive hedges and high gates and long driveways.

'This one,' he panted. 'I've sussed it already.'

He led her quickly across the road to where overgrown privet bordered two iron gateposts. They were immediately illuminated as a car turned the corner and sped towards them, its lights whitening Martin's face for seconds that felt like minutes. She pressed her cheek close to his chest, feeling his heart racing away in there as a whole bucket of love tumbled through her. The car zoomed past and they were plunged into sudden darkness.

'Here. Look—' He pulled her closer into the hedge; the twigs and stems cracked under their pressure. The sudden close heat of him was intoxicating. She glanced up. His eyes glittered brightly in the shadows.

'We're definite on this one then? It's empty?'

'Yeah.'

'Did you bookmark it?' she whispered.

'Yeah.'

She said it casually, but that was only to show that she'd been listening to everything he'd told her. He'd explained how you could tell if the occupants were away: put a little tag of Sellotape on the door in an inconspicuous place and then come back two days later. If the tape was intact, then the owners were away. It was that simple.

'And are we taking the stuff very far? It nearly killed me last time,' she giggled.

He glanced over at the front of the house. His jawline was strong and confident and her heart sang with delight and adoration. This was what she loved: they were fearless and self-assured; they pushed boundaries without a care for authority. Martin was a man, not a boy – a man with ideals and principles, taking risks to do good.

He looked back at her and kissed her nose. 'Not too far. I heard about an old guy who lives not far from here. He's on his own now, his wife died a few weeks ago. The bastards stopped his pension while they sort out his single allowance. He's got no one now and nothing to live on.'

'He will have tonight.'

'Yeah, he will have tonight,' he grinned back.

'Wouldn't it be fantastic to see his face, though? To see his expression when he comes down to all the goodies laid out on his table like Father Christmas has been? Wouldn't it be brilliant to see that, just once?'

'It's not *for* us.' Martin was still smiling, but there was a seriousness in his tone that made her falter. 'The government doesn't care. The welfare people don't care, the charities and the do-gooders don't give a toss really – they're all operating within the system; they're part of the system and therefore part of the problem. We're not. We're the outsiders. We don't play by their rules. We steal from the rich and give to the poor – how activist is that?'

She felt breathless. The words he spoke were like magic: they were incantations, spells, drawing her in. Whenever he spoke, she believed in him, totally. He was more than a man: he was someone she knew she would give her life for.

'Are you ready?'

His eyes were bright with excitement and purpose. She nodded.

'I found a gap here in the hedge. See?'

He glanced around him once and then crouched down, quickly lifting the leaves to reveal an arched hole where the branches hadn't grown. He gestured quickly and she knelt, crawling through the dirt, slipping like a feral cat down through the shadows. They slunk in the darkness round to the back of the house, huddling conspiratorially for a moment. She glanced up, checking and mapping. Every window of the house was striped with diamonds of security shutters in the moonlight.

'I like your style,' she whispered, smiling. 'You've worked out my favourites.'

Any bars or grills on doorways or windows were a fantastic bonus. Perfect for hand and footholds, and very sturdy ones at that.

Martin pointed upwards soundlessly. 'Up there,' he mouthed.

She looked to the third floor. There was a tiny fanlight, probably to a bathroom, which was open about two inches.

'If you can get up there and slip your hand through, there's a bigger window next to it. You should be able to get to the main catch.'

She assessed all the access points. It wasn't going to be easy.

'I just was wondering if—'

'Don't worry your head,' she whispered. 'This is my bag, not yours. You just leave it all to me.' She half stood, half crouched for a second, assessing and then looked around.

'Now... Come on.'

They followed the line of shadows to where a huge sea of dark lawn and trees lay in front of them. Down the other side of the garden, there were clumps of whippy-looking trees dotted about, the first cluster about six feet away from the side of the house wall.

He followed her gaze.

'But they're not strong enough!' he hissed.

'Not for you, no.' She tiptoed quickly over, glancing around to make sure she hadn't been spotted. Dipping down, she crawled under the first tree, crouching to peer upwards into the branches. She parted the bottom twigs and signalled to him with a thumbs-up. 'Yep, perfect. Piece of cake.'

Before he could say another word, she'd reached up, swinging herself through the lower sections like a tiny monkey. Keeping close to the trunk, and winding her way as though it was a staircase, she scaled higher, and then paused to get her bearings. Peeping through the leaves she could make out where the first level window grills jutted out but they were at least four feet away; she'd never make the leap. Her brain zig-zagged, re-calculating... Then she had an idea. Climbing another two branches up, she peeked out again. If she was clever and quick, she could actually do this.

Testing the flexibility of the branch as best she could, she began to work her way along it. *Concentrate, Frankie. Concentrate.* Gritting her teeth, she inched, hand over hand, letting it bend with her weight until she got within striking distance of the window. One reach further and she should be able to feel just how much it would bend and bow – if she went a stretch too far she knew the thing would snap completely. There would only be seconds, but seconds were all she needed.

Taking a breath, she gathered herself and shifted all her weight forward. The branch groaned and creaked alarmingly. Gathering her knees up, she altered her centre of gravity and suddenly found she was dropping far quicker. The window grill flashed for a second in front of her eyes, and in that instant she let go of the branch. There was the swift and scary whistling whip as its leaves skimmed past her face, but she managed to land tiptoed on the sill, her fingers immediately grabbing for the wrought iron. Breathing heavily, she signalled an okay sign to Martin's upturned face and without pausing, began her climb to the next storey and the bathroom window. This bit was simple. Crouching on the ledge, she slipped her hand into the gap and unhooked the catch on the bigger window levering it wide.

She was in.

The only sound was the ragged air leaving her lungs. She collected herself for a moment, wrinkling her nose at the smell. The bathroom reeked of old lady soap and mildewed towels. Wishing she had a torch, she felt her way across towards the door where the moonlight lit up the landing. The house sat in its musty stillness, the floral carpet leading her to the top of the stairs. Slipping swiftly down, she headed for the front door. Sliding the bolts back, she opened it to find Martin grinning widely as he stepped into the hallway, swinging his rucksack forward and pausing to grab her hand and kiss her cheek.

'Clever girl.' He looked around him. 'Down here, I think.'

Pulling a torch from his pocket, he led her down a hallway that opened up into a wide, square kitchen. In the centre was a big wooden table and old-fashioned solid units and cupboards lined the walls. The torchlight bounced around.

'Right – the plan of action is these cupboards first; any packet or dried goods, or tins, whatever you can find, and then we'll look for cash. We don't touch anything else, no matter how tempting.' He gave her a look. 'There should be enough here anyway.'

He pulled open a large dresser on the wall. Stacked on the shelves was all kinds of stuff: cereals, vegetables, soup, baked beans.

'Bingo!' he said softly.

'Why are we whispering?' she giggled back. Her voice sounded unnaturally loud and she giggled again. 'We can actually make as much noise as we like! Look—' she opened the fridge door and closed it with a bang.

Martin nearly dropped the light. 'Shh!!' he hissed. 'Stop that! We never take those kinds of chances!'

She felt her face colour and burn and was thankful that it was so dark he couldn't see how much of a kid she felt. He didn't seem to have noticed; he was too busy loading the rucksack and filling his pockets. She chewed her cheek, embarrassed. Now she'd made herself look stupid. She desperately wanted to make amends and show how capable she was. She opened the fridge door again and pretended to look inside.

'Martin.'

'What?' He didn't stop loading his bag.

'There's all kinds of stuff in here.'

'Yeah. Good.'

She picked up a half-full carton of milk and unscrewed the top, bringing it up to her nose.

'This is fresh.'

'Uh-huh.'

She didn't think he was really listening. She frowned.

'How long did you say these people have been away?'

'Why?'

A crack from above their heads and they both snapped up. Neither of them moved, breath held, hands stilled at the definite creak of footsteps. There was the squeal and clump of a door opening and then the sound of someone walking down the stairs.

Martin's eyes looked huge in his face as he blinked rapidly. Suddenly grabbing up the bag, he swung it onto his back.

'The front door's open. It's my only way out,' he breathed. He sounded scared. 'I'm going to have to chance it. That'll draw them away from the stairs. See if you can get out the same way as you got in. No one will imagine you'd do that. Okay?'

She nodded frantically. Her heart was in her mouth. She couldn't think, couldn't speak, couldn't move.

He jerked forward and kissed her on the forehead, then, just as suddenly, he was gone. She stood motionless, not knowing if she should make a run for it now, not knowing whether to hide or run or—

A woman's voice called out, shouting and tremulous, echoing through the hallway. Frankie couldn't make out the words, but it was enough to get her feet moving. Slipping quickly along the passageway, she listened as the voice grew louder and more urgent as the woman shrieked with anger. Frankie peered through a gap in the door. There were the stairs. A cold blast of air whistled past. An elderly lady was standing in the open doorway, brandishing a stick and clutching her dressing gown to her throat as she yelled into the darkness. Her fingers were fumbling with what looked like an alarm around her neck. Frankie watched as she shambled her way out onto the front step, her slippers crunching on the gravel, still bellowing loud enough to have the whole neighbourhood come running. There would only be seconds to spare if she was going to make those stairs.

She took her chance.

Keeping tight to the wall, she sneaked as fast as she could along the hallway and rounded the first few steps, not daring to pause or to look back, all the time waiting to hear a barking order telling her *to stop right there!* – but it didn't come. She threw herself along the landing and ran to the bathroom where the window sat exactly as she had left it. Jumping onto the windowsill, she glanced around, realising the tree was the absolute worst option. The old woman's voice wavered out into the dark. She was stuck. She'd break her neck if she tried to jump. Her brain went into overdrive. There was a drainpipe, that was the most obvious choice, but she knew it was inches out of reach – she'd never make it. Then she had a thought.

Unbuckling her belt, she pulled it through the loops and slid the buckle over the window latch, pulling it hard and winding it around her fist. As long as she kept the tension on it, it might just give her the extra reach she needed.

*With a little levering swing... With one more push...* Her shoulder jerked sideways, and she made a grab for the downpipe, feeling the cold iron under her fingertips at the same time as her foot left the wall. There was a nano-second as her toes searched for the bracket – and then they hit home.

Breathing hard, she let the belt go, the rubber soles of her trainers squealing as she manoeuvred her way down the pipe until she got to the metal grille. Every muscle shook with relief as she squat-landed heavily onto the ground just as the wail of sirens echoed shrilly into the night. In a flash, she hunkered down through the shadows along the side of the house, and then dipped to where she thought was the hole in the hedge – but immediately froze. The old lady was out there with her stick and a torch, smashing and poking the shrub-line, stooping right down and peering hard, almost as though she knew what they'd done. Frankie shrank into a tight ball, crouching painfully, her chest pressed against her thighs, her breath aching in her restricted lungs, every inch of her body flinching as the splintering bushes shook around her. She couldn't stay there, that was a fact. A panic gripped her: if she made a run for it she'd be spotted for sure. There was a whole swathe of open lawn to cover. She was sunk.

A pop and crunch of tyres and the pummelling of the bushes paused. She took a glance up. A load of emergency vehicles had squealed up to the kerb; their circling blue and red lights illuminated the driveway.

A dark figure paused by the gates, its shadow wavering and elongating through the spooling lights. A policeman. So close. One look down and he'd have her. She was done for.

'Frankie,' said a low voice.

She almost fainted with relief: Martin.

'Move towards me *now*. I mean *now*.'

She scrambled out of her hiding place quickly pushing her way along the privet and through the hole to where his legs were blocking the view. He was still wearing his rucksack. Arm aloft, he had his hand cupped to his eyes as though mesmerised by all the activity. She went to stand, seeing that his jacket had swung open, giving her the perfect cover. He looked like a student out for an evening stroll. He ignored her completely, gazing away and up at the house and then around at the police cars as though he was a curious bystander. She was just about to say something, when his arm slipped around her shoulders as though she had been next to him the whole time.

A policeman's radio twittered just a couple of feet away, but she didn't dare look round.

'Which direction have you just come from, son?'

Martin pointed away down the road. 'We were just walking from that way. A load of cop cars whizzed past me and we wondered what was going on.'

'Did you happen to see anyone running along this road, or acting strangely in any way?'

She was concentrating hard at staring into Martin's neck. She could see the pulse of nerves in his throat as he turned his head to gesture up and down the street.

'No,' he frowned. 'I haven't seen anyone. We were only walking this way 'cos we missed the bus and there's a cut-through up there back into the centre of Chester.'

'Is that where you live?'

'Yeah. We're both students at Cheshire College.'

The copper turned his attention to Frankie. He opened his mouth but the driver in one of the police cars called out to him and he was forced to turn away. He nodded back at them.

'Thank you for your time, son. You pair just need to be on your way.'

She almost giggled as the nerves flooded through her.

'No problem.' Martin lifted a hand in salute.

They started to walk awkwardly up the road. Behind them she heard the slamming of car doors and radios clamouring as the police cars began to pull away. She found she'd gone from trembling to a full-bodied shake. Martin still had his arm around her, and her hand inched its way around his waist, her fingers clutching at his jumper, too scared to let go. She felt like dropping to her knees right there on the pavement, and giving in to total hysteria.

'You okay?'

She nodded. She wasn't sure her legs would take her any further. Neither of them dared to speak and then she realised Martin was shaking too. She glanced at him.

'How about you?'

'Jesus,' he breathed. He was almost laughing. '*Jesus*, Frankie! How the hell did we get out of there alive?' He shook his head. 'Did any of that really happen?'

'Did that woman see your face?' The thought suddenly struck her. A tremor of real fear jolted her back to reality. It had gone from just some mad stunt to something far more real.

'Nah. Definitely not. A hundred per cent... She was a feisty old bird though, wasn't she?' They turned down an alleyway. He was chuckling properly now. 'Fuck, can you imagine what she was like when she was younger? It's a good job I legged it, if she'd smacked me with that stick she'd have probably caved my head in.' He grinned round at her, the tension easing and lifting as a sudden wash of adrenaline gushed through her.

*They'd done it. They'd really done it. They had. The two of them together.*

She felt closer to him than ever. Pulling his arm close around her and turning her face, she nuzzled into the wooliness of his jumper, wanting to blur the lines between them, to meld herself to him. She wanted him more than she'd ever wanted anyone or anything before.

'It's here.' He pulled away from her, breaking the spell. They were halfway along an alley. Martin dropped the rucksack from his shoulder and hoisted himself up on the wall to peer over.

'What is?'

'Where we're delivering.'

She looked at him, wide-eyed. 'We're going in there?'

'Don't worry. This old chap never locks his back door. He says if someone wanted to break in and steal stuff they'd be sadly disappointed, and if they broke in and murdered him it would be a blessing.'

'That's sad.'

'Yeah, and d'you know what's really the saddest thing of all?' The anger came off him in waves.

'That this poor old bugger lives only round the corner from that lot.' He thumbed over his shoulder. 'They have more than they know what to do with, and he has nothing. How can that be right?' He bent to lift a broken bit of fence panel. 'Here you go, we can squeeze through here.'

She took half a step forward and then stopped. 'I can't, Martin. I just can't.'

'Yeah you can. Don't be scared. You've done the scary bit.'

'Really, I can't. Not after…' She gestured weakly. 'Seriously. Seriously. It was too much. Please don't ask me.'

He stood coolly watching her for a few moments, not saying anything.

'You're not going to do this again?'

The disappointment in his tone was almost more than she could bear

'I didn't say that—'

'Then what are you saying?'

She'd failed. It was like a punch in the gut. She'd been set a test and she'd let him down.

He took her hand. 'Frankie. Look…' He chafed her fingers. 'All this… this stuff we do. It's outrageous and it's uncomfortable. We have to push ourselves beyond our own boundaries, and that's exactly what you've just done. Don't retreat back into your old life now. You were brave, you were ballsy, you took control… Changing people's lives takes all that. You and I are a rare breed.' He tugged her hand a little towards the fence. 'Please. Please come with me.'

She looked into his face: into those eyes. She found her fingers turning over and finding the warmth of his palm.

'Yes?'

Her banging heart steadied a little. The shaking paused. She took a breath and gripped on tight. 'Okay,' she said.

'Good.'

The splintered board lifted easily. Glancing round, he knelt and pushed the rucksack through before gesturing for her to follow. She immediately found herself crawling into a dark tunnel of wet weeds before she entered a bit of a clearing and managed to stand. He was right behind her.

'This way… The old fella's as deaf as a post. He won't hear a thing. He'll just have a fantastic supply of food left on his kitchen table. Look, I'm even leaving this just in case.' He laughed and rummaged about down the side of the bag before producing a tin opener. She managed a smile.

'See? Someone needs food, we feed them. Someone needs shelter? We find them an empty house. Someone needs money? We take from the rich and give to the poor. We don't do things by the book. We're the kinds of people who see injustice and fix it, yes?'

'Yes.'

He was so sure, so impassioned; he radiated certainty. Of course, he was right, it was so obvious a child would understand the simplicity of it.

'Then don't let go of those ideals. They're why we're here, so let's do this.'

He gestured for her to go in front. She wouldn't disappoint him, not this time. She nodded, letting go of his arm and threading her way determinedly through the wild garden to the back door. She paused before forcing herself to reach out and turn the knob. The door shuddered open, catching on the torn linoleum floor.

Of all the places they'd been, this was the worst. It was supposed to be a kitchen, but the only indication was the chipped stone butler sink with a cold tap above it. The cooker, if you could describe it as that, was a rusted box with a filthy door. A flimsy table sat next to it with two plates on top and a knife and fork.

'Appalling, isn't it?' Martin whispered. 'A human being lives in all this… Come on, we'll leave the stuff through here.'

He led her through a hallway that was so dark, she was only just aware of him moving in front of her. The darkness lifted, revealing a small, high-ceilinged room. It was sparsely furnished with an old dining table pushed against one wall and a couple of wooden chairs either side. There were two floral covered armchairs positioned in front of an empty grate, with a TV on a stool in the hearth. It felt as though no daylight would ever be able to force its way in there.

Martin dumped the rucksack on the floor and began pulling out the tins and packets, piling them up in the centre of the table. She stood back, watching him work, her eyes darting this way and that, ears pricked, listening for movement from above, but the house stayed quiet.

'Won't he wonder where this has all come from?' she whispered.

'When people are lonely and sad and desperate, they don't ask too many questions,' he said grimly. 'They're just grateful for a bit of kindness.'

Frankie nodded. How often she'd seen that with the girls in care, running from one lad who mistreated them to another, looking to fill some terrible dark pit of loneliness – and then the babies, born in the hope that they'd bring a tiny bit of love into their lives. She shook her head silently. Thank god for Martin.

The moonlight showed a single lightbulb hanging down from a kinked flex, and shadows of damp spreading dangerously across the ceiling and down the walls. She looked a little closer at a darkened patch by the window, and realised that what she'd thought of as a blotch of mildew, was actually a faded black and white photograph. She took a step closer. In the dim light, she could see it was a woman, a girl really, high-cheeked and pretty, the whole of her face filling the frame. There were white patches in her hair that she realised must be flowers. A wedding photograph.

'That was his wife. She was seventeen.' Martin put the last of the boxes on the table and came over to stand beside her. 'Pretty, isn't she? He got the album out one day when we were chatting. I had it framed for him as a surprise.'

'What a lovely thing to do.' The fact that she was the same age as this beautiful girl hadn't escaped her.

'Yeah, the damp's got into the back of it and spoiled it a bit. They were married for seventy years.'

'Wow.' She couldn't even imagine what that amount of time would look like.

'That'll be us one day.' He paused and tickled the side of her face with one bent finger. 'We should be going.'

Her heart began to sing. *Did he really just say that? Would that be them?* She followed him out of the house as though she was walking on air. She felt like laughing and shouting up into the night sky.

'I'm in the mood to celebrate.' He offered a hand to help her through the fence. 'Let's go and find some place to party.' He dipped his head, kissing her fingers and she breathed in the scent of the skin of his cheek for a second. She felt completely intoxicated.

'Where, though?'

'Oh there's loads of places. Tons of all-nighters going on.' The cut-through led them straight onto the main road.

'Just stay out, you mean?'

'Why not?' He laughed at her expression. 'We've just got to get you back home before anyone's awake, that's all.'

Nothing mattered apart from being here with him, right now. She didn't care – she felt free and light and excited.

'We'll have to get some booze then. Is there somewhere near here?'

'Already sorted.' He dived into the rucksack and pulled out a bottle of wine. 'Courtesy of the old lady's larder.'

'I thought it was all for the old guy?' she frowned.

'Aw, I left him the whiskey,' he grinned. 'I'm sure he'll appreciate a tot of the hard stuff far more than a cheapo bottle of this crap. What do you think? Or do you want me to go back?' He paused and waved the bottle towards the house.

'No, no, god, no!' she laughed pulling at his arm. 'Waay enough drama!'

They began to walk down the road. 'Jesus, when that copper came over…' She shook her head.

'He had no idea though, had he?'

'Who would've thought of standing outside a house after blagging it? That was inspired,' she grinned.

'Yeah, what house-breaker would do that? It messes with their heads, see?' Martin laughed and tapped his temple.

She felt as though she was brimming with good things: the excitement and magic of tonight; the joy of Martin. She squeezed his arm tighter.

'Always hide in plain sight. That's the thing; the more obvious something is, the less people see it.' Martin chuckled as they saw a bus trundling around the corner. 'Let's grab this one. I think it's going more or less where we want to go.' She knew she'd go anywhere he asked her to. He swung the rucksack off his shoulder in readiness. 'I once met a guy who'd just come out of the nick for breaking and entering, and he told me: d'you know the very best place to hide a key?'

She shook her head. Just listening to him talk was enough.

'In a box full of keys.' He laughed as the bus drew up and the doors hissed open. 'Clever, eh?'

They found a seat on the bus and he slid the rucksack in between them. She reached down and gripped his hand, making him look round at her.

'Thank you,' she said.

'What for?'

'My life. I didn't have one before I met you.'

He smiled and kissed her cheek. 'That goes both ways, you know.'

'Maybe,' she said, although she knew that wasn't true.

'You don't believe me?'

She could feel the weight of his look on the side of her face.

She gave him a faltering smile. 'I'm not as strong as you. I don't know stuff.'

'Never underestimate yourself, Frankie, you hear me?' He gave her hand a little shake, bringing it up to kiss her knuckle. 'You're far more capable than you think. There'll come a day when you'll be asked to show it.'

'I can do anything if you're by my side.' She turned their linked hands over and pressed the back of his hand to her lips. 'I *will* do anything.'

'Be careful,' he grinned. 'I might just hold you to that.'

# *Chapter Five*

They could hear the party as soon as they got off the bus. The buzz-thump of music came at them in waves. Frankie looked around. She thought she might know this area. The Victorian houses here were imposing but studenty and run-down: their blackened rooflines disappearing into the September evening sky. The downstairs windows were open and she could see silhouetted bodies lounging and sitting out on the ledges. Behind them the ceilings were strobed with coloured lights.

They picked their way along the path as a scatter of voices rose and fell and a gaggle of girls emerged from the shadows. They were all clearly pissed.

'Come on, my weave's getting blown about!' There was the clackety-scuff of heels as one of the women with ironed, straw-like hair shoved at the front door. There was a sudden tumble of light and noise and the hallway opened up. It was thronging with people and unbelievably loud. Groups of beautiful twenty-somethings crowded up a magnificent carved staircase that spiralled high into the sweet fug of dope smoke. A dusty chandelier overhead twinkled through the garlands of fairy lights and lanterns.

A young man in a dishevelled open shirt threaded his way down touching hands with each person he met. Everyone seemed to know everyone; they oozed chic self-assurance. Frankie blinked into the dim haze. There was a girl sitting on the stairs gazing at her through the struts of the bannister. She was dressed all in black and had long blonde hair that was held back with a red hairband. Her kohl-rimmed eyes blinked languidly. Frankie immediately felt out of place and ugly; a silly, nail-bitten kid in a room full of wonder and enchantment. Her clothes felt wrong, her hair felt wrong; she knew her make-up was hard and garish. She glanced up at another couple of lads coming down the stairs. One boy with a white buzz-cut picked up a lock of the girl's hair and ran his fingers through it as he passed. She glanced up at him and smiled, holding her hand out to meet his and he caressed her fingers.

'Drink?' Martin mimed the action, nudging her elbow, but all the while his eyes lingered over the girl.

'Yeah. Great. Whatever,' she hollered back, but she saw how his eyes kept flitting that way, landing like a butterfly towards the stairs again and again. There was an immediate and overwhelming rush of jealousy.

She watched him pushing his way through the elbows and backs to get to the kitchen, suddenly feeling very alone and itching inside her own skin. She was acutely aware of being totally invisible and horribly conspicuous at the same time. But no one was looking. They were all too busy focussing on the girl who absorbed the attention like a right. Frankie felt herself bristle.

The gaggle of women who'd arrived in front of them were gathered into a squawking gang, shrugging out of their coats and mussing up their hair.

'Shah! *Charlotte!* Whoop-whoop!' A peal of child-like squealing rang out behind. Frankie made a half turn as Blonde-Weave elbowed her painfully in the cheek. Without even saying sorry, she bounced, arms aloft, waving frantically before lurching into the tide of bodies and throwing herself towards the stairs. The girl, Charlotte, only gazed at her with mild interest as she draped herself around her shoulders in an over-enthusiastic embrace. Frankie wished she could stop looking.

'Your long-lost sister?' Martin appeared at her side with two plastic cups, handing one over. 'Vodka. No tonic I'm afraid, I couldn't find any, but the voddie's straight out of the freezer… Anyway… Cheers.'

'Cheers.' She took a little sip. The ice of it burned like fire. 'What do you mean, my sister?'

'You look a bit like her.' Martin let his gaze drift over to the stairs again. 'Wow – she looks like she's well out of it, though.'

The Blonde-Weave's voice cackled up. The whole group sounded like they were very pissed or very stoned.

'She seems to be getting a lot of attention.'

'Yeah,' Martin nodded, distracted. 'She's one of those girls people are drawn to. She's like a magnet. There's just something about her…' He trailed off but then suddenly gathered himself, slipping an arm around her waist.

'You were amazing tonight, you know that?'

'Was I?' The alcohol had hit her empty stomach; she felt a bit sick and close to tears.

'What's the matter? You know you were,' he smiled.

'I don't know anything.'

'Hey! What's wrong? What's happened?'

'Nothing.' She really did feel like a kid now.

He looked at her, shocked. 'It's not that girl, is it?' He was almost laughing. Frankie's temper soared with the vodka.

'You seem very interested in her.'

'Christ, you've got this all wrong.' He shrugged awkwardly as they were jostled by even more people squeezing past. 'She's involved in the party scene. I've just seen her around, that's all.' He deliberately moved away, drawing Frankie towards the room where the music was so loud she felt it shivering inside her ribcage.

'Mart!' A male voice suddenly shouted over the thumping din. 'Mate! You okay, man?' They turned. The lad with the buzz-cut pushed through the mad jungle. They clasped hands and enveloped each other in a man-hug.

Martin pulled back a little. 'Oh, this is Frankie.'

'How do, Frankie.' He grinned and raised the bottle he was clutching in greeting, but neither of them offered his name.

'Frankie's my girl.' Martin gave her a look, slipping his hand around her waist again. 'And my partner.' Some of her resolute truculence left her, and she let herself be hugged.

'In crime?' the lad chuckled.

'Yeah,' she said boldly, staking her ground. 'That too.'

The lad and Martin shared a look that she couldn't decipher.

'Let's chill later, yeah?' Skinny boy nodded from one to the other. 'Catch you soon.' He raised his bottle again and disappeared into the crush.

Martin bent to her ear. 'I don't want to be with all these people, do you?' His breath teased her neck and gave her goosebumps.

'No.'

'Come on. Let's go outside.'

He took her hand and led her towards a set of French doors that opened onto the gardens. The sweet air hit her like a balm. There were trees hung with coloured bulbs that cast weird bobbing shadows onto the path that wound away in front of them. The rest of the garden was thick with darkness. They could hear voices on either side of them coming from the bushes but couldn't see anyone.

'Ow!' She caught her ankle on an upturned brick. 'How far are we going? There aren't any lights down here.'

'That's the whole point. Mind, there's a tree stump.'

The sulky jealousy left her as though it had never been, dissipating into the night sky. She was here, with Martin and all these amazing people, nothing else mattered. She felt giggly all of a sudden.

He paused, checking and toeing the ground in the gloom, and then guided her to where the trees grew denser and the light went from shadows to completely black. The thud of music grew fainter and a peal of laughter from somewhere near the house rang through the air.

'This way.'

Flicking the torch on his phone, he guided her deep into the undergrowth where a bed of thick leaves made a dry circle. He pulled her down to sit and she squinted into the glare. There was a musk of damp earth: a mushroomy smell, warm almost. His face was lit ghoulishly in the strange light and then it went out. She giggled, feeling the heat of his palm on her neck. He gently brought her face closer and kissed her softly, the alcohol on his breath tasting sweet and sugary, his tongue tipping softly across her top lip as everything around her swam a little. She wanted him so badly. She pulled his jacket from his shoulders and then began to unbutton his shirt. She felt him tremble as the breeze caught his bare skin. He peeled up her T-shirt and pulled it over her head, kissing her as he reached down for her jeans and she heard the jink of his belt as he began to wriggle out of his own.

'You're truly beautiful.' His voice was husky in the darkness.

'But you can't see me,' she breathed into his mouth. She loved being naked with him; the pitch darkness making it more exciting and more thrilling than she could ever have imagined. Skin against skin. The heat of him – Her heat. Their being together made her feel totally complete. When he pushed inside her, it was as though he was pushing the rest of the world away. There was nothing but him and her: one joined body.

Afterwards they lay together, her head on his chest. He touched the side of her face with the tips of his fingers like a blind man: reading her. 'That was the feeling I've been looking for, Frankie. That was the connection that people search their whole lives for. You know that, don't you? We became the same person... Or maybe we became another person. Did you feel that? Does that sound weird?'

'I felt it.' She put her hand on his chest and felt the thud of his heart beneath her palm: so visceral, so alive.

'I don't want us to move – not an inch.' She could hear the urgency in him. 'I don't want the real world to ever find us. I want us to disappear to another place: a better one.' His voice sounded disembodied in the blackness. It felt like he was all around and yet so close.

The drum beneath her fingers grew stronger.

'I don't want us to be like other people. I don't want us to be ordinary. I want this to be special: *extra*ordinary. Different. I want us to be vulnerable and' – he let his fingers travel down her neck to the mound of her breast, her nipple tightening under his touch – 'completely as one.'

His hand landed on her thigh. She closed her eyes; she thought she might die right that moment. She leaned in to rest her forehead against his. He kissed both her eyes, the bridge of her nose, her top lip. When she opened them again all she could see was the glitter of his eyes: so close. He had a strange look on his face.

'What?' she smiled slowly.

'This is more than love.'

'Yes,' she said. 'I know.'

'No boundaries… No going back… That's what we said, wasn't it?'

'That's what we said.'

'Will you come with me then, if I asked you?' he murmured. 'Somewhere very special?'

'Anywhere. I'd go with you anywhere.'

He reached back for his jacket, finding the pocket and bringing out a little bag. The whiteness of the pills gleamed in the strange light. She looked at them and then at him.

She shivered although she didn't feel cold.

'Come here then. Open your mouth.'

She did as he asked. She felt him reach out again and then there was the soft give of the plastic cup against her fingers. She lifted the rim to her lips and took a hard gulp, feeling the tablet sticking to her tongue for a moment and then she swallowed with a gasp as the liquid burned. He took the cup from her and did the same before slipping his arm around her back, pulling her to him to lie on his chest. She listened to the steadiness of his breathing, feeling his heat against her face, her lips almost tasting the scent of his skin.

She began to feel the first shiver of magic, because it *was* magic. He'd conjured it. The dry leaves beneath them made a carpet, lifting them up, carrying them both, weightless, to a place away from everywhere. She felt herself slipping in between the layers of dimension: not outside anymore, not inside, just surrounded by air that was thick and soft, slow and pillowy, where no one could reach them. She felt warmth: perfect like the skin of a peach, its velvety softness stroking her face. A flash of singular perfection; this was the one moment where everything was pure and right and entirely good, and she was soaring.

–

She opened her eyes.

She was lying with her belly against his back. Her arms were wrapped tightly around him and she lifted her head to nose the hair behind his ear. He grumbled and moaned in his sleep, his eyes flickered, but he didn't wake.

Her mouth felt as though it was full of cotton wool. All she could think, right that moment, was that she needed water – and lots of it.

Casting about for her clothes, she found them, pausing for a moment, before bending forward to kiss him, gently. 'I adore you too, you know,' she whispered, pulling the scraps of clothing to cover him. 'I won't be long.'

Crawling from the bushes, she made an attempt to stand, but then staggered and nearly fell. The ground beneath her feet was heaving unpleasantly and her stomach automatically rebelled. She glanced up. The lights from the house blurred and focussed. Swallowing, she chose her route, not daring to look down, but managing one foot in front of the other until the French doors loomed up. Her hands grasped the frame and she hauled herself inside.

The air was thick with sweat, the dancing bodies pushed closer and closer until she thought she might suffocate. Blinking painfully into the flashing lights, she fought her way through, concentrating hard on the square of doorway, aware that her nausea was rising steadily. She paused at the kitchen, fearful that she'd pass out or throw up and cause some terrible scene.

Her tongue drifted stickily. She was desperate now, really desperate. The stairs were no longer packed with party-goers and she scrambled her way up on all fours, reaching the top and looking frantically for the bathroom. Two girls with glittery stars on their faces glared down at her, their arms folded.

'There's a queue,' the first one said.

Frankie had to clutch onto the wall to get herself upright. She attempted to waver a smile, but they didn't smile back.

'Is there any chance…?' Her voice didn't sound as it used to. She gestured weakly at the door. 'Like, I really have to get in there.'

'No,' said the first girl.

'Yeah,' said the second. 'You look like you do.' They exchanged glances and second girl shrugged. 'We don't want her puking on our shoes though, do we?' She unfolded an arm and thumbed at the door. 'Go for it.'

There was the click of the catch shunting back and Frankie winced at the sudden dazzle of white light. It opened wider and she felt her entire body shrink back as Charlotte stepped past her in a wash of musky perfume. There was a moment when their eyes locked, before Frankie managed to stumble over the threshold and shunt the door closed.

It was as though Charlotte was still there. Even the taps smelled of her as she turned them, bending her face to the chilled rush of water. She drank greedily, splashing her face and neck, and then straightened to take a look at herself in the mirror. A complete sight stared back. She had twigs and leaves in her hair and her make-up hung in great hammocks of grey and black under her eyes. She looked pale, and drawn, and very sick. She closed her eyes and the room swam in one appalling queasy wave, as suddenly she heaved, bringing the water and vodka back up in one great gasping torrent. The relief was like a weight lifting, and she leaned heavily on the basin edge, breathing deeply.

Throwing up felt so, so good. Rubbing her nose, she reached across for the toilet roll, but her eye caught something lying on the floor. A red strip of what looked like fabric was lying between the foot of the basin and the bath, and she bent to pick it up. It was Charlotte's hairband. She held it for a moment, smoothing the silky flowers and breathing in that scent as it drifted up. Placing it carefully on the side of the bath, she meticulously pulled each sprig and dry teasel from the ends of her hair before running her fingers from root to tip until it lay across her shoulders in slippery waves. Sliding the hairband over her brow, she pushed it back over her forehead. Tendrils of curls hung prettily around her face. Running the tap, she used wads of toilet paper and began to wipe the dead make-up off. Her young, pink skin began to shine through. She looked so much better.

Pressing her lips together and pinching her cheeks, she unlocked the door and, mustering what remained of her dignity, made her way past the two staring girls and back down the stairs into the cacophony of noise.

Her stomach felt hollow and empty. She really didn't want to be here anymore. Part of her longed to be at home in her bed. If only she could take Martin back with her.

If only they could snuggle beneath the covers together, it would all be okay. Her head thumped with a grinding ache and she started to feel like puking again.

She got to the bottom step. There was a couple with their backs to her, blocking her way. The girl was spinning round, dancing, smiling and flirting with her arms aloft. The man leaned in to whisper in her ear and suddenly the sick feeling in her stomach lurched.

It was Martin.

And Charlotte.

She saw his dark head leaning in against her blonde hair as he tried to hear what she was saying.

They hadn't seen her. Frankie froze. She was aware of her hand gripping the bannister as the scene unfolded like a drawn-out nightmare. She saw the sudden silly grin lighting up his face, his nodding interest, the way his eyes ran up and down Charlotte's body as he drank her in like a greedy dog. The girl only observed him from the side of her eye, coolly, totally self-contained and in control, smiling and pursing her lips as though she was dealing with an over-eager puppy. Martin wanted her: anyone could see that.

Martin. Wanted. Her.

Two guys moved past them on their way out. One barged into Martin's shoulder, making him lift his head and turn. He immediately saw Frankie: his face instantly withdrew. He took a step back and Charlotte looked round.

There was a sudden silence in Frankie's head.

'What are you doing?' She could feel her chin trembling with anger and tears. 'What are you doing with her?'

Her voice didn't sound as she wanted it to. She heard her petulant tone, like a whining six-year-old, but inside she felt an absolute adult rage.

'We weren't doing anything.' The ridiculousness of the statement as it fell out of his mouth made it worse. 'I mean – not in the way you think. It's not like—'

'My hairband!' Charlotte suddenly announced in surprise. 'Where did you find that?'

Frankie stepped back defensively, the tears threatening to cascade any minute.

'What about before?' She gestured weakly in the direction of the garden. 'What about all that you said? What about us?'

Martin opened his mouth and closed it again. 'It's not—' he started.

'Can I have my hairband please?' Charlotte reached out a hand but Frankie slapped it away, her eyes ablaze.

'Don't you dare come anywhere near me! I don't want the thing – it stinks!' She ripped it from her head but Charlotte went to take it from her. The audacity of the action made her refuse to let go. She really did feel like a kid now. There were seconds of tugging and yanking, neither of them giving in. Frankie pushed her in the shoulder, somewhere between a punch and a shove. The girl staggered.

'Hey! Oi! Hang on! Hang on!' Martin got between them, holding his hands up. 'Stop! Just stop.' He blocked Frankie. 'Calm down, Frank, seriously. It's nothing. You're getting mad over nothing… really.'

She searched his face looking for the thing that had been there between them: that special thing that made them so different from everyone else, but she couldn't find it anymore. It wasn't there. He'd become ordinary and small right in front of her eyes.

With a frustrated yell, she chucked the hairband at Charlotte. Frankie's eyes desperately raked Martin's. *Why? Why would he need to do this?* He'd humiliated her, embarrassed her in front of the one girl that she couldn't bear to be humiliated by. She spun round. The front door was open and she made a bolt for it, the night wind slapping her tear-washed cheeks as she started to run. Her feet pounded the pavements; her breath was hot and jagging in her throat. She had no idea where she was going, she didn't care who saw her or what they might think.

*How could she have been so stupid? Why hadn't she seen what he was before?*

The choking hiccoughs that racked her chest finally stopped her from running any further. She slowed, her breath stinging and burning, her tongue dry and aching. She couldn't cry properly because her lungs wouldn't let her. She was far away from anywhere and everyone she knew.

She came to a stuttering halt, resting her hands on her knees as she bent to catch her breath. She stared down at the pavement. Everything was wrong now, the world looked wrong. She thought of him sauntering back into work tomorrow, casually picking up where he left off, laughing and chatting with Jude and those girls, and no one knowing a thing. She thought of all the houses they'd broken into and all the things he'd taken and how there would be no consequences for any of it because no one knew what he'd done. A sudden rage slammed into her belly. She'd been picked up and manoeuvred just as easily as he'd picked up those bottles and tins. She was clearly nothing to him: a useful thing, a kid to be strung along and she'd fallen for the whole spiel. He'd suckered her in, big-time. Was she going to let him just get away with that? *Was she?* The hell she was.

She began to retrace her steps back along the streets until the noise told her she was close to the party. There were people still standing in the doorway as she barged past and into the hallway. An awful thought suddenly struck her: *what if he was hooking up with Charlotte right now?* The idea almost slayed her. Fighting back the threat of tears, she turned the whole lot into anger. Grabbing up a full bottle of wine from the table, she stormed up the stairs, banging each of the bedroom doors open in turn. A number of surprised faces peered back at her from amongst the coats and jackets but none of them were Martin or Charlotte. Stomping back down the stairs, she bulldozed her way through the horde in the living room and practically fell out of the open doors into the garden. *She wouldn't let them see what they'd done to her; she wouldn't give them that satisfaction. But she'd make sure they felt the full force of it: all her pain and fury was coming their way. Yes, they could definitely have some of that.*

Taking a big slug from the bottle, and then another, she marched down the path. Where were they? Smashing her way through the bushes, she tore and ripped at the stems, knowing that people were staring but she didn't care. The lights above her swayed in the breeze and a tremendous weight of unbearable sadness fell around her shoulders. *She would not cry*. She staggered a little. There were the bushes where she'd lain with Martin, and a lump caught in her throat. Taking another gulp of wine, she pushed her way into the undergrowth and listened again. She couldn't hear anyone. *They're here though... they must be here... Why would he do this to her?* She gulped back a sob and scrubbed at her face. It was wet, and her neck was gritty with dirt and tears. She licked her lips and tasted… blood. Pushing her way back onto the path she realised that her palms were sticky with it; the skin was cut up and sore, and her nails were broken.

The wine buzzed loudly in her ears; the pills and the alcohol heaved together in a sudden squall in her gut. She closed her eyes as a wave of giddiness caught her and she sat heavily on a tree stump. *What was she really going to find out here?* Only more hurt and more pain. The garden came into focus and then drifted away again. *Blot it out. Yeah. Blot the whole fucking thing out.* She tried to stand and failed – tried again and dropped back, hard.

'Are you okay?'

A voice came from somewhere behind, making her jump. She swung her head round in a wave of dizziness. There was a man, a bloke anyway, his leather jacket creaking as she felt the warmth of his hand cupping her elbow, helping her to her feet.

'Doan worry 'bout me,' she mumbled. 'Mm fine… juss need to—'

'Your face. You're bleeding.'

'No I'm not, iss my hands, I was—'

'Hang on.'

There was a rustle as he delved into his pocket and she felt the papery touch of a tissue against her cheek and palms. 'You're in a bit of a state.'

'Mm alright.'

'I don't think so.' The voice was kind, concerned. 'Let me get you a cab.'

'Nah.' She got up, swaying slightly. 'I wanna walk.'

'I don't really think you should—'

But she'd pushed past him before he could finish.

'Let me make sure you're safe, at least!' he called after her.

But she didn't want to listen, she just wanted out of there. Surprisingly, her legs complied, allowing her to stumble her way back through the house and out onto the street. Glancing briefly over her shoulder, she saw he was following. *For fuck's sake, go away!* She took every sidestreet and turning, repeatedly doubling back on herself, using the tactics that Martin had taught her, until she found a front garden that was shrouded in shadows and slid into them, crouching, waiting until he had gone.

*Martin.*

The things he'd taught her.

He'd changed her life. How she'd love to just forget she ever met him.

But he'd never forget he'd met her.

She stood unsteadily. If he wasn't at the house, then she knew where they'd be. The streets were silent. She knew exactly where she was heading: she'd seen the blue finger-post signs marked 'Footpath' and where it was pointing to.

It took her half an hour to get down to the canal. She couldn't remember exactly where he was moored – she'd only been there once before – but she thought she could find her way there. The towpath was murky and deserted. The canal tunnels loomed black in front of her. The only sounds were those of her own feet as her soles pinged, their echoes ricocheting unsteadily across the water's surface. It was a different world down here: the ages-old wet mustiness of bricks and lichen, and the slow clopping of the water inside the lock gates.

*Frankie.*

Startled, she whirled round. The voice had been in her ear: so close, right on her shoulder. But there was no one there. The shadows around her feet elongated like weird puppets – they began to move to her left and right, independent of her, not hers at all, her head becoming cartoonish, the hands wild and gesticulating, but she wasn't moving them. Heart drumming, she looked around. The path behind was quiet. She looked back. No shadows. No waving figure. Nothing. She swallowed.

*Drugs. That's all. Just the drugs. Come on, Frankie, keep it together.*

Up ahead, the canal boats reared like sleeping monsters out of the gloom. Using the torch on her phone, she shone the beam along the water's edge, trying to make out the names: *Annabella, Gypsy Rose, April Star*— and then she saw it and instantly recognised the name: *Morning Mist.* Her eyes searched the length of the boat, peering painfully at the windows as she slowed her pace, searching for the sight she dreaded: Martin with Charlotte. And then she saw it. A faint gauzy yellow glowing through one of the closed curtains. Something gripped her gut.

She stopped, listening. Her breath was high up in her chest and she blinked muzzily. She could see the door to the cabin was slightly ajar with a beading of light round the edge. If they were in there, she'd hear them. The boat rocked a little in its moorings as the sound of a voice made her turn her head.

Heart thudding, she walked to the back of the boat. One foot forward and a flip of that door to swing it wide and she would see what her heart wasn't ready to see. She put a hand on the rail. The boat moved alarmingly and her fingers gripped the metal tighter as she stepped onto the edge. Her fingers grazed the tiller. Noiselessly, she grasped the wooden end and pulled it free from the rudder. It felt heavy in her hands. She staggered a little, swaying with the motion. If she opened the door now... She imagined the look on their faces. They'd be scared of her, terrified. She'd show them that you can't treat people like something that can be used and thrown away.

Softly and very gently, she put a fingertip on the edge of the cabin door. The light arced into a geometric shape at her feet. She dipped her head below the roof edge. The black shadow of her outline loomed up in front of her like an uninvited guest.

Everywhere went suddenly very quiet. The stink of Charlotte's perfume filled her nostrils and she jumped as a flock of ducks squawked and flapped, skimming across the water's surface. The end of the bed revealed itself; the bedclothes were rucked and tumbled onto the floor. She couldn't see Martin or Charlotte. Where were they?

She stepped inside.

# *Chapter Six*

She didn't remember how she got back to the home. She knew she was running; the juddering hammer of pain in the top of her skull; her breath hissing through her clenched jaw. There was a screaming in her head that wouldn't go away. She couldn't see or hear or think. The drumbeat of her heart pounded until she thought it might rip through her chest wall. Suddenly she was back in the familiar street with the shape of the house coming up in front of her. *Tonight hadn't happened*, her head told her. *None of it was real.* None of the horror: none of the sights or the sounds. Nothing. She'd dreamt it. She knew she would wake up in her bed, and everything would be just as it was. But something inside said different.

The birds of the dawn chorus twittered all around and a chill gathered down her spine. She stopped running. It had happened to someone else. Her head felt heavy, as though it was on a stalk that she could barely hold upright. No matter how hard she tried, the images fluttered and drifted, the pictures before her eyes rushing up to her as though on a surging tide before being dragged away again. She couldn't hold on to her thoughts. *Let them go; you don't want them.*

Her window was still slightly ajar. The house was silent. As she had done so many times before, she scaled the first bracket of the drainpipe, back onto the porch roof and onto her windowsill. Within moments she was back inside her room. It was exactly as she'd left it. Pushing down the backs of her sneakers, she crawled fully clothed beside the hump of pillows, putting her arms around them, and holding on to them tight. She closed her eyes. A shock lurched through her jerking her arms and legs, but she only held on tighter and tighter, squeezing everything out – *Don't let it in, shut it all out*, until oblivion dragged her down to a place that she really, really wanted to go.

–

Her surface dreams were full of grief, great, roaring waves of it, deep and all-consuming that kept breaking into her consciousness. She didn't want to wake up; she didn't want to remember. Her brain dragged and thrashed over a multitude of terrible fears. Someone was crying and begging; the wailing got louder and louder until she was forced to open her eyes. The roaring was real. Her eyes batted as she tried to make sense of the sound. There were voices. Two of them, coming from downstairs; they were loud, rising and falling. She lifted her head from the pillow. Somewhere in the background she could hear Martin. Her heart leapt and then utter despair kicked in. Shoving the covers away, she managed to stagger her way to the door. She could hear Jude, but not what she was saying. Easing herself quietly onto the landing, she tiptoed down the first few steps.

'But I *know*, Martin. Don't you get that? All this rubbish you're spouting – it's pointless!'

Martin said something in reply, but she couldn't quite catch the words.

There was a whispered chatter from the hallway, and she realised she wasn't the only person to have been woken up by the ruckus. She went down a little further, peering through the bannister to find Nat and Jaden perched on the bottom step. They both turned, saw who it was, and looked away again in disgust.

'Come to gloat, have you?' Nat sneered.

'What?' She tried to move her tongue against the roof of her mouth, but it felt as though it was coated with sawdust.

'Martin's in the shit 'cos of you."

Her eyes ached with a dull, angry throb.

'What are you on about?'

'Jude knows you wasn't in your room last night. She's blaming him. She says you was with him and says she's gonna call the Old Bill.'

Frankie felt her eyes widen painfully. *The police?* A shunt of fear lurched through her. No... If Jude called the police, if Jude asked them to question her...

Pulling herself together, she slipped down the last few steps, marching straight into the office without knocking. Both Jude and Martin turned round in shock.

'What's going on?' She pushed the door closed behind her and tried to keep her voice low, knowing those ears would still be flapping on the other side.

Jude was bright pink with anger, but on seeing Frankie she tried to calm herself.

'Ah. Good. I'm glad you're here. Have a seat.' She gestured to one of the comfy chairs next to the coffee table that was supposed to make the residents feel comfortable and relaxed. It never worked. Frankie sat, not willing to catch Martin's eye. She stared stonily at the carpet.

'Let's cut to the chase.'

Frankie could sense Martin's tension.

'Two things have been brought to my attention: I know you weren't in your room last night, and I've been given information that there's some kind of inappropriate relationship going on.'

'Whatever Nat's told you—'

'Let's leave Natalie out of this, shall we? She's got enough going on.' She paused. Frankie knew she was trying to read her body language. She kept completely still. Her fuddled brain tried to work out who might've seen them. She licked her lips, still refusing to look up.

'I was explaining to Martin here that this behaviour has crossed a line. I know he's only here as a volunteer, but we still may have to inform the authorities that—'

'But he hasn't done anything wrong!' Frankie quickly blurted.

'Frankie...' Jude was using her patient voice.

'He was covering for me.' Her brain went into a whirl of plausible excuses. 'He knew I was sneaking out at night and that you lot had no idea. He was afraid of bad things happening while I was out, so he kept following me to make sure I was safe.'

She couldn't look at either of them, but Jude was suddenly out of her seat and bending to examine her.

'Frankie, what's that on your face?' She sounded alarmed. 'And your hands...?' She gently turned them over. 'You've got blood all over your hands.' She lifted her chin into the light. 'Look, it's all down the front of your shirt too.'

'I think I must've got a cut without realising.' Frankie studied her palms. 'It's nothing.'

'How is that even possible?' Jude crouched at her side and searched her eyes. 'Where did you go last night, Frankie?'

Frankie sniffed and studied the spot on the carpet again. 'I wandered about the streets for a bit. Then I heard a noise, like there was a party on or something, so I went there.' She glanced away awkwardly.

'And you're saying Martin followed you?' Jude frowned. She didn't look convinced.

'Yeah. He followed me. But he's kinda annoying and embarrassing, y'know? Having some bloke following you round like he's your dad or something.' She clicked her tongue and shook her head, but still she wasn't going to look at him. 'So I pretended I was leaving the gaff and I gave him the slip. It worked.'

'Then what did you do?'

Frankie shrugged. 'Scored stuff, drank a bit, went out into the garden to chill.' She shrugged again. 'That's when I must've done this.' She turned her palms over. 'Don't remember. Then I came home and got back in my room and went to bed. No drama. Nothing to get all vexed about, anyway.'

She could feel Jude's eyes boring into the side of her face and then her attention shifted to Martin.

'And you just walked the streets looking for her, did you?'

She could make out Martin's head nodding from the corner of her eye.

'Yeah,' he said. 'Yeah. I was worried. Young girl out of her tree, wandering about. Anything could happen, couldn't it?'

'And you tried ringing her?' Jude's gaze was piercing.

'He doesn't have my number,' Frankie said quickly. 'So he couldn't. Here – check if you want.' She reached for her phone from the back pocket of her jeans, knowing that they had agreed never to phone each other for that very reason.

Jude didn't offer to take it. She got up and perched on the edge of her desk, looking straight at Martin.

'So why didn't you bring your concerns to me?'

Martin held out his hands imploringly. 'I've been told how Frankie responds to authority, and some of the other staff said that when she's challenged it just makes things worse. I was coming off my shift last night when I happened to catch sight of her as she was climbing out of the window, but she saw me and ran off. So I went after her.' He paused. 'It's all totally my fault, Jude, I should've alerted you right then, but I panicked. I thought if I could persuade her to come back it would all be okay. When I saw she was headed to that party, I knew she could get herself into some serious shit.'

Jude leaned back and folded her arms. She was seriously angry, but she was still listening. Martin could clearly sense that too.

'Once I lost her, it didn't take me long to realise I was out of my depth and that I had no idea what I was doing. So call it arrogance, call it inexperience, but I can tell you categorically, I've learned a huge lesson.' His shoulders dropped. He sighed and shook his head. 'Clearly I got it wrong. I got it wrong right from the beginning and for that I am so, so sorry.'

Frankie watched his performance in amazement. He looked like he truly believed his own story.

He leaned forward, his fingers linked as he shifted nervously. 'Look, I understand totally if you think I'm not cut out for this kind of work. I fully respect whatever decision you make, Jude. Even if you suggest I stop volunteering here. I wouldn't blame you. I totally get it.'

Jude stayed silent for a moment, looking from one to the other. Her arms unfolded and there was a shift in the atmosphere.

'Well actually Martin, given Frankie's past problems, this outcome is fundamentally a step forward.' Frankie let herself breathe. 'She didn't stay out all night and force us to call the police as she normally would.' She felt Jude's beady eyes on her. 'She got herself back home, relatively unscathed.' She gave her another meaningful look. 'That's a massive plus from where we were six months ago. I'm not saying the way you behaved was right, Martin, but the result is the right result, and if you had a hand in making that happen then I commend you. But I have to tell you – no more, you understand me?'

Her gaze forced them to look at each other.

'If there's a next time, I will have to take it further.'

They nodded in unison and Frankie got up and walked towards the door. She paused.

'Thank you, Jude,' she said in a small voice.

'Yeah, thanks Jude,' Martin echoed.

Frankie opened the door and Nat and Jaden nearly fell head-first through the gap.

'Show's over,' said Frankie sullenly. 'You're going to have to make your own entertainment.'

'Ah, you two,' Jude called out. 'I'm glad you're both here. Can I have a word?'

Jaden and Nat glanced at each other.

'Oh, and Frankie? You missed the house meeting yesterday where we discussed what's happening with Natalie. Nat, do you want to tell Frankie yourself or do you want me to tell her?'

Natalie looked steadily at Frankie. There was a pause. 'Y'know what happened yesterday – our fight?'

'Yeah?' Frankie looked at her, puzzled.

'Well, the reason everyone went bat-shit about me fallin' over, is 'cos I'm pregnant.'

'What?' Frankie stared back at her.

'Yeah, but I'm having it adopted.'

Frankie couldn't find the words.

'It's for the best.'

No one spoke. Nat stood there, chewing her cheek and then she looked away. 'Yeah well, it's no big deal anyway… It's sorted now. An' I'm sorry I went into your room and took stuff. I shouldn't've… But my head's been all over the place.'

Frankie instantly felt terrible. 'I had no idea, Nat. I feel awful. I shouldn't have pushed you. I'm sorry too. It was stupid. I shouldn't have done that either.'

Nat gave a quick nod and carried on chewing. The unhappiness came off her in waves.

'Well, there we are then.' Jude clapped her hands and looked at them both. 'Situation resolved, I think. With all of us.' She included Martin in her gaze. 'Can we all get back to some kind of normal now, is that possible?' She smiled. 'Okay, Nat have a seat and I'll talk you through what's going to happen at your appointment with the adoption caseworker, and I'll see you two later. Close the door behind you as you leave, please.'

Frankie pulled the door shut with a click. She turned to go but Martin caught her arm.

'Wait a minute.'

'Take your hand off me,' she said stiffly. 'I've got nothing to say to you.'

'Well I've got plenty to say to you.'

Twisting her arm out of his grasp, she stalked away from him, very aware that he was close on her heels as she stomped up the stairs.

'I don't want to hear it.' She felt ill, she felt tired, she felt like crying. She reached her room knowing that part of her longed for him to say *something*, anything to make all this go away.

Wordlessly, he put his finger to his lips and pushed the door open, gesturing for her to go inside. She debated for a second, and then went and sat sulkily on the rumpled bed. He closed the door behind him and then came and crouched in front of her.

'So where did you go?' He went to touch her cheek, but she snatched her face away.

She stared ahead sullenly.

'I came looking for you, you know that, don't you?'

She wouldn't even blink.

'I know you don't believe me, but I'm not interested in Charlotte. I was just talking to her – I was actually remarking how similar you two looked.'

'Really.' Her voice was dull and hard.

'Yes, really. Then you come down the stairs and all hell broke loose.'

'I went to your boat.'

She saw his face tighten.

'There were lights on and then I heard voices.'

'I always leave the lights on when I go out, and you can't have heard—'

A terrific banging on the front door stopped them in their tracks. They both leapt up. Martin went over to the window and looked out.

'Shit.'

'What is it?'

She peered over his shoulder. Outside were two police cars parked askew, their lights whirling madly. The battering of the front door went on and on as though they might break it down any moment. She heard Jude's voice and the jabber of radios.

'Jude said… she promised she wouldn't take last night any further,' Frankie stammered. 'She *promised*.'

Martin went out onto the landing and looked down.

'You don't have two cop cars and all those Old Bill for that.' He hesitated before walking down the stairs. Frankie was right behind him. 'Something's kicked off. One of the girls is in trouble, maybe.'

They reached the bottom. She was aware of the black figures filling the hallway as the police and Jude turned to look at them.

'Are you Martin Jarvis?' one policeman said.

'Yeah, why?'

'And you currently reside on a houseboat named' – the officer consulted his notebook – '*Morning Mist*, that's moored just north of canal bridge number 137. Is that correct?'

'My boat is called *Morning Mist* yes, but I don't know any bridge numbers. Why, what's happened?'

'In that case, I would like you to accompany us to the police station, sir. We'd like to ask you a few questions.'

Martin looked at each of their faces as though wondering if this was a joke. Jude's face was a mask of shock.

'The body of a young woman was discovered this morning in the canal.' The policeman looked at Frankie and then back at Martin.

She felt something crawl across her scalp.

'The body was found in the water next to your boat, Mr Jarvis. We don't have a formal identification as yet, but a girl fitting her description didn't come home last night. She was reported missing by her parents.'

Frankie's knees wouldn't hold her any longer, and she sat down hard on the stairs.

'We were wondering if you were able to give us any information, or help in any way?'

She watched the back of Martin's head. It swung back and forth. He didn't make a sound.

'We know you were present at an address in Cheyne Road at a party, Mr Jarvis. We have plenty of witnesses putting you there. We also have CCTV footage that shows you and this girl together. Maybe I can jog your memory a little. Would that help? The missing girl's name is Charlotte. Charlotte Vale.'

# *Chapter Seven*

*Now*

She watches Alex's face as he stands there in the doorway. His hand is still clutching the edge as though he's afraid to let go.

'So you think this guy stalking you is someone you used to work with in a care home?' He looks down blankly at the note.

'Yes.'

'What was his name again?' He tips his head.

'Matthew Jarrow.'

She has no idea where that name came from.

'So, your managers knew about his behaviour: this over-familiarity, and eventually they got him transferred?'

'Yes.'

'And that was the last you heard of him?'

'Until someone told me that he's just come out of prison.'

Alex stares down at the piece of paper in his hand again. She's glad he's not looking at her face. The lie scours her cheeks.

'And we don't know what he was in for?'

'No.'

'But you definitely think this is him?' He lifts his head.

'I don't know.'

'And that phone call?'

'I – I don't know. I really don't. It could've been. It's just silence, normally.'

She realises the way she's phrased it is a mistake.

'So this isn't the first time?'

The appalling snowball of the pretence begins to pick up speed. She needs to stop it somehow. This is mad, stupid.

'How long has this been going on?'

She can't breathe.

'And why didn't you just tell me?'

Her jaw clenches painfully. She rubs a tired hand across her face so that she doesn't have to look at him. 'Alex – look, I don't know. I should've... Maybe I thought... Well, you've got enough going on without all this.' She casts a hand across the notes.

'I'll ask again: how long?'

'A few weeks – a month maybe.'

'*Jesus*.' He watches her, appalled. 'And the shit state of my life is the only reason you haven't mentioned it?'

Her head snaps up. 'Of course!'

'So why now?'

She looks at him, puzzled.

'What?'

'Why is he contacting you now after all this time?'

She can't bear this. 'Because he's been released, maybe? Maybe he blames me. Maybe he's obsessed. I don't know.'

'*Christ*.'

She is aware of him searching her face. He must see it, surely? The burn of shame: the lie, upon lie, upon lie. How she wishes she could tell him the truth, but she can't. She can't go back and undo everything.

Alex reaches out and grabs her hand suddenly.

'Frankie.' He clasps it; his eyes are soft with tenderness. 'Y'know the worst thing?'

She wishes he wouldn't look at her. She despises herself.

'The worst thing is, I can't bear the fact that you felt you couldn't come to me. I can't live with the idea that you've had to go through this thing on your own. I've been completely self-absorbed, I know that. I am so sorry – so, so sorry. I've punished you – I know I have.'

'It's okay. It's my fault. I should've said…' She's stunned and appalled to find him drawing her to him, relaxing against her, burying his forehead in her shoulder and wrapping his arms around her. She thinks he might be crying. She has truly never felt more terrible, more awful than she does right now.

'Shh… Honestly… it'll be okay, Alex. It'll be fine.' She hates herself.

'It will once we go to the police.' He pulls away, abruptly. 'We go to the police with these letters and we'll tell them everything. If you're right and this guy has been released, then they need to know that he's threatening and harassing you.' He kneels down on the carpet and begins to push the papers gingerly back into the envelope. 'Fingerprints. There could be fingerprints,' he mutters.

She watches the feverish gathering.

'And the phone. Bring something with the account number on it. They'll want to check out the call log too. Come on.'

'What, we're going right now?' She looks at him in astonishment.

'Yep, now.' He's very definite. 'You've got some bloody nutcase stalking you. Of course we're going to the police. We should've gone to them weeks ago. Now, come on.'

# *Chapter Eight*

Frankie sits across a grey desk in an even greyer side room, giving her statement to a policewoman called Julia. Julia was just about to go off duty after a nightshift but is glad she can help them. Julia sounds as though she's been on a Community Relations course.

Frankie tells her tale, hoping that this policewoman was sent on the course because she's struggling at work, and is, this moment, too tired to pick up on the finer points. Her eyes look a little glassy but she's diligent and careful to ask the right questions in the right way, constantly keeping eye contact, nodding and smiling and making sure that Frankie is comfortable at all times.

'Do we know if this Matthew Jarrow has been released, then?' Alex leans forward, his knee jiggling with tension. Frankie just wishes he'd stop.

'We'll certainly be checking into all the details you've given us and be reporting back everything we find.' Julia clearly wants to sound reassuring. 'We'll be doing everything we can, Mr McKenzie. We do take these things very seriously. Your wife's safety and your safety are our priority. Absolutely. Number one.'

It's a pat response and Alex sits back. Frankie can tell he's not satisfied with her answer. A whole load of questions run through her own mind, the first of which is, what will she tell Alex when the police ring back and declare that there's no Matthew Jarrow on the database – either in or out of prison? What will she say then?

'And you say everything you've received is in here?' Julia puts her hand briefly on the plastic wallet.

Alex looks at Frankie questioningly.

'Yes.' Frankie nods. 'That's all of it.'

The lie slides from her lips. She thinks about the envelope still sitting beneath her desk. There's truth and there is pain. Sometimes terrible truth and terrible pain go hand in hand and, right now, Alex doesn't need either.

Her elbow squeezes the slight bump of the hairband in her pocket. She told Julia about it, showed it to her even, but she really isn't on the ball when it comes to securing evidence.

'I think your statement is pretty comprehensive.' Julia scans the statement sheets in front of her and makes some minor adjustments before swivelling them round for Frankie to read.

'Have a good look through and see if there's anything you want to add. I'll just pop out and speak to one of my colleagues and check if we've already got anything logged on the system that we can tell you about this Matthew Jarrow.' She walks briskly to the door. 'Back in a tic.'

Frankie pretends to read the sheet, her eyes moving back and forth across the page without taking anything in, praying and hoping that she can register the right reaction on her face. She knows she needs to look shocked when she's told that there is no Matthew Jarrow. Her reaction needs to be plausible and Alex needs to see and totally believe it.

She can feel his calm gaze on the side of her face. She looks back at him. He has a slight smile teasing the corners of his mouth. His eyes have an odd look. For one tiny, split second, she wonders if he knows she's lying, but suddenly the warmth of his fingers inch across her own in her lap. He lifts her hand and kisses it.

'From now on, we're in this together, yeah?' He searches her face questioningly. 'No more secrets? Something happens and you tell me. Is that a deal?'

'That's a deal.' She manages to nod, but the deceit echoes hollowly.

The door opens and the hollowness turns to dread.

'I'm afraid the computer's down.' Julia bustles over to the desk. 'How are we doing here?' She puts a finger on the paper. 'Any amendments or additions?'

Alex looks at Frankie, but she shakes her head.

'No, it's fine, thank you. And thank you for all your help.' Her stomach unravels a little.

'Absolutely no problem at all. I've passed all the information to the team. So, if this individual contacts you again, or if you're concerned even slightly, here's my mobile and direct line. Remember, I'm totally on your side.'

She walks them to the main doors, shakes both their hands and they step out onto the early morning street. It feels quiet and strange out here: the buildings and shops around them are still shuttered and closed, the streetlights casting pools of gauzy yellow into the half-light. Frankie looks up and takes a deep breath in. It's just starting to rain.

'You okay?' Alex puts an arm around her waist.

She lets it slowly out again. Her shoulders are trembling with the stress of the last hour. The rain begins to come down harder and Alex quickens his pace, ushering her along the pavement towards their car.

'You got your keys? I'll drive.'

She delves into her bag as he hurries round to the driver's side and blips the car immobiliser. She yanks the passenger door open and slips into the seat.

He gets in beside her, breathlessly. 'No. Jesus.'

She looks over. He's holding a folded piece of paper. Something inside her contracts.

'It was under the wiper blade.'

He opens it and holds it out for her to see.

> *I'm close. You'll just never know how close I really am.*

Frankie looks back at him in horror.

'Right.' He puts a hand on the door and goes to get out.

'Alex. Don't.'

'Yes I am, Frankie. I'm taking this straight into the station. Now.'

'Alex, please—' She grabs his arm.

He is breathing hard. The windscreen fogs.

'For me. Please.'

The rain hits the glass like thrown gravel. A mist has risen outside and in. She feels a contraction in her stomach that begins to shiver into fear. Her whole body is tense and on high alert.

'Why not?'

'I don't want to be left on my own… Don't you see? This means he was right here. It means he knows our movements.' She snatches a look behind her. 'He must've followed us. He must've been outside the house. He's here, Alex. Out there. He must be watching us right now.'

She sees the look on his face: his eyes are wide and staring as he takes in the enormity of what she's saying. A gust of wind rocks the car and she clutches his arm tighter. 'Let's get out of here, Alex. Please. Now.'

She can see it's against every instinct, but he reaches down and turns the ignition. The misted window makes it feel as though everything is closing in: there are shapes out there, piles of rubbish sacks casting weird shadows in the yellow streetlights. Alex opens both side windows; she daren't look round.

'We'll have to wait a minute for the windscreen to clear.' He peers out, blinking.

Out of the corner of her eye she thinks she sees a figure. She turns her head, seeing the bulk of shadows through the fog, hearing the growl and hiss of the truck behind them. The black plastic bags flap in the wind, but something else moves. The headlights of a stationary car on the other side of the street suddenly light up, and the figure crosses the road in front of them. She stares at the shape, willing it to pause and face her. The mist bundles in waves and then clears a little. *It's him, it has to be him.* He's always been out there hovering in the periphery of her sightline, that man, just she remembers him, that twenty-one-year-old, conjured up; a man she wants to hate. It's been a long, long time. Fifteen years gone and now he's found her, just as she always knew he would.

A patch on the windscreen clears a little. Alex puts the car into gear. They go to pull away just as the figure passes by her window. It turns its head and looks straight at her.

It's not him.

# *Chapter Nine*

## *Then*

'How do you plead?'

Frankie sat up in the public gallery, tucked away in a corner, her hands clasped between her knees, leaning anxiously forward. The whole room was designed to absorb the daylight: the dark Victorian benches, the arched, ornate ceiling, the scrolled, panelled walls closing everything in. The outside world didn't exist. This had been life for the last few days. This was her only life.

'Not guilty.'

She stared at the shape of Martin's head, unable to drag her gaze away. She closed her eyes for a second, remembering how, just a few months ago, the sight of him from her bedroom window sent her stomach somersaulting. All those feelings were still there, as intense as they'd ever been. How she wished they weren't. She opened her eyes. The clusters of dusty pendant lights gave everything a muted, jaundiced haze and the room felt dry and overheated. Her eyes kept being drawn back to him over and over, as though an invisible thread connected them that nothing, not anger, or hurt, or time could ever break.

The judge was speaking; he was a jowly man, old and wrinkly, like the judge in a cartoon. He droned on, speaking a language she didn't understand.

They'd taken him away that day, questioned him and eventually charged him, gathering their evidence and their paperwork, mapping out his movements that night, weaving and knitting until it all fitted together like a jigsaw. The next day he'd rung the care home from HMP Moreton Wood where he was being held.

'No, I'm very sorry, that simply isn't possible.'

She had been passing Jude's office door when the call came through. She instantly knew it was Martin: Jude's voice had that stiff, professional clip.

'Please… Let me speak to him. Jude, please—'

But Jude only carried on talking, waving her away and shaking her head.

'Let me speak to him,' Frankie insisted. 'I need to know what he's told the police.'

Jude paused with her hand over the receiver and Frankie took the tack that she knew would work.

'Look, *you* need to know what he's told the police. I'm seventeen and I'm still in your care. It's in all our interests. If he drops me in it, it'll all come back on you. Think about it Jude.'

'Precisely. This is for me to deal with.'

'It's my life too. I got Martin into this by going to that party, didn't I?' She held out her hand. 'Come on… Please… Two minutes. Just let me speak to him.'

There was a moment's hesitation and then reluctantly, very reluctantly, Jude handed over the phone, but made it clear she was going nowhere.

'Hello?'

'You don't know what it's like just to hear your voice,' he breathed.

'What's happening?'

'They're saying I did it.'

'I know.'

'It doesn't matter what they say, you know I didn't. You *know* that, don't you?'

'Yes,' she said.

She closed her eyes. If she concentrated hard, she could shut out all the flashing images that came back to her: the darkness, the water, the boat, that queasy rise and fall sensation beneath her feet. By closing her mind, she could make it fade around the edges and start to go black until there was nothing there. Nothing. None of it.

'So what did you tell the police about me?' She was aware of Jude's piercing eyes.

'I didn't tell them anything; there's nothing for them to know. Look, all this will get sorted, but I need to ask you a qu—'

'What's he saying?' Jude stood suddenly. 'Give the phone back to me.' Her fingers began to wrestle the receiver from Frankie's hand.

'Ow!'

'Is there anything else I can help you with, Martin?' She was breathing hard and her face was set and stony. 'No? Good. Right then. Thanks so much for getting in touch. Goodbye.' And the phone went down. She looked up.

'Sit, please.'

Her tone said there was no choice.

'I might as well be very straight with you, Frankie. You're a bright girl and you have a chance of a proper future, but you know better than I do that someone with your sort of background is often never given a first chance, let alone a second. Are you listening to me?'

'Yes.'

'Stay away from all this chaos with Martin Jarvis.'

'But—'

She held up a hand. 'I know you feel responsible in some way because of going off to that party, but you're not. There were clearly things going on with him that just need leaving alone. Let the court deal with him.'

She had a frightened tight feeling in her chest.

'I should never have agreed for him to work here. I did the usual: I gave him the benefit of the doubt and it was stupid.'

'Benefit of the doubt?'

'Yes, I know how he comes across – he's a likeable, charming, intelligent young man. All that is true, but there's another truth – the care orders, the juvenile detention, the probation monitoring, I just thought he was past all that.'

Frankie's head snatched round.

Jude looked at her, surprised.

'I thought you knew – the other girls were chattering on about it so I assumed everyone did. He was one of my lads from a previous life. He was on my unit. Didn't you know that?'

'Unit? What kind of unit?'

Jude took a breath and then paused as though deciding how much to say.

'He used to have... well... anger management problems. Let's call them that. But anyway, I really thought he'd turned it around. I knew he'd been sleeping rough but once he started working on that old canal boat he'd found, it really seemed to give him a focus. Then he started talking about college and working with youngsters, and I thought, "Brilliant! I'll help him in any way I can to get on his feet." Hence him working here.'

Frankie shook her head slowly. She'd had no idea.

'And now…' Jude held out her hands. 'Now look where he is. God alone knows what he's done or what he's got mixed up in. That poor, poor girl…' Her thoughts seemed to drift for a moment and then snapped back. 'And that's the thing, Frankie. That's how easy it is to get drawn into the wrong place at the wrong time with the wrong people, and suddenly your life changes forever. So don't fall into that trap. Don't put yourself anywhere near his world. You're not responsible, so stay well out of it.'

'But he's innocent!' blurted Frankie.

'You have absolutely no idea whether that's true or not.'

Frankie felt the tears beginning to gather.

'A girl has *died*, Frankie.' Jude lowered her voice and her eyes narrowed. '*Died*. We don't know how, but people are saying that she was held under the water and drowned, do you understand that? So they're saying someone *did* that to her. Some animal, some monster.'

Frankie flinched. A whole barrage of images flashed unbidden into her head. She saw black water and felt a sudden undulating judder beneath her feet.

'You didn't see or hear anything at that party, did you?'

She could hear the veiled panic in Jude's voice, but she could only shake her head – if only she could shake away what was in there.

'And you're sure of that? It's as you said: you gave Martin the slip and you didn't see him again?'

Another grim shake. She didn't know if Jude believed her or not, but she obviously wasn't going to press it.

'I don't want you anywhere near this, Frankie, do you hear me? Martin has told you he's keeping your name out of this whole thing and I want your face kept out of it too.' Jude came and sat next to her and put her hand on her arm. 'Look at me for a moment.'

Frankie lifted her head.

'You think I'm ancient and therefore blind and daft and stupid, but in fact, I'm only one of those things.' She nudged her playfully. 'And being ancient doesn't mean I was always old. I was young, once. I know what attraction looks like and I could see you were attracted to Martin.'

Frankie opened her mouth, but Jude quickly cut across her.

'I don't *need* to know, and I don't *want* to know. Right now, there's nothing to be gained from having that conversation. This is a life lesson for you: no one ever knows anyone. Not really. They think they do, but they don't.'

She found herself swallowing.

'There's going to be a trial, Frankie. It's going to be in every newspaper and on every screen for a while so prepare to be shocked. I've been in these situations before; everyone involved will have their own spin and their own take, so you won't know fact from hype. I can see that you care for him, my love, but they'll open him up and peer into his innermost depths until the Martin you thought you knew will disappear. Whatever happened to that poor girl will come out. Trust me.'

# Chapter Ten

Martin was sitting with a prison officer on either side of him. He looked lost and very alone. He wasn't going to look at her no matter how hard she stared. She studied his shoulders, the nape of his neck, remembering the sweet scent of the skin behind his ear; the sheer heat of him against her cheek. The thoughts and sensations wouldn't go away. She swallowed.

The prosecution barrister was droning on, his voice whining, insect-like. He had small, thick-lensed glasses that kept flashing as though the eyes behind them were absent. The tone wavered like a dying bluebottle. The judge was staring down with his hand propped against his forehead. She wondered if he'd gone to sleep.

The jury shifted uncomfortably, some of them glancing at their watches. The lunch break seemed a very long way away. She needed to get back to school and show her face before she could manage to sneak back into the court again, later. She shouldn't be here at all, she knew that. She promised Jude, but then she'd promised Jude a lot of things and they weren't happening either.

She gazed at the other people at the far end of the gallery. There was a woman in a pink jacket sitting next to a sandy-haired man with a round, kind face. In front of them was a boy wearing a denim jacket. She had a feeling she might've seen him somewhere before.

'May I bring the CCTV footage of the towpath to your attention.'

There was a shift in the atmosphere and the jury suddenly sat up and took notice. Several of the large TV screens, placed strategically around the courtroom, flickered into life. A grey gauzy background told them something was about to happen. The barrister picked up a small remote control and pressed the 'Pause' button as a line of white numbers and letters denoted the time and the date frozen onto the screen.

'This shows the early hours of Saturday the sixth of September at three thirty-seven in the morning.' He pressed the 'Pause' button again and the screen formed a picture. It showed the black and white footage of the stretch of canal where Frankie had walked that night. There was the exit of the tunnel and the lock gates just up ahead. Three boats were moored on the left.

'Please keep watching.'

All eyes were on the screen as two figures appeared, staggering slightly, from the mouth of the tunnel.

'The figure on the right of the screen is Charlotte Vale,' said the barrister.

There was a slight gasp from somewhere in the gallery, making Frankie turn her head. The woman in the pink jacket had her fist pressed to her lips.

'And the figure on the left is the defendant Martin Jarvis.'

Frankie stared and then stared again. *They'd got that wrong. That wasn't him. He'd told her, hadn't he? He'd said that... What had he said?*

She looked at the back of Martin's head. He didn't flinch, he didn't make any movement at all. A gripe of something acidic washed through her stomach. It felt like fear. Martin had his arm around Charlotte's shoulders. She had her head bowed. Her hand kept coming up to her face and then dropping to her side again.

'And here, on the next camera, we have the defendant, Martin Jarvis and Charlotte Vale boarding the narrowboat *Morning Mist* – the boat that is owned by Mr Jarvis.'

Frankie watched, her horror rising as Martin and Charlotte stepped onto the side of the boat, Charlotte steadying herself as Martin opened the cabin door and they both disappeared down the steps. The footage ended and the barrister turned off the screen.

The judge peered across his bench. 'Ah, we have further footage from this point onwards, do we, Mr Bain?'

Mr Bain looked slightly uncomfortable. 'Erm... No... Unfortunately, the Prosecution has been unable to secure the footage from these frames onward.'

The judge continued to peer at him, saying nothing.

'I believe it got wiped, Your Honour.'

'Wiped?'

His voice boomed as though he hadn't heard the word before.

'Er, yes, Your Honour. We have no further footage of the defendant or the victim from this time-point onwards. An administration error I believe, by the Canal and River Trust.'

The judge looked at him as though he had to be personally responsible. He sat back abruptly.

'Please continue.'

A tiny trickle of sweat ran down between Frankie's shoulder blades. Martin looked across to his left so that she was able to see the side of his face. His chin lifted and his eyes batted upwards as if assessing the air. He knew exactly where she was. She willed him to catch her gaze, but knowing, absolutely that he wouldn't. He couldn't bring himself to look at her.

*He'd lied.*

She needed to see his eyes.

*He'd lied.*

She'd known he was lying all along. She'd challenged him at the party and in her room, knowing, deep down he was lying to her – and she'd wanted him to lie because she couldn't bear to know the truth.

*She was just an impressionable kid: easily duped, easily manipulated. A mug.*

And then suddenly he lifted his head and his eyes caught hers and her heart folded.

Her rage and her anger went to war with the hurt and betrayal. She battled fiercely with the tears that burned and stung her eyes.

His head shook slowly as he stared at her. What was he saying? That he was sorry? That the footage was wrong? That it wasn't what it seemed? What?

She looked away, concentrating on the rail in front of her. How did anyone turn off their feelings? There wasn't a switch or a button. It was all still there: that pull, that yearning, bringing her back to him again and again.

*She would not cry… Find something. Concentrate. Close it down.*

'Can I refer the members of the jury to a particular point to your evidence bundle.'

She lifted her head, blinking. Mr Bain flipped over several papers on the table in front of him and there was a tidal wave of rustling as the jury did the same.

'Section C, pages eighteen to twenty-one. Can I draw your attention to page eighteen, the photograph labelled "Seven" where you can see the police evidence photo of the interior of the cabin? The next photograph I would like you to consider is the photograph identified as "Number Eight", showing where the DNA evidence was identified. You will see the red arrows pointing to the pillow on the left-hand side of the bed, the bedside cupboard handle, the drinking glass located on the top of said cupboard; all have been identified as containing DNA evidence and fingerprints belonging to the victim, Charlotte Vale.'

He paused to let that information sink in. 'I believe none of this information is contested by the counsel for the defendant, Your Honour.'

Mr Saunders, Martin's barrister, nodded in agreement and looked back at his desk.

Mr Bain turned to address the judge. 'So I think it is safe to say that we all agree that Charlotte Vale, the victim, was indeed present in that cabin at some point that evening. The DNA evidence is strong and undegraded, thus indicating that her presence there was very close to the time she was last seen – sometime after three thirty-seven on the morning of the sixth of September.'

He carried on speaking, but Frankie couldn't hear any of the words. She kept imagining and picturing the scene: she saw Charlotte's naked shoulder just peeking from beneath the covers, the indented pillow, the blonde head that would leave behind those few strands of pale hair, the glass on the bedside cabinet being put there by a slim white hand, the fingertips just trailing, leaving their mark before she slid from the side of the bed. *None of that had happened, it couldn't have.*

'I would like to call the defendant, Martin Jarvis, to the stand.'

All eyes turned as Martin stood up. Frankie had never seen him dressed like that: the ill-fitting suit, the tie, the collar of his shirt slightly awry. He walked with strange jerky movements to the witness box where he mounted the steps, his face totally devoid of any expression. His skin had a pallor to it, a ghostly translucence, as he was asked his particulars. He answered calmly and precisely as though this might be something that happened to him every day.

She listened to the muffled rise and fall of voices as though she was one side of a thick plate of glass. Mr Bain, the barrister, then began to press questions about Martin's whereabouts that night. Martin was speaking, but her ears couldn't bear to listen to him: hearing his voice was sheer agony – this was the voice that had whispered to her; those were the lips that had told her so many lies. Her heart was thudding so hard she couldn't hear his answers. The sound of the questions came in and out of focus: Why had he been at that party? Who did he see there? Who had he spoken to? She was terrified that at any minute she was going to hear her name. She waited. She waited some more. It didn't come.

'So can you tell the court, Mr Jarvis, the sequence of events after you left that party? You say you invited Charlotte Vale back to your canal boat?'

'Yes.'

His voice was barely audible.

The saliva in her mouth tasted bitter.

'And in your opinion, she was going with you willingly? Happily, even?'

'Yes.'

'Would you mind speaking up, Mr Jarvis?'

'Yes.'

A knife-like pain stabbed through her gut.

'And you maintain that she went with you willingly because she'd been to your boat on several occasions before, I understand?'

The judge peered down intently.

'That's correct.'

The knife drove in further, twisting, slicing her in two.

He told them how he'd left Charlotte sitting on the bed in the cabin. He said she'd been upset about something, but she wouldn't say why. He said he'd offered to go and buy wine from an off-licence, but the local shop had been closed and he didn't go any further afield. When he got back, Charlotte had gone. The cabin was just as he'd left it and he just thought she'd changed her mind and gone home.

The judge suddenly coughed.

'Can I just clarify that we definitely have no CCTV footage from the streets to confirm or repudiate what the defendant is alleging here? Is that correct?'

Martin's barrister, Mr Saunders, got to his feet. 'That's correct, Your Honour. The CCTV does not show my client or the victim, Charlotte Vale, again. There is nothing *whatsoever* connecting Ms Vale's death with Mr Jarvis.'

The prosecution barrister got to his feet and Mr Saunders was forced to sit down.

'Can I ask the witness a simple question? Were you, or were you not, in a sexual relationship with Charlotte Vale?'

Frankie closed her eyes. Her stomach came up to meet her throat but she held on.

'Objection!' Mr Saunders shot up. 'That has no bearing on the case.'

'Overruled.' The judge harrumphed. 'Please answer the question, Mr Jarvis.'

'No, I was not.'

There was a murmuring hiss from somewhere over to her right that grew more menacing.

'Yet there were marks on Charlotte's body, scratches around her neck. I wondered if she had got them during or before intercourse took place?'

Her stomach rose again.

'Object—'

But Mr Saunders didn't get any further. The explosion was immediate.

'*Liar! You fucking liar, Jarvis!*'

It took a second for Frankie to register the shock of someone screaming. The boy with the denim jacket was on his feet, his fists raised and then slamming down on the rail in front of him again and again as he leaned over to yell a stream of obscenities. Martin had shrunk down in the witness stand and was gripping the sides as if any moment the guy might launch himself through the air from the public gallery and tear him to shreds. Suddenly everyone in the courtroom began to speak at once above the *blam-blam-blam* of the judge's gavel. Within moments, two guys in security uniforms appeared, grabbed the lad and hauled him bodily away, his shouts and yells echoing all the way out into the corridor. Frankie stared at the space he had left and, with a shock, realised where she'd seen him before.

That party.

The lad with the white-blonde hair who had come up to them. She stared blankly at the empty seat. The woman in the pink jacket had a tissue pressed to her mouth and her eyes were swollen. The sandy-haired man had an arm around her shoulder. He looked as though he was just about keeping it together.

'No, no, no, no, no,' the woman was whispering. 'Not to Charlotte, not with him… Not with him… What did that monster do to you, my baby? What did he do?'

She remembered the bed of leaves, the heat of them, the whispering in the darkness.

*'This is more than love.'*

*'Yes, I know.'*

*'No boundaries… No going back… That's what we said, wasn't it?'*

*'That's what we said.'*

That was it. The vomit that had been threatening for so long came up in one terrific rush. Her palm came up to her mouth to stop it. She bolted for the exit, out into the corridor and straight to the Ladies' where she hung like a rag doll over the toilet bowl, sobbing and coughing as her insides turned out. Everything left her: every shred of self-respect, every hope she'd ever had; her whole world was flushed away in an instant.

*The moment she'd seen them together, she'd known.* From that moment the magical world had turned grey; there was nothing special there; just old and dirty and monochrome. *Why had he done those terrible things?* Why did he have to come into her life bright and burning, and then turn out to be ash like everyone else?

The hard edge of the enamel pan cut into her cheek and she closed her eyes. She was empty now; there was nothing left. There was no way forward, and definitely no way back. She was lost: utterly lost.

'Oh!… Oh my goodness! Are you okay?'

She felt a pressure on her shoulder, and she opened her eyes. There was the scuff of feet behind her and the cubicle door bounced a little against the wall.

'Gosh. Oh dear, you poor thing. Hang on.'

She heard the drum of copious amounts of tissue paper being pulled from the dispenser.

'Here. Let me get some paper towels and wet them. Don't try and get up. Stay there.'

The feet moved away. There was the sound of water gushing. She managed to pull herself up onto the closed toilet to sit, her forehead in her palms as she let herself breathe. The touch of something damp and cool against her fingers made her jump and she peered upward. A woman with tawny hair and kind eyes was crouching in front of her. Frankie dropped her hands.

'Oh!' The woman lurched back, her hands flailing to save herself. 'Oh my god!'

'I'm sorry! I'm sorry!' Frankie blurted. The woman's eyes filled with agony.

'No, no it's me. I'm the one that's sorry. It's just that you look—' Her eyes welled. 'Oh my goodness…' Her fist moved to her chest as she stood, trying to control her breathing as though she might pass out.

Frankie stared at her in horror. Pink jacket.

Charlotte Vale's mother.

She felt instantly queasy again.

'You look like… I'm so sorry. I shouldn't be saying this…' The woman shook her head over and over. 'But you're not. Please forgive me… you just caught me off guard. It was such a shock, that's all.' She sniffed and tried to gather herself. 'Never mind me, look at you, you're not well. You don't need me and all my silliness. Come on – let me help you.'

She put out a hand and Frankie reluctantly took it.

'I'm Vanessa, by the way.' She managed a smile.

'Frankie.' She licked her lips, hoping that she didn't smell of puke.

'So how are you feeling now?' Vanessa scanned her face.

'Better than I was.'

'Well Frankie, shall I go and get someone? Who did you come with?' Her face was kind, so, so kind as she glanced round.

But Frankie only shook her head. 'No one, but honestly, I'm fine, really. I really should go.' She gently pulled her hand away.

'You haven't got anyone with you?' Vanessa looked immediately concerned. 'Well, they've adjourned for lunch, so how about you and me go and get a cup of tea somewhere, hmm? My husband, Peter, has gone to find out what's happening with my stepson, Jack. I can't go, I just make them both more upset, and I think we're all upset enough, don't you?' She attempted a smile, but her chin wobbled. 'Anyway, there's a café just around the corner. I hate sitting in places on my own, so you'd be doing me a big favour.'

'Well...' She wasn't sure this was a good idea. It all felt pretty weird. Too weird. She took a step forward but staggered a little.

'That sorts that, then,' Vanessa said decisively. 'You need a hot drink at least. Look at you – you're incredibly pale and such a skinny-minny.' She smiled but the pain in her eyes was like a flash of light. 'Did you even have breakfast?'

The thought of breakfast was even worse.

'Then I'm going to ask you to put up with my company, I'm afraid. Even if it's only for half an hour.' She put her hand briefly on her arm; it was a comforting gesture. 'I promise, with a bit of food inside you, you'll feel tons better.'

–

The café was thankfully only a few doors away. Vanessa fussed around Frankie for a few moments, settling her at a table before going to the counter and ordering food. She kept glancing back to make sure she was still there, but Frankie knew the only place she was possibly running to was the toilet. She grimaced and tried to ignore the horrible metallic taste in her mouth.

'Here we are.'

A mug of tea descended over her shoulder and Vanessa sat down opposite with what looked like coffee.

'I took a guess… Sugar?' She slid the pot of sachets over.

'No thanks. This is fine. Great… Thank you,' she added. She picked up the mug and took a sip. The heat of the liquid was comforting.

'My pleasure.'

She could feel Vanessa watching her over the rim of her cup. She dreaded what might be coming next.

'Shall I just' – she put the coffee down. '—Address the elephant in the room?'

Frankie couldn't take her eyes off a lone crumb that was caught between the wooden slats of the table.

'I think I knew most of Charlotte's close friends – the ones who would be close enough to come to…' She waved the circumstances away with a flinch.

Frankie kept her eyes on the crumb.

'So if it's not Charlotte, then I'm assuming you know Martin Jarvis.'

It was a statement and not a question.

'And I'm also assuming that a very young and pretty girl like yourself knows him…' She paused. '…Romantically?'

Her neck muscles wouldn't let her nod.

'I'm not surprised you got ill.' She didn't sound angry or judgemental; she just sounded sad. She reached across suddenly, touching the back of Frankie's hand. 'It all came as a shock, didn't it?'

She had never had someone touch her so instinctively. The warmth of Vanessa's fingers became her whole palm. Her skin was red hot. Frankie thought she might cry again. She glanced up. Vanessa was leaning across the table, her eyes searching her face. 'Don't feel awful, Frankie, don't punish yourself; you're just as much a victim as we are.'

She swallowed and then picked up her tea to cover it.

A waitress appeared with two plates. Vanessa glanced up with a grateful 'thanks' as they slid onto the table. She gestured to Frankie to help herself.

'Are you okay with my choices? You'll feel so much better. Come on, get stuck in.'

She gazed at the array of different dishes.

'If not, I can always pop over and get something else.'

There was a toasted cheese and ham sandwich, a bowl of chips, and a mound of delicious-looking guacamole with triangles of toasted pita bread sticking out of the top.

She felt her mouth watering but with hunger this time.

'It looks lovely.' She picked up a piece of pita and reached for the guacamole, loading it up and taking a bite. 'Mmm. Thank you.'

She hadn't realised how good food could taste.

Vanessa watched her approvingly as she chewed, before taking a slab of sandwich and cutting it daintily into smaller chunks.

'I'm sorry about my reaction before. I'm all over the place. I know this sounds odd and mawkish, but the fact you look a little like Charlotte makes me feel strangely comforted.' The knife paused. 'It's like there's a bit of her sitting here and we're doing something ordinary together. Does that creep you out?'

She shook her head but wasn't sure that was the truth.

'So tell me all about yourself, Frankie.' Vanessa smiled and this time her face relaxed. She picked up a bit of sandwich but then paused. 'I have to say this is a very funny way to make friends, isn't it?'

Frankie smiled back. *Were they friends now?*

She told her the pat story that everyone got told: that she'd been brought up in care, that it hadn't been too bad, that it was like belonging to a big family. None of it was true but it got people off her back.

'So you weren't ever fostered?'

The question was simple enough and so was the answer.

'My birth mother left me when I was three. People don't generally want three-year-olds, they want babies.' She shrugged.

'And do you remember her? Your mother?'

'Umm… Only bits. Nothing much. I think she was very young. I don't think she could cope.'

Vanessa seemed happy with the answer. They both ate in silence for a few minutes. 'Young and unable to cope' made people feel better. She had no idea what the truth was. She had no memory of anything. She'd seen the police report though, the one about how she'd been abandoned in a derelict house just before Christmas. She was only wearing a T-shirt. No one had any idea how long she'd been there or who might've left her. A homeless man called Frank had found her. She'd crawled amongst the filth and the garbage and had eaten newspaper to stay alive. She was left out with the rubbish. That's what had always stayed with her. And the simple kindness of a stranger. That stayed with her too; hence the name Frankie.

'She must have been very scared, your mum. You mustn't be angry with her.'

'No.'

'And you seem a lovely girl, so something in the care system clearly worked.'

*Did it?*

'People do all kinds of things when they're not coping.' Vanessa sighed deeply.

'Peter, my husband, isn't coping at all.' She pushed her plate away wearily. 'He's not himself. It's as though he's pretending that nothing has happened.' She glanced away for a second. 'Here he is, a well-respected professional man who works for Children's Services, who's around therapists and counsellors and guidance people all day – and the irony is, he's a man who's utterly lost.' She shook her head. 'I just worry what will happen when he stops pretending and reality hits him.' She blinked the thought away. 'He's not Charlotte's dad, he died ten years ago, but Peter has always seen her as his own… *Saw*,' she hesitated. 'And Jack – even though he was only her half-brother, he's always been super protective. That outburst in the court is how we're all feeling. I only wish I could get a hold of my rage and scream and shout like that – I'd love to.' She grimaced. 'I think we're all numb and angry and exhausted with grief, and we're all dealing with it in different ways.' She gazed blankly off. 'I don't think Peter or Jack can go through another session of all that. That's why I've said they should go off together this afternoon.'

She placed her knife and fork very neatly on the plate of half-eaten food. 'But I have to be there, Frankie. It's like a compulsion. I want to feel something. Anything: any amount of pain. It's the only way I can cope. It's like I see the white-hot flames of this horror and I have to put my hand right in the middle.' She stopped and wiped her fingers on a serviette. 'Sounds mad, doesn't it?'

'No, I think I understand.' *Did she?*

'But maybe not quite as mad as being in a café with me must feel to you,' Vanessa smiled. 'But maybe we're both sitting in that court because we're trying to achieve the same thing. I'm guessing you're looking for answers that you know you won't find anywhere else. You want the whole picture so that you can try and make sense of all this, just like I do. Is that anywhere close?'

She hadn't thought of it like that, but that was exactly how she felt.

'I have this terrible, terrible driving need to know. No matter how excruciating, no matter how horrific, I have to be there and hear every single one of the details and know, precisely what my daughter went through.'

The sheer enormity of what she was saying crumpled her face into a mask of pain. Her hands came up to her mouth as though trying to stop the words, but now she'd started, she just couldn't stop. She began to weep: sobbing and sobbing behind those trembling fingers. Frankie stared at her in horror.

'I carried her inside me for forty weeks and then her birth – the long and agonising twelve hours of it...' Her voice whispered. 'We went through the blood, the sweat, and the tears together, and at the end I held her in my arms and she held my little finger. I made a promise to her then, that I'd be by her side through everything. That she would never have to face anything alone.' She took a massive breath and her eyes widened in shock and horror at the realisation. It was as though Frankie wasn't there.

'But I broke that promise, didn't I?' She began to cry again then, great convulsions of grief, not caring that people were looking round and wondering what was going on. 'If I can hear it… If I can make myself listen to what she went through, if I can picture every second of what she endured, then it'll be like I kept my promise and I never really left her.'

Her weeping got louder. Frankie was suddenly jolted out of her trance. Her eyes searched around frantically as she pulled a whole load of serviettes from behind the sugar holder and pressed them across the table.

'I'm sorry, I'm sorry, I'm so sorry…' Vanessa kept saying. 'I shouldn't be talking to you like this. I shouldn't be saying these things… Look at me, I'm supposed to be the adult here, looking after you.' She wiped her eyes with the back of her hand and then went to grab another serviette. 'Please forgive me, Frankie. This must all seem very strange and uncomfortable—'

But Frankie suddenly caught her hand. 'Vanessa—'

The sensation of the touch felt weird but strangely nice.

They looked into each other's eyes.

'Vanessa, I wish—' She broke off and looked away. 'I wish someone like you had been my mum.'

The pain in Vanessa's eyes burned.

'Thing is, I've never had a mum. I've never had what you've just described. No one's ever told me that they'd be with me, no matter what.'

*Everyone lets you down in the end. Even the people who are supposed to love you.*

Vanessa let go of her hand to dab at her cheeks. 'That's so sad, Frankie. So incredibly sad,' she sighed. 'No one should have to go through any of that alone, that really is the worst thing...' She gave a watery smile. 'Hey, maybe we can help and support each other Frankie, what do you think?'

She had no idea how she could help anyone.

'I think we both want the same things... I think we both want to know the truth, however hard it might be to hear it.'

Her antennae twitched an alert at what Vanessa was saying.

'I mean, you're discovering things about this boy that you thought you were in love with. We both want to know exactly what happened that night.'

Frankie's gaze didn't waver.

'This all must be excruciatingly painful for you,' Vanessa said as though she'd read her mind. 'But you know things, details, that I don't.'

'Oh, I don't think—'

But Vanessa started to gabble. 'I know, but there could be things, couldn't there? Tiny things. Things he said that night, things he did – clues. His state of mind. It would tell us – tell me... it could give me the answers I need. You *know* things, Frankie, you just don't realise it.'

'I really don't.' She felt another frisson of alarm.

'You haven't made the connections, that's all.'

'I don't know anything.' She instantly began to back-pedal.

'But you don't know that,' Vanessa pushed. 'If you would agree to meet me again – talk to me, just chat, that's all I'm asking. I mean, did you know, or suspect he had some kind of relationship with Charlotte? Did you ever argue about it?'

The desperation came off her in waves.

A split-second image of that fight over the hairband sprang up as Frankie slewed her chair back.

'I have to go now.' She had a sudden surge of panic. She didn't want this. What was she doing here?

'Please. Frankie—'

'I really have to.' She stood abruptly.

'I'm sorry... I'm so sorry.' Vanessa's face was lined with pleading. 'I shouldn't have said all that.'

Some of the other customers were looking round.

'Please.' Vanessa smiled around the café as though it was all fine. 'Please, Frankie, finish your food. Finish your tea. I'm sorry. You're right, you're right. I don't know what's the matter with me. This was all supposed to be so nice and now I've spoiled it... Please, don't go.' The begging eyes made her sit.

'I promise I won't ask you stuff like that again.' She dipped to look at her. 'I give you my word. I totally understand how you feel. I know how I come across. Peter says I'm too full on; I suffocate people so they end up not wanting to be around me. Charlotte couldn't. She shut herself away... I know she kept secrets from me. If I'd known her secret was someone like Mar—'

She realised what she was saying and looked up suddenly.

'God.' She bit her lip and looked as though she might cry again.

Frankie felt an immediate rush of pity. 'Please don't get upset, Vanessa. Please… I'm not walking out. You've been nice to me and kind to me. You're a lovely person. Please don't do this to yourself.'

Vanessa brought the bundle of napkins to her nose again and wiped her streaming eyes. 'You even chose the guacamole,' she laughed sadly through the tissues. 'Charlotte's favourite.' She paused as though considering whether to say something and then took a breath.

'Don't end up like Charlotte, Frankie,' she said suddenly. 'Protect yourself from men like Martin Jarvis. Stay away from people like him. You have a chance right now: walk away, do something positive with your life. Don't drag his darkness around with you – cut all ties and move on. No good will come of people like him, no matter what they tell you.'

Frankie sat back in her seat and picked up the mug of tea again and drank deeply.

'I know that's not something you want to hear, Frankie, but something positive has to come from Charlotte's death. If it means that you live a life that's free of those sorts of men… If it saves one young girl from all that trauma, then none of it was pointless.'

'It's too late.'

'No, no, no, that's madness talking.' Vanessa reached across the table and touched her elbow. 'It's not too late! You don't have to choose that way. You're really young, you're really smart, you're really—'

'Martin has my heart,' she said simply. 'I gave it to him: all of it. I'm his now: for good or for bad, whatever happens.'

Vanessa studied her with a tight smile. 'I know it feels like that right now. At your age all your emotions are so intense they overwhelm you. But as you get older, you'll see things differently, I promise you. Martin Jarvis will become just a name.'

'You don't understand.' Frankie lifted the mug and finished the remainder of the tea. 'He won't, you see. He never will. He'll be in my life forever until the day I die.'

'No, Frankie, please don't say that. Please.'

She placed the mug gently down on the table.

'He will. Because I'm having his baby.'

# Chapter Eleven

*Now*

'You're not seriously going out?'

Alex looks at her as though she's lost her mind.

Frankie squeezes her feet into her shoes and picks up her bag. 'If I'm going to be disciplined then I need to look at Keeley's file. I need to speak to Declan at the home and find out what's been said. I don't for a minute think that he made a complaint about me. He's not that kind of guy.'

'But that could be seen as interfering with the investigation process, and anyway you said you were scared – terrified, even. How can you go out? And I thought after the police and the note this morning... You honestly can't take these kinds of chances.'

'I've decided I'm not letting him ruin my life, Alex, even if I *am* bloody petrified. I'm not letting him do that.'

'Then let me come with you. Let me drive you at least. I'll sit outside in the car and wait. You said he was watching you, Frankie. It's not safe.' He looks around for his jacket. 'Actually, I hope he does turn up.' He snatches it up aggressively. 'I *want* him to show himself so I can explain, in very clear terms, what being harassed and terrified really feels like.' He pulls on one sleeve but Frankie grabs his hand.

'Alex, don't.'

'Don't what?'

'I'm the regional manager, I don't need to be chaperoned. I can't be guarded twenty-four hours a day. I'm only going to the home and back. Twenty minutes each way, that's all.' She sees the look on his face. 'Oh Alex, don't look at me like that! – how about I ring you? Does that put your mind at rest? I'll ring you when I get there and when I'm leaving, how about that?'

'But you were—'

'Seriously. It's a promise. If I say I'm going to do it then I shall,' she says definitely. 'What's the time now?' She glances at her watch. 'It's ten forty-five. If I go now I'll phone you in twenty-five mins, max.' She leans forward to kiss him, but he pulls her into a hug and holds her close.

'I'm scared for you, Frankie. I'm scared this bolshieness will make you take risks.'

'I will be careful. I've said. I promise.'

He doesn't look convinced. 'Well, I'm going to ring the police station this morning and leave a message for Julia – tell her about the note on the car and ask her what she's found out about Matthew Jarrow. I'm not having an arsehole like that dictating our lives.' He bristles. 'If the police won't protect you, then I will.' His jaw works angrily.

She's instantly worried. 'Hey, hey now, promise me you're not going to do anything stupid.' She looks closely into his face. 'I need you by my side, not in some bloody police cell, do you understand?'

He nods defensively.

'I'll ring you when I said, right?'

He's still standing on the doorstep watching her as she gets into the car. She lets out a long sigh of relief. Here feels like an oasis of privacy. She realises he hasn't moved as she quickly dips to start the engine. Being with Alex feels like acting a part. She lifts a hand to wave before reversing off the drive, watching his outline getting smaller and smaller in the rear-view mirror.

She'd already made the call to Declan while Alex was in the shower, to talk over what happened. She also told him that she might pop in for a chat later. That should cover it if anyone asks. Watching the road unfolding in front of her, she tries to quell the rising alarm at what she's about to do. The desperation is moving as swiftly as the lies. There's a black hole up ahead and a moving walkway that's heading in one direction.

*How will this all end?*

Badly.

*Who will be hurt the most?*

The thought nearly paralyses her.

Checking the time, she slows down and begins to indicate, before pulling into a lay-by. She waits, and then makes the call to Alex.

'Yep, it's me. I'm there already. I don't know how long I'll be, but I'll ring you when I leave, okay?' She keeps her voice steady and reassuring. He's not happy but at least he's not suspicious. She ends the call, hating herself, hating what she's doing, but it feels like she has no choice. Her fingers plug in the phone number that she thought she'd never ring again. She rests her head back, staring up at the sky, amazed that it's trying to connect. Her heart is making the connections too: squeezing with nerves and an appalling, shaky, hope. She closes her eyes as a voice answers.

Her mouth opens but no sound comes out.

'Hello?'

The shock of the voice on the other end is like electricity.

'Hello?' it says again.

*So many years.*

'Vanessa, it… it's Frankie,' she stammers. 'You still have the same number… I was scared you'd changed it and I wouldn't find you.'

It's a ridiculous thing to say. She cringes.

There's a silence on the end. Then: 'What do you want, Frankie?'

'Can I see her? Please. I wouldn't' ask, but—' She breaks off.

There's a moment's pause.

'No.'

'I need to.'

'I don't care. I don't care what you need. The answer is still no. We're fine. We don't want you.'

'You don't understand—'

'I understand everything. He's out and it's brought it all back.'

The punch takes her breath away.

'You know?'

'Of course I know. We're Charlotte's family. We're the victims.'

The terrible guilt weighs around her heart like a stone.

'He's following me.'

'And?'

'I'm scared what he's going to do next. He's sending me letters. I've seen him outside my house. I don't know what he wants.'

'Of course you know, Frankie.' Her voice is hard and flat. 'I'm glad he's following you, obsessing over you. I'm glad he's vengeful and possessive and driven and angry.'

Her voice is brittle with fury and pain. 'It's what you deserve.' She hears another voice murmuring in the background.

'Let him. It'll be justice for both of you.'

There's a beep as Vanessa cuts her off and she's left holding the phone, listening to her own silence.

*We're fine.*

*But we're not all fine, are we?*

Frankie stares out into the quiet lay-by.

*Some of us haven't been fine for fifteen years.*

*No matter how many kids' lives have been made better: the smiles, and the hugs, and the hand-holdings, the sitting on beds and stroking faces – no matter how many roofs she climbs and daring rescues she throws herself into, there's always that one child she didn't save.*

*The one she chose not to.*

*Her own.*

# *Chapter Twelve*

'I shouldn't be here.'

She says it out loud. Her voice jars oddly into the car's quiet interior.

She checks out all the houses in Vanessa's street. The rooflines are just as she remembers them: the front doors, the gardens: everything has stayed the same. It's like a kind of grotesque dream: something from a very long time ago that comes back to her in pulses of appalling recollection. The horror begins to grind. The old memories come at her, one after the other, a picture-terror that makes her want to gun that engine, put her foot down and get out of there as fast as she can. But her heart won't let her. Not now.

–

'I shouldn't be here.'

She said those words once before as she stepped over the threshold of Vanessa's house.

'Nonsense. Why ever not? I've invited you, you're very welcome. More than.'

She walked into the tiny hallway, feeling Charlotte's whispered presence like an immediate draught of cold air. She shivered.

'There's no need to feel uncomfortable. It's awful for all of us sitting in that court day after day and you have no one to go home to. I only wish we could do more. Pete and Jack will be in for a cup of tea soon. Come and sit down. Relax.'

Vanessa patted the back of an armchair and Frankie sat, perching on the edge. The room was pleasantly neutral and very neat – fawn carpet, sisal coloured sofa, a glass coffee table – but it felt like a church with old graves under the floor, the bodies lying there, dead and gone, but their creepy company very much alive.

'There we are. I'll go and put the kettle on.'

Vanessa bustled into the kitchen as something inched its way up Frankie's spine. She looked around, moving her eyes but not her head, acutely aware that Charlotte's touch was on every surface – that her fingers had lingered on this, and that: this table, that chair – she could maybe even detect a tiny note of lingering perfume, but when she tried to breathe it in, it disappeared.

*Why had she even agreed to come here?*

She knew why: it was like her punishment. She deserved to see every second of what they were going through. Their pain should be her agony.

'Hello! You must be Frankie.'

She jumped. Vanessa's husband was standing in the doorway to the kitchen watching her; his jumper was filthy, and he had mud on his face.

'I would come over and shake your hand, but I'm not allowed on the carpet.' He grinned and scratched his chin, smearing the mud a bit further. 'I was just saying to Vanessa that you're very welcome to come out and join me and Jack outside while the weather's not too bad. You can bring your tea if you like.' He smiled at Vanessa who had appeared at his elbow with a tray of steaming mugs. 'Do you like gardening?'

She was aware he was talking to her as though he'd known her for years.

'Jack and I are just sorting out what we'll plant next spring. We like to get the ground prepared. It takes our minds off things. Come on, let me show you.'

So she joined the family, standing in a pair of borrowed wellies watching Peter as he turned the compost heap, and Jack, incongruous in his anorak, pulling weeds as the four of them chatted about unimportant things. None of them mentioned Charlotte. Vanessa was right: it was as though the horror of it hadn't happened.

Vanessa made dinner that first night, a meal that no one really ate, but their family rituals were there: the sharing of food, the passing of plates, including Frankie into their family as easily as if she'd been around that table all her life. For one second, one split second, she wondered if it was Charlotte's seat she was sitting in, and in that same split second, she realised it didn't feel wrong; she felt accepted in a way she'd never felt before. Part of her wished she could stay here forever, but part of her knew she should run.

-

'By the way, I've lied for you. I've told Jude I've seen you at school.'

She nearly fell over Nat who was sitting on the turn of the stairs.

'Jesus! You nearly killed me!'

'I've said you're in some of my classes, but I know where you're really going every day.' Nat glanced at Jude's office door, like any minute she was thinking of grassing Frankie up.

Frankie glared sullenly down at her hunched figure, wondering where this conversation was going: some kind of blackmail, probably. She waited to hear how much she'd have to shell out.

'I geddit.' Nat eased her legs from under her. 'I know why you're doing it. You're in the same shit as me.' She glanced pointedly at her belly. Frankie instinctively drew her forearm across her waistline.

'I dunno what you're on about.'

'Yeah you do.' Nat nodded and lowered her voice. 'I've bin in your room, r'member? Your boxes of tampons haven't moved, an' I found the tests you tried to hide in the outside bin.'

Frankie looked at her, incredulous. 'You've been through the *bin*?'

Nat looked smug. 'See? I should be a detective. If they weren't yours you wouldn't have reacted like that.' She saw the expression on Frankie's face. 'S'alright. No one else knows, 'specially not Jude... But you are, aren't you?'

'You need to mind your own business.'

Nat only glanced into the hallway. 'I'm just tryin' to help,' she twitched huffily. 'I'm telling you, once they find out, you know they'll never let you keep it. They say they will, 'cos they have to, but then they come up with all kinds of reasons why you can't. They'll take it off you and you won't have a scooby where it's gone. You'll never see it again.'

Frankie looked into her face.

'You don't believe me, do you?' She gave a sad little smile and put the flat of her hand on her stomach. 'This is my second. I fought for the first when I was fourteen, but they took him off me.' She glanced around her. 'I've told them they can have this one for adoption, but that's only to get them off my back. What I'm really gonna do, is look for my mum… I'm gonna see if I can find her. They want babies to be in families, see? If I can persuade her and her boyfriend to take me back, then they'll have to let me keep it.'

-

She looks up at the windows of Vanessa's house, scared of seeing, and at the same time, scared of not seeing movement there – but the pane stays disappointingly blank. That's Jack's room at the front. She remembers the hours and hours they spent sitting playing *The Tomb Raider Legend*. It was the closest she'd ever come to having a brother; there they were, two seventeen-year-old kids messing about playing video games. She often thought about Jack: what it must have been like for him back then, how hard it all was, yet he was always there for her: always had her back. He was always her rock even when things got really bad.

Once, mid Tomb Raider game, she realised he was watching her.

'Do you feel as weird about this situation as I do?' He said it so matter-of-factly it shocked her, but then she saw he was smiling.

'Yeah.'

'Good. That means we're being dead honest with each other.' He was still smiling. 'We shouldn't though.'

'What?'

'Feel weird – It's like Vanessa said, you're a victim just like we are.'

She couldn't answer.

He shrugged. 'It's messed-up. Like, life is messed-up. I'm so sick of hating and fighting. Why would I hate you? You haven't done anything wrong.'

She went to get up. 'I think I should go—'

His eyes followed her. 'I mean, I wasn't sure at first – like, why Vanessa would ask you here? And then I was even more surprised when you said yes.' His cool gaze searched her face.

She stood. 'I really should go.'

'What's the matter?'

'Nothing. It's just...' She waved a hand. 'You're right, this is weird.'

'But you keep coming round... I mean, I like it, I just wondered why, though?'

'You're right, it's probably best—' She bent to pick up her jacket.

'I remember you that night at the party.'

She froze.

'It took me a while to think where I knew you from.' He started to rush. 'I-I saw you. Later on. When you were totally out of it – I didn't know what you'd taken, but you were in a state. I'm really sorry for you, you know?' He looked at her, concerned. 'I realised you'd got caught up in something without knowing it.'

'Vanessa thinks I know stuff about Martin – I don't.'

'Vanessa's always trying to make connections that aren't there – ignore her,' he said bitterly.

'That's why she wanted to talk to me in the first place. She thinks I can tell her something that'll help her understand what happened with Charlotte, but I can't! I don't remember a thing. Honestly!'

'Shh…' Jack grabbed her hand. 'It's okay, you don't have to feel bad, Frankie, seriously. It's not you, it's her. Vanessa feels as guilty as hell about Charlotte; she thinks her control-freakery drove Charlotte away. Maybe it did and maybe it didn't. But I do know once she gets her claws in you, she doesn't let go. You become a possession. My dad's her possession.'

There was something about the way he said it that sounded off: strangely angry.

'She was very kind to me though, that day at the court.' Frankie almost felt like she needed to defend her. 'She made me feel…' She shrugged but it felt like a flinch.

'Yeah, I know how she makes people feel.'

There it was again.

'She made me feel like she was listening to me. Not judging me, y'know? Girls like me are judged all the time. They shove us in a box as though being brought up in care means you've been branded, here.' She made a stripe across her forehead. 'It's invisible but everyone can see it.'

'You would've liked her, y'know.'

Something shunted inside her.

'Who?'

'Charlotte. You would've got on. I know you had that row, but—'

She lurched.

'You saw us arguing?'

He nodded. 'Dunno who else did. No one I know has said anything – but they wouldn't. All my kind of tribe leave the police alone and they leave us alone… Yeah, I think you would've liked her. Some people said she thought a lot of herself, but she didn't: quite the opposite. She always wanted people to like her – and if they didn't, it cut her deep. A bit like you, really.' He smiled. 'You stay away from people so they can't hurt you. I know that. I think you recognised something in her, too. Not just the way you both looked. I think she fascinated you.'

Frankie felt herself falter.

'You were staring at her that night at the party, weren't you? Yeah, I remember now.'

She swallowed involuntarily.

'And I've seen the way you are in this house. That's why you and Vanessa have this weird connection: it's like you're both haunted by her. I see the way Vanessa looks – it's like Charlotte's come back. And then I see you, your eyes flitting everywhere as though you're scared her ghost will suddenly appear. Is it because you feel guilty?'

Her neck jerked back.

'About the row you had? You shouldn't. People have rucks all the time. Oh I'm sorry, – that was a crappy thing to say – I just wanted you to understand that I get how you feel, and I don't want you to feel bad.'

'I have to go. I told Jude I'd be back by nine.'

'Frankie—'

She heard him saying something else but she had pulled the bedroom door closed behind her. The sound of her feet on the stairs drummed out all his calls for her to stop. The TV was booming in the living room. She was aware of Peter's head swivelling round at the sound of the front door opening.

It was black outside and the rain was coming down in rods. She'd only got her little denim jacket with her. Pulling it over her head she started to run down the road, her feet splashing through puddles soaking her thick tights and skirt, making her skirt stick like a sheet of wet rubber against her thighs. She didn't know where she was going or how she planned to get back to the home – *Shit!* As she trod on a loose paving slab, a tidal gush of rainwater flew up. Whatever bit of her hadn't been wet before, was now soaked. Running was pointless. Dragging her jacket from her head, she looked up and down the street. The main road was just up ahead. She'd find a bus shelter or a doorway and wait it out. She didn't have enough money for a cab and the indignity of phoning Jude and asking if she could come and get her was more than she could stand. Plus there'd be questions – and she didn't want questions.

*Frankie!*

She thought she heard someone say her name. She took a look round.

*Frankie! Over here!*

Glancing across the road, she saw the black shape of a car, headlights flashing through the needling rain.

The window was wound down and Jack's face was bobbing in the gap. 'Hang on, my dad'll turn round.'

The lights swung across the road, illuminating just how sopping wet she really was, and then the car pulled up alongside her; the back door opened.

'Come on – hop in!' Peter was blinking up at her. 'You can't be out here in this. Get in, you silly girl!'

'I'm too wet!' she shouted back. 'I'm fine, honestly. I need to get back. I'll get the bus. Really. It's very kind of you but—'

'There aren't any buses. There's been an accident on the main road, nothing's getting through either way. Will you just get in this car, Frankie? I'm getting as wet as you are!' He was laughing and she suddenly felt a bit stupid standing there arguing in the pouring rain. She got in, squashing herself into as small a space as possible on the back seat and tried not to drip everywhere.

'I'd already rung Jude.'

She shot a look up at Peter who was watching her in the rear-view mirror.

'Sorry?'

'I'd heard the local news so I gave her a quick ring to tell her you were safe at our house. I hope you don't mind. I didn't want to disturb *Tomb Raider* at a vital moment.'

She felt her mouth fall open.

'It's okay, I said you were a friend of my son's. Well, that's true, isn't it?'

She was aware of him peering at her reflection. 'I couldn't see the point of complicating things that don't need to be complicated.'

She sat very still, her knees pressed together, feeling the water running from her hair down her cheeks and neck.

'And she didn't ask anything?'

'I think she assumed I must be talking about someone at school. She sounded quite pleased, actually.' Peter smiled at her and she managed a smile back.

'So what did you tell her?'

'I said, given the circumstances, we were quite happy to give you a bed for the night. Which we are, of course.' He peered up again. 'More than happy. And so was Jude actually. I think she likes the idea of you being around a family. She said it was 'encouraging' that you were making friends. Yes, that's the word she used.' He grinned at her in the mirror.

*God, if only she knew.*

Jack twisted round in the seat, hanging onto the safety belt. 'That's okay, isn't it, Frankie? You're okay with all that?'

She knew what he was asking: he was asking if he'd upset her earlier? Had he said too much? Was she totally weirded-out? She could feel Peter's eyes on her, waiting for her response. What else could she say? What alternative was there?

'Thank you very much,' she nodded. 'This is all very kind of you. I don't deserve it.'

'Don't be daft.' Peter pulled a face. In the odd light his eyes became black pits full of shadows. 'You deserve all of this and more.'

Frankie stared out at the road tunnelling away in front of her. She had no idea what she felt. There was Vanessa, and Charlotte, and Jude, and Martin... and now a baby... So many things were whirling around in her head that she couldn't think straight. She stared out into the night not able to say anything. The blackness beyond the street lights pressed in on either side, the headlights only going so far as though the car might be heading into the darkness towards a cliff edge – as if they might be driving off the end and into nothing.

–

'My God, look at the state of you!'

Vanessa was standing in the doorway as Frankie got out of the car.

'I said to Peter "that child's never gone out in this, has she?" What on earth were you thinking?'

She enveloped Frankie in a warm bath sheet, soaking clothes and all, as soon as she stepped into the hallway.

'Keep this wrapped round you, get those shoes and socks off and get yourself upstairs. I'm just running you a hot bath.'

She stood there, tutting, as Frankie picked apart the sodden laces on her trainers, struggling to get them off, and peeled her socks off, inside out.

Peter and Jack bustled in behind her, shaking off the rain like a couple of over-excited dogs.

'I'll put the kettle on, shall I? Actually, who fancies a hot chocolate? I bet Frankie does.' Peter grinned round at them all before sloping off into the kitchen. He was over-jolly and bright. He'd left Jack standing in the doorway. Jack's eyes were large and watchful as his father walked away. He gave Frankie a pointed look and then there was a tiny shake of the head.

'Yes, she'd love one, I'm sure.' Vanessa pulled the towel further around her. 'You have to look after that baby of yours, you know. You can't just go roaming about in all weathers. Now come on, let's get you up those stairs.'

Vanessa went ahead and Frankie glanced back. Jack's face was stony.

'Are you coming or are you going to stand there shivering?' Vanessa paused, smiling, mid-step. She didn't have much choice.

Going into the bathroom, Vanessa bent to turn off the taps before bustling from the bathroom to one of the bedrooms, finding more towels and dry things to put on and a dressing gown and toothbrush.

'These might be a bit big, you're only a skinny thing and I'm probably a size bigger.' Vanessa held out a pair of joggers. 'But these have a tie waist so you should be okay.'

She shouldn't be here; she knew that. It allowed them to think all kinds of things about her – things she knew they'd hate if they ever found out the truth.

'This way.' Vanessa walked ahead past two tightly closed bedroom doors. 'I've put you in here.' She pushed open a door revealing a part guest room, part office.

Frankie paused on the threshold, putting a protective hand on her stomach.

‘Are you okay?’ She looked at her, concerned.

‘Just a bit tired.’

‘And we’ve got another long day at court tomorrow.’

The baby quickened again inside her, or was it her heart?

‘I hate going to that place.’

‘I understand completely.’ Vanessa’s eyes were kind and sad. ‘Some things are just too hard to listen to.’ She patted her arm. ‘Look, you need to lie in that bath, relax, and think about nothing but nice things for a while. I’ve put some bubbles in, that’ll have you sorted in no time.’

‘What shall I do with all this wet stuff?’

Vanessa smiled. ‘No problem. While you’re soaking, I’ll put that lot in the washer dryer and we’ll leave these comfy clothes on the radiator. All you have to do is let me look after you, Frankie, if only for one night.’ She gave her a mock stern look.

The thought was almost too tempting. She could easily have lain down right there on the floor and gone to sleep.

‘Okay,’ she said.

‘Good,’ smiled Vanessa. ‘That’s settled then.’

–

She lay in the bath watching the steam condensing into rivulets down the walls. The wind whistled around the side of the house and the window jiggled a little in the draught. She didn’t dare close her eyes. The draw of sleep dragged at her eyelids and she struggled to keep awake. Her eyes batted open as things began to dawn on her. Charlotte had lain here; she’d looked at the tiles on that wall, she’d seen that bit of a gap where the grout had missed. Her hands had touched the sides of this bath…

She gingerly put the tips of her fingers over the edge. She felt a momentary out-of-body slide: she saw the walls and the door as though it was footage from an old film… someone else's eyes… Eyes that belonged to a dead girl. She blinked, and the room came tumbling back.

*She should've kept walking tonight. This was more than a mistake. This is wrong.*

A wave of guilt rose up again and bit her hard. She took a big, deep breath. *So wrong.* It would all come out and they would see her for what, and who, she really was.

She'd been to see Martin.

The shame of it twisted her insides.

She knew as soon as the Prison Service envelope landed on the doormat at the home. She could have left it there or put it straight in the bin, but she didn't. She picked it up, snaffling it away before anyone else could see it. She knew what it contained and what he wanted. The thump in her gut told her she hated him and loved him and neither was winning. If she went to see him then everyone would hate her. If she didn't go, she knew she would always hate herself.

She'd made a call.

'Gavin?'

'Yes?'

'It's Frankie Turner.'

Gavin was her social worker: a genuine, nice, but slow kind of guy. Not very good at his job, but no one wanted a social worker who was on the ball, so he was pretty much perfect.

'I think I should have been to see you or something, shouldn't I?' There was the rustle of what sounded like a whole pile of paper. She imagined his desk. Poor Gavin.

'I think we're overdue.'

Gavin's 'overdue' made it sound like it was weeks rather than months late.

'You sound a bit upset. Are you upset?'

'I'm not upset, Gavin, I just need your help.'

'Ah.'

There was more crackling of paper. She knew he had no idea. He was the same with all his clients which made him a total plum when it came to wanting a favour. Gavin was ripe for the picking.

'I need you to come with me into a prison.'

She could've probably asked him for two bottles of voddie right that minute and he would have obliged.

'Say that again?'

'I'm not eighteen yet. I need an escort, and someone who's not going to blab. I know you won't blab, will you Gavin?'

He stalled. 'Well… Er… I don't know… What's making you want to go into a prison, Frankie?'

Gavin always had to pretend he was following some kind of protocol. They both knew where this was going.

'There's someone I really want to see.'

'Ah.'

She stayed silent.

'Would you like to share who that someone might be?' Gavin's voice wavered, a little uncertain.

'I'd like you to trust me, Gavin.'

That put his protocol to the test.

'Oh! I see… Well… erm… When were you thinking?'

She smiled. *See, Gavin? That wasn't so difficult, was it?*

'How about this afternoon?'

–

She had never been inside a prison before. The noise struck her first and then the smell. The Visits Hall was a long, cavernous warehouse of a building, with no natural light. Single prisoners sat in their orange bibs at low coffee tables that were bolted to the floor. Her eyes picked out Martin as though he was sitting in a spotlight. She watched his gaze lift as he drank in the sight of her. She carried her jacket across her stomach, her shoulders straightening defiantly as she walked purposefully towards him. He looked shocked that she'd turned up and she felt stupidly pleased.

His gaze drifted over to Gavin who had been at great pains to show how much he trusted her by not asking any awkward questions. He manfully thrust out his hand, and Martin, looking unsure, took it.

'I'm Gavin,' he said, smiling. 'How about I go and get us all some drinks and cakes and give you two a chance to catch up?'

He wandered off. Frankie quietly sat and waited for Martin to speak. He looked different. His skin was grey and unhealthy. His deep-set eyes had dark purple circles under them. But he was still Martin underneath it all. She could feel her resolve faltering.

'Thank you for coming to see me, Frankie.'

Her arms folded across her stomach, bundling up her jacket. She licked her lips.

'You had sex with Charlotte Vale.'

He looked shocked by the blunt force of the statement.

'I did not. I did not…' He shook his head emphatically. 'That did not happen.'

'You were in a relationship with her then. You were seeing her.'

'I was not. I swear to you.'

'You didn't tell me you'd gone back to the boat with her.'

'There was nothing to tell, Frankie. I wasn't doing anything wrong. She and I spoke at the party. I told her that you two looked alike – we joked about it. I told you this! Then she started asking me some weird questions.'

'Like?'

'Like if I'd ever taken roofies? Rohypnol, y'know, that stuff that really knocks you out.'

'And?'

'Christ, no!'

'Why was she asking that?'

'I don't know. It was just like an odd, off-the-wall conversation; she didn't seem stressed or anything. She came across as relaxed and happy. She was having a nice time, she was a bit high – she was dancing—'

'Yes, I saw.' Frankie's mind immediately dragged up the image – *sinuous, sexy, laughing.*

'But that wasn't the first time you'd seen her. You'd seen her loads. You admitted it.'

*She would not cry. There would be no tears.*

Martin waved a hand dismissively. 'She'd asked me a few times if I knew where she could buy a bit of dope, that's all. People know I have bits and pieces. It's not a huge deal. I do a little here and there. I said I had a bit stashed and she came to the boat to collect it. Nothing major, nothing big, just a bit of draw, a few pills on a couple of occasions, that's all – Frankie, look—'

'So why did you take her back to the boat that night?' The tears threatened but she held tight to her anger.

'It wasn't like that, Frankie.' He held out his palms towards her. 'You ran off. You disappeared. I'd gone into the street trying to find you and suddenly there she was.

I told her I was looking for you and suddenly she started crying. She asked me not to leave her on her own – I couldn't just abandon her, could I? So she walked back to the boat with me. I thought you might have gone there. She was sobbing, but she wouldn't tell me what was wrong – Look, Frankie, I swear to you...' He leaned forward. 'I did *not* murder that girl. Everything I said in that court was true. I didn't touch her. I asked her onto the boat because she was upset – nothing else, I swear to you. I went to buy booze. When I came back, she'd gone.'

Pictures came to her mind in grainy flashes: the black water, the pitch and roll of the boat, the hard feel of the wooden rudder in her palm as her fingertips curled around the edge of the cabin door... the corner of the bed, the discarded covers. *She hears a voice and there's a shifting movement. The door at the far end is open. It's dark, but in the light from the moon she sees...*

It's a blur. *What did she do?*

She studied Martin's face, the impassioned, open, pure honesty of it. He looked so real, so genuine. She could look into those eyes and see the truth – but at the same time knowing that what she was seeing was only what she wanted to see.

She glanced around the room. Men with shaved heads and teardrop tattoos on their cheeks sat thin and hunched at the tables.

'Why didn't you answer any of my emails or letters?'

She couldn't drag her eyes back to his face.

'I've needed to see you. Do you know what it's been like in here without you, not knowing what's been going on?'

She gave a little shake of the head. She was hearing the words but wanted to shut them out.

'I need to ask you something.'

'About?'

'That night.'

She saw a flash of a silhouette, bent over.

'You were there. You said you came to the boat.'

She remembered the outline of his shoulders with his back to her against the carbon blue of the night sky – so absorbed in his task that he didn't hear her tread. And then a girl's voice... and she sees—

*Charlotte.*

*And Martin.*

*He was lying.*

She remembered her rage – white hot. She felt it again now: the sheer thundering fury that made her grip that piece of wood and metal, feeling her fingernails biting into the heel of her palm. She remembered looking down and seeing that red stripe of discarded hairband lying on the deck, and then feeling the slippery wet of blood on her palms as the cuts opened up, the anger in her silently boiling higher – and then the next thing she was aware of was running, the pounding of her feet and the pounding of her heart—

'Yes.'

*She knows why he's asking these questions.*

'And you saw nothing?'

She watched his face, savouring the moment, letting him know that she knew, letting him feel her power.

'It's just... Frankie, when I saw you the next day... You had blood on your face and hands. I know they found DNA that they have no match for... I don't know how to ask this...'

'I come bringing gifts!' Gavin's moony face appeared, plonking a tray with tea and cakes in cellophane on the table in front of them. He chuckled from one to the other and then realised that no one was joining in.

'Oh dear!' he said nervously. 'Should I go away again?'

They both looked at him.

'I'll go away again then, shall I? Maybe see if I can find the facilities.'

He trundled off like a little cartoon character in his flat suede shoes. Frankie put her jacket on the table and drew her shoulders back. Martin's gaze stayed glued to her face.

'I don't remember anything about that night.' She stared intently back.

'You don't remember anything?'

'I was stoned, I was drunk. I don't remember.'

His gaze didn't waver. He swallowed.

'You didn't see Charlotte?'

'No.' She didn't drop her eyes.

'You're sure that's true?'

'Yes.'

He breathed and his whole body slumped with relief. 'I don't want you back at that court again, Frankie. As much as I love the idea of seeing you, it's not safe.'

She stayed silent.

'I don't want the police to see or think anything where you're concerned. I want you to keep right out of it.'

Jude's warning came back to her. She was a girl from a care home. She was poor. She was trouble. She was easy prey.

'Will you do that for me?' His eyes dropped down briefly, and a stunned shock of realisation coloured his face in that instant. The round 'O' of his mouth wouldn't let the words out.

'Frankie—'

'What?'

'You're...'

He was struck dumb. His mouth worked oddly at the realisation she was pregnant.

'Why didn't you tell me?'

She gave a little jerk of her shoulder.

'Jesus.' He rubbed the back of his neck. 'I don't understand. Why wouldn't you tell me?'

'I didn't know what I was going to do.'

'What you were—?' He looked at her. 'You wanted to decide without me?'

'I had to decide without you.'

He stopped and his hand fell. 'What do you mean?'

She stayed silent.

'You're cutting me out,' he said dully. His eyes winced, painfully. 'You believe what they're saying about me and Charlotte being in a relationship.' He studied her. 'Is that what your heart says?'

Her heart felt as though it was bleeding from a thousand cuts.

'Have people got inside your head, Frankie? Is that what's happened? Is that why you haven't told me about the baby?'

'No.' She shook her head stubbornly.

'Is it Jude?'

She put her hand on her stomach. 'She doesn't know.'

He looked at her in disbelief. 'How can she have not noticed?'

'In exactly the same way you didn't.' Frankie smiled grimly. 'Only one of the girls knows and she won't say anything. I've worn baggy clothes and I've been staying out and going back late.'

'Staying out? With who?'

'No one. Just out.'

'Frankie.' He took a deep breath in. 'Just tell me.'

'Charlotte's parents.'

'Charlotte's par—?' Martin's face fell in shock and then terror. His head dropped into his hands and he groaned like a wounded animal.

'What have you done, Frankie? What have you done? Why them, for pity's sake?'

Martin looked like a man in pain. She was glad. She wanted to sit here and let him feel every blow she could muster. *Him and Charlotte. Charlotte and him.* The liar.

'Her mum. Vanessa. At the court. She found me. She looked after me, when…' She stopped at the pain of the memory. 'I didn't know it was her. I didn't realise at first, and then…' She looked away. 'She was nice to me.'

'Why would you want to be anywhere near that family, Frankie? And they know about you and me, do they?'

She gave a tiny nod. *There was no her and Martin. She was alone – Again. There was just a man sitting across a grubby table, one that she had been stupid enough to come and see. That's all there was.*

'It just doesn't make sense… I can't get my head around it. None of it. A baby… You being pregnant…' His head swung slowly from side to side. 'This changes everything, you know that don't you, Frankie? Everything. They have nothing to convict me on – not really. They can't prove I did it. There's no concrete evidence tying me to her murder – and I did not do it, Frankie. I swear on… on…' He glanced round. '…On that baby's life. I didn't kill Charlotte Vale.'

'Don't!' Both arms came to protectively cover her belly.

'I've not mentioned your name at all: not to anyone. I've protected you from being involved all this time, Frankie. So will you do this one thing for me?'

Her guts felt like stone.

'You have to give me a chance when all this is over.' His eyes burned into her. 'You have to say you'll be there for me when I walk out of that court. Don't throw away what we had – and definitely not now. I'm walking out of that dock and straight back to you if you'll have me.' He went to reach for her hand.

'Oi!' said the voice of an officer over by the desk. 'No touching!'

'We're going to be together, the three of us: you and me and that baby, Frankie. Nothing is going to keep me away.'

–

The steam on the bathroom walls had turned to running tears of condensation. She listened to the crackle of the foam as it disappeared around her.

*Who was there for her now?*

No one.

*Who could she confide in?*

No one.

It was all impossible; life on her own with a child felt impossible. Her head and heart wrestled with a mess of intertwined emotions that she just couldn't untangle.

*She'd loved Martin with all her heart.*

*She hated Martin to the core of her soul.*

*Martin.*

*Charlotte.*

She had bound herself to him in a way that couldn't be broken. She was having his child.

*But you can't love a man who's done these things to you*, her head said.

*I can't, I can't. I don't*, she said back.

*He's a liar and he betrayed you*, the voice was insistent now. *He deserves to be punished.*

But punished for what? What happened that night?

She tried to bring back the white rage she had felt, but couldn't. She tried to conjure up the sound of the water, the girl's voice; there'd been the splash of birds, hadn't there? But it was as though the tape-loop ended: stuck in a freeze frame. Her mind stumbled and floundered.

Lifting her hands from the water, she pressed the heels of her hands into her eye sockets until she saw stars. God, how she wished she could erase all this horror. How she wished there was a reset button and she could make all of it disappear – *Wouldn't that be something?* The sheer joy of rubbing it all out. She took a deep breath and opened her eyes. A pure and perfect fantasy where there was no Charlotte, there'd been no party, no boat, no past, just present. Her heart lifted: just two clean slates waiting for the future to be written. Their tiny family could become—

The lights went off.

She shot up, her heels squealing against the enamel as the sudden crack of the door opening behind her had her wheeling round in a tide of water. She groped for the towel, but her fingers only closed on thin air. She was aware of the light from the landing sending a shaft through the darkness. In the doorway was a figure: a black silhouette. Her breath dragged into her lungs in a gasp of shocked air.

'Who's there?'

But the darkness was silent. The silhouette swayed slightly.

Gathering herself, she scrambled to the other end of the bath, her shoulder blades pressing painfully into the taps as she drew her knees up to her chin.

'Who is it? Jack? Peter? What do you want?'

'You're so beautiful,' the blackness whispered. 'I love seeing you naked.'

She watched, horrified, as the shape came towards her. Her hands and feet scrambled for purchase on the slippery enamel, her breath catching tight in her lungs, her mouth paralysed with shock as a cold draught moved swiftly, the dark figure looming closer as it bent and dipped, forcing her to turn her face away in terror. She screwed up her eyes as a tiny warmth of breath whispered across her cheek and the pressure of fingers touched the top of her spine.

Her foot slipped. She heard a sound, a strangled cry coming from deep inside her as the water slammed into her ears and eyes. Her lungs screaming pointlessly. Hands flailing, she fought and floundered, grasping on the solid sides of the bath and hauling herself up, coughing and heaving and instantly blinded as the light came on.

Spluttering, she shook the water from her eyes as the sound of running feet and someone shouting rammed its way into her muddled brain.

'*Frankie! Frankie!* What is it?'

Vanessa's frenzied yells hurtled up the stairs. She crashed through the door and stood panting in the doorway, eyes blazing with panic, before rushing over to grab her, hauling her out of the bath and grabbing for a towel. Frankie's teeth chattered wildly inside her head. She couldn't stop shaking.

'My god, what's wrong? What happened? Are you okay?' She rubbed the towel vigorously up and down

Frankie's shoulders, patting and holding her close and stroking her hair back.

'There-there was someone here.'

'What?'

'There was. There was someone here in the room.'

'Who? What are you talking about?'

'I don't know. It went d-dark. The lights went out.' Even as she said it, she could hear how mad it sounded.

'No one came out of the bathroom, my darling, I would've seen them.' Vanessa cupped her cheeks in her hands. Her palms were hot. Her eyes searched her face. 'And there was no power cut, and the light's on – See?'

'What's going on? Is she okay?'

Peter appeared in the doorway, peering anxiously at the two of them. 'Has she hurt herself?'

'No, no I don't think so.' Vanessa smiled round at him. 'She slipped, I think. No bones broken. She's okay… aren't you?'

She nodded dumbly but felt like she might burst into tears.

'I think there's a lot going on for all of us at the moment.' Vanessa smoothed Frankie's wet hair back from her forehead. 'We're all exhausted. Things happen when you're exhausted, but we'll be fine.'

Vanessa's gentle touch made the tears well and she gave a little sob. 'I don't know what happened, I'm so sorry… I must've fallen asleep. I think I was dreaming or something… I saw a shape…'

'I thought something had happened to the baby.' Peter shook his head in shock.

'The baby's fine, I'm fine – I think.' Her teeth were chattering. 'I'm so sorry about the carpet.'

'Oh don't worry about that, I can clear all that up, so long as everyone's alright. You just go and get yourself dressed and warm, Frankie.' His kind, smiley face beamed at her as Vanessa ushered her along the landing.

'Here, put this on.' She pulled a dressing gown from the radiator. 'It'll be nice and warm for you… My goodness, you gave me such a fright!' She slipped Frankie's arms into the sleeves, chuckling as she steered her towards the door.

'Thank you for being so kind, Vanessa.' She meant it; she really did.

'I would do anything to make sure you're okay.' She reached forward and snuggled the collar around her neck. 'Quickly now. Don't get chilled. Hot chocolate will be ready as soon as you are – where's Jack, by the way?'

'Oh he's still downstairs, oblivious, with his headphones on,' Peter grinned. 'He'll only respond to sign language.' He hauled a vacuum cleaner up the last few stairs and disappeared behind the bathroom door.

'He loves that Wet and Dry toy,' Vanessa grinned ruefully. 'You've given him a perfect excuse. Just come down when you're ready.' She leaned forward and kissed her cheek. 'Don't be too long.'

Frankie brought her hand up to where Vanessa's lips had been as she watched her trot down the stairs. *Was this what it felt like to be cared for?*

As though in a dream, she tentatively pushed the bedroom door open as Jack leapt up off the bed. Her hand came to her heart.

'Jack!'

'I didn't know she'd put you in here. Sorry, my fault.' He laughed nervously and made a move towards the door. 'I'll let you get dressed.' The sound of the vacuum cleaner droned loudly in the background and he paused with a hand on the door edge. 'Are you sure you're okay? I heard the commotion—'

'No, honestly. I'm fine, I'm fine.' She glanced around. 'I feel a bit silly now, actually… God – I must've been dreaming, but it really freaked me out.'

'Don't feel bad, seriously. There are things you should…' He went to say more but then stopped. 'Look, I'm only across the landing. Once you've changed, we'll go downstairs together.' He glanced towards the bathroom. 'Don't go down on your own, okay?'

She frowned, unsure what he was meaning.

'Vanessa can be a bit—' he rolled his eyes. '—Full on with her mothering instinct. Just tap on my door. I'll wait for you.' He smiled, pulling it closed behind him.

She got dressed slowly, putting on the joggers and sweatshirt, feeling their heat seep into her back like a comforting blanket. She didn't really get what he was talking about; Vanessa was just being kind and caring. There were slipper socks on the radiator too and she pulled them on. Padding out into the hallway, she tapped gently on Jack's door. The gap creaked wider.

'Come in.' His voice came from somewhere inside and she pushed the door a little.

He was sitting on the side of the bed holding a book.

'Yeah – come in for two minutes. Let me explain what I was blabbering on about.' He closed the book carefully and put it down beside him. 'Just push that door to, would you?' He glanced at it as though he was afraid of someone hearing.

She stood there uneasily, trying to read him.

'I wanted to ask you something. Do you remember the conversation you and I had about Vanessa? – About how she's like a dog with a bone?'

'Uh-huh,' she nodded.

'And how she thinks you know stuff about the night that Charlotte died?'

She rubbed her forehead anxiously. 'It was just like you said, Jack: I was out of my head on stuff. I don't remember anything. Seriously, honestly.' Her heart shunted up a gear.

He sat back a little, his hands in his lap. 'It's okay, it's fine. You and I just need to be totally straight with each other. I can shield you if I know exactly what's going on in your head.'

She looked at him, puzzled. 'Shield me? What do you mean?' The thudding behind her ribcage intensified.

'Vanessa and my dad. They latch onto things... Ideas... People... and they can't let go. Vanessa's obsession becomes my dad's obsession. I didn't want you to get blindsided by them both, that's all.'

'She's already told me that she can be a bit like that.'

'Yes, well, that's part of the grooming process.' Jack looked down into his palms. 'She tells you those kinds of things to disarm you, so that you don't see it coming.'

Frankie went to speak, but Jack held up his hands.

'I know they don't mean to do it and I'm not trying to be horrible.' He shook his head. 'But it's like they close in on you. It's so tiny at first, you barely notice it.' His teeth caught his bottom lip. 'Until you find you can't breathe. Which is what happened to Charlotte. They adored her and so they smothered her. She was running wild because she couldn't cope with their adoration.' His face looked haunted, but he covered it with a rueful smile, and shrugged. 'There are definite benefits in being the son that no one's interested in.'

'I'm sure they're interested in you. I'm sure they love you.'

He snorted. 'Haven't you noticed? Didn't you see the way my dad was downstairs? All the attention goes immediately to you. You're their replacement daughter.'

Her spine itched with discomfort.

'Watch their eyes if you don't believe me. They can't stop looking at you; they can't stop wanting to be with you, they always want to touch you. They think she's come back.'

Something walked over her grave. She shivered.

'And me?' The rueful smile was pained. 'I think as far as they're concerned, the wrong child died.'

'Jack!' She was horrified. 'No!... They don't think that!'

'What did you see?'

'What? When?' She jerked in alarm.

'What did you see in the bathroom?'

'I was dreaming. I must've fallen asleep.'

'Tell me what happened? You said you saw a shape.'

'Nothing really.' Her heart drummed wildly. She didn't want to think about it, let alone speak about it. 'I told you, it was a kind of dream... like a nightmare.'

'A sort of hallucination?'

'Maybe... I'd rather not—'

'What did you see, though?' he pressed. 'Was it a man?'

'Jack, seriously... What is this?'

'Charlotte told me something.'

Her whole body froze. 'What kind of something?'

'She wouldn't sleep in that room.' He nodded to the far wall.

'Her bedroom?' Frankie glanced over nervously.

'She said someone kept whispering to her.'

The itch crawled.

'It was a shape, a black figure. She was seriously, seriously scared out of her mind.'

Frankie watched his face, horrified, but Jack only grinned nervously and shook his head.

'I told her none of it was real, that it was the crappy drugs she was doing. She never knew what shit she was buying – it was probably cut with all kinds of stuff. You don't know, do you?'

A creeping dread wormed its way through her gut.

'She asked Martin about Rohypnol.' Her head moved from side to side as she tried to shake the information away.

'Did she?' A shadow moved across Jack's face. 'No one could believe it when Jarvis got a job working with vulnerable kids. He clearly conned someone to get a role like that. It just goes to show that he's capable of conning anyone. Don't ever beat yourself up, Frankie. Trust me, loads of people have been taken in by him.' His eyes flinched at the memory. 'Charlotte was a mess and he exploited that. I know they used to talk; she wouldn't say what about.' He shook his head. 'I think Martin Jarvis got in her head, y'know?' Jack tapped his temple. 'I think he messed with her mind. If she was getting roofies from him, Christ alone knows what that was doing to her.' His mouth set in a hard line. 'This man she kept seeing, this thing in her room, whatever...' He sighed, 'it kept getting worse. Every hallucination got more intense.'

Her heart thudded painfully.

'Yeah,' he shook his head again. 'She was terrified to go to sleep. She said it was whispering.'

Frankie stared at him, not wanting to hear this, not wanting to comprehend.

'Whispering?'

'Yeah, that's what really freaked her out. The night when it touched her neck.'

# *Chapter Thirteen*

They sat downstairs drinking hot chocolate. The TV was on; Vanessa had recorded some gameshow that contained a lot of screaming. She and Peter kept shouting in unison and laughing, but it came across as sad and forced like they were pretending to be having fun. Frankie hugged the hot mug close to her chest, aware that Jack's eye kept flitting in her direction.

'You look a bit knackered,' he said eventually.

'Thanks.' She wavered a smile. 'You know all the right things to say.'

'Why don't you go on up?' Vanessa turned to look at her. 'I put your electric blanket on half an hour ago. It'll be lovely and snuggly.'

Frankie tried to look appreciative but the memory of what had happened in the bath tingled into her hairline. Vanessa's gaze didn't drop. Her unease prickled.

'Okay.'

She slid the mug onto the coffee table and shuffled forward.

'Goodnight, then.'

'Night night. Sleep tight.'

She wondered for a second if Jack would get up too, but he didn't offer to move.

'See you in the morning, then.'

Their three faces looked up at her. 'I've washed and dried all your clothes,' Vanessa smiled. 'I'll run an iron over them tonight. They'll be all ready for the morning. Big day tomorrow.'

'Yes, big day,' she repeated. 'Night.'

–

She made her way softly up the stairs. The boom and chatter of the TV was comforting as she stepped onto the landing. The air around her crackled with a faint static charge.

*Charlotte.* She felt suddenly very close.

The landing light cast grey triangular shadows down the walls. The air was thick with her presence. There was a tiny movement: a flicker in the darkness over in the corner, but she couldn't bring herself to turn her head. If she looked… But she didn't want to.

Her eyes tilted.

Charlotte's bedroom door that had been tightly closed before, now sat slightly open. A faint breath of perfume eased through the gap. She recognised it immediately.

Her hand came up. It was like a compulsion.

Listening for a moment with tightened breath, she put a finger on the door. The muffled sound of the TV was still rumbling on in the background.

*You want to do this*, something inside her said. *You need to.*

Poking the edge of the door gently, she watched the landing light spreading its geometric shape as the room opened up in front of her eyes.

A single bed sat neatly under the window. One wall held a white chest of drawers with an ornate, white-framed mirror sitting above it. At the foot of the bed was a cream sheepskin rug that she'd be terrified to even put a foot on. There was a full-length white bookcase rammed with books on the opposite wall. She had never seen so many books in her life. She glanced back down the stairs, and then took a step forward.

Charlotte's presence was as real as if she were sitting quietly on the side of the bed. In the light from the landing, she could see her, painting her toenails: one knee crooked, her heel balanced on the edge of the mattress, head bent and concentrating on the sweep of the tiny brush. She blinked. Of course there was no one there.

A light glinted dully and she turned her head. But the mirror only reflected her own image, paused, as though she'd just been asked a question and was about to answer. Somewhere over her shoulder, the shape of Charlotte drifted past. She looked around quickly. She wasn't there. She really wasn't.

But the urge to touch her things, was.

She went over to the bed and smoothed her hand across the covers, her fingers grazing the deep pink pillows – *She'd been here, and here, and here.*

Imagining, imagining...

Charlotte's face turned sideways in sleep. She could almost hear the quiet draw of breath, her hair splayed out, creamy gold against the rose pillowcase. Next to the bed was a dresser with a shaded lamp. In front was a box full of all kinds of makeup and a pot of brushes. Her hairbrush – wooden and expensive-looking, still had a few stray hairs clinging to it. She picked it up, bringing it to her nose. Charlotte was there, as real and as solid as if she'd just whisked the bristles through her blonde curls. Frankie's fingers copied her movements: gently brushing the ends of her hair, feeling the snag and catch, the strands mingling with Charlotte's… She stopped.

*No.*

Hastily putting it back, her eye caught a small wooden trinket box. It sat, quiet and square. She licked her lips.

*There was no harm, she was only looking.*

The lid opened easily. Inside were finer bits of jewellery: gold hoop earrings and rings with set stones. She lifted out a chain, the strand twirling and glinting prettily. A cut crystal pendant slid to one end, tipping into the light. There, in the centre of the ball, the letter 'C' came and went in a hologram.

'Nice isn't it?'

The room went suddenly dark.

She spun round. Vanessa was standing in the doorway, blocking the landing light.

'I bought it for Charlotte.'

'Oh god! I'm so sorry! I shouldn't have been looking… I didn't mean to—' She found her hands were shaking as she tried to put it back. 'I wasn't going to take it or anything!'

'No, no!' Vanessa was laughing. 'The idea never crossed my mind!' She came over and put her hand out. 'It's fine! Honestly, it's fine.' She chuckled. 'I didn't want to startle you. Please don't feel bad.'

'Sorry. Sorry…'

The necklace tangled around the box hinge, catching clumsily. She was terrified to yank it.

'Don't worry. Hang on, let me.'

Vanessa took it from her and pulled the chain safely free. 'Look. Here you go, let's put the light on.' She reached for the lamp switch. 'It's so lovely, isn't it?… Let's not shut it away in the dark. It's too pretty. Would you like it?' She held it out.

'Me? Oh no, I couldn't. I really couldn't!'

'Yes, you could.' She reached for Frankie's hand. 'I want you to have it. It's a gift from me to you. A thing like that is meant to be worn and loved, not lie in a box.' She dropped the pendant into her palm and closed her fingers around it. 'I gave it to Charlotte to show how much I loved her. Your wearing it would be keeping that love alive. It would mean masses to me, Frankie, more than you can imagine. Take it, please. Would you do that?'

Frankie felt the glass, hard against her palm. Vanessa's eyes looked huge.

'If not for you then for me.' Her hand pressed firmly. 'I mean it.'

Frankie looked down. 'Okay. For you,' she nodded gently. 'But only if you're sure. If you ever change your mind—'

'I won't. I assure you.'

'Okay... Well... Thank you.'

'It also means you're a part of our family now too.'

Somewhere over Vanessa's shoulder, she saw a movement, and instinctively knew it was Jack.

She felt appalled that he might've heard that conversation. She needed him to know that this wasn't her doing.

'Right. Now off to bed with you.' Vanessa ushered her out of the bedroom and pulled the door closed behind them. Jack had disappeared.

Vanessa paused on the landing with one hand on the bannister. 'Right, have you got everything you want? Would you like a glass of water? A book to read? Anything?'

'No really, I'm fine. Oh… and thank you again.' She gazed down at her palm. 'I'll treasure it.'

There was a flicker of movement at the bottom of the stairs. She felt wrong and unsettled; Jack had warned her. She should never have agreed to stay here. Now this.

'Goodnight then.' Frankie paused with a hand on her bedroom door.

Vanessa was already halfway down the stairs.

'Yes, sleep well. See you in the morning. Night-night my darling.' She turned and blew her a kiss. 'It's so lovely to have you home.'

–

Frankie lay in that bed, wide awake, hearing her own rustling heartbeat against the pillow, trying to calm it into a steady rhythm. *Eight or so hours and she could be out of there; just keep it together.* She stared up at the ceiling watching the shadows move: the unfamiliar shapes and patterns, listening to the odd noises of water running and a toilet flushing, and lights being switched off as everyone settled down for the night.

The thudding inside her ribcage shook the covers as her eyes cast nervously about the room. There were metal shelves stacked with files of paperwork against one wall. A desk in front of it, a computer screen, a printer. Each shape contained its own squat blackness. She memorised it, so that she could tell if anything moved.

Nothing did.

Sleep was impossible. Her thoughts began to tumble over themselves: *whispering shadows… Charlotte… Martin… Vanessa… the necklace… Jack…*

The wind sent a scramble of rain against the window and the curtain twitched.

Sighing, she closed her eyes briefly and then opened them, staring into the darkness. *Nothing's going to happen*, she told herself. *Just get through these next few hours, that's all. You'll be fine.*

A few minutes passed, maybe more, when suddenly she became aware of a band of light. It moved slowly across the floor, stretching under the door in a thin strip of pale moonlight. She watched as the line came and went, came and went, as though something was moving through it, slowly back and forth. There was a rustle and a soft creak of a floorboard and she realised that it was the sound of someone pacing.

Her eyes swept madly; the seconds felt like a lifetime. All the images of earlier in the bath came flooding back: the shape, the sound of the whispering, the feel of those fingers touching her spine. Then the pacing stopped. She watched the patch of darkness growing deeper. Something was moving closer. She stared, willing it to stop – and then, to her horror, she saw the door beginning to inch open.

Her eyes wildly scanned the black gap opening up before her. She gripped the covers closer to her chin. The door stopped. The moonlight replaced the blackness in a stripe of grey light.

There was only silence.

She held her breath.

Still silence.

A gust of wind moaned again, the rain smacking the glass, harder this time. The edge of the door juddered a little, shivering in the draught, as it moved gently back and forth. She let her breath go.

*The bathroom window… It didn't close properly, did it? That was all. Just the bathroom window and the doorcatch not latched.*

Swinging her legs from the side of the bed, she reached for Vanessa's dressing gown and pulled it on. Tiptoeing onto the landing, she waited a moment, hoping she hadn't woken anyone. The house was quiet. She glanced toward the bathroom door; she could feel the chill even from here. She took a careful step, trying to remember if any of the boards creaked. One tiny tiptoe as she eased her bodyweight forward, the carpet cushioning each tread.

*Two more, and she'd be at the top of the stairs.*

Her fingers brushed the wall to steady herself. She reached the doorway of Charlotte's room but something made her look round.

An eye looked back at her.

It was red and blazing, a hooded outline beneath it hung there, long and shapeless, its silence dark and black and staring.

The shock sent her stumbling forward, her hands flailing for the bannister as she slipped with a shriek down the first few steps, skidding and juddering until she landed in a heap at the bottom.

There was an immediate blaze of light as Peter appeared, bleary but wide-eyed, scrambling down the stairs after her.

'Oh my god, Frankie!' He reached down to grab her, but she was already hauling herself to her feet. Vanessa was close on his heels.

'What's happened? What's the matter?'

She immediately scooped her up, arms around her, holding her up, smoothing her hair and the tears from her face.

'Frankie, Frankie, Frankie,' she kept saying.

'I saw...' she blubbered. 'I saw...'

'What did you see? Are you hurt?' Vanessa kept checking her up and down. 'Another nightmare – was that it?'

'I wasn't dreaming – I wasn't.'

She saw Peter and Vanessa exchange a look as they both began to lead her into the living room to the sofa where they banked her up with cushions and a throw that Peter pulled over her knees and tucked in.

'What's going on?'

Jack appeared in the doorway rubbing his eyes.

'Another nightmare.' Peter looked over at him. 'That's all.'

Jack knelt at the side of the sofa and took her hand. 'What did you see, Frankie? What was it?'

'Let's not go there right now Jack, shall we?' Peter snapped. 'She doesn't need interrogating.'

Frankie saw something in the glare that passed between them.

'I saw an eye.' Frankie looked from one to the other. 'An eye staring at me. In Charlotte's room. The door was open.'

Peter looked up at Vanessa. 'Go and see what it could have been, could you, Nessa? Just to put Frankie's mind at rest.'

Vanessa nodded. The three of them stayed silent as they listened to her soft footsteps creaking their way up the stairs. There were several minutes, and then the sound of her coming back down again.

'No, that door is firmly closed.' Vanessa came to stand in front of her. 'As in, pulled shut.'

'It was open,' Frankie insisted, staring up at them. 'I swear to you, that door was open.'

Peter bent and put his hand on her knee. She could feel the heat through the blanket.

'Well, it's not now. Do you want to go up and check for yourself?'

She felt the pressure of the squeeze. Her eyes caught his, but his expression stayed the same: kind and concerned as ever.

'No,' she said with a little shake of the head, sniffing. 'No, I don't. Thank you, though.'

'Good. That's good.' He patted her hand and straightened, smiling round at Vanessa and Jack. 'There we are then.'

She felt her cheeks colouring.

'It was my fault,' Jack said suddenly.

They all looked at him.

'I told Frankie a ghost story earlier. Well, kind of a ghost story. Something Charlotte once told me.' He looked at his father. 'I shouldn't have. It's my fault.'

'A ghost story?' Peter's eyes narrowed.

'Stupid, really.'

Peter opened his mouth to say something else but Vanessa interrupted. 'Hey, look, we've all got a heavy day tomorrow so let's not get involved in a fight. Now, are we all ready for bed?'

'Would you mind if I didn't?' Frankie suddenly blurted. She couldn't face the thought of going back up there. 'Would it be okay if I stayed down here? I don't think I'd be able to sleep anyway.'

'Of course you can!' Vanessa soothed. 'I'll bring the duvet and pillows down and we'll make you a nice comfy bed on the sofa. No problems at all.' She disappeared upstairs and then came back with armfuls of bedding.

'Here.' She slotted one of the pillows behind her. 'You can watch TV if you want, too.' She picked up the remote.

'I'll stay with her,' Jack said firmly. 'To keep her company for a bit.'

He sat, making it clear he wasn't going anywhere.

Vanessa smiled uncertainly. 'Okay then. If you need anything, Frankie, you know where we are.'

'Thank you, I'm fine.' She smiled back.

'We'll say goodnight, then. See you in the morning.'

Peter stooped forward and kissed her briefly on the forehead. She was aware of his breath, the sudden closeness of the stubble on his chin. There was a smell about him: strangely sweet, like rotting apples. She felt herself go pink.

'We'll look after you, Frankie. That's all you need to remember. You've given us so much just being here. Never feel embarrassed about feeling overwhelmed – our home is your home.' He stood, surveying her for a moment before collecting himself. 'Okay then. Night-night you two.'

She and Jack waited, listening to them making their way up the stairs and the click of their bedroom door. Frankie hugged her knees and Jack let out a massive sigh.

'I warned you, didn't I? I warned you what they were like.'

'I did see something though, Jack… And that door *was* open.'

Despite the warmth of the duvet, she found that she was shivering.

He glanced at the door and she anxiously followed his eyes.

'Frankie… Frankie… Hey, come on.' He took her hand. The pressure of it was comforting. 'What I was trying to say earlier – it came out wrong. It's not that my dad and Vanessa are bad people, they're just stuck. It's their grief and their pain that brings its own kind of weird energy into the house. Everything is heightened. I don't know if you're hooking into that weirdness, but whatever it is, it's not healthy. I told you, now you're here, it's like they've got her back.' He looked at the door again. It was making her nervous.

'And once you leave and if Martin Jarvis gets off tomorrow...'

Just the mention of his name made her feel ill.

'I think it will kill them. After losing Charlotte. I don't think they'll survive it.'

Frankie saw the score lines under his eyes and around his mouth. He looked older than his years. He lifted his head to look at her. 'And then there's you, Frankie. You must be torn both ways: part of you must want him punished; part of you must hate the fact that he'll be leaving you with a kid.'

Frankie hugged her knees closer, trying to protect herself from his words. The baby quickened and turned inside her.

The pain lines in Jack's face deepened. 'Charlotte's death is at the centre of everything. It's like we're all haunted by her: what we did, what we didn't do. We're all thinking we could have stopped it happening in one way or another: if Vanessa and my dad hadn't smothered her, if I hadn't gone with her to that party, if you hadn't had that row with her, *if only, if only, if only* – and the truth is, until we can put her ghost to rest, none of us will get any peace.'

# *Chapter Fourteen*

## *Now*

The sound of her phone slams her back into the present.

There are seconds where it drills and jangles into the car's quiet interior before she manages to look at it.

*Christ*, Alex.

'Hello?'

'Where are you?'

'I'm—'

'And don't say you're with Declan. I already know you're not.'

Her brain swarms into panic. 'I wasn't going to say that.' *What's Declan said?*

'You were going to phone me. You said you wouldn't leave me to worry. So where are you?'

She glances quickly at the clock. *Shit*.

'You can tell me the worst, whatever the truth is. What's going on?'

She wonders for some gut-churning minute if he followed her here and is sitting in his car watching her right now. She takes a surreptitious glance around, but if he's here, she can't see him.

'Has something else happened at work?'

'Sorry?'

'Diane.'

'What about Diane?'

'I thought that's why she was trying to get hold of you. She didn't reach you then? She said your phone kept going to voicemail, so she rang here. I thought maybe it was bad news.'

Frankie quickly glances at the screen and sees there are three voice messages.

'Ah – no – I don't know how I missed them. I'll contact her now. I called into the office – I realised I needed some files that I can't access at home. Christ, the time ran away with me. I—'

'Oh, and the police rang.' He doesn't sound convinced.

Her stomach does a little flip. 'They rang you?'

'Yeah… It was a really odd conversation. Julia said they couldn't find a Matthew Jarrow on the system who'd been convicted or released recently. She said they couldn't find anything on the police files about him at all… Strange, isn't it?'

She opens her mouth to speak.

'So I asked Diane about him.'

Her mouth closes again. There's a moment's silence.

'Did you hear me? I asked Diane about this Matthew Jarrow and him harassing you. I told her I needed to know exactly what kind of man he was.'

She thinks she's forgotten to breathe.

'And what did she say?'

Everything stops.

'She said it must've been before you worked for her, while you were still at the Ellesmere Port office. She said she remembered several cases where—'

But his voice fades as her brain scrambles. She feels light-headed with relief. Diane, bless her, had taken the question in her stride.

He pauses. She realises he's asked her a question.

'Sorry, the phone cut out. Say again?'

'I said I was sorry for storming off this morning.'

The guilt of where she's sitting right now, washes up and over her in a hot tide of shame.

'It was stupid and childish and could only make matters worse. There are two sides to every argument, and you feeling that you couldn't confide in me makes me feel terrible… More than terrible. I hate the way I found out, but I hate even more that I was going to just walk out. That's not how a partner is supposed to behave—'

She wishes she could stop him talking right now. The guilt squirms and burns.

'There's no need, Alex. There really isn't.'

'Yes, there is. I want you to know how bad I feel. I'll make it up to you, I promise.'

'Alex—'

'I've got to go over to the community centre this afternoon. I'll go shopping for dinner on the way back. You're coming straight home now?'

'Yes.'

'So how about we talk about stuff over dinner tonight? Like, properly talk. I want us to be a team again. I want it to be us against the world.'

'Yes. Yes, so do I.' She tries to breathe normally.

'—Oh and Frankie?' She can hear the smile in his voice. 'I love you, you know.'

'I love you too.'

'Bye, love.'

'Bye.'

The call ends and her hand drops. The phone lies there warm against her palm. She stares at it for a few moments. He's going to find out; he's going to find it all out and then he'll see her for what she is. This is madness. She feels as though she's standing in front of a wall of water. She can hear the sonic boom of it, a great roaring in her ears that's getting louder and louder. She glances up as a shaft of sunlight dazzles from in between the houses. She raises a hand to shield her eyes. She knows she can't stop it; it's coming for her and right now she's utterly powerless.

The sunlight glints and moves and then she notices the figure by the gate. It's oddly familiar. She pauses, and then there's one great leap of realisation. *It's Jack*. She almost laughs out loud at the sight of him. He takes a look back at the house, and then comes walking around the front of the car. He hesitates for a moment, pretending to look right then left as though checking for traffic but then quickly opens the door and slides into the passenger seat.

'Oh my God, *Jack!* Is it you?'

He grins back at her. Real and solid and right here, sitting beside her as though the last fifteen years haven't touched him.

His head ducks to look up at the house again. 'Can I make a suggestion?'

'I can't believe—' she starts.

'I suggest you start that engine pretty smartish.' He leans back in the seat so that he's not visible from the windows. 'You drive, then we can talk.'

Her hands respond automatically as she starts the engine, managing to the end of the road where she halts with a jerk and looks round.

'Which way?'

'Any way you please, we can just pull up somewhere.'

She drives a little further, finds a turning and pulls into it, yanking on the handbrake and slumping back in her seat.

'Jack! I cannot, *cannot* believe—'

He shakes his head, as though he, too, is stunned to find himself here.

'When you rang earlier, I had this premonition that you'd turn up. I've spent all morning trying to distract Vanessa—'

'That was you, in the background?'

He nods. 'I visit her. I live nearby to keep an eye on things.' He twitches a small smile.

'It's been too long.' She studies his face. Still the same, kind, Jack.

'Far too long. I'm sorry I didn't—'

'No, don't be.' She holds up a hand. 'I know how difficult it was back then. I wouldn't have come here Jack, it's just—'

'I know. You're scared. We're all scared. None of us know what he's going to do. If he goes to social services; if he alerts people to the situation—'

*The situation. What they did.*

Neither of them speaks as the memories come flooding back.

He clears his throat. 'I thought of you a lot you know, over the years.' He looks at her with real affection. 'I still feel terrible. I could have, should have, helped you more—'

'You don't have to feel anything, Jack. I was a kid, a child, who was having a child. It was impossible.'

'It didn't have to be impossible.' He sounds almost angry.

'We were both kids. We were both in a mess. I don't suppose we could have helped anyone, least of all each other.'

'Yeah, you're right there,' he says bitterly. He rests his elbow against the door ledge and touches his forehead gently with his fingers. 'I knew though, didn't I? I knew it, I was there, warning you, and yet we both blundered into it blindly like we were sleepwalking or something.' He rubs his forehead as though he would like to erase the memory.

'You make it sound like—' She stops before saying the words.

'A trap,' he says sullenly. 'That's what it was: a grief-driven, ghost-ridden madness that we all got sucked into.'

Frankie shook her head.

*She'd left her baby.* Christ. *Was that the way it had been?* No. It wasn't like that. It wasn't all planned and orchestrated, they wouldn't have gone that far. It just happened – a whole train of events: one, then another, and another. That was the truth. Wasn't it?

# *Chapter Fifteen*

## *Then*

April the sixth. Bright, cold sunshine, a brisk wind and white scudding clouds.

The day is all wrong from the start.

April the sixth. One year ago today she'd met Martin for the first time: a grinningly handsome dark-haired lad, full of front, and charm, and clever talk, and now here she was sitting in a courtroom, pregnant, staring down as they talked about death, and murder, and violence. *How had it come to this?*

There was an open folder on the jury bench showing Charlotte's body: the marks, the bruises, the report on her lungs, the contents of her stomach, the drugs in her system, the state of her clothes. Frankie sat, head bowed in her seat, her shoulders heavy with an invisible weight as every piece of evidence sliced and stabbed and punched into her as though she'd been physically beaten and might never stand straight again. She listened to it all, but became aware, even with her limited knowledge and understanding, that although this terrible, monstrous thing had happened, there was nothing to tie it to Martin. The DNA evidence showed that Charlotte had been in the cabin, but that was all. There was no transfer of fingerprints from Martin to her; neither her hair nor her blood were on his clothes; the drugs in her system could have come from anywhere. The Prosecution were struggling, and that was becoming more and more evident.

The look on Jack's face was enough to tell her how the family were feeling. Peter hadn't been able to listen any longer and had walked out. Vanessa stayed mute and stony-faced, but the enormity of her hatred for Martin came off her in waves. They could all see this was a foregone conclusion – Martin Jarvis was going to get off. Vanessa and Peter would be eaten up with their own grief; they'd lost Charlotte, and now they would lose what was left of themselves to anger and sadness.

Her hand came up to her throat to touch the pendant that Vanessa had given her. It felt strange and unfamiliar around her neck.

Some forensic guy was talking. Nothing he said made any sense. Everything was swirling round in her head, making it ache. She closed her eyes and rested her cheek on her hand, feeling the bones of her knuckles digging in.

'You okay, Frankie?' She realised that Vanessa was leaning across to her, concerned.

'Just a bit hot in here, that's all.' She smiled weakly back.

Vanessa grimaced in sympathy, but her eyes were unbearably sad. 'Not long now.'

No, not long until they would be forced to live with the knowledge that the man that had killed their daughter was going to walk free – and then what? Then what would happen? What would she do?

'I'm going to go for a walk during the lunch break,' she whispered.

'I'll come with you.' Vanessa put her hand in the middle of Frankie's back.

'Would you mind if I went by myself? Is that okay?'

'Of course! But if you still feel unwell, you ring me, yes?' Vanessa frowned, concerned.

She watched the judge's face, waiting for the signs that he was about to wrap up the morning session. As soon as he leaned back in his chair, she gathered her jacket and was on her feet.

'I'll ring.' She managed a quick smile back. 'I promise.'

Her quick footsteps echoed down the stairs as she made her way to the ground floor. Her palms were sweating and her hair was sticking to her forehead. *Air*, that's what she needed. To be able to think straight, to be able to—

The doors of the courtroom suddenly opened.

'Ah good! I was hoping to bump into you!'

She stopped abruptly.

'You're Ms Turner, am I right?' A chubby-cheeked man with pale-coloured hair, stood there with an armful of papers. She realised it was Mr Saunders, Martin's barrister. She felt her face colour.

'I was on my way out.' She made a weak gesture towards the door.

'Yes, yes…' he said distractedly as though that was of no consequence. 'Mr Jarvis tells me that he's been trying to get to speak to you.' His voice boomed, unnaturally loud, and she winced, looking round nervously.

'He saw you in the public gallery and said that if I saw you, I should have a word.'

She suddenly felt very hot and dizzy.

'Oh my goodness! Are you alright?'

She thought she might throw up.

'Dear, oh dear!' He immediately ushered her to the row of chairs behind them. 'Let me get you some water…' Dumping the papers on the seat beside her, he went over to the water cooler and pulled a plastic cup from the stack. 'Here we go.'

He handed her a half-filled cup. She drank greedily and then held the wet plastic against her cheek.

'I'm sorry… I'm really sorry.' She swallowed thickly. 'I'm fine now. It was a bit too warm in there, that's all.' She fanned her face and smiled.

'Ah good. As I was saying…' His eyes were sympathetic and kind. 'Mr Jarvis has asked—'

'I can't talk about it all right now,' she interrupted and made a move to get up. 'It's too difficult. He's acting as though what happened is nothing – he's already saying that after he gets out, he'll want—'

'Gets out?' Mr Saunders gave her an odd look. 'I'm not quite following—'

She took a deep breath. 'The way the case is going, I mean. They'll release him, won't they? He'll be out.'

'I think…' He faltered a little. 'I think we should have a little chat.' He took the cup, refilled it, and passed it back. 'That's why Mr Jarvis wants to speak to you so urgently I believe, so that you're fully aware of how the case has changed.'

'Changed?'

'Regarding the charges. He hasn't told you?'

'No.' She started to feel dizzy again.

'Oh now, now! Don't upset yourself!' He stopped, suddenly making a decision. 'Look. Miss Turner, I know this is a little irregular, but I have to go and speak to Mr Jarvis now and I was wondering if you'd like to come with me?'

'Me? Here?' she sniffed, drying her eyes. 'Is that allowed?'

'It is if I say it is,' he smiled kindly. 'He's downstairs in the cells. Would you like to see him? It would give us a chance to talk, just the three of us, and I can explain what's happened. It can only be literally a few minutes but perhaps it might make this whole horrid situation feel a little better.'

'Okay.' Her head was buzzing.

'That's settled then.' Mr Saunders bent and swept up the papers from the chair. 'Come with me.'

He strode away with her trotting behind trying to keep up. He halted at a plain wooden door with no handle. There was just an intercom and a bell-button that he pressed and then waited, staring impatiently off into the middle distance. It felt like an age. There was a faint fizzing noise and then a bored voice crackled.

'Yes?'

'Mr Saunders and Ms Turner to see Martin Jarvis.'

More silence and then the door buzzed and opened.

They made their way down a blank set of concrete steps to where two prison officers sat; one had his feet on a chair that he only just managed to lift in time for them to pass. The narrow corridor had nothing of the ornate grandeur of upstairs. Here, the plain tiled walls were grimed with the hundreds of bodies that had passed by them. The lino floor was the colour of dirty luncheon meat.

'Cell three,' the officer called out behind them.

Mr Saunders raised his hand in mute response as they stopped at a cell door. The officer came up behind jinking a set of keys, and with a metallic clatter, the door swung wide.

The man sitting there wasn't the Martin she knew. Her heart cleaved wide. He looked up, startled, and the eyes she knew caught hers. He looked small and beaten.

His expression changed. 'Why's she here?' He gave Mr Saunders a nettled, questioning stare.

'You wanted to speak to Ms Turner, and I just happened to bump into her.'

Martin gave a sullen nod.

'Please.' The barrister gestured and pulled out a plastic chair for her to sit. Martin perched on the end of a narrow bed that jutted from the wall.

Frankie sat with her knees pressed together. She was within inches of Martin but they didn't touch.

'What's going on?' She tried to read his face. 'Mr Saunders says the case has changed?'

'Things have got complicated.' Martin couldn't look at her.

'What? How complicated?' Frankie's eyes moved from one to the other.

'Shall I go through it with her?' The barrister moved around the small space like a caged animal. She found her thighs were shaking. Martin gave a brief nod.

'The night of the party, I don't know if you're aware, but Martin allegedly broke into a property. A leather belt was recovered at the scene. The said belt has Mr Jarvis's fingerprints on it. Mr Jarvis's fingerprints are on the police database and there is no doubt about the match.'

She swallowed involuntarily.

'The elderly lady at the house also gave a description of the intruder. She described Martin quite precisely.'

The shake got worse.

'The lady had a heart condition. She was hospitalised after the break-in. And I've just received notification that she very sadly—'

The shake stopped.

'—Died. Last night.' He stopped pacing.

Martin's face was the colour of stone.

'So there is talk from the prosecution that the added charge of aggravated burglary will be withdrawn and a charge of manslaughter laid in its place.'

'I really thought it was best that you heard this from Martin or myself, in private, where you can ask anything you need to know. I thought it might come as a bit of a shock, and in your condition, along with everything else—' He broke off as someone in the corridor called his name.

'Ah sorry, just one second—'

He flapped out of the door. Frankie stared after him but Martin grabbed her hand.

'I will never, ever tell them that you were in that house, Frankie. Do you hear me? I will never tell them that you were anywhere near my boat. They've got me for all of this. That's enough. You need to go out there and live your life. You and the baby.' His hand dropped to her belly. 'All I need in return is one thing; it's a huge thing, but I need an answer.'

'Martin—' She couldn't cope. This was too much to deal with.

'No, listen, I'm deadly serious. I need to know that you're out there waiting for me, Frankie. I need to know that our connection is still solid. I *need* that. I feel like I'm suffocating in this filthy place. I can't breathe.' He lifted his chin as though searching for air. 'The thought of you is like oxygen. As long as I can hold onto that, I'll be able to survive.' He gripped onto her fingers even tighter. 'I'm serious, Frankie. Without you I won't even—'

She saw his eyes startle suddenly. His hand slowly lifted to hover in mid-air at her throat.

'Where did you get that necklace?'

She instinctively touched the tiny crystal.

'I said, where did you get it?'

Her brain floundered for an answer. She didn't know what to say.

'Why?'

'Frankie, this is important. Just tell me.'

'I found it.'

'Found it where?' His face had gone white.

'I can't remember.'

'You can't remember? What do you mean, you can't remember?' He grabbed her arm and shook her a little. His grip was tight, getting tighter. 'Tell me, Frankie. Where did you get it?'

'Martin, don't, I—'

'Where, Frankie? Where did you get it?'

She watched his face go from white to angry red. He let go and stood suddenly. Her eyes jerked up with the movement. Her mouth mumbled over the truth. Vanessa. She couldn't drag Vanessa into all this – she'd been through enough brutality and pain. She just couldn't do it to her.

'On-on the street,' she stuttered. 'Maybe outside the house where that party was. I-I can't remember exactly.'

The sound of voices from the other side of the door got louder and Mr Saunders bustled in.

'Right. Where were we? Ah, yes.' He seemed unperturbed as he riffled through the papers in his bundle and peered across at Frankie.

'Miss Turner, would it be okay if I asked this very pleasant prison officer to escort you back upstairs, please? There are several points I need to go through with Martin before we resume this afternoon's session.'

Frankie stood; the room spun a little.

Martin gripped her hand and pulled her to him. 'And that's the honest truth, Frankie?' His eyes burned into hers.

She swallowed, nodding. 'Yes, that's the truth.'

'I'm sorry, you really need to say your goodbyes.' Mr Saunders fluttered his papers.

Martin dipped and kissed her full on the mouth, his hand snaking around her waist to draw her in. The taste of him was sweet like honey. She let the feelings flood in – they felt so easy – so simple. How she longed for things to be as they were.

The officer gestured for her to go through the door. She glanced back; Martin was sitting, hands clasped and head bowed, not wanting to watch her leave. She could hear the barrister's voice getting down to business. The door began to close behind her until all she could see was a tiny glimpse of Martin's cheek in the gap.

'Now...' She saw the barrister lean forward a little in earnest. 'Let's look at this in the cold light of day. These rape charges—'

She saw Martin nod. The door closed but the barrister's voice resounded in a muffled echo.

'—Thankfully the amount of time the body was in the water has washed away all traces of DNA...'

Her hand reached out for the wall. The officer's footsteps ricocheted back at her. Her head turned back to the door.

'Are you alright, miss?'

But the words just kept on coming.

'—The police won't be able to substantiate the charges, Martin, so they haven't been brought, but—' floated through the air.

She couldn't breathe. The atmosphere felt thick, like treacle. She tried to drag oxygen into her lungs but it wasn't happening. Stars began to burst in front of her eyes; a tunnel of darkness was moving towards her at lightning speed.

'Oopsy-daisy.' There was a man's voice and she felt hands circling her waist as the stairs pitched and rolled.

The tunnel zoomed up. She was enveloped in blackness. Flashes came back to her: that night, the boat, the pitch and swell of the water. There was a sudden stink of boat diesel... She saw the yellow rectangle of cabin light that her hands had reached for as her head dipped to go inside... She had the sudden recollection of the girl's voice... Not just the voice this time, but the words.

'*You don't want to do this. You know you don't.*'

The way she had pleaded. She'd sounded scared: panicky.

'*You can do whatever you want, I promise I won't say anything.*'

She knew in that split second: this was Charlotte begging for her life. This was Charlotte begging not to be raped.

The last few stairs beneath her feet came back; her hands groped for the wall as she hauled herself back through the door and she collapsed: her cheek and chin hitting the marble floor, the shock of its coldness and the taste of blood as her lip split wide.

'Jesus Christ! Bloody hell... Hang on there, let me get someone.'

'Frankie...?'

There was a squeal of shoes and she lifted her head. Peter was walking swiftly towards them. 'Frankie? Are you alright?'

She tried to lift her head but the floor kept dragging her down.

'My god!' Peter was kneeling at her side. 'What the hell's been going on?'

She watched his face as though from very far away.

'She's been visiting a prisoner,' the officer said.

The atmosphere instantly changed. The room was tilting around her, blurring, coming in and out of focus.

'Can someone call an ambulance please?'

'I don't want an ambulance.' She suddenly found her voice, tremblingly managing to sit up, and pushing the hair back out of her eyes. She wiped her mouth on the back of her hand and then took the tissue that Peter was proffering. It instantly went red. The tears started, running down her face, unstoppable. She needed to speak; she wanted to speak. She struggled, grabbing onto Peter's arm for support as she saw a sweep of black gown about to walk past. It was the barrister for the Prosecution who turned towards her, clearly wondering what the commotion was all about.

'Mr Bain!' Frankie held up her hand to stop him. Everyone looked round. 'Mr Bain!' Her lip felt thick and stupid as she scrambled to her feet. She realised, in those seconds, he was going to keep on walking.

'It's about Martin Jarvis!' she called to his retreating back. 'I was there!'

He paused and slowly turned. 'I beg your pardon?'

'I was there, that night, on the boat!' She was aware of Peter's eyes on her face, the paralysed shock, the disbelief; she was making some sick kind of joke, wasn't she?

'I'm sorry, do you know what you're saying? Are you being quite serious?' Mr Bain came towards her, the thick spectacles making his eyes look small and pig-like. They stared at her, unblinking.

'I was there that night. The night that Charlotte died. I was on the boat. I saw them – Martin and Charlotte Vale. I was there when he—' She stopped, bringing the tissue to her mouth. She couldn't look at Peter, knowing the profound agony that would be drawn in his eyes. But she would say it; she had to say it; she'd *make* herself say it.

'I saw things. I heard things. The night she was raped.'

She was aware of the movement of her bruised lips forming the words, listening to the echo of a voice that didn't sound like hers, saying things that couldn't possibly be true, but knowing, until she was sick to her heart, that they were.

*Charlotte*. This was for Charlotte.

'I heard her crying out – she said–'

She told him what she'd heard, and she told him what she'd seen. She watched as the last shreds of her love disappeared into the appalled frown on the barrister's face.

And then she stopped with a gasp. There was sudden, acute pain, like something giving inside her: a stabbing punch that knifed into her belly and slammed into the top of her skull. She instantly doubled over.

'Frankie… Frankie? Can you hear me?'

The floor came up to greet her. All she was aware of were endless shoes moving in front of her eyes in a strange kind of dance. They moved oddly, and then white trainers took their place as the marbled floor began to billow slowly in an ever-increasing ripple.

'I'm only twenty-nine weeks so I'm fine,' she heard herself say. 'The baby won't be born yet.'

She didn't remember much else.

–

There were the snatches and drifts of memory, like a camera angle that was focused off centre. Other recollections were sharp and clear: a stretch of ceiling lights, ribboning above her head in a dizzy stream of yellow, the sound of sirens, a patch of sunlight on a wall, a box of surgical gloves with the cardboard top torn raggedly, dust motes spiralling in a cone over flashing and beeping machines. She knew they were there to keep her daughter alive. *A daughter*, someone said. *You have a girl.*

She remembered the feel of her head on the pillow turning to look at her baby's tiny frame. The drugs twitching her frog legs taut, her tiny chin shivering. Frankie closed her eyes and thought about the things she wanted to tell her: how she'd always be there to look after her, how she'd never leave her alone, how she'd face the worst horrors in the world just to make sure she stayed safe. She remembered a doctor and a nurse sitting on her bed with that look on their faces. She knew exactly what their look was saying: *was she capable of any of those things? Could she even look after herself?*

She kept her head under the covers for what felt like days. She remembered hearing Vanessa's and Peter's voices as they sat by the side of her bed for hours as she pretended to be asleep. She couldn't face them. *What had she done?*

Slowly, she emerged. The hospital noises grew louder, the curtains swished back and forth a hundred times a day. She ate, she drank. She didn't allow herself to think. She sat watching her little daughter in that fish tank of a plastic crib, knowing that one day she would take her away from this place, because she would get better; she had to get better. Hours and days passed. She thought of where they might go: somewhere quiet, the seaside maybe, just the two of them. They would sit and watch the waves, listening to the sea grass rattling beside them and watching the sunset blazing into pure lilac. They'd sit in hollowed dunes with the soft pink shadows creeping, hiding them from everyone. 'Your name is Chloe,' she whispered through the plastic wall. 'And you're all mine.'

## *Chapter Sixteen*

'How are you both doing?'

'Oh!'

Jude was standing behind her in the doorway. She was smiling, gently, looking round at all the machines and wires. Frankie's embarrassment stung: hot and smarting.

'I'm okay. We're okay.'

Jude tiptoed over and peered into the incubator, the shock of such a tiny little thing registering on her face and then she smiled.

'You don't have to look like that, Frankie.' She raised an eyebrow and gave her a sideways look. 'Vanessa and Peter have stayed in contact with me. They told me you were pregnant.'

Frankie looked at her, stunned.

Jude gave her a wry smile. 'The three of us came to an agreement. They convinced me you were being looked after properly, so I knew you were safe.'

*She had no idea.*

'I could have intervened at any point, but I've learned over the years that being 'text-book' doesn't always give you the best outcome, Frankie. After all, I knew where you were, even if the circumstances weren't what could be described as…' She chose the word carefully. '…Umm… Orthodox.'

Frankie bit her lip.

'So now I understand why you were so keen to get involved in going to court,' Jude said gently. 'I get it now. You did a very brave thing there, Frankie.'

She didn't feel like that at all.

'It wasn't brave. I was a total coward. Vanessa and Peter—'

'Vanessa and Peter just want to help.'

'But they must hate me.'

'I know how it must feel, Frankie, but they don't. I've spoken to them at length. They are genuinely warm, kind people. They see you and that baby as victims of circumstances beyond your control. You two are innocent in all this as far as they're concerned.'

'But I'm not though, am I?'

'Well, yes, they feel angry, yes, they're upset and confused over what you did and didn't do, but they also know that you're just a kid. That you got mixed up in something that was way, way over your head. No, you didn't do the right thing in the beginning – you should have told the police that you saw Martin and Charlotte together – but you did the right thing in the end, and that's what counts. Your testimony and witness statement will be crucial in making sure that Martin goes to prison for a long time. Vanessa and Peter have been told it could be fifteen years. That has to be something, doesn't it?'

The idea of that length of time made her head swim. It felt like a lifetime.

'Martin Jarvis is the guilty one here, not anyone else. That's what you have to remember. All this blaming yourself for not coming forward sooner,' she waved the idea away. 'That just lets him off the hook. We all need to concentrate on building positive relationships. You have your whole life in front of you, Frankie. Vanessa and Peter know that. That's why they're offering you a home, you and…' She looked at the name plaque. '…little Chloe.'

Frankie felt her eyes widening in shock; she'd never dreamed…

'You're eighteen in a couple of months. You're an adult, a free agent to live where you choose. Take the offer. Live with Vanessa and Peter. Let them provide you with a firm family base while you get yourself some qualifications and a job. Be your own woman, Frankie. Put all this behind you and move forward. Don't drag the past round with you forever; let it go.'

She nodded silently. She couldn't bring herself to speak.

'Thank you,' she whispered finally.

'Thank yourself,' nodded Jude. 'You're the one that's going to be amazing.'

# *Chapter Seventeen*

Which meant Jude signed the paperwork for the remaining two months of guardianship. Chloe was doing well, so there was no reason she couldn't be discharged. Vanessa and Peter came into the hospital smiling and happy and Frankie immediately burst into tears.

'Hey, hey...' Vanessa's arms went around her. 'There's no need for all that. You did the right thing. Without you, Frankie... without you...' She stopped and pushed her back to look into her eyes. 'He's not going anywhere for a long time, but we know where he is. That, at least, gives us a little peace for a while.'

Frankie looked into her eyes and believed her. She believed because right that minute she would have believed anything. She was so tired, so exhausted. *Tell me what to do and I'll do it, tell me what to think and I'll think it.* It was as though she was functioning but with someone else pulling the strings. All she wanted to do was lie on the floor and close her eyes until the world stopped spinning and she could finally get off.

She'd done everything that was required. She'd filed the witness statement for the court, given evidence, *in camera*, so that she didn't have to face Martin. She allowed everyone to think that she had changed: grown up, taken the right path and done the right thing. *So why did she feel so dead inside?* It was as though she was on a moving tread-mill, being taken into a foreign country where everything felt wrong and bizarre. Vanessa was always there by her side, constantly smiling. *This was the right thing… Of course it was… Giving her statement against Martin… Telling the truth… Agreeing to live with Vanessa and Peter… Of course it was the right thing.*

The day she moved in she stood in the living room. Jack was sitting sullenly on the sofa as Vanessa and Peter flapped around her, manoeuvring her towards an armchair and gently taking Chloe from her arms and laying her in a brand new white and pink bassinet with matching covers.

'This is too generous.' She looked up at them. 'You've already bought the car seat and you've told me about the cot and changing table. You mustn't keep buying things.'

But Vanessa waved her away. 'Oh, it's nothing. We like getting bits and pieces, don't we Peter? It gives us something nice to focus on.'

Peter was already in the kitchen, whistling tunelessly as the kettle boiled.

'I'll make us all sandwiches, shall I?' She fussed excitedly. 'I've got tuna, and cheese and tomatoes and salad…' She went through the whole lot, reeling off lunch and then what she had planned for dinner as Frankie watched Jack's face growing more and more bleak and stormy.

'Sounds perfect,' Frankie attempted to reassure her. 'Anything, really. I'm starving.'

Vanessa finally pottered off into the kitchen still twit-tering about food, as an uneasy quiet descended.

'Go and look upstairs, quick.' Jack jerked his chin, glancing at the ceiling. 'Go and look what they've done.'

Frankie glanced at the kitchen door and then at the sleeping Chloe before creeping into the hallway and tiptoeing up the stairs. The door to Charlotte's bedroom was no longer closed. It sat open now. The bookcase against the far wall was still there, but that was the only remnant of the past.

It had become a nursery. The wallpaper was sprigged with pink flowers, as were the curtains. The bed had gone, and a white cot stood in its place. There was a white changing table stocked with nappies and creams and wipes, and a rocking chair was laden with big, blush velvet cushions. She gazed at it all in shock and then went to the room next door. It was spartan and functional as before: the computer, the printer, the bed pushed against the wall; it was all still the same.

She made her way back into the living room and Jack raised his eyes to meet her gaze. *See?* his expression said and then he flashed a look towards the cot. Frankie immediately went over but Chloe wasn't there. She panicked. She could hear Vanessa cooing and crooning in the kitchen as she stormed her way in. Vanessa was sitting in the saggy old wicker chair with Chloe in her arms, feeding her from a bottle.

Frankie's breasts ached. Her arms longed to take her.

'What's going on?' She tried to say it as calmly as she could. Vanessa glanced up.

'Oh, you weren't there. She was hungry.'

'I only went upstairs.'

But Vanessa only smiled and shrugged and stared down at the baby again.

Peter was standing at the sink, gazing out into the garden, seemingly lost in thought. 'If you want things to be perfect, it's all in the planning,' he mused to no one in particular. 'I'm so glad we did all the groundwork. That's the secret to success, really.' He turned to look at her, smiling. 'I think I'll get out there for a bit while it's still sunny. Now, wellies… are they in the porch or did I leave them in the shed? That's the question.' He went to move past her, brushing the back of her hand as he did so. A jolt of alarm tingled up her forearm and she moved it away.

'Gosh, I bet you're shattered, Frankie.' He paused, wrinkling his nose in concern. 'I think we've got this all covered down here. Why don't you go for a lie down, hmm?'

Frankie stared at Vanessa's bowed head. She was humming to the baby as she fed her but then stopped suddenly and lifted her eyes.

'Look at us!' She gazed round with a strange smile on her face. 'Look at us, a proper little family again!'

Peter went over and crouched next to the chair, reaching out to gently stroke the baby's cheek. Frankie felt a whole surge of protective rage coursing through her veins.

'It'll be wonderful to watch her grow, won't it?' Peter smiled round. 'We'll be here to see her bloom and blossom into a young woman. Don't you think that'll be amazing?' He caught Frankie's expression. His smile froze.

'Why don't you take my advice and go upstairs for a little sleep, eh? Your room's all ready and waiting for you. Don't fret about Chloe. We'll take good care of her. She's in expert hands, don't you worry about that.'

# *Chapter Eighteen*

Frankie lay in her room listening to the sound of her baby crying downstairs. The tears leaked from her eyes, clucking into her ears and making the world go silent. She'd had weeks of this. The milk inside her swollen breasts felt hot and sore. It was excruciating. The thought of moving an inch brought her out in a cold sweat. A tiny sob hiccoughed in the back of her throat as she listened to Chloe's cries getting smaller and smaller and Vanessa's soothing tones. There was nothing to do but cry: for the pain she was in, for her hatred of Martin, for what had happened to Charlotte, for all the things she'd done and hadn't done in her life. How she would love for everything to go silent and just stop. She really prayed it would – that she would never have to hear or see anything ever again. She honestly wished she were dead.

Chloe hated her.

She knew it.

She felt it every time she picked her up, feeling the baby kick and squirm and turn her face away. Each shriek and wail said the same, her tiny fists punching into the air, furious and rejecting – until Vanessa picked her up. Then she would lie against Vanessa's shoulder, hiccoughing as her sobs faded, her big grey eyes staring in accusation. *I hate you*, the look said. *I've seen inside you. I know what you are.*

Everything Frankie did was wrong; every way she held Chloe made her scream. She could hear the tut in Vanessa's voice as she bustled over to the rescue, trying to show her for the hundredth time how to hold her properly, how to change a nappy, how to get her into her onesie – how to be any kind of mother.

She was rubbish; she knew it. She'd been abandoned in that house with the rubbish for a reason; it was clear for everyone to see.

–

'I did try and tell you what was going to happen, didn't I?' Jack was standing in the kitchen doorway.

She was at the sink rinsing Chloe's bottles. *A bottle.* An instant reminder of what a failure she was.

'It's not you, it's them.' He deliberately kept his voice low. 'I told you what they'd do but you didn't believe me. They're taking away your confidence with your own child – they're constantly undermining you. I can hear them; I see them doing it whenever you go near her. Chloe is fine, but they're making you feel like you're crap. You're not. They're trying to take over. You know deep down what's happening. What I don't understand is, why aren't you fighting back? Why don't you fight for your daughter?'

She looked at him.

'Don't you see? They're trying to replace Charlotte.'

The horror of his words struck something deep inside her. She didn't say anything; she just looked back at her daughter lying asleep in the baby chair. Chloe's lips twitched a little as she dreamed her baby dreams.

'You have to get out of here, Frankie. Somewhere they won't know where to look.'

'And go where, and do what?' She shook her head. 'They're right. I'm not any good for her. I have nothing. How would I live? I know I won't be able to look after a baby on my own. I'll never manage. For a start, the authorities will never let me. I'm still in Vanessa and Peter's care, remember? There'll be case workers and social workers and health workers and court hearings, until they decide I'm unfit to look after her.' She realised she was breathing hard. 'And maybe they're right. Maybe I'm just being selfish, and it is impossible.'

'Unless I was with you.'

She thought she must've misheard him. Her hands paused in the running water.

'What did you say?'

'You heard.'

She shook out a bottle and put it on the rack. 'That's a lovely, kind, generous offer Jack,' she smiled sadly. 'But we both know it's a fantasy. That's not real life.'

'It is real, and I do mean it.' The stairs creaked and they both anxiously looked round.

'Jack—'

'I have money. I have friends who'd help us.' He glanced quickly over his shoulder again.

'You have money?' She frowned a little. 'But a bit of money won't go very far. It's really sweet of you, but—'

'No, I mean I have *money*. Proper, serious money. This is no life for either of us here. We have no future. This is what I want: you and me and the baby. We'll disappear. People do it all the time.' His eyes were wide and desperate. 'You're eighteen really soon which means you'll be free… But would you do it, though? Would you take the risk? It'd be massive.'

She almost laughed out loud. *This could not be happening.*

'You mean all this, don't you?' She knew it was just talk, but it felt as though a weight had been lifted. It was lovely to pretend that she could have a life; not the one she'd dreamed of, but a life that wasn't about being managed and controlled. She felt like screaming hysterically, the stress of all the last few weeks bubbling up inside her ready to explode.

'Let's do it.'

She could see by his face he was deathly serious.

'Sorry?'

'Let's do it.'

She shook her head at the impossibility of it all.

His face lit instantly with excitement. 'Just leave it all to me. I know how to make it happen. We'll go quickly, we'll take very little; it'll make it easier. After we've gone, I'll tell Dad and Vanessa that we're fine and not to worry about us. I'll sort it, I promise.'

'But when?'

*Was she actually considering this? Really? Truly?*

'Soon. Play the game, Frankie. Don't let them think that anything is wrong. As soon as we're both ready, we'll be gone.'

–

For the next few days, she tried to let it all sink in. An excitement kept fluttering in her stomach. *Could they? Could she do this?* She forced herself to behave normally, but it was hard. She and Jack stayed away from each other. Vanessa was clearly losing patience with her. She began snapping angrily when she didn't follow her instructions precisely: she wasn't passing things over quickly enough, she wasn't anticipating Chloe's needs, she didn't organise and manage her time properly... The list went on and on.

'It's just easier to do it myself,' she kept saying. Peter was different with her too. Gone was the nice, smiley man. In his place was a man with strange eyes. Sometimes she caught him looking at her as if he couldn't quite work her out. She wondered if he suspected anything. Jack was right. Jack had been right all along. *Jack could make this happen. They really could leave. So she just had to put up with it all for a little while longer… It wouldn't be long now…*

Each night, she secretly packed bits and pieces for herself and Chloe into a tote bag that she kept stuffed down the side of the bed, leaving the zip in such a way that she would know if anyone had touched it. Each day she checked it minutely to make sure, and each time she checked she was instantly reminded of Martin. She couldn't carry on like this. She had to get away and start again. The zip stayed just as she'd left it, but the memories of Martin stayed there too.

## *Chapter Nineteen*

'This afternoon.'

'What?'

She was folding Chloe's clothes trying to follow Vanessa's instructions so that she wouldn't moan at her again.

'It's this afternoon,' Jack whispered over her shoulder. 'Make sure everything's ready. We'll leave at different times, but we'll meet up here.' He gave her a piece of paper with an address on it. 'This is the address of the friends I was talking about. These are the people who will help us.'

She nodded quickly, shoving the paper into the pocket of her jeans.

'One o'clock, yes? That just gives you an hour. Do you think you can manage it?'

She nodded again and Jack kissed her cheek, the heat and excitement of his breath still warm on her skin as she heard him in the hallway calling out to Vanessa that he'd see her later.

She carried on folding, not really aware of what she was doing and glanced at the clock. She knew why Jack had chosen today: Peter was at work, and Vanessa had told them she was going out to meet a girlfriend for lunch. She wouldn't be back for a couple of hours, by which point they'd both be well away.

Pulling out her phone, she found Uber and quickly tapped in the address as Vanessa clip-clopped down the stairs and into the kitchen carrying a laundry basket.

'What a mess you've made of that!' she laughed, glancing at the pile. 'Leave it, I'll do it when this lot's dry.'

Frankie quickly slipped the phone back into her pocket; her face felt hot and bright.

But then she caught sight of the laundry basket.

'My friend cancelled at the last minute,' Vanessa shrugged. 'Very annoying. We're going on Friday instead.'

'Friday?'

'Doesn't make any difference to you though, does it?' Vanessa hoisted the basket further onto her hip. 'I'll just put this load on the line and then it'll be time for Chloe's feed.' She glanced up at the clock. 'Won't be a minute.'

She watched dumbly as Vanessa went out of the back door to the washing line. Her brain went onto automatic pilot. Dropping everything, she raced up the stairs, dragged out the tote bag from the side of the bed and then gently scooped up Chloe and wrapped her in a load of blankets. Lifting her onto one shoulder, she pulled out her wallet and opened it. There were some pound coins but not much else. Head buzzing, she carefully made her way back down the stairs, peering along the hallway to make sure Vanessa was still in the garden. She glanced down; Vanessa's open handbag hung from the stair post with her purse sitting on the top. Dipping her hand in, she pulled it out, swinging the tote bag onto her back and making for the front door. She hurried down the path, finding her phone and checking the time. She was too early for the Uber. She snapped a look up and down the street, praying and hoping—

'Frankie?'

A car drew up, its indicator flashing.

There was Peter, his window was down with his anxious face filling the gap. She looked around desperately, her heart hammering.

'Are you off somewhere? Hang on, isn't that Vanessa's purse?'

Chloe started to cry. Her wails rang up and down the empty road as Peter bounced out of the car, abandoning it, and marched across the road towards her. She began to back away, dropping the purse, the cards scattering into the gutter. Her backing away broke into a run; Chloe started screaming. Peter was shouting things that made no sense about lying and betraying. *if she could get around the corner she could lose him...* Chloe's screams went up a pitch – she was really bawling now – and then suddenly all hell broke loose. She glanced back. Vanessa was pelting up the street towards them, her white face frozen into a mask of terror. Frankie looked frantically: left and right, but there was nowhere to go. She felt Peter's hand gripping her arm, swinging her round as his words tumbled thick and fast through the air. He was incandescent: What was she thinking? Running off with a new-born premature baby? Where in god's name did she think she was going? There were accusations of theft, of putting Chloe in danger, threats to ring Jude and social services –

'No, Peter! No! Stop this!' Vanessa was shrieking.

Chloe was beside herself. She was yanked from Frankie's arms. Peter was shouting and shouting. He grabbed the phone from her hand and they both watched as the piece of paper fluttered to the ground.

He immediately recognised the writing.

'Jack.' He looked at Vanessa, breathing heavily. 'Jack. She was going with Jack.'

Within seconds she found herself back inside the house and Peter turned to dead-lock the front door.

'You have no idea, do you?' He glared at her. 'You're just a stupid, stupid girl.' He stared down at her phone for a moment. 'Ring him,' he said bluntly. 'Ring him and tell him to get himself here before I do something terrible.'

-

Jack stood in the centre of the living room with his head hanging and his shoulders slumped.

'Tell her.'

He couldn't even lift his head to meet her eyes.

'Tell her,' Peter commanded. 'Tell her what will happen to you if you leave this house.'

Jack's face was bright red. She thought he might be crying. He sniffed. Her heart nearly broke.

'If I ever leave this house...' he choked.

There was a pause.

'Go on. What? Say it Jack.'

'If I leave this house, I'm dead.'

She stared at his blood-red cheeks in horror. 'Why? I don't understand—'

'I got involved with dangerous people – I mean, seriously dangerous. Drug people—'

'What?' She couldn't take it in.

'I-I saw what Martin Jarvis was doing with his little deals here and there, and it looked so easy. I thought doing small stuff was stupid – I thought I was cleverer.' His eyes lifted toward his father and then batted away again. 'I got way out of my depth really quickly. I got in very deep shit. My dad has had to pay them off every month.' His shoulders hunched around his ears. 'I have to stay here and out of circulation. If they find me back on the streets again, they'll kill me.'

Peter snorted. 'Exactly. I have to pay your debt. All our savings, my job and all my future earnings.' He waved a hand around the room. 'This house and everything in it so that you won't die some horrible, tortured death.'

Jack nodded dumbly.

'So what the fuck is this?'

She had never heard Peter use that kind of language before.

He bent and picked up a holdall from behind the chair and dropped it onto the coffee table. It hit the glass with a thud. Reaching to unzip it, Peter upended it, shaking out three brick-sized rectangular packages.

A jolt of alarm shot through her.

Jack's eyes didn't move.

'So what was the plan?' He glared at him. 'I have nothing else to give, Jack.' Peter's voice trembled with anger and fear. 'Nothing else. It's all gone. All that's left now is your life, and I would have honestly, truthfully, given mine for yours. You're my son. But not this time. This time you're out on the streets; you're gone. You can take your chances out there.' He thumbed over his shoulder.

Jack stared at Peter and then at Vanessa in shock. No one said anything. The only sound was Vanessa weeping and Peter's ragged gasp of emotion.

Then she heard Jack take a breath.

'It's mine.' She heard her own voice leaving her throat as though it was coming from someone else. Jack's head snapped up in shock. She wouldn't look at him. She had no real idea what she was saying.

'That's why I needed to see Martin in the cells that last day at court.' The words slipped easily from her tongue. 'It was all to do with Martin. It's nothing to do with Jack.'

She couldn't allow Jack to be punished after all that he'd done for her. She looked from Vanessa to Peter. She could see they wanted to believe her. Vanessa's mouth was open and unchecked tears were streaming down her face. She made no attempt to stop them. Tiny whimpering cries left the back of her throat. Peter only stared at her stonily.

'Don't call the police or social services. I'll leave now,' Frankie said quickly. 'No one has to know anything. I can make all this go away. I'll be out of your lives and you'll never have to see me again.'

She bent to pick up the packages, pushing them inside her jacket and then picked up Chloe's blanket from the arm of the chair. 'I'll be gone, Chloe will be safe, I'll make sure of that, and… I'm sorry,' she added quickly. 'I'm sorry for everything I've done. I'm not a bad person, you have to believe—'

But Peter cut her off.

'You're not taking Chloe.'

Her spine stiffened. 'What?' She straightened jerkily.

'You're not taking her.'

She stared at him and then at Jack.

'You're not capable of looking after a tiny baby. You're associated with drugs and murderers and chaos. She wouldn't be safe with you. We can give her security and love and every chance to be happy. You can't give her any of that.'

'You can't…' She felt her mouth trembling. 'She's mine. I'm nearly eighteen. You can't…'

'You're seventeen and you're in our care. Once you're eighteen,' he waved dismissively, 'I shouldn't think they'll even remember you were on their books. Girls like you don't exist. They live in squalor, they die in squalor, and apart from being a number on a benefit claim, no one even knows who they are.'

'No. You can't do that. She's mine, I'm taking her.'

'Okay then, Frankie, you take her.' He folded his arms. 'The moment you set foot outside that door, I'll be ringing the police and social services about everything you've done. You're already on their database, remember? You're the girl who's been in trouble all her life who no one wanted to adopt; you're the girl in a relationship with a murdering rapist, the girl who watched our daughter being attacked and did nothing to help her. You lied, you manipulated us. You're that girl, Frankie.'

The breath wouldn't leave her lungs.

'You've got several kilos of coke there,' he nodded at her jacket, 'with your fingerprints all over them. You'll keep Chloe for a while until you go inside and then she'll be taken into care and probably be adopted. You'll have no idea where she's gone or who she's with, or even if she's still in this country. You know as well as I do, they'll cut all contact with you because it'll be in the best interests of the child. You know the reality. So – there we are. Walk out of here now and take that filth with you. Be a rubbish mother – we've seen all the evidence for that.'

'No... No, Peter, please!' The tears began to flood down her face. She gulped painfully.

'Or, alternatively, tell Jude and the local authority that you're still living here and Chloe's fine. That way you might get to see her again. We'll be reasonable. We'll give you money to live on. We'll act as guarantors for landlords and suchlike. You won't starve or be on the streets. We're reasonable people.' His smile wasn't pleasant. 'The choice is yours, Frankie. You helped that man take our daughter, now we take yours. It's entirely up to you.'

# *Chapter Twenty*

## *Now*

Frankie stares through the grimed windscreen listening to the intermittent rush of cars passing on the main road. Jack is quiet beside her. She can tell they've both been thinking about the past. He reaches into his jacket and draws a rectangle of white paper out.

'I thought you'd like this.'

She turns it over. It's a photograph of a young girl. The sunlight is behind her; her hair is like a curly blonde halo. She's wearing a sunhat and is squinting off into the distance.

'I took it when she wasn't looking.'

Frankie realises her thumb has creased the paper, from gripping it so hard. 'This is Chloe now?' She looks at him in wonder and then back at the photograph. She sees herself in that face, around the mouth and chin. Her heart clenches with another emotion: she sees she has Martin's eyes. She traces a finger down her cheek. 'Oh my god, Jack. You don't know what this means.'

'I can imagine.'

'You were always so kind to me. I don't know what I would have done without—'

But he puts a hand on the photograph. 'Please stop. I should have done more, had more balls. I was spineless. I know you must hate me. I caused you years of pain.'

She looks across at him. She can see how awful he feels.

'After everything that happened, I think I was in shock for a long time...' She speaks slowly, choosing her words carefully. 'It was as though I couldn't think, couldn't feel stuff. And then, I have to admit, I was angry: beyond furious, particularly the way Peter and Vanessa stopped me from seeing Chloe after they promised I could. But you weren't to blame for their actions, Jack. You were at the mercy of them in the same way that I was. Think of us – we were bits of kids, that's all! How could we have taken on Peter? A man that worked for Children's Services, for pity's sake! There was no way!'

Jack shakes his head angrily. 'You know what really gets me? There he was with a job like that; with *power* like that, all those people falling over themselves to hang on his every bloody word – and yet at home, what had he got? A son he could walk past in the street and a step-daughter he obsessed over.' His face goes hard and dark.

'And the danger you were in from those people, Jack! What happened to you?'

He looks out of the window. 'Well, I'm still here and breathing, so I clearly have my uses.' His mouth sets in a grim line and he shakes away whatever thoughts have gathered. 'You remember that address you went to... Sean's house?' Frankie nods. 'Well, I picked up the packages from there. My dad thought he'd paid my debt and that would be it – Of course my dad is naive about these things – The truth is I'm caught in their net until the day I die.'

Frankie shakes her head, appalled.

'Which is one of the reasons I'm here now.'

'Why? What do you mean?'

Jack hears the panic. 'Hey... No... I didn't want to scare you, it's just—'

'What's the matter?... Has something happened? It's not Chloe is it?'

'No, she's absolutely fine. She's happy. She's a very together kid.'

'So what is it?'

'It's my dad, he's—' He breaks off, shrugging.

Frankie looks at him. 'What?'

'He's got problems. Serious problems. It got so bad that he and Vanessa split up.'

'But I thought...?' She replays the earlier phone conversation. She had no inkling.

'Things with him got worse after you left. I did tell you I thought that might happen, didn't I?' Jack looks out through the windshield at the empty street. 'High-powered job, loads of stress and totally unsuited to that kind of work. He was a ticking time-bomb waiting to explode.' He blinks away at the houses. 'I think he had some kind of breakdown when Chloe was about five. That was the catalyst for it. He was hospitalised on and off for the next five years and then they finally parted. I got to see a bit more of my dad then. It was nice, y'know?' He looks across with a sad smile. 'Without Vanessa controlling him. I got my dad back. But then—'

'Go on.'

'It was the obsession with Martin Jarvis; it brought them back together: Jarvis came up for parole. It's been like a wound for them both that would never heal.' He looks at her. 'But Chloe has been like a bright light in the middle of their darkness. She's kept them going. They've told her she's adopted; I don't think she's asked many questions. She thinks her dad died.' He shakes his head. 'They don't want her to know the truth.'

'And me?' she blurts suddenly. 'What have they said about me?'

'I don't know.'

He looks away but she knows he's lying. The thought crucifies her. She suddenly can't bear to hear any more. Her hands come up to her eyes to try and shut it all out.

'Hey… Frankie.' His hand reaches out for hers again and she feels the comforting warmth. 'Stop punishing yourself.'

She nods, knowing all the time that she can't.

His palm flinches for a second and he takes a breath.

'Listen to me, Frankie. I have to tell you what's going on.'

'What?' Her heart thuds.

'My dad, like I said: he's not thinking straight; he's not in his right mind. He lost his job, his friends, his self-respect. Jarvis comes up for parole, and then Vanessa's back on the scene—' He pauses. 'Things happened. He ended up in court and got sent down.'

'Oh my god!'

'I don't want to talk about what he did, but he blames Jarvis and he blames you, Frankie. He thinks that somehow none of these things would have happened if it weren't for you two.' He shifts uncomfortably in his seat. 'He's seriously unwell. I'm petrified he's out of control. His thoughts, the stuff he's doing – he's not right. I can't go anywhere near the police, not in my position, but I'm really, really shit scared.'

'How scared?' Her hand comes to her heart. 'I mean, is he really that unwell? Is he dangerous?'

Jack nods slowly. 'Dangerous enough for me to believe he'll try and kill Martin Jarvis.'

# *Chapter Twenty-One*

The journey back home is a blur.

*Would Peter do such a thing?*

The craziness whirls around and around in her head.

Martin's face… Martin's face keeps coming back to her. He's grinning; that infectious playful grin that even now wipes out everything and sends her stomach somersaulting. How she wishes she could hate him cleanly and sharply, like a razor blade slicing through skin – the pure, unadulterated loathing that Peter and Vanessa feel – but she can't. She feels a great, churning tangle of old emotion that's now full of a terrible panic. *But the idea of him being killed?* The fear rattles and rattles… Her brain goes into overdrive.

The screen in the console jangles into life and Alex's name flashes up.

'Hiya!' She tries desperately to sound upbeat. There's a slight pause on the other end.

'That's a very long journey home.' His voice is flat.

She snatches a look at the time. 'Oh! God, Alex… I'm sorry! I'm so sorry. I was—'

'Please don't bother,' he interrupts. 'I've heard it all before,' he sighs. 'I said I'd cook dinner, didn't I?'

'Uh-huh, you said—'

'That we should talk about stuff.'

'And we should.'

'But I really can't see the point.'

'Alex—'

'Why would I, Frankie? You don't invest in us. It's like you can't see or think of anything apart from that job. Even now, even now with a lunatic prowling about, you're still behaving as though your feelings are the only ones that matter. You carry on as though there's no one to consider but yourself.'

'It's not like that, it's—'

'Stop trying to justify the unjustifiable, Frankie. Just take a moment and think. What about me, Frankie? Consider me for once.'

She goes to argue but stops herself. 'You know what, Alex? You're exactly right.'

Her reply takes the wind out of his sails. He hesitates.

'I've been selfish and I'm sorry. I want to make things better between us.'

'Right, then. Well, that's a start. So convince me, Frankie. Convince me that you're in this marriage as much as I am.'

'I am in this marriage, Alex. I want to be with you.'

'Then change.'

'Yes, I will, I'll talk to Diane—'

He sighs, huge and exasperated. '*No*, Frankie. Not Diane – I mean *change* by changing your life. Change *our* life, for god's sake! Leave that bloody job!'

She stares silently into the road in front of her, wishing and wishing that they weren't having this same old conversation right now. That somehow, it could be different.

'I'm really close to home.'

'Are you?' He sounds doubtful.

'Can we talk then?'

'I'm still at the community centre, but yes, let's talk later, Frankie. Let's talk about changing both our lives. Let's put a time band on it for a brand new start. Can we agree to that?'

'Let's agree to talk – yes, definitely.' She tries to sound as definite as her words.

'Okay. I'll see you later, then. Bye.'

'Bye.'

The depression leaches over her in a blanket of pure exhaustion. *Yes, give up your job, run away from all this*, her head tells her. *So what if Peter kills Martin? Why should you care? Move away where no one will ever find you, leave it all behind, and start again – No Martin, no Chloe, no Vanessa or Peter or Jack. None of them ever existed. Start again.*

Could she do that?

Looking up, she realises she's almost home. Pulling on to the drive, she practically stalls the engine. Her head feels like a pressure cooker that's ready to explode. If she screamed out here, no one would hear her.

There's a stillness in the house as she walks into the hallway. She's thankful Alex is out. She thinks her head might burst. The thought of Chloe's photograph keeps coming back to her in a stunned, dragging ache. All those feelings that she's pushed down hard for years are now simmering in a great surge that she can barely keep contained. She puts her hand in her pocket and brings out the photograph that Jack gave her.

*Chloe, Chloe, Chloe.*

It's an immediate compulsion. She doesn't even pause to take her coat off. Walking quickly upstairs, she goes into the bedroom and pulls out a cardboard box that's hidden at the back of the wardrobe. The pink ribbon has frayed and dried out with age. She sits on the end of the bed holding the box on her knees. It's been a long, long time.

The pain forms a stone in the centre of her chest as she forces her fingers to slide the dusty band over the end and tip off the lid. Inside is the plastic hospital wristband with her name 'Frankie Turner' on it. Underneath it are two tiny ones: 'Chloe Turner' they both say, one for her ankle and one for her wrist.

She slips her fingers inside them: so, so small.

*How could she have done what she did? How could she have done any of it?*

She didn't. She couldn't have. It must have been some other person, someone who lived some other life…

How she wishes that were true.

She picks up the little bits of things one by one. A single scratch mitten, a tiny hat, a necklace chain that she unwinds holding it up to the light. The tiny crystal 'C' dances there. '*C*' *for Chloe*. Undoing the clasp, she puts it around her neck, stroking it with the tips of her fingers. *Chloe.* A miniature onesie that looks like it could have belonged to a doll. She brings it up to her nose. The scent is still there; it's unmistakable. It's a primal smell that tells her they were once joined in a way that no one else could ever be joined to her: not Vanessa, not Peter, not even Martin.

Jack had gathered these tiny memories for her to keep. Smuggled them out to the house where his friend lived; the place they should have been going together, but where she ended up going alone. He got his packages, and she got these small lifelines. He sent her photos too, little video clips of Chloe as a baby that he took when no one was looking. She didn't know how she would have coped without him in those first few weeks and months. They let her see Chloe in the beginning, once a month at a park or a shopping centre – somewhere there were lots of people in case she thought of snatching her – but they would never let her hold her. She saw Jude twice in that time, who asked lots of smiling questions and she gave her lots of smiling answers. Martin had sent letters, she was told. 'Burn them,' she'd replied. Jude was happy with that. Everyone was happy, apart from her.

She feels the mask of depression tightening behind her eyes. The time gaps between the contact meetings got longer; there were always reasons and excuses to soften the blow, but she knew what was coming. Her baby was being taken away from her, but the truth was she'd never been hers from the start.

She drops the mitten back into the box, her stomach hollowing out with grief and she bends double suddenly, her breath suddenly sucked away.

She needs to leave the memories alone.

The realisation comes like a shaft of light.

Leave her alone for good. Do what Alex is asking her to do: pack everything up and move to the middle of nowhere – start again, have a baby. The thought makes her heart race. *Could she do that? To mend her marriage?* She would be giving him not only a new start, but the possibility of a new family. Replace the old with the new: the past for the future. Her whole being rebels. She feels dizzy with the thought of it, but she holds on tight.

She could do that.

She could.

Straightening up, she looks at the box in her hands. All these things – these letters, this baby stuff – these things are the real ghosts. They are dead things. What's the point in her turning them over and over in her hands like dirt from a grave? Chloe isn't this tiny baby anymore; she's a fifteen-year-old girl on the cusp of womanhood. And Martin Jarvis is a name on a prison discharge list, one of the many hundreds of men who walk through those gates, the mess and the pain and the agony they've caused floating away with the free air they're now breathing – ready to inflict their misery all over again.

Only he's not going to do it to her.

Not anymore.

Gathering the box together, she goes into her office and kneels beneath the desk. Prising open the board at the back, she drags out the hidden envelope and then takes the whole bundle downstairs to the Rayburn where she opens the fire door. She pauses for a moment, weighing the things in her hands, feeling the searing heat radiating from the stove as the wood crackles. She knows this is destroying a part of herself that has been an open wound for the last fifteen years. She needs to heal; it's the only way, and this is all part of her penance.

Wavering for a moment, she pulls out one of the letters from its envelope.

*I miss you.*

She lets the piece of paper fall from her fingers. A quick spool of smoke curls up and then a lick of bright flame blackens the papery edge and the words melt one by one.

*We were meant to walk through this life together*
*and never be apart*

The second note lands on top of the charred flakes and is consumed quietly as though it had never been there.

A great gulf of sadness threatens to consume her too. She could sink to her knees right now as she watches that seventeen-year-old self, who was so trusting, who was so in love and so vulnerable, go up in smoke with his words.

*I'm waiting for you Frankie*

Each piece gets fed into the flames, one by one. She feels a track of something running down her neck and only then realises she's crying. She rubs her nose with the back of her hand, sobbing her grief into every message that she's letting go. He dirtied everything they had. He soiled her; ground her into the muck with the heel of his shoe and left her there. So why couldn't he just leave her be now? Why did he have to drag her back into all this? Hadn't he destroyed enough? The terrible night of Charlotte's death had murdered something inside her too.

A key rattles. There are voices and her head snaps round.

*Alex.*

In a heartbeat she's closed the stove and stuffed the remainder of the notes into the shoebox, pushing the whole lot under the dresser. She turns to find him standing in the doorway. He's clearly been laughing; as he sees her, his smile drops. 'Oh! You just coming in or going out again?' He looks her up and down and she realises she's still wearing her coat. There's a curtness in his tone. She looks back at him.

'Oh yeah.' She scrubs at her face. 'A bit of both… and neither.' She attempts to make light of it.

'What's the matter?'

'Oh, just worrying about this work thing, that's all.' She brushes the tears away, realising that there's a figure behind him waiting in the hallway.

'You've got a guest! Great! Hang on, let me get out of your way.'

She ducks to squeeze past him as Alex crosses her path, walking into the kitchen.

'Come through! Come through! Cup of tea, mate?' he calls over his shoulder. 'Or maybe…' His voice fades into background noise. She doesn't hear the rest of the sentence, because her entire body has lurched with a shock as powerful as a bolt of lightning. She stumbles back.

'Where's she gone?' Alex's voice rings out and she manages to keep herself in one piece by pressing her back to the wall.

'Ah, this is Martin.' Alex holds out a palm of introduction. 'From the community centre.'

'You must be Frankie.' Martin stands there in front of her, his expression inscrutable. Her seventeen-year-old self freezes in that instant; the years fall away, time spins backwards, and there she is and there he is and nothing else exists.

'Alex has told me a lot about you.'

She hears the words and watches his mouth moving. His face is different but his eyes: his eyes look straight into her soul.

# *Chapter Twenty-Two*

She doesn't know how she got out of that hallway.

Martin's eyes had bored into her as he walked past and through into the kitchen. Alex was asking about milk and sugar and biscuits which gave her a chance to get up the stairs before her legs gave up on her completely. Dragging herself into the bathroom, she locked the door and sat with her back against it as the shakes got to her, an uncontrollable, pummelling quake that shook her to the core. She hears the low rumble of voices from downstairs and the occasional guffaw of laughter, and closes her eyes.

*What the fuck just happened?*

Resting her forehead on her knees, she tries to force her head to comprehend the thing that cannot be real. She had taken one look at Martin and the whole world, the hallway, the kitchen, Alex, had disappeared. All that was left was the two of them standing in a space like the eye of a tornado. A hundred buried emotions, sensations, bloomed and burst in time-lapse photographs.

She lifts her head, staring wide-eyed around the bathroom: her bathroom that looks the same as it always does – and yet downstairs in her kitchen, her and Alex's kitchen, is the man who changed her life forever.

*No. No. No.*

He had walked into her house as though it was any other house on any other day and she was any other person. Her head rests back on the door and she grinds her scalp until she can feel the ridges of the panel bite. So he had found her, and watched her, and in so doing, had found Alex too – such a simple way into her life, a way that would ensure she was completely cornered.

There's a soft knocking on the door.

'You okay in there?' Alex's muffled voice comes from the other side.

She doesn't think it's possible to be further from okay.

He taps again gently. 'Frankie...?' The tapping gets more insistent.

She gathers her legs under her. 'Yes... Yes, I'm fine. I-I was just leaving you two alone to...' She can hear her voice trailing off as the enormity of the situation begins to dawn. Her ears begin to buzz with tension, her ribs constrict her lungs. She clutches hold of the side of the basin and tries to breathe... *just breathe*...

'One minute. Hang on a sec.' She unlocks the door and steps back.

'You sure you're okay? You look... Did something happen? That weirdo guy... He hasn't—' He puts a protective hand on her arm.

'I'm fine, honestly.' She shakes her hair back and attempts to smooth it so he won't see the tremble in her hands.

'I didn't know you'd be back so soon... I thought—' He pauses and takes a breath. 'Look, I've been meaning to mention Martin before, but things got—' he waves. 'It's part of this life-change stuff I'm talking about – I can't spend my time alone in this house, driving myself slowly insane. It's not fair on me and definitely not fair on you. So I thought, okay, I'll make some positive changes. The first thing I'll do is start making new friends… That's a good thing, isn't it?' He gives her a puzzled look.

'Yes… yes, of course. It's a great idea.'

'And Martin's a really nice guy. We got chatting at the centre about a month ago and really hit it off. He's in much the same situation as me, I think. He's recently moved into the area, so he doesn't know many people.'

'Right. Yes.' She thinks her head might explode.

'So I invited him round for dinner tonight.'

'Tonight? But I thought—'

Alex shrugs. 'I wasn't even convinced you'd turn up, to be honest. I didn't want to eat on my own again.'

She stares at him open-mouthed. 'I have to go.'

'Go—? What?… Why?' He's instantly irritated.

'I rang Diane back…' she stumbles. 'It's about the meeting on Monday. I have to prepare for it… See her and talk to her, maybe. I'm not sure.'

*Please go, please go, please just go…*

At the mention of work his face sets. 'And this is because I've invited someone round, is it?'

'Sorry?'

'All this' – he waves a hand – 'what shall we call it? This performance. Are you sulking about what I said on the phone, is that it?' He narrows his eyes. 'Is all this because my attention isn't solely focussed on you?'

'What? No!'

'You seem to use Diane and work as an excuse for everything. Sure, I get it – you're under pressure, but you do manage to turn everything back to you and your problems: your needs.' He's not even attempting to keep his voice down. 'Y'know what, Frankie? How about doing something purely for me for a change? See how that feels, huh?'

He pulls the door closed with a definite thump and she lets her knees give way as she slumps backwards onto the laundry box. There's a flood of relief that he's left. She catches sight of herself in the mirror. Her reflection looks like it's a long way away. The face is white and pinched, the eyes are round and startled-looking. They're reddened and bloodshot and mad.

She has to get out of this house. She can't bear it a second longer.

Opening the door slowly, she stands on the landing, heart pounding, and listens. Her ears pick out Martin's voice instantly as though he has a frequency all of his own. How she wishes she could block him out, stop her ears and run, and keep on running. She tiptoes down each tread to the front door and grabs her bag. Fumbling with the door catch, she makes it out onto the driveway and heads for the car.

'Frankie!'

She freezes with the door open and one hand on the wheel. Behind her there's the tread and scuff of feet. The passenger side opens and everything stops. Alex's face dips to appear in the gap. She's trapped.

'Actually, Martin was just telling me he needs to get the bus into town, but I have no idea how often they run. If you're going out, maybe you could drop him off?'

She is aware that Martin is right there behind him on the drive. She tries to collect herself but fails.

Alex is looking at her questioningly. 'What's the problem?'

'Nothing... I...'

Irritated, he turns away from her. She can't watch as the two men exchange goodbyes and she hears them making arrangements for this evening. She feels the car bounce a little as Martin gets in beside her, slamming the door and reaching for the safety belt. He raises a hand to wave to Alex as she closes the door and starts the engine.

She drives, aimlessly. Her entire body is screaming but her brain just feels numb. She feels his gaze resting on the side of her face.

'Hello Frankie.'

Her eyes manage to make a forty-five-degree sweep, taking in the bottom of his jeans, *blue*, his shoes, *trainers*, his knees with their acutely familiar shape, but she can't get any further. She yanks the car into a lay-by and a car horn blares out behind her.

'I've missed you so much.'

'Stop this.' Her voice comes out in a kind of croak.

'Have you missed me?'

'I said *stop*.'

Her eyes sweep across to take him in properly. *Christ, she hadn't realised how much he'd changed*. The shock makes her giddy. His hair is longer; there are lines like furrows down the side of his face. His hand is resting on his knee; she sees the age on the back of it, the grime around the knuckles that sends a jolt through her heart.

'How did you find me?' She realises she's breathless.

'Find you? I never lost you.'

'You need to stop this, Martin. You have to leave me alone.'

'You know you don't want that.'

'Yes, I do. Yes, I *do* want that. I want that more than anything.' She feels fear, but it is coupled with anger.

'Why did you do it, Frankie? Why did you give the court that statement?'

Her anger rises. 'How can you even ask that question? You disgust me, you are abhorrent, you are—'

'I wrote to you in the very beginning. I told you what happened. I told you that you'd got it all wrong.'

She rounds on him, the anger taking over fully now. She bites down, hard. 'I'm not interested in your lies, Martin! I don't want to hear your excuses; not then, not now. Jude burned everything you sent.'

'Burned my letters?' He looks incredulous.

'Look! You need to leave me alone, for fuck's sake! I don't want you, Martin! What you did – what happened…'

'You do want me, you always have. Neither of us can forget what we had.'

It's as though he can't hear her; his face is full of tenderness.

'We have nothing – do you hear me? You murdered a girl. You raped a girl. You're a monster!' Her voice rises to a shriek.

'I don't know what you thought you saw that night, Frankie, but it wasn't me. You know that on some level. You know it wasn't me.'

Her hands snap up to clamp her ears; she can't hear this. She can't listen to any of this anymore.

'I've been to the police; I've shown them the stuff you've been sending.'

He pauses, searching her face for a second and then his head shakes slowly from side to side. 'No you haven't.' He starts to smile.

'What are you talking about? I *have*, I—'

'Because if you'd given the police my name, they would have recalled me by now.'

'I – I—' She can hear the words blundering pointlessly.

'I think you were pressurised back then.' His mouth is set in a grim line. 'I think you said those things to the court because you were a confused and pregnant kid who could be led to say all manner of things and end up believing they were true.'

'No one wanted to lead me anywhere! I *know* what I saw, Martin! Can you imagine what it was like? Listening to a girl begging for you not to hurt her? Can you imagine that, you… you—' But he talks over her.

'They wanted someone to pay for what happened, Frankie, and I happened to fit their plan.'

'"They"? Who's "they"? What plan?'

He looks at her wide-eyed. 'Charlotte's parents.'

'Vanessa and Peter? Don't be ridiculous!'

'They would have done anything – you could see that in their faces. They were out of their minds with grief. They could have suggested all of it to you… Fed you the lines… told you—'

'No… *No!*' She shakes her head vehemently. 'None of that happened.'

'So what did happen?'

'I told you!'

'I mean about our child.' He's looking at her with those eyes and an odd smile.

She hates him; she hates this. 'We don't have a child.'

His smile drops. 'What are you saying?'

She stares resolutely out of the window.

'You owe me that much, Frankie.'

'She was adopted.'

He blinks, taking a moment. 'She,' he says finally. 'A little girl. I can't quite get my head around that.'

'Arrgghh!' She slaps her hands on the wheel. 'We can't do this, Martin.' She skews round in her seat, forcing herself to look directly into his eyes. It's as though the person she once knew is behind a deeply lined mask that's bruised and scarred.

She swallows. 'You are nothing to me. I am married to Alex. I have a life with him, a home.'

'But you don't have a child with him. You have a child with me.'

'I wish I didn't.'

'You don't mean that.'

'We don't have anything, Martin. She's not ours.'

'We made her. She's ours. Who adopted her? Do you know where she is?'

'No.' The lie caught in her throat. 'But listen—'

'No, you listen.' His face changes completely. 'I found you. I can find her.'

'No, no—' She shakes her head from side to side. 'You can't do that, Martin. For god's sake, haven't you done enough?' She feels the heat in her face growing. 'You can't.'

'Of course I can. She's older now, what? Fifteen? She'll want to know—'

'No! No, she won't!' Frankie almost reaches out a hand to touch him but then snaps it back to her throat. 'She needs to be left alone to live her life. Don't drag her through the dirt, too!'

She knows she's pleading; she feels as though she's pleading for everyone. 'We all need to be left alone; don't you understand that? You've destroyed so many lives: Charlotte's, her family's, mine… You have to go away somewhere. Anywhere. You can't stay here. It's too dangerous.'

'Life's dangerous.'

'I'm being serious, Martin. You'll be dead. Charlotte's stepfather wants you dead – don't you get that?' She brings her hand down in frustration and catches the chain around her neck. It breaks, the pendant rolling into the footwell. He dips to pick it up.

'You still have this…'

She goes to snatch it, but he closes his hand.

'You never told me where you found it.'

'I didn't fi—' Her fingers and his fist pause.

He stares at her hand and then his eyes lift to meet hers. 'What did you just say?' Frankie feels her cheeks burn.

'You didn't find it?'

'I—' She stumbles at the lie.

'So where did you get it?'

'Vanessa.'

'Vanessa?'

'It's nothing to do with you.'

'Listen to me, Frankie. This is really, really important.' He opens his fist.

She looks down at the broken necklace in his palm.

'Charlotte was wearing this necklace the night of the party.' His gaze bores into her.

'Which means she was wearing it the night she died. You told me you found it on the street, but you're now saying Vanessa gave this to you?' His gaze won't let her go. 'Is that the truth?'

'Yes.'

'So this necklace got from around Charlotte's neck the night she died and somehow got back to Vanessa? You understand, Frankie, I couldn't have put it there, could I?'

She tries to make sense of what he's saying.

'So if I couldn't have put it there, then someone else did. Someone else was there that night on the boat. Do you accept that?'

'Martin, stop this.'

*Vanessa would never hurt Charlotte, never in a million years.*

But a fault line in her memory begins to falter.

He pulls his hair back. 'Maybe the same person who gave me this—'

A huge curve of a scar runs from behind his ear down the side of his neck.

Her hand flies up to her mouth. 'Jesus, Martin!'

The tips of his fingers gingerly trace the line. It looks fresh: the skin is still rippled and sore where it's knitted together.

'It was a present from Peter Vale.'

The fault line begins to crack and crumble.

'Peter Vale?' She repeats the name but she feels like crying. She shakes her head. 'Charlotte's stepbrother warned me... He told me – he said Peter knows that you've been released and he's out looking for you. He hates you. He hates me. He thinks we should both be punished. Oh, Christ, Martin...' she can't stop the tears now. 'When did this happen? Have you been to the police?'

But he shook his head. 'It was on the wing. The others jumped him, otherwise he'd have killed me.'

'The wing?'

Something appalling begins to dawn. Her head swings dully. She's not comprehending this properly. She doesn't want to comprehend it.

'Peter Vale was in the same nick. He got out a few days after me.'

Her hand drops into her lap. She feels sick suddenly. 'Seriously Martin, he wants you dead.'

'I know, but he can't show his face on the street. People know, you see. He has to be careful.'

Her brain can't take it in. She doesn't know what he's saying.

'They know what?'

'What he was in for. Indecent images of kids. Thousands of them.'

Something drops like a stone.

'He got sussed by the other cons while I was still in the hospital wing. They found him out. Peter Vale is a sex offender.'

## *Chapter Twenty-Three*

'Get out of the car.' She doesn't know how she's able to articulate the words.

'I'm not going away, Frankie.'

'You need to get out. Get out. Please.'

'You know I can't leave you alone, not now. I want to see our daughter. I want to find her. Will you let me see the adoption paperwork? Will you do that for me?'

She is trying really hard to hold it all together, concentrating on a piece of lint that's caught in the air vent. It waves like a tiny finger. Her eyes lift; she is more afraid now than she's ever been.

'I understand why you wouldn't tell Alex. I understand why you'd want to forget the past, but the thing is, Frankie, it happened; it's a part of who you are. I mean, what will you say if our daughter decides to come looking for you?'

She is beginning to feel frantic. 'Please get out now, Martin. I need you to get out.'

'You can't be sure she won't – and if she does then Alex will be devastated that you didn't tell him yourself.'

*Get out get out get out.*

'You'll have to explain why you've lied all these years. You're living on borrowed time, Frankie.'

'You don't know anything...' Tears start to sting, blinding her.

'Alex told me you'd talked about children, but he wasn't sure they were on your radar. Wouldn't it be better to tell hi—'

'*Now, for Christ's sake!* Get out of the car *now*!'

Stunned, he reaches for the door catch, swinging the door wide.

'*Now! Get out now!*' Her hands slam repeatedly onto the wheel. 'Leave me alone, can't you?'

Martin leaps from the car as she guns the engine. The door jerks wildly and crashes closed on its hinges but she doesn't care. She accelerates, hard, over-taking blindly, and swerving to miss a lorry coming the other way. All she can think about right now is Chloe.

She glances in the mirror. Martin is exactly where she left him in the lay-by: a lone black figure getting smaller and smaller. The roads and hedges flash past the car windows yet it feels as though she's driving through treacle. Every car in front is deliberately slowing down, every traffic light makes her want to scream. The engine wails in resistance; her foot is hard on the floor as painful sobs rack her dry throat.

*A sex offender. Peter. My daughter was in that house with a sex offender*. She could scream it, yell her terror as the roads whizz past her, not caring about lights or cars or danger, as Vanessa's street lurches into view and she jams on the brakes.

Banging on the front door as hard as she can, she begins to shout, not caring who can hear her.

'Vanessa! Open this door! Vanessa!'

Silence.

She bangs again, standing back, frantically scanning all the windows, begging to see some movement.

There's nothing.

Snatching the phone from her pocket, she finds Vanessa's number with shaking fingers, listening to the bland tone ringing out, giving nothing in return. Glancing up at the windows again, she makes her way around the side of the house, cupping her hands either side of her face and peering in every gap in the windows she can find.

The back door slams open.

'What the hell do you want?' Vanessa stands there, pink with anger. 'I told you—'

'Where the hell is he?'

'Where's who?'

But Frankie has already barged past her, pushing her way into the kitchen. She can smell him. It stinks of him. *Peter.* He's been here. She knows it. She rounds on Vanessa.

'I know,' she snarls. 'I know about your sick, sick, bastard of a husband... And you... Both of you. Don't tell me you didn't know.' Her hands come up but she doesn't know what to do with them. Her eyes are burning with violent tears of rage. 'How could you, Vanessa? How could you have stood by and... Oh, Jesus Christ!' She whirls round, tearing at her own hair. 'This is absolutely beyond anything possible...' She can't find the words. 'You took my baby, you sick bitch. You took my baby knowing... *Knowing*...'

Vanessa shrinks back against the door edge. The pink in her face has turned to white. The fear in her face translates into anger. 'Get out of my house! I don't know what you're talking about!'

'Peter. That's what I'm talking about. *Peter.* Your husband. The sex offender. The man who...' She can't bring herself to articulate the words, to let her lips even form them. Her mind shows her pictures of his hand on her knee, squeezing it. The smell of his breath on her face as he leaned in to kiss her goodnight. The black figure in the bathroom touching her – *Yes. Yes. She can see it all.*

'Sex offender…? Don't be disgusting! This is bizarre and absolute rubbish! Why would you concoct such filthy lies? You *know* Peter! You *know* him, you know he would never, ever do anything to a child. You know that Frankie! Stop this! Stop!'

It's as though she's in some kind of bizarre state of denial.

'Where is he?' Frankie stands panting, her blood is singing in her ears. 'Where is he? Where's my daughter, Vanessa?' She wheels round, angrily. 'I want to see her. You can't keep her from me anymore! Do you hear me?' She marches into the living room with Vanessa right behind her. Every wall, every angle, every object in here is so familiar that the past is instantly dragged back to the present.

'Is she upstairs?' She puts her hand on the door to the hallway and pulls it open.

But Vanessa blocks her.

'I won't have this, Frankie! I won't!' Her whole demeanour is charged and indignant. 'You can't barge in here, shouting the odds about Peter, throwing your weight around as if you owned the place! Who the hell do you think you are?' She uses her weight to force the door from Frankie's fingers. She knows she'll have to lay hands on her to get past.

'Where have you suddenly got all this crap from?' Vanessa stares at her and then her face changes as it dawns. 'Oh… you've seen that bastard Jarvis, haven't you? Oh my god, you've spoken to him and he's fed you all this filth! Of course he has.' Her mouth drops open as she shakes her head. 'Even after everything he's done to you, done to this family, you're still there, aren't you, Frankie? Standing in his shadow and watching from the sidelines. Have you any idea of what that man actually did to us? What he continues to do every moment he's still alive and breathing?'

Frankie flinches but holds her ground. 'I'm not in his shadow Vanessa. I'm not being manipulated by him.'

'Ohh no of course you're not! You never were, were you Frankie? – you with your drug-soaked, booze-raddled life where you turn a blind eye to a girl being raped and murdered! You're never duped are you?'

The guilt grips Frankie's heart. She can hear her own breath whistling high in her lungs.

'And then you turn up here in your fancy clothes and your fancy car shouting and demanding to see Chloe. Look at you! You're the same piece of rubbish you were back then. You're not a mother!' She sneers at her, up and down. 'You could have walked past her a hundred times in the street and never known it! What kind of mother is that?'

Frankie recoils at the truth.

'You helped destroy our lives, Frankie. Peter lost everything – his job, his dignity, everything. And so we decided that piece of filth needed to lose too.' She's shaking uncontrollably. '*Sex offender?*' she scoffs. 'I'll tell you the truth, shall I? Peter sacrificed the tatters of his life and got himself put inside to have one good go at him – one good go. And I know he nearly got him.' Her lips break into a terrible leer. 'He very nearly got him. So near and yet so bloody far.' The taunting mouth stretches wider into a grin, baring her teeth. '"Never mind," I told him, "better luck next time..." And there will be a next time, Frankie. Martin Jarvis might try all the tricks in the book, but we'll make sure he spends his life looking over his shoulder. Peter only has to get lucky once; Jarvis has to wake up every day wondering whether this is the day that it's going to happen.'

Frankie feels the fight draining from her.

'Oh for god's sake, look at you!' Vanessa turns and yanks at the door. 'You're pathetic. So go on – throw your life away on that man. It's what you were born to do.'

She reaches for the front door catch and holds it open.

'Chloe—' Frankie starts, but Vanessa takes a menacing step forward.

'Let's get one thing absolutely clear here, Frankie. If either you or him come anywhere near my daughter, the revenge I'll take will be on a level you can't imagine. Death will be a sweet release from what I'll do to you. She's mine, Chloe is mine. We told you that in the very beginning. You took our daughter, so we took yours. Is that clear enough?'

-

The car is as she left it: the door slewed open and parked as though it's been abandoned. She gets slowly into the driver's seat and puts a hand on the wheel. The pent-up anger courses through her arms and legs in a torrent of emotion. She catches sight of her eyes in the mirror. They are the eyes of a hunted animal, startled and wary, but her whole body is slick and pumping with adrenaline. Every nerve-ending is on jangling high-alert.

The mirror holds her gaze and her eyes flit to the reflection of the house.

*My daughter*, she'd said.

*Mine.*

Vanessa's face: the twisted mouth, the years of hatred scored into every pore.

But all Frankie can think of is Peter. That she'd left her baby in a house with Peter Vale. *She'd known it all those years ago but somehow it never made sense.* Sheer revulsion courses through her. *She just hadn't trusted her feelings back then. She'd dismissed them because she was a child, because Peter looked like a nice man.* The whispering in the darkness… the eyes in the shadows… the touch on her neck…

The adrenaline turns to ice.

Jack had always known something wasn't right in that house too. He'd been a kid just like her, but Jack had known, he just couldn't articulate it.

*Jesus… Jesus Christ…*

Her phone suddenly pings, and she pulls it from her pocket. It's a text from an unknown number.

> Vanessa just told me what's happened. Try the Saturday Club at Lakebank High

It gives the address.

> Ring me. Jack.

*Chloe.* The thought of actually seeing her… Like, *really* seeing her?

With fingers that feel like thumbs, she makes the call. He answers straightaway.

'Thank you, Jack. Thank you,' she breathes, 'for giving me this chance.'

'They've kept you away from Chloe for too long, Frankie. I know Vanessa. She refuses to see my dad for what he is. She believes everything he says; even a six month prison sentence hasn't convinced her. I'm really worried she's going to let him back in that house. I know Probation and the police are monitoring him. Because of the nature of the offences he can't go back to that address straight away, but Vanessa is fighting them, arguing that he's not a risk.'

She feels an immediate rush of fear. 'My god, Jack, what am I going to do?'

Her heart thuds in terror.

'I'm sorry I couldn't bring myself to tell you before.' He sounds as though he's out of breath. 'I was the one who...' He searches for the words. '...Who found stuff—' He stops. 'I'd heard them whispering about Martin Jarvis and I decided to go snooping. That's when I found the files on his computer. Kids – Young girls. It was awful. I was the one who confronted him. Vanessa went mental – screaming, hysterical, all sorts. She said someone must've hacked his account – that he clicked on something by accident... You know how it goes. But I wouldn't let it rest. I went to the police.'

She goes completely cold.

'Suddenly the penny dropped... Like Charlotte and that room and her obsession about a man watching her—' His voice breaks.

'I didn't believe her, Frankie. I said it was just the gear she was doing. I made fun of her. Looking back... *Jesus*... I keep going over and over it. She was *scared* of something happening to her, Frankie. I mean, *really* scared.' He falters and swallows. 'Thing is... Now I know this sounds completely crazy, but is it possible he was involved in how she died? Did he have some connection with Martin Jarvis that night? Is that even possible?'

Frankie stares straight ahead.

'I can't risk it happening to Chloe, Frankie. I can't let Vanessa allow my dad back into that house.'

Checking her phone, she punches in the postcode for the school. She has to find her.

'I'll think of something, Jack. I'll find a way to get Chloe out of all this. I don't know what or how, but I will.'

'Get my dad back inside, it's the only way,' Jack says suddenly. 'It's the only way to make sure she's safe. I can't be seen going to the police again, it's too dangerous for me, I might be seen, but you could. You could, Frankie. They'll listen to you.'

'Thank you, Jack,' she blurts. 'Thank you for everything you've done. I know the cost.'

'You don't know the half of it,' he chuckles sadly. 'But I'm glad I could help.'

Frankie ends the call, checks the mirror, and drags the wheel round.

*She couldn't protect her daughter last time, but that's not happening again.*

*She'd rather die first.*

# *Chapter Twenty-Four*

The playground is deserted.

*Has she missed her?*

*Will she even know if she sees her?*

She clutches at the photograph in her pocket and surreptitiously takes a glance at her daughter's smiling face. A terrible thought grips her insides and Vanessa's words come back to her: *You could've walked past her a hundred times and not known it.*

That's so close to the truth it hurts.

A double door to a building bangs open and she looks round. Small gaggles of kids begin to appear – boys and girls in sports gear swinging bags, chatting and laughing. She scans each face desperately *A real mother would know her own daughter.*

The reality of the situation shames her. *That's the kind of mother she is: trying to find her own child from a photograph.*

They're coming out quicker now; she's surprised how many kids are here and loads of the girls are blonde; this feels impossible.

The noise level gets closer. They're coming towards the gate. She steps back a little, not wanting to be seen, chin lifted and searching. Could it be her? Or her? Or her?

A small cluster of kids start to hustle through the gates, heading for a crossing where there's a chip shop and news-agent on the other side of the road. There's the incessant *beep-beep-beep* of the crossing lights and she desperately scans round and back to the gates. Her heart comes into her mouth.

There she is.

She's dawdling, looking at her phone, her bulky bag slung over one shoulder. Her gangly legs in their yoga pants look as adorable as a new-born colt. She hitches the bag further onto her shoulder, her eyes don't leave the screen, even for a second. Her hand comes up to smooth a long swathe of blonde hair, absent-mindedly pulling it across the bottom half of her face like a veil as she begins to chew the ends. Frankie's heart cleaves wide with an immediate rush of love. She takes a few steps forward.

*Her daughter.*

There she is; just like her picture. Frankie drinks her in, every inch, her eyes like a camera-shutter: skinny little hands, bitten nails, her face a bit too pale, big eyes, heavy-lidded and beautiful.

*I'll make sure he can't come near you.* A sudden grip of anger replaces the love. *I'll keep him away.*

The squawking of the children outside the shop grows louder. She sees Chloe look up, not letting go of her hair and pausing on the pavement edge. She's close now – a few more steps and she'll be within speaking distance.

Chloe smiles and waves at a group of girls on the other side of the road when a sudden movement catches Frankie's eye.

A car comes around the corner.

Chloe steps off the pavement.

Frankie's body responds on instinct. There's a flash of blue and the glint of a wing mirror as the car slams on the brakes with a screaming wail of tyres. There's a sudden hot stink of rubber and the round 'O' of shocked faces from the girls on the other side of the road.

Frankie's body is propelling her forward before her brain even tells her what's happening. Her fingers close around an arm, a shoulder as her weight meets Chloe's. The air leaves her lungs in an exhaled punch as the tarmac zooms up before her eyes.

There are moments of dull numbness, before she manages to gaze around, dazed, into an expanse of sky as a searing pain ricochets around her body. There's a sudden whirlwind of faces that appear and disappear, all moving dizzily as they circle. A car door slams and there's a crunch of feet.

'Hell,' breathes a man's voice as a face appears in her sightline. 'Are you okay?'

She wipes the blood from her lip, unable to speak. Her fingers are still gripping Chloe's blazer as though she's never going to let it go. Chloe struggles to sit up; her yoga pants are ripped and there's a bright trickle of red oozing from a gash on her knee.

'I think we should call someone. Can we ring for an ambulance?' The man looks around the stunned group. No one offers to move. Suddenly another face appears, a curly-haired woman in gym clothes, a teacher possibly, pushing her way through the group.

'Oh my god!' She kneels in front of them both. 'Chloe? Are you okay, my love?'

Chloe is sitting up examining her palms. 'Yes, yes, I'm fine – I just—' They're studded with grit and dirt but amazingly uncut.

'Let's find a clean tissue for that knee.' The teacher delves in her pockets.

'This lady—'

Chloe looks over shyly at Frankie. Frankie realises she's hearing her daughter speak for the very first time.

'This lady… Um…' She flickers an embarrassed smile as she takes the tissues. 'This lady stopped me from walking in front of that car. I don't know what I was doing… I'm sorry…' She looks up at the teacher and back to Frankie again. 'It was stupid. I wasn't thinking.'

'Are you okay, though?' Frankie manages to kneel beside her. 'Have you got any pain anywhere?'

'No… no, I don't think so.'

'Shouldn't you call an ambulance, to be on the safe side?' The driver glances over his shoulder.

'I'm fine… Honestly, I'm fine…' Chloe scrambles up, wincing and colouring bright pink.

'Maybe you should pop back into the school for a sec.' The teacher peers at her. 'Just to make sure.'

'It's okay, my mum will be here in a minute.' She dusts off her hands. 'She's picking me up.'

There are only moments before Vanessa's voice peals out from somewhere behind them.

'Let me through! Please let me through!'

She appears, panicked and breathless, launching herself between Frankie and Chloe.

'Ah, Mrs Vale, I think we're all okay,' soothes the teacher. 'I think we're just a bit shaken up, but no bones broken, mercifully.'

'It's okay, Mum. It's okay.' Chloe disappears as she's suddenly enveloped in Vanessa's arms. 'This lady saved me. It's okay.' Her voice is muffled in Vanessa's shoulder.

The teacher quickly tries to diffuse the tension. 'Gosh, it could all have been so much worse, so I suppose we should be thankful to this la—'

'Have you got all your things?' Vanessa cuts across her abruptly, glancing at the ground.

Chloe nods.

'Then I'm taking you to A&E.'

'Mum! I'm fine, I'm okay! Honest!' She looks back at Frankie apologetically and Frankie yearns to reach out and touch her again.

'I think we should be grateful—' The teacher tries again, but Vanessa wheels round.

'You should be the one who's grateful, Mrs Stephenson, grateful that I don't take this incident further,' she snaps hotly. 'Maybe you should have been out here supervising these children properly and not leaving them to the mercy of any odd passer-by.'

She glares with hate-filled eyes as she clutches Chloe firmly around the waist and helps her away, leaving Mrs Stephenson and Frankie gazing at each other.

There are shouts from across the road. Some of the boys have made their way to the scene to get a better look at the excitement.

'Okay kids. Let's all move away now, shall we?' The teacher begins to usher them into a manageable bunch. 'If your parents are picking you up, can you make sure you stay inside the school gates, please?'

The voices get louder and more excitable as they begin to discuss who saw what and when. A boy with red hair starts toeing at the tyre mark on the road with the tip of his trainer and talking animatedly about 'crime scenes'. The driver of the car touches the teacher's arm.

'Err, excuse me, I was wondering if you needed me to fill out any reports or anything?'

'Oh, thank you, that would be very helpful, just in case there's any comeback.' She winces a smile at Frankie.

'Actually, could you both spare a couple of moments to come to the school office and I can jot some things down? I'm probably going to get hauled over the coals about this. I'm newly qualified, you see.' She grimaces, embarrassed. 'Mrs Vale – Charlotte's mum, I'm sure she didn't mean to come across as—' She stops. 'The family's had a difficult time recently, and—'

'The dad's a nonce!' The boy with the red hair shouts over his shoulder. '*Nonce alert! Nonce alert!*' he yells at the other kids, and starts prancing about and swinging his bag.

'That will do, Tom!' Mrs Stephenson snaps sharply. 'Stand over by that wall where I can see you and don't move!' She rolls her eyes and gestures Frankie and the driver towards the school office.

Frankie doesn't want to be here right now. She can't waste any more time.

'I'm sorry – I was thinking... I was wondering if I could pop back later... Or ring you?... It's just...'

There's a sudden whoop of shrieking behind them. They all turn to look. About six or seven boys have joined in with Tom's cat-calling. They swarm around each other in a strange flock formation, shouting over-excitedly, jabbing and pointing. Mrs Stephenson is answering her question, only Frankie isn't listening. She's watching the children as they point and jeer. There, by the school gates is a lone figure. His hands are hunched into his pockets as he stares mutely forward. Frankie stares across the yard, not quite believing, as her heart sets up a frightened thrumming. She knows who the figure is.

It's Peter Vale.

# *Chapter Twenty-Five*

*Tonight.*

*Whatever she is going to do, it has to be tonight.*

*Peter Vale watching Chloe.* The thought tumbles over and over in her mind as she drives home. She'd raced across that playground with the gang of schoolkids watching, shocked and in awe, only to see Peter disappearing into an alleyway. Hurrying to her car, she'd driven around the streets for half an hour, but it was pointless; he was far too clever.

She walks into the kitchen. Alex has his back to her but she can't gauge his mood.

'Oh hi, how did it go with Diane?' He glances up from the cookery book he's reading.

'Oh, fine. I think we've got it sorted.' The deceit makes her squirm.

Her brain struggles to connect with the lies. She feels like a puppet operated by strings.

'They've added a no-climbing clause into your contract, then?'

She manages to grimace a smile. 'Something like that.'

'And so how are you feeling?' He raises both eyebrows. She looks back at him in a nervous query.

'I'm fine. I'm okay.'

Alex's face relaxes into a smile in response. 'Good… Hey, I'm sorry about earlier.' He shrugs. 'I think we're both under a bit of pressure and neither of us are behaving at our best at the moment.'

He's trying: he's really trying.

'Did you mention anything to Diane about leaving?' He picks up a chopping board and knife, and then reads the look on her face.

'Please, Alex – I will. I just don't want to go over it all again right now. Can we leave it there? Is that okay?'

He regards her blankly for a moment, and then his expression softens.

'You're right. Let's just enjoy the evening. Fancy a glass of something before dinner? That red's open.' He nods across to a bottle. She sees that the table is already laid. 'Martin will be here about seven.'

Her stomach flips a little.

'Okay.'

Sliding a wine glass across the table, she glugs a couple of inches into the bottom. 'I'll run a bath and take this with me.'

'Great idea.' He begins to slice a tomato. She can't cope with it all.

Making her way up the stairs, she goes into the bathroom, turns on the taps and sinks into the chair, burying her face in her hands. A slick of anxiety winds itself into her gut: a tightening sensation that makes her want to scream. She has no idea how to handle any of it: Alex, Martin, the idea of going to Vanessa's house tonight.

She takes a gulp of wine to steady her nerves.

*She should tell Jack.*

But what will she tell him?

She'd gone over the scenario all the way home in the car, imagining what it would feel like to find Peter at the house. What would she do? Would she be afraid of him?

What would she say? Challenge him? Threaten him? With what? The police? What would she do there and then?

A thought slams into her mind.

*Kill him?*

No.

*Would she kill to protect Chloe?*

She takes a breath. She might. She really might.

*My god.*

Every possible outcome of tonight wheels endlessly.

*You don't know this man. You don't know what he's capable of.*

*He's already tried to kill Martin...*

Balancing the glass on the side of the bath, she strips off, sinking into the water, letting the searing heat prickle her skin.

*Martin.*

*Martin is coming here for dinner.*

The very thought of it sends her head spiralling along yet another track. She's suddenly aware of the water cooling and it jerks her back. He will be down there, in her house, sitting at that table, those eyes searching out her own as her defences against him teeter.

'Penny for them.'

'Oh Lord!' She reaches for the wine glass. 'Alex! Don't do that!'

'Sorry, I thought you'd heard me come in,' he grins. 'I just wondered how you were doing?'

'Christ! I *was* doing okay.'

'I was really worried about you earlier, you know.' He pulls the chair round and sits with his elbows on his knees.

'I'm fine, honestly, but thank you.' A terrifying thought suddenly comes to her. *Has he just been through her phone?*

'You're sure it isn't anything to do with this Matthew Jarrow guy?'

She hides her face by putting the glass on the floor. 'Honestly.'

'Honestly?'

She nods. *Jack's message and his number on the call-log.*

'So Diane's on your side?'

'Yes.'

'And everything's okay? She's reassured you?'

'Yes, she did. She was really great. Can you pass me that towel?' She gestures over to the rail without looking at him.

Alex gets up, pulling the bath sheet after him. She goes to take it, but he holds it just out of reach.

'Where were you really?'

'What do you mean?' Her heart shunts up a gear. She makes a grab for the corner of the towel but misses.

'I said, where were you really?' He lets her have it but holds on to the other end as though he's afraid to let go.

'I heard the question, I just didn't understand it.'

She tries to bury her face in its soft, fluffy warmth. There's a black hole of deceit and she's inching further towards it.

'You didn't see Diane,' he says simply. 'So why did you lie?'

She finds her mouth opening and closing pointlessly.

'You see, I lied too, Frankie. I haven't spoken to her today and I know you haven't because I went to your office – where you told me you'd be.' He gives her a look. 'And Diane's assistant was there. Diane was a guest today at a colleague's wedding, so I think it's unlikely that she'd be having meetings with you, don't you think?' He raises an eyebrow.

Frankie finds her throat constricting involuntarily. It makes an odd, frightened sound.

He falters, choosing his words carefully.

'So. Where were you?'

Her heart contracts. His mouth is working awkwardly as though he might cry.

'What's going on? Although I don't know why I keep asking,' he rubs his forehead aggressively, 'because nothing's going on, is it? There's no kind of relationship here. Certainly not with me, anyway. Even when you're here you're not. You're always somewhere else: physically and mentally. Just tell me: do I know him?'

'What? No! No, Alex… No!' She desperately clutches at his arm.

'Who's this Jack?'

She thinks her heart might have stopped.

'Alex.'

But he closes his eyes and holds up both hands.

'No. You know what, Frankie? Don't tell me. I can't bear to hear any more of it. Every time you open your mouth, I don't know if it's the truth. Every time you make a promise, you break it. You can't even ring me when you say you will. All I know for sure is, I'm not first on your list, Frankie. I barely even make the top ten.'

'Alex, please—'

'Look, Frankie, I know I'm not very exciting—'

'No. Stop.'

'But I can't lose you.' His eyes glisten with tears. 'I just can't.'

'Stop this, Alex… don't… You're not going to lose me. I'm not going anywhere. I'm not having an affair. I'm really, really not.' She shakes her head in frustration.

He rubs his nose with the back of his hand and looks at her with reddened eyes.

'I feel as though you are so far away from me, Frankie. I *miss* you, don't you get that? Just tell me the truth. If it is another man, I can deal with it.' He grabs her hand and holds on, tightly. 'Let me in, Frankie. Just tell me the truth. Please.'

The doorbell rings and they both snap round.

Alex lets go of her hand and roughly scrubs at his face. 'Oh, hell. Look… After he's gone this evening, yeah? After he's gone we'll sit down, you and I and you'll tell me everything? And I mean everything. However horrific it is, I'll handle it. Will you do that Frankie? If nothing else, I just need to know what's going on.'

She finds herself nodding, clutching the towel as though it's some kind of lifeline. She hears Alex clattering down the stairs and clumping his way to the front door. Then there are voices – Martin and Alex. They are talking as though all this is ordinary and normal. In a very short while, she will have to walk down those stairs and join them. They are going to share a meal together, drink wine, talk about all kinds of stuff as though what's happening isn't really happening. And then later, much later, she's going to have to tell Alex that the whole of their married life has been a façade, a theatre production, a betrayal of the absolute worst sort – and she also knows, right that moment too, that Alex is never going to forgive her.

Slowly, very slowly, she gets out of the bath and puts on a dressing gown and walks into the bedroom to dry her hair and apply her make-up. She selects the right clothes from her wardrobe and pulls them on. Standing in front of the mirror, she smooths her top down over her stomach and tucks her hair behind her ears before walking quietly to the top of the stairs and treading her way down, listening to the footfall and creak of every step. It feels more like approaching an execution than a dinner party. She puts her hand to her throat, instinctively feeling for the necklace that is no longer there, listening to the rise and fall of voices. The hallway feels like it's closing in on her: there's no way out, and no way back. She puts one hand on the kitchen door. She knows she's just about to face the absolute and bitter end.

## *Chapter Twenty-Six*

'How about some port? Yeah, why not? Frankie, could you get some glasses?'

Alex slews his chair back and stands unsteadily.

There's a terror at the thought of him leaving her alone with Martin and she finds she's on her feet far too quickly. They both turn to look at her.

'She's keen.' Alex winks, grinning. 'I didn't think you liked the stuff that much.'

He eases around the table and makes a grab for the back of the chair to steady himself as he lurches towards the door. Martin's eyes are immediately on her.

'I need to talk to you, Frankie,' he hisses. 'I need—'

But she doesn't want to hear it, any of it.

'No! This has to end, tonight, Martin.' She leans across the table, glowering steadily. 'I don't want you here. I don't want you in my life. This can't happen.'

There's the sound of Alex searching in the cupboard under the stairs and muttering to himself. She knows she only has minutes.

'Frankie, listen. This is really important. You have to—'

'I mean it, Martin. No more coming round, no more phone calls or following me. Are you hearing this? I'm going to tell Alex the whole story, and from that moment on, you don't exist. No more blackmail. Are you listening?

Otherwise I go to the police. I don't want to do that to you, but if you force my hand, I will.'

'Phone calls? Blackmail? Following you?' His face furrows. 'I don't know what you're talking about.'

Frankie glances at the door. 'Stop it. I don't want to live in the past. The past has gone, Martin. Gone. Dead. No more. Please.'

'But I really haven't—'

'Maybe there's a new bottle in that box in the garage,' Alex's voice calls out from the hallway. 'I know we've got some somewhere. Hang on.'

They listen to the front door opening before she gets up, reaching beneath the dresser where she had shoved the box of letters.

'Here – look. This is what I'll take to the police.' She opens the box and pulls out one letter at random and then pulls another from its envelope. 'The rest are at the police station already. You were right, I didn't give them your name. I gave them a fake one, but I can just as easily tell them the truth and it would—'

But he's frowning and shaking his head. 'No, no, no – this isn't me.'

'Not you? Of course it's you.'

'No it's not. Look.' He reaches for his jacket from the back of the chair and pulls a bit of paper out of his wallet. 'Here.' He puts it on the table, turning both bits of paper round. 'This is my writing – see the way the "y" loops and the curve of this "r" there? Yes? Now look at this one. This clearly isn't me. You don't know my writing?' His eyes search hers.

She can only stare, dumbfounded. 'I told you – I – Jude – burned your letters.'

There's the clatter of the front door closing, and Frankie hurriedly pushes the papers back into the box and drops it next to her feet. Alex walks back into the room with a bottle of port held aloft. The bottle slowly descends onto the table as he looks from one to the other.

'Sorry, did I interrupt something?' He's smiling sarcastically and clearly very drunk.

'Frankie was just telling me about her work.' Martin picks up his wineglass and finishes the dregs. 'I've been hearing about kids in care. Heart-breaking isn't it?'

'Oh yeah, heart-breaking.' Alex sways a little. He seems like he's debating taking the sarcasm further but then changes his mind. 'Just goin' to the loo. Back in a tic – Where's those glasses, Frank? C'mon! C'mon! Chop-chop!' He pushes the bottle towards her and disappears out of the door.

Martin listens to the creak of the stairs before he glances round.

'How long have you been getting these letters?'

She looks back at him, stunned. 'Um… A little while… I don't know, I just assumed you'd got out and—' She stares at him. 'You're honestly telling me that these aren't from you?'

He shakes his head.

'Then how do you explain this?' She reaches down to the box and finds the jiffy bag and slides it across the table. Martin carefully opens it and cautiously shakes out what's inside. The red fabric makes him jump back in his seat.

'Fuck! *Fuck…*' he says. '*Jesus Christ*, Frankie.' He pokes it away from him. 'Someone sent you that? My god…'

'You remember it?'

'Yes… Yes, of course I do. Charlotte was wearing it the night… Jesus…' He pauses, staring at the hairband, appalled, but his brain is clearly working.

'I told you, this is Peter Vale,' he says suddenly. 'It's obvious.'

Frankie watches his face. 'You can't mean that.'

'This—' He waves his hand. 'I get it. I understand now. The necklace – who else could have got it back into that house? I'm telling you, this is all Peter Vale.'

'No!'

'Look at it, Frankie! Think about it! It's him. It has to be. But why would he do it to you? Why now?' He frowns for a second. 'There's a connection here, somewhere that we're just not seeing. There has to be.'

She stares at it all, dumbly.

She feels his eyes scanning her face. 'What is it you're not telling me, Frankie?'

'I can't Martin. I can't.'

There's a crack of floorboards on the landing.

'You can. There's something, isn't there? What is it?… You know something about Peter Vale, don't you?'

She can't bring herself to tell him.

'Have you remembered something about that night, Frankie? Think back. You didn't see me that night on the boat, did you? Was it him?'

Her head instantly swims with the scene on the boat, but she tries to fight it.

'I know you told the court that it was me but can you absolutely say, right now and beyond all doubt?'

Jack's words about Peter Vale come back to her – '*is it possible he was involved in how she died?*'

'I thought…' but she doesn't know. Not really *know*.

'All this, Frankie, all of it has to come out, you have to come clean about all this – about everything. You have to tell me, the police, Alex—'

'I'm dealing with this.'

'Dealing with what? You have to tell me. Please.'

'I can't do this now.'

'Yes, you can. You don't have any choice. There are things you're not telling me. I've been convicted of a crime I didn't commit. Please, Frankie. You owe me that much.' He doesn't drop his gaze. She's scared that if she lifts her eyes—

There's the sound of footsteps on the stairs and she instantly gets up to fetch the glasses as Alex walks back into the room.

Martin stands suddenly. 'It's getting late.'

'Hey, hey… We were just about to get started on the port! Hold on, hold on… You two not had a tiff, have you?'

Frankie glances quickly over at Alex. He's far drunker than she thought.

Martin looks instantly embarrassed. 'Thanks so much for dinner. It was really great, really delicious.'

'It's the only thing I'm proficient at now.' Alex laughs but there's no humour in it. 'Must be all the practice.'

Martin goes to make a move towards the door, but Alex stumbles into his path. Frankie can't tell whether it's accidental or deliberate.

'You must come round again, mate.' Alex grips his hand and grabs him by the shoulder. 'Oops!' He staggers a little and giggles like a little boy. She almost can't bear to watch.

'You'll see him out, won't you, Frank? You'll like that. See y'mate!' He swipes the port bottle from the table and starts clattering about with the glasses.

She gestures for Martin to go ahead of her into the hallway.

'Thank you for coming. It was nice to meet you.'

She is acutely aware of his physical presence as he walks past her, fixing her eyes to the floor as he makes his way to the front door.

He goes to turn the lock but struggles.

'Here, let me.' She reaches forward and their fingers brush. A crackle of static fizzes between them and she snatches her hand away, opening the door and stepping back into the safety of the hallway.

''Night then.'

'Frankie.'

'No, Martin.'

'You can't keep pretending.'

'Just go.'

'Here—' He dips into his pocket and pulls out a bit of paper which he pushes into her hand. She instantly drops it.

'Please,' he says again. 'We need to—'

But she's already closing the door, aware of him getting smaller and smaller in the gap. The catch clicks, but her fingers won't let go. His shadow looms through the glass. Her whole being yearns to open it again, but she won't allow herself. Flicking off the light, the hallway is plunged into darkness. He's gone, her heart thuds, she doesn't want him back.

Turning sharply, she walks quickly into the kitchen where Alex is standing with his back against the dresser. It's not port he's drinking, it's whisky.

'Well, that was nice.'

The fumes of alcohol waft towards her.

'Yes, it was. Shall I load the dishwasher?'

She can feel his eyes on her as she crosses the room.

'Go on. You're going to tell me.'

She has her back to him. She daren't turn round.

'You might as well. Nothing can be more painful than what you're putting me through now. Nothing.'

She pauses for a second, shoulders hunched. She would love to beg for a few more minutes before she tears her whole world apart. How she'd love to go back and rewind the clock to just a few weeks ago when the past was just a nightmare at the back of her mind.

'You'd better sit down.' She turns to face him.

'That bad, is it?' He cradles the glass against his chest. 'No thanks, I'll stand and take it like a man.' He grimaces unpleasantly. 'So. You were telling me. You're having an affair with…?' He waves the glass.

She almost laughs. 'If only it were as simple as that.'

Alex narrows his eyes and purses his lips. He watches her silently.

She takes a deep breath.

'I know Martin.'

His face goes very still.

'I knew Martin when I was a kid – when I was seventeen. He was a voluntary worker at the care home where I was living. I – We…'

Alex's face falls. 'But you said you were a kid, Frankie! He must've been… what? Early twenties?'

'We got involved.'

'Involved,' Alex says sullenly.

'I got pregnant.'

The room is silent.

'At the same time that he was arrested for the rape and murder of a girl.'

He closes his eyes in disbelief and sways slightly.

'It was my evidence that got him convicted. What I saw that night.'

'What you…? Jesus fucking Christ, Frankie.' Alex rakes a hand through his hair and looks at her. He suddenly appears completely sober. He stares down into the rim of his glass. His eyes are bloodshot and full of agony.

'And the notes? Who sent those?'

'I thought it was him.'

'But you told the police and me that it was someone called Matthew Jarrow.'

'Yes.' She can't look at him.

The silence grows thicker. 'So that was a lie. That was a lie to protect Martin.'

'Yes.'

'Because you have feelings for him, is that it?'

'No!' Her head snaps up to look at him. His eyes are full of terrible, terrible pain.

'So why didn't you tell me any of this?' He tries to stop his voice cracking.

'Because of what I did.'

He frowns in query.

'I left the baby.'

There's a moment where he can't speak. 'You left the baby? What do you mean, you left the baby? Where? How? Who with?'

Frankie shifts uncomfortably. 'It wasn't that straightforward.' She tucks her hands behind her thighs to stop them shaking. 'I left her with some people. I thought they were good people. I was a *child*, Alex. I didn't feel as though I had any choice.'

He struggles to get the words out. 'People? What people? But you were in care, Frankie... there would have been adoption. There was fostering. There's a whole raft of support services...'

She hangs her head. 'I left the baby with the girl's parents.'

'The girl?'

'The girl that died. The girl that was murdered.'

It's as though someone else is speaking. She cannot be saying these things. The words don't have any meaning.

Nothing moves. She can't lift her head. She almost dare not breathe.

'I didn't feel I had a choice,' she mumbles.

'Yes, so you keep saying, but of *course* you had a choice.' Alex's voice goes up an octave. 'You had choices, and you made a decision.'

He's angry, really angry. She can't tell him about the drugs, she just can't.

'Where are these "people" now? Do you even know?'

'Don't you think I feel bad enough, Alex? Don't you think the guilt and the shame of what I did has stayed with me? I've never forgotten the terrible thing I did, never! I've had to live with that.'

'And I've had to live with a person I didn't even fucking know.' He glares at her. 'So why couldn't you have told me any of this, Frankie? What kind of ogre have I been all these years, eh? How terrible a person?' His narrow eyes glare at her. 'I'll tell you, shall I? *Not at all.* The truth is, I've spent fifteen years of my life showering you with love, and support, and protection, and *money*' – he spits the word – 'trying desperately to make up for the appalling start you had in life. I alienated myself from my family to back you up. We moved miles away – *miles* – from family and friends who sneered at me for being with you. I gave up everything, and now—' He breaks off. She can see he's close to tears.

'Because that's not the whole truth is it, Frankie? There's more. Even now at this eleventh hour, I know there's more.'

She falters for a split second and that's all it takes.

'See? And there we have it.'

'No Martin, it's not that—'

'Oh, but it's *exactly* that! What is it between you and this *offender* that's so special that you'd lie to your husband for the whole of your marriage? You read in magazines about women like you, don't you? Warped obsession – is that what this is?'

'Alex—'

'Oh yeah, I'm supposed to be supportive and understanding of your past "trauma", aren't I?' he sneers. 'I'm supposed to suggest we sit around in a circle doing bloody counselling and act like a saint – well, y'know what, Frankie? I'm sick of being a bloody saint. I'm sick of trailing around after you being supportive and waiting for you to drop some crumbs of affection. I'm sick of being the understanding good guy in the background while you run off for hours and days "finding yourself". You're a selfish bitch, Frankie, and the irony is, you've become the person my family said you were – a liar, and a user. Well, well...' He begins to clap slowly. 'Go figure.'

*Clap. Clap. Clap.*

'Stop it.'

'Bravo, Frankie! What a performance it's been! The performance of a bloody lifetime – literally.' He smiles, chuckling horribly and then the smile falters as his eyes suddenly focus on the middle distance. 'So... let me get this straight. Me meeting Martin Jarvis wasn't by accident. This stranger who walked into the centre and presented himself as a vulnerable ex-offender has actually singled me out in order to get to you, is that right?'

Everything she can think of to say just makes this all worse.

'Martin Jarvis… Matthew Jarrow…' Alex pauses for several seconds as a whole raft of realisations flood across his face. 'You let me sit in that police station, worrying myself sick for your safety. You wasted their time chasing some newly-released offender that didn't even exist! Oh my god! Oh my god!' The glass swings wildly as he levers himself up to confront her. 'You and him… It's been you and him all along… Why the fuck didn't I get it? Christ, you and Martin must have laughed together this evening. It must've been like old times!'

'Stop it, Alex. Stop it. It's nothing like that. You don't understand—'

'Oh, I understand only too well, Frankie. That's the whole problem,' he growls. 'The ridiculous rose-tinted veil of loving you has well and truly dropped from my eyes. I see you for what you are, now. Finally… *Finally*.'

'No, Alex listen, you're right to hate me but you don't understand that the child, my daughter is—'

'I don't want to hear it.' His eyes flash with fury. '*That's* why you wouldn't talk about having kids with me, isn't it?' He starts to laugh, a low bubbling stream of hatred. She watches his face with growing horror; she's never seen him like this. 'That's why – because you had one already. Jesus… You know what? Go on, get out. Go and have a life with some murdering sex-offender if that's what you want.'

'Alex, I don't want—' She takes a step towards him and puts a hand on his arm.

'Don't fucking touch me! Don't you dare!' He swings her off.

'If you'd only let me explain—'

'Get off me, Frankie!' He's really shouting now, pushing her away. She staggers back, shocked.

'Alex—'

'No!'

She doesn't feel it, but she hears the whistle of the glass tumbler as it skims through the air past her head. She instantly ducks, hands pressed to her ears as it hits the far wall and shatters. Shards of scattered diamonds shower her feet.

'Get out! Get out!' he roars, his footsteps crunching behind her and then suddenly the kitchen door crashes against its frame. Running along the hallway, she grabs her bag, lurching to the front door and yanks it open. A tiny piece of paper flutters in the draught. She glances down. There, in the pool of moonlight, is the little folded rectangle. Bending swiftly, she picks it up, striding quickly to her car. Alex doesn't come after her. Sitting behind the wheel, she stares at the writing in the muted interior light. She looks up. The house sits there in a pool of bitter, grey shadows, closed-down and grim. She deliberately keeps her mind blank. She doesn't dare let herself think, but what she now knows keeps coming back to her: *Martin didn't send those letters… He couldn't have had anything to do with the necklace…* Things begin to piece together, and she begins to make sense of it.

Starting the engine, she backs off the drive in a scree of gravel. Punching the phone icon on the screen, she holds up the bit of paper into the passing streetlights and repeats the digits slowly. The phone bleeps loudly into the silence as it tries to make the connection. Her mind is empty of everything but Chloe. She knows what she's done to Alex. Her betrayal is enormous, but protecting Chloe overrides everything.

'Hello?' says the familiar voice.

'I'm coming to get you,' she says. 'Where are you?'

'Where I've always been.' She can hear the smile in his voice. 'Waiting for you to find me.'

# *Chapter Twenty-Seven*

The flat looks like a kind of wartime bunker. She pulls up to find Martin standing in the doorway, jacket already on and zipped. He runs over, scrambling to get into the car. He's excited and breathless. She knows what she's about to tell him will change his life forever.

'I never really thought you'd ring.'

She pulls out of the shabby, run-down estate and onto the main road.

'It was my one and only chance to persuade you to talk to me, but I never thought you'd agree, I thought—'

'Stop talking,' she says abruptly. 'Stop talking, Martin, and listen.'

She hauls the wheel round to the kerb, rams on the brakes with a jerk and kills the engine.

'This isn't about you or us. This isn't about Charlotte Vale, or Alex, it's about Chloe.'

He looks puzzled at the name.

'Our daughter.'

His eyes quicken with surprise but also fear.

'She wasn't put up for adoption.'

He turns his head slightly towards her. His cheek flinches, unsure.

'She wasn't?'

'I was staying with Peter and Vanessa Vale when I had her. Jack – you remember Jack at that party? – He's their son. He got involved with drug dealers, and I helped him – only Vanessa and Peter caught me. I lied to cover for him, and they took Chloe.'

Martin is staring as though she's fantasising.

'It's all true. What were my choices? I was seventeen and living in a care home. I'd just been caught with three kilos of cocaine; what chance do you think I would've had of keeping a baby?'

He looks back at her in disbelief.

'The answer you're looking for is none. So I lied. I told Jude I was still living there. Once I was eighteen no one bothered checking. Kids like me usually end up on the streets or worse. There's no safety net, no one cares. I knew Chloe would have a good life with them. Jack sent me photographs and little videos. I got to see her at first. If they'd taken her into the system I would never have seen her again.'

'Peter Vale had our daughter?'

Something terrible is happening to Martin's face. It doesn't look human. His mouth contorts as though he might scream or roar or…

'Peter Vale has our daughter now?'

Frankie puts her hand on his wrist. The feel of his skin beneath her fingers makes something inside her give way.

'I'm back in contact with Jack. He's always been on my side. He was the one who went to the police about the images he found on Peter's computer. It was Jack who got him put away. But Peter's out now, and Jack's worried that Vanessa will let him back into that house. He's lurking around. I went to the school today – Chloe's school. I saw her.'

'You actually laid eyes on her?'

Frankie nods emphatically. 'All grown up and gorgeous. It's the first time I've seen her since she was a little baby. She's fifteen, Martin. She really is beautiful…' She smiles, but then swallows it. 'But I saw Peter Vale too. He was hanging around by the school gates. Vanessa doesn't believe he's done anything wrong. Jack says we have to get Peter Vale put away again. It's the only sure way of stopping him.'

'We can maybe do that.' Martin looks quickly at her. 'The notes, the necklace: we have those. You remember at the court there were unexplained marks around Charlotte's neck? That was from the necklace they never found. The one you were wearing.'

Frankie's hand comes up to touch her throat where the pendant used to be.

'If you want to hide something, do it in plain sight, remember? I'm telling you, it's Peter Vale. He's the one.'

'And the hairband?'

'If that's got his DNA on it, it could be vital… Jesus, Frankie, it's like he's taunting you, like he wants you to know these things.'

She doesn't say anything, but she can guess why. *He's getting off on it*. She thinks back to how Peter made her feel: the way he looked at her, the way he made her skin crawl. He'd killed Charlotte and got away with it. He wanted her to know as a kind of sick torture. He'd been at the school gates in full view: provoking and gloating, not caring if she saw him.

A dawning of some terrible realisation slides into her stomach. The stalking, the notes, the phone calls had all started when Martin was released. She and Martin were the only two people who could possibly work out what he did – *He was enjoying the fact that they knew.*

*The hand on her back.*

*The finger on her neck.*

*The whispering in the darkness.*

'I really believe that he's…' She can only just say the words. '… He's out of control. He's got away with it once. He thinks he's untouchable.' The disgust in her throat tightens. 'He's sick, he's dangerous and he's free. He wants us to see him, he wants us to work out what he did, Martin.' She swallows thickly. 'He wants us to know he's after Chloe.'

## *Chapter Twenty-Eight*

She parks a little way down the road. From here they have a good view of Vanessa's house. A light is burning behind the living room curtains. Every so often there's a flicker that tells them whoever's inside is watching TV.

'You know the layout of the rooms, yes?'

'Perfectly.'

'And you'll know exactly how to get in?'

'Of course. I've already thought it through.'

They look at each other in the gauzy interior darkness. She feels seventeen again. Martin is twenty-one. For those few seconds, they're the people they used to be. She looks down into her lap. Her hand lies flat on her thigh, her wedding ring glinting dully in the street light. She isn't free to have these feelings. They are not hers to have.

'I understand,' he says simply. 'I know it's too late for us, but not for our daughter.'

They both look up at the house, lost in their own thoughts. A light comes on in the hallway: it spreads up the stairs and then moves to the front bedroom. A figure appears, cruciform for a moment as it tugs at the curtains.

'Probably Vanessa,' Frankie whispers. 'That's her room, there.'

'Does Jack know where Peter is?' Martin whispers back.

'I don't know, but I can find out.'

She pulls out her phone and sends a brief text. It instantly buzzes back.

'He says he can find out. He's asking what we're planning?'

'Very good question, I'd say.' He gives her a sideways look. 'You'll need to share it with me, at least.'

Frankie checks the clock. 'Chloe has Charlotte's old room. Peter's office used to be right next to it. There may be still stuff of Peter's there. We just need to find a connection to tie him to those notes: a sample of his handwriting, maybe? I don't know. This is Peter's home, this is where he feels safe. He knows Vanessa is on his side. If he's going to leave evidence anywhere, it'll be here.'

There's a movement at one of the windows and Martin dips his head to see clearer.

'The light in the front bedroom has just gone off.'

'Okay.'

'And we think Chloe will definitely be in bed by now?'

Frankie checks the time. 'She's fifteen and it's gone midnight. I would think so.'

'Okay.'

'Okay.'

Her phone buzzes.

'Jack's checked. Peter's at home in his bed-sit. That means we'll have stacks of time.'

'Right.'

She can feel the anxiety coming off Martin in waves. He stares out of the windscreen as ten minutes pass, then twenty. In the quiet, she hears him take a breath.

'My daughter's in there.' It comes out in a choked rasp, as though he can't believe it.

Frankie holds on to her own feelings, tight and hard. She feels her neck flex with tension.

'Shall we do this?' She looks across.

He looks back at her. 'Let's.'

They get out of the car. Softly clicking the doors closed, they walk quickly across the road. She tries to clear her mind.

*This is a house, like all the other houses they'd broken into, nothing more, and nothing less.*

Checking up and down the street and keeping close to the shadows, they make their way around the back. She looks up. The curtains at Chloe's window are closed. The ones in the next room are open. Her guess was right then. The bare pane stares down like a blank eye. She points upward and Martin nods in agreement. There's the small bathroom window. Even from here she can see that the catch on the fanlight is still faulty, its edge standing a little proud from the frame.

'Use this.' Martin whispers, pulling a Swiss Army knife from his pocket.

'Thanks.'

The soil pipe makes it an easy ascent, but the last fifteen years doesn't. Her muscles and joints object loudly, creaking and groaning and refusing to flex in quite the way they used to. Ignoring the pain, she crams the tips of her trainers into the back of the iron brackets, and hoists her way up, foot by foot. Panting, she reaches the sill and takes a look down. Martin is standing there with his arms folded. He gazes up at her with an expression she remembers so well. Her heart folds a little. Running her fingertips around the edge of the window frame, she feels gently, looking for the loose catch and then levers the knife into the gap to flip it open. Reaching inside, she pats around for the latch and unhooks the larger window.

Within seconds, she's inside.

It's a very odd feeling. For a moment the familiarity of everything makes her falter, but she gathers herself, listening for any sign of movement. The house stays silent. Creeping from the bathroom, she pauses again on the landing, aware that the bedroom doors are shut tight. Soundlessly, she makes her way down the stairs to the front door where she can see Martin's shadow weaving through the glass. Leaning her weight against the door, she turns the catch, easing it open without even a creak. He slips inside. They meet each other's eyes, and she signals for them to make a start.

Peter's office.

Frankie leads the way. She prays that the door won't stick. Putting her hand on the handle, she looks back. Martin has stopped by Chloe's bedroom door, his head slightly cocked and listening. She watches as he lifts a hand. With all five fingertips balanced gently, he wordlessly presses the wood as though feeling for his daughter on the other side. The look on his face tells her more than words ever could. He nods quickly.

*Let's get on.*

She eases the handle down and opens the door. The curtains are drawn back, and the bright moonlight bathes every surface in grey light. A laptop is sitting neatly on the desk and she goes over, flipping open the lid as the screen flashes blue into the darkness. She beckons Martin to start on the drawers. She sees they're full of paperwork: innocuous stuff, boring minutiae of old bills and bus timetables, parking machine tickets and bits of grubby Post-It notes. The laptop whirrs gently, lighting up and immediately letting her in.

'This must be Vanessa's,' she whispers. 'There's no password.'

She goes through clicking on the files, one after another after another. She frowns: this looks more like Peter's stuff. There are gardening tips and planting timetables, seed suppliers; nothing dodgy at all. She double-clicks onto others: there's reminders from the National Trust, Over Sixties' holiday brochures. Exasperated, she begins on the browsing history. It's all the same tedious, everyday rubbish. She glances at Martin. He's pulled out great swathes of paperwork and is holding up a document that looks as though it's something to do with the house. The torch on his phone flickers across the page. It's a typewritten letter addressed to Peter, and on the back, Peter has drafted a handwritten reply. Martin focusses the torch and Frankie peers closer.

It's nothing like the writing on the notes; the script is totally different. It has an upward left to right slope and the writing is pinched and tiny.

She looks up at Martin and shakes her head, puzzled.

'And the laptop?' he whispers.

She shakes her head. 'Maybe we just don't know enough about how these people work,' she hisses in a low voice. 'They're secretive. They know how to hide stuff so that it all looks innocuous.'

'So what do we do?'

'Let's take this.' She unplugs the laptop. 'We'll find someone who knows how to dig deeper in to the memory. If there's nothing there, then we have to find Peter and we threaten him,' she whispers, wide-eyed. 'We tell him what we know. We make sure that he's aware we're watching him. And we *will* watch him, and we'll keep watching him for as long as it takes.'

There's a sudden sound and they both snap round.

Frankie can hear Martin's breath, high and scratchy. Neither of them moves a muscle. There it is again… a tiny creak coming from the next room.

Holding her finger to her lips, Frankie slips closer to the door and puts her ear to it.

Martin is frozen to the spot. Frankie holds up a hand, hesitating in mid-air. She listens.

*Is it Chloe?… Where's she gone? The bathroom?* For one terrible moment she thinks she might have gone in to Vanessa and woken her.

She holds her breath.

There's another crack and the slight squeal of a door.

She waits. It all goes quiet. She points at the bedroom wall and holds up a hand. Martin nods.

Time stands still. Nothing moves. Carefully, very carefully, she eases the door open, glancing back once to make sure that everything is as they found it. The landing is dark. She beckons Martin forward to where the stairs begin. Just a few steps and they'll be down them and out of there… Just a few more steps.

There's a soft shushing movement from behind Chloe's door.

They freeze. Only Martin's eyes move in the darkness.

The door is no longer closed. A shadow in the gap moves a little. Frankie thinks her heart might burst at any moment. She can't look at Martin. They stand, paralysed.

'*Fraaankie…*'

Her whole spine turns to ice.

Slowly, almost in imperceptible degrees, her eyes move towards Martin. His face is like a ghost.

'*Fraaankie…*' A giggle, tinkling like a child. '*Mummy…*'

The door begins to open. Bit by bit, inch by inch, it widens to reveal the moonlight dappling across the sheepskin rug, a duvet, thrown back. A dented pillow.

No Chloe.

Frankie reaches out, cautiously touching the door edge. She can feel Martin close behind her. They step into the room. There's no one there. They stand, unsure, blinking into the shadows. There's a movement: a red eye blinks right back, as a cloak of darkness shifts and it turns to face them.

The door slams.

The light goes on.

Jack is standing with his back to it. He smiles suddenly. His look is indescribable: the eyes are mad, glassy: drugged up.

'Well, well,' he chuckles. 'Well, well… It's just like old times.' He smiles broadly at Martin who only stares back at him.

'Jack? What are you doing here? What is this?' she starts.

'Why did you have to come back into our lives, Frankie?' Jack shakes his head. 'Why couldn't you have just gone away like you were supposed to?'

'I don't understand…' she grapples. 'What's going on?'

'You had to turn up on our doorstep when everything was just ticking along nicely.' He takes a breath and tuts. 'I had it all sorted: Dad and you and Vanessa and Chloe. But you had to keep turning up and I had to keep finding ways to head you off.'

'Where is she?' Frankie takes a step towards him but instantly feels Martin's hand on her arm. She sees his gaze flicker downwards. Jack is holding a can of lighter fuel.

'Of course she's not here. Vanessa thinks you're the devil incarnate.' He smiles. 'You're so easy to wind up and manoeuvre, Frankie.' He grins widely. 'All that sitting outside the house, and being a nuisance at the school; you're such a nut-case. So she's taken Chloe away.' He cocks his head on one side. 'I had to make sure she's safe. She's my prize possession.'

'*You* orchestrated all that?' Cold air slips into Frankie's lungs as her brain tries to process what she's hearing.

'Chloe looks just like Charlotte, she sounds just like Charlotte, she *feels* just like Charlotte.' The grin becomes a wet leer.

Frankie gasps in fury. She wants to scream and claw his face off. But Martin's grip on her arm tightens.

'Don't worry. I haven't touched her yet. She's a dish that's yet to be savoured. The anticipation is as delicious as the first spoonful.' He licks his lips.

'It was you.'

The sound of Martin's voice snaps her round.

'What was me?'

'It was Peter Vale and you.'

'No, no.' Jack grins his strange grin. 'No, my dad is a fine upstanding chap, everyone knows that. That's why his fall from grace was so dramatic. There was this fantastic family man, who would do anything, *anything* to protect his family. But then, you'd know better than anyone, Martin – You know he would. You've got the evidence in that scar around your neck.'

Frankie's eyes flit down again to the fuel can that he's gripping and loosening at his side.

'You killed Charlotte,' Martin says flatly. 'You and him.'

'Me?' His hand flies to his chest like he's some second-rate actor. 'No, dear me, no. I was having far too much fun with Charlotte to want to kill her.' He smiles at Frankie. 'And you, lovely girl. I was just beginning to have a bit of fun with you. Remember the bathroom? "*You're so beautiful*," he hisses, giggling. "*I just love seeing you naked*." The sniggering breaks into a throaty laugh. 'Christ! The look on your face!'

Frankie suddenly can't find any air.

'I loved seeing Charlotte naked too... Did you know she wanted to be a model?' Jack cups the back of his head as he strikes a pose. 'And I just obliged. Silly bitch,' he sneers. 'She thought it made her look powerful and sexy, but she didn't see all the dirty-minded men using her pictures to spill their filth into. That's how powerful she was,' he laughs. 'You're all silly bitches. Her and you and all the others.'

Martin jolts beside her as though he's woken from a trance.

'So that's why she couldn't tell me what was going on: because it was *you* Jack! She only hinted at what you were doing to her... And the indecent images – they were yours, weren't they?' Martin shakes his head, incredulous. 'That's the bit we missed. Peter took the rap for you.'

Jack only looks back, blankly, for a moment. 'It was my idea,' he says suddenly. 'To kill two birds, as it were. You and my dad.'

'Why would you do that to your own father?' Martin looks at him, horrified.

But Jack's face clouds. 'Have you got any idea what it's like to be neglected all your life, hmm? To be the child that doesn't exist? Have you?' He glowers. 'All I ever wanted was for him to see me, but he never did; it was all Charlotte, Charlotte, Charlotte.' His mouth grimaces. 'So bit by bit, I took her away from him until I took her away for good. It didn't take much to convince my mental father to kill the man who had murdered her – It all seemed so sweet.' Jack looks directly at Martin. 'But the incompetent old fucker didn't kill you, did he, Martin? He ballsed up and you get to make a nuisance of yourself with her.' He points the can at Frankie. She sees that the cap is off.

'How I wanted you dead, Jarvis.' Jack's grimace turns to anger. 'You just couldn't keep your hands off anything, could you? Charlotte was mine and you had to go and touch her.' His face hardens. He grips the can until it makes a denting sound, *in and out, in and out*. 'And she wasn't yours to touch.' He pulls a lighter from his other pocket.

'Jack, you're not serious,' Frankie starts. 'Put that down. What do you think you're doing?'

'He touched her.' Jack doesn't take his eyes from Martin. He rolls the lighter wheel again.

'But I didn't touch her Jack! She came to me a few times and we talked. That's all! That night at the party was different: she was crying. She was shit-scared. Now I realise she was scared of you, Jack – you were everything she hated… It was you.'

'You're a liar.' Jack flicks the lighter once, then twice. 'You were telling her to get away and leave me. I knew it wasn't her saying that shit. You put the words in her mouth.'

'She was terrified. She said something really bad was going to happen to her. I told her to go to the police, but she said no one would believe her.'

'See? See?' Jack's head snaps back. 'You couldn't help yourself. We were fine until you came along. She was happy—'

'You're not going to do any of this, Jack. You're not that stupid.'

Martin glances at the lighter can and then at the flame that keeps popping and fading from under Jack's thumb. Frankie shoots a look at him in warning. *What was he thinking, antagonising him?*

'Don't you tell me what to do.' The flame sends weird dancing shadows across the glint of Jack's eyes. His thumb pauses menacingly. 'You're not in charge here, Jarvis: I am.' He eases the door open behind him. 'All this and you...' he waves the can across the floor and a spray of fluid patters across the carpet, '... are going up in smoke.'

There's a sudden blur of movement.

Martin lunges for Jack, knocking the can from his hand. A spray of lighter fuel fountains into the air, pattering across Frankie's face, leaving her gasping. There's a crash as the two bodies hit the wall. A whole shelf of books topples, smashing to the floor as Martin makes a dive for the can but misses.

'Frankie!' he yells.

Jack has grabbed him, pinning him to the floor; his elbow is at his neck. Martin thrashes wildly, his fingers reaching for Jack's face. He rakes at his mouth, digging his nails in and tearing downwards. There's a howl from Jack and a sudden spurt of blood from his lip as Frankie suddenly jerks into action, leaping onto Jack's shoulders and using her whole bodyweight to haul him backwards. He stumbles, floundering madly, wheeling her round and crashing blindly into the bookcase. A load of books topple, and then he has her: his fingers dig into her windpipe, squeezing and squeezing as she claws frantically at his clothes. There's a buzzing in her ears, the sound is getting louder as the room begins to fade around the edges. She's aware of Martin somewhere, his voice sounding very far away, getting fainter and fainter… then there's a sudden release of pressure and she takes a huge gasp of air.

Martin is shouting, she doesn't know what. Jack's weight lifts and her senses come rushing back. She finally hears the words he's yelling. Her fingers fumble to her pocket and suddenly she has it: the Swiss Army knife is in her hand, the blade pulled and pointing and she thrusts forward, not knowing what she's doing or where it's aiming.

Jack screams, and both men pitch backwards into the bookcase. She is aware of the sound of splitting wood and looks up to where the shelves used to be. In their place is a camera, its hooded black snout pointing in her direction, its red camera eye blinking and flexing, and what she saw that night begins to fall into place. Jack is crouched on all fours, bleeding from a cut on his face. Martin is lying slumped against the far wall. Disorientated, she becomes aware that there's paper, lots of it, bits of paper dropping from the back of the smashed shelves. *It's not paper*, her brain tells her… This isn't ordinary *paper*… These are photographs.

Hundreds of them.

She grapples to make sense. Pale naked images of flesh slide across the floor towards her – she sees arms and legs, breasts and buttocks… Photographs… loads of them, slipping from their hiding place and floating to the floor. Charlotte. Charlotte… more of Charlotte. And then her eyes catch another: it's Chloe, partly dressed, her arms crossed above her head as she takes off her top… Then there's Charlotte again: her bare back and shoulders. Frankie's hand reaches out to touch it, as a sudden yell rents the air. She turns to see Jack. He has crawled and grabbed the lighter. He raises it in the air as their eyes lock. The moment seems to last an eternity as the blur of Martin moving in front of her paralyses everything. There's a flash of what looks like lightening, and a piercing shriek from Jack. She shields her eyes in the sudden flare, as the heat, a searing, sudden heat, crackles all around and a caustic stink scours her nostrils.

'*Frankie!*' She can hear someone bellowing. '*Frankie!*'

Then there are hands around her waist, pulling her backwards. All she can hear is a terrible screaming that goes on and on and a smell that's so, so dreadful… She gags and retches, bending double. Dragged by a sudden massive force, she finds herself on the landing and half-stumbling, half-falling down the stairs and out through the front door. She gags and retches again, hands on knees, coughing and spitting, her eyes streaming with tears as she fights to get the words out.

'Jack…' she splutters. 'Jack…'

She glances up. Martin's arms are still around her as he hauls her out into the street. Palls of smoke are billowing high into the night air. There's a terrific crack and roar of flames and suddenly the upstairs window shatters, sending shards of glass tumbling down into the garden.

She sees Martin with a phone and is yelling, panicked. '*Please!* Fire brigade and ambulance!… *Hurry!*'

She looks back up at the house with tears flooding down her face. 'Oh my god…' she whispers softly. 'Oh my god…'

But Martin's arm tightens around her. 'Come on,' he says gently. 'Come and sit in the car. There's nothing we can do. Leave it, Frankie. Just leave it.'

She allows herself to be guided. Her feet feel as though they're barely making contact with the ground. Martin holds the door open, helping her into the passenger seat. She's not really there; her hands and face feel numb. He slips off his jacket and wraps it around her.

'Your shirt—' she can barely get the words out. 'Look at your shirt—'

He looks down. He's soaked in drying blood.

Clamping her jaw, she swallows hard. 'W-What happened, Martin? W-What the hell just happened?' Her eyes are full of grit and smoke. She can barely see. Martin doesn't reply. He looks round into the wall of blue and red flashing lights that are coming down the road towards them. His face looks pinched and weird in the maddened light.

'What's that?'

Her eyes follow his.

She realises she's clutching one of the photographs. The room is Charlotte's bedroom and in the foreground is a face she instantly recognises: Jack. He's looking back over his shoulder, smiling impishly into the camera lens.

'I don't know,' she says automatically, but even as she utters the words, she knows that she does.

He gently takes the photograph from her, tipping it into the light. There's a sudden glare of headlights and the photograph is lit in all its obscene clarity.

There in the background is Charlotte, naked and asleep on the bed, one arm sprawled above her head, one hand clutching the covers part-way across her breast as though seeking a little modesty. He pushes it back at her.

'I don't want to see that. I don't want that filth in my head.'

There are shouts from the fire fighters and a group of police begin to swarm from their cars.

'We'd better go and speak to them.' He sounds utterly exhausted. 'Or I will. Yes, you stay here, Frankie. They're going to want to talk to both of us, but I'll tell them we're going to the police station.'

She watches him walk slowly towards the officers, his gait leaden with weariness. They can't escape. She leans her head back against the head rest. Martin is a black outline against the blaze of lights. Groups of people in their dressing gowns have gathered on the pavement to watch. Every face is a mask of disbelief. Somehow, in the midst of the horror, she feels a kind of appalling relief that Chloe is safe, that Vanessa is with her—

*But Jack.*

She can't get his face out of her head. *Jack.* What he told them; none of that could be true, could it? She knew Jack. He was kind to her. They laughed together, chatted together. The person in that house tonight wasn't the boy she knew. She starts to cry, the tears and sobs choking and unstoppable down her face as the recollection of what took place tonight plays over and over. He caused such unbearable suffering, such horror… how could he have done all that? *Jack – The other Jack. The one she didn't know.* The tears start to flow, as the darkness of her reflection stares back at her in the window. She rests her forehead against the glass, grinding the bone until it's painful.

'*What didn't you see, though?*' a voice inside her says. '*How blind are you? You never see what's right in front of you.*'

# *Chapter Twenty-Nine*

'We're holding your boyfriend for questioning.'

Frankie's eyes follow D.S. Markham as she walks around the table and sits down opposite her again. 'Can I get you a cup of tea?' She smiles casually, as though they are a couple of old friends having a catch-up.

'He's not my boyfriend…' Frankie watches as she settles herself, organising her pen and pad of paper. 'You're holding him on what charges?'

'I'm not at liberty to discuss the details of the people we're detaining, I'm afraid.' The D.S. looks at Frankie disapprovingly. She rests her hands on the pad, fingers linked, leaning forward slightly as though waiting for Frankie to speak.

'I've told you everything.'

'Really?' The D.S. twitches an eyebrow. 'Okay. Well… Let's look at that from our point of view. A man has died in a house fire, in a house that you broke into through a window, using Mr Jarvis's Swiss army knife. Is that correct?'

Frankie nods.

'You've already told us that you were intending to remove a laptop from the property, but which is no longer in your possession, and all the evidence you claim to be proof of his sexual offences, has been lost.'

'But there was a camera—' Frankie starts.

'Many houses have security cameras, Ms Turner. It's not that unusual.'

Frankie stares across at this woman who is probably only a few years older than herself. She can tell what she's thinking: she's an open book. Her eyes move from Frankie's hair to her nails and then to the state of her jacket. They're assessing and judgemental. Her gaze says a lot: that she may have designer clothes, a nice car, and a fancy rural postcode, but the smell of her background comes off her in waves. There's the stink of trouble in her DNA, and they both know it.

'Jack Vale was involved with drugs,' Frankie repeats for what feels like the millionth time. 'I'm telling you, he killed Charlotte, his stepsister. He told us. He said—'

'He told you? You're absolutely sure that he said that: word for word?'

'Not precisely, but he—'

'So he *didn't* say it?'

'He told us that she was "his" and he was angry that Martin had touched his property.'

'He was angry that Martin Jarvis had murdered his sister?'

'No!'

'He *wasn't* angry, then?'

'*Christ!*' Frankie slams her hand on the table.

'*You* seem very upset, Ms Turner.' D.S. Markham sits back, frowning a little. 'Would you like me to get you that cup of tea?'

'Look. We went to the house because Jack told me that Peter Vale was a danger to Chloe—'

'Jack gave you information to protect your daughter?'

'Yes.'

She can immediately see how contradictory this all sounds.

'Although you haven't yet explained how Chloe came to be living there without you. Odd isn't it? She's only fifteen, after all.' The D.S. puts her head on one side like a bird, but that's where the resemblance ends: there's clearly nothing small and sweet about her at all.

'I – She—' Frankie stumbles. 'She wasn't there alone. She was with me for a while—'

'—A "while".' The D.S.'s head moves to the other side. 'We'll need to define what 'a while' means, I think…'

The lie burns hot in her cheeks.

'But let's come back to that later,' the detective switches tack, smiling.

Frankie can feel the threat being applied as leverage.

'So let's get back to where we were.' The D.S. picks up the pen and taps it on the table. 'You're saying that Jack Vale, this drug-dealer, confessed that he had indecent images of his stepsister, which his father, Peter Vale, took the blame for, and indeed was prepared to do a six-month prison sentence for. Have I got that about right?'

'Yes,' Frankie nods emphatically. 'Martin knew that Charlotte Vale was scared out of her mind and that something bad was happening to her, but she wouldn't say who, or what, she was scared of. Jack had a hidden camera in her room. I saw the photographs that he'd taken… I saw one of Chloe—' She breaks off suddenly remembering the photograph of Chloe that Jack had given her in the car. '*I took it when she wasn't looking.*'

His grinning face comes back to her and she's instantly repulsed.

'I don't know what Jack did to Charlotte. But I know it was so awful she couldn't even talk about it.'

The D.S. consults the pad in front of her.

'The police believed that Charlotte had been sexually assaulted; that she'd been raped.'

The hardness of her statement shudders the air.

'But the DNA evidence was washed away by the amount of time she was in the water.' Frankie can feel the D.S.'s eyes raking her face. 'I read all the statements that are on file, Ms Turner, and it was your evidence, your very compelling evidence I might add, that put Martin Jarvis behind bars. Are you now saying that evidence was a lie?' She gives her a quizzical sideways look.

'It wasn't a lie… Not a lie, no. I was mistaken, I made a mistake—'

'But you said you *saw* Martin Jarvis. You said you were sure of it.'

'I said I saw him, yes—'

'But now you're saying you *didn't* see him, and that you couldn't be sure, which means that what you said in a court of law, Ms Turner, was, indeed, a lie.'

Her head tips to the other side again.

'So how do you explain the necklace and the hairband?' Frankie feels suddenly exhausted and close to tears.

'The necklace and the hairband?'

'The night she died, Martin said Charlotte was wearing a necklace.'

'Martin Jarvis said.' The D.S.'s tone is unpleasant.

'Yes. When her body was recovered from the water, she had marks around her neck that were never explained, and the necklace was missing. Until Vanessa, her mother, gave it to me as a gift. Somehow it got from Charlotte to her jewellery box.'

D.S. Markham's eyes flicker. 'You have this necklace?'

'Yes. At home.'

'And the hairband?'

'It was sent to me – with the letters... Stalking-type notes. I came in and told the police about them. You have all this on file.'

The D.S.'s chin lifts a little in query. 'But you've already said that someone called Matthew Jarrow sent you notes when he got out of prison. And the hairband doesn't appear in the evidence file.'

Frankie falters. She takes a breath. 'Matthew Jarrow: that wasn't the truth, and I took the hairband... My husband didn't know the whole story, you see, and—'

'So more lies, then?' She gives her an odd look.

'I can see how all this sounds, but—'

'Hmmm... Yes, I'm sure you can.'

There's that tone again.

'Yes... yes... I can. But look, I have a photograph. One of the photographs that Jack took.' She puts her hand in her pocket, and then the other pocket and then checks her jeans. 'Martin has it,' she says. 'Martin had it in the car. Speak to him. He'll tell you.'

D.S. Markham lets out a long sigh and raises her eyebrows. 'It looks as though we're speaking to Mr Jarvis about quite a few things, so we'll add that to the list.' She smiles grimly and pushes her chair back to stand. 'I'll get you that tea shall I?'

'Do Vanessa and Peter know what's happened to Jack?'

The D.S. doesn't reply; instead she pauses for a moment.

Frankie looks up at her. 'Peter will confirm what I've told you about Jack. He did all those things because he was protecting his son and he believed that Martin had murdered Charlotte.' Frankie shakes her head. 'God, what a mess.'

The D.S. bites her top lip. 'Do you take milk and sugar?'

'You will be talking to him though?' she presses. 'You will speak to him?'

The D.S.'s mouth contracts slightly into a thin line.

'I may as well tell you. Peter Vale's body was found earlier this evening. His throat had been cut with a short blade knife similar to the kind of knife you described belonging to Mr Jarvis. Mr Jarvis is also sitting in our interview room covered in blood.'

Frankie finds her jaw has dropped open.

'Martin Jarvis is on licence, as I'm sure you're aware. That means he can be recalled to prison at any time, and that's exactly where Mr Jarvis will be going.'

Her jaw closes with a snap. She knows that the D.S. is watching her face.

'As I indicated earlier Frankie, there are lots of unanswered questions that I will want to put to you and I'm sure there's lots of "evidence" that you'll want to produce for me.'

She says the words like they're all part of a tired joke and she's heard the punchline a million times.

There is a pull, deep in Frankie's stomach as she realises she's not going home for a long while yet.

'Is that okay, Frankie?' The D.S. is still smiling as she nods dumbly in reply.

'Ah, tea! Silly me! Actually, I could do with a cup myself. I'll tell you what, we'll have one together. I'll scrounge some biscuits too if you like and we can have a *good old chat*.'

# *Chapter Thirty*

Her phone begins jangling the minute she steps out of the station into the quiet street.

It's Alex.

Where are you?

The message bats onto the screen.

She checks it, realising she's got thirty missed calls. It flashes again into the grey light. She presses the 'Call' button.

'You're safe! Thank god, you're safe! Oh Christ! I've been going out of my mind… How could you just walk out like that? It's four o'clock in the morning, Frankie. Where the hell are you?'

She halts, mid-step. 'You told me to get out.'

'I was really pissed. I was upset and angry…' He falters a little.

Her brain stumbles and snags. It's all a mess, everything is a mess.

'Please come home, Frankie. I've been so worried about you. We need to talk.'

*Talk?* She has no energy. There are no words.

'I want to make this right. I shouldn't have said what I said. I can't tell you how much I need to hold you and touch you. I was so afraid—' There's a catch in his voice.

'Will you please just come back? To chat things over. That's all I want right now – you and me, two people, two adults – a truthful, open, honest conversation. Please, Frankie.'

'I'm over an hour away. You'll have to give me time.'

He takes an inward breath of relief. 'You can have all the time you want.' His voice is soft. 'You can have anything, you know that, Frankie. You've always known it. You can have all the time in the world.'

She goes and sits in the car, unable to drive, unable to think. It feels as though the world is carrying on, but she is perfectly still. A flock of disturbed starlings chatter and fight in the tree across the road. They tumble and swoop across the front of the car and disappear into the blurred rooflines. She realises it's close to dawn. She must've been in the station for two or three hours. Her body aches and she knows she stinks of god knows what. Her head is thumping. She's too wired to sleep and too exhausted to stay awake. She wishes she could fall unconscious and have the whole lot of it drift away like a terrible dream.

The D.S.'s face comes back to her. She may have let her go, but she's not free. How can she be? No one would believe what happened, let alone an experienced detective. Frankie stares glumly at the clock on the dashboard as it clicks from one number to the next. It's a game of cat and mouse, and she's being reeled in. But reeled in to what?

–

'Two people have died tonight.' D.S. Markham blew across the surface of her tea and took a sip.

'Stop. Please stop. I can't hear any more.'

*Peter, dead? Peter can't be dead. Jack's dead.*

'And both you and Mr Jarvis have blood on your clothes. Would you like to talk me through that?'

'Jack and Martin fought. Jack attacked me. Martin got the blood on his shirt from the fight.'

'So neither you nor Martin had blood on you before you went to that house?'

'No!' She looked up at the detective, shocked.

'You know that for a fact?'

'Sorry?'

'You saw Martin's shirt before the fight?'

Frankie tried to think back… His jacket was zipped up when he got in the car.

'But he didn't know…' she blurted. 'He had no idea where Peter was; neither of us had. He didn't know that Chloe was even living with Peter and Vanessa. He was totally shocked when I told him.'

D.S. Markham pulled a face. 'What? Peter Vale attacks Martin Jarvis so badly that he ends up in the prison hospital but doesn't tell him that he has his daughter living with him?'

*You took my daughter, so I took yours.* Vanessa's words came tumbling back to her.

Frankie's brain blundered around, trying to tie it all together.

'Listen! Jack orchestrated it all! He was going to kill us!'

The D.S. regarded her as though she was looking at a naive child.

'The question is, Frankie, do you trust everything Martin Jarvis has told you?'

The D.S.'s head tick-tocked again. She pursed her lips as though she was trying not to smile.

'Let's look at the options here, then. Let me play devil's advocate for a moment. Let's say Martin Jarvis was involved with Jack Vale in some very dark and shady enterprises. We already know that Martin and Jack are associated through drug-dealing—'

Frankie interrupted her. 'But Martin wasn't a dealer like Jack! He only did bits and pieces. He was just small fry, recreational, that's all—'

The D.S. continued as though she hadn't spoken.

'—Martin and Jack become involved in some shady stuff and somehow Charlotte Vale gets lured in, but she doesn't like what she finds. She's going to spill the beans, so she gets murdered to shut her up. But Martin does the prison time for it and resents Jack for walking away scot free.'

'But Jack already told us—'

The D.S. held up her hand. 'Now just go along with my theory for a while and let's unravel it a bit further. Martin believes Jack owes him. Martin threatens Jack. So Jack gets his father involved, hoping he'll kill Martin in prison, but Peter messes up. Peter Vale now knows too much, so Martin takes him out too. Martin then goes into that house with you, finds Jack there, and sees an ideal opportunity to get rid of him once and for all. How about that?'

Her whole tone was ladled with glib sarcasm. Frankie stared at the desk. She concentrated on the scratches and whorls on the tabletop, seeing patterns and faces: a goblin with a hooked nose, an elephant with three legs, a leering pumpkin with hollowed-out eyes.

She looked up suddenly, 'Where are Chloe and Vanessa?'

'We haven't been able to locate them. We don't know where they are right now. We're trying, though. A neighbour said they'd just gone away for a couple of days. But we will trace them, rest assured of that… Now, come on, tell me what you think about my Jack and Martin scenario?'

But Frankie could only think about Chloe. She felt her mind drifting: Vanessa's plan was obvious: Jack had told her to get her as far away as possible. But what would she do now Peter and Jack were dead? There was no one to corroborate anything.

'Okay Frankie, let's do this your way.' The D.S. pushed her chair back a little and put her hands flat on the table. 'None of what I've said is true. It's Jack Vale from beginning to end: he's a sex offender, a murderer and a drug dealer, yes? So this vital evidence, this hairband, this necklace, this photograph, just explain how come you've got it all? Seems odd, doesn't it?' She looked at her awry. 'You said you told the police all about it in your earlier statement, but all we have are a few hastily scribbled notes. Why didn't you give this hairband and necklace to the police if it was so crucial to this murder?'

Frankie shook her head.

'There are so many things and actions that you don't seem to be able to explain, Ms Turner.' D.S. Markham paused. 'And just so you are aware, Martin says he doesn't have the photograph of Jack Vale that you referred to.'

Frankie's eyes batted up.

'He also says that you and Charlotte had a fight at the party the night she died.'

There was a pause where the two women looked at each other. The moments ticked by. *So what was Martin doing: Shifting? Deflecting? Denying?*

'What we've got so far is a dead girl's necklace and hairband in your possession, and her step-brother and step-father dead on the same night. Is that right?'

She noted the colour of the D.S.'s eyes. They were a kind of washed-out blue: muddy and a little dull, not sharp and bright and full of clarity.

'And you're wanting me to believe, what? That it wasn't Martin Jarvis who killed her, but Peter or Jack Vale. Is that right?'

Frankie looked down into the surface of the tea and watched the steam rise.

'So take me through it, frame by frame, Frankie. That night when you went down to the canal boat. What did you do? What did you see?'

*She remembered the keyed-up pounding swirl of emotion. She'd wanted a row – to scream out – but when it came to it... When she saw...*

Frankie scoured her memory.

'I thought it was... I assumed it was... But now I think—'

*What did she see?*

*Charlotte was gone.*

*Jack was gone.*

*Peter was gone.*

*Martin had done fifteen years of a prison sentence that she had orchestrated.*

*All she had was a broken necklace and a hairband and a bunch of weirdo letters pointing nowhere.*

*Nothing she had to say now was going to change anything. No one wanted to open this case to get justice for an ex-offender with dodgy background.*

She frowned. 'I think I've got it all wrong. I was only seventeen. I was drunk, I'd been taking drugs. It was dark. I'm making connections where there aren't any. Maybe Charlotte was wearing a necklace that night, or maybe she wasn't – who knows?'

'Who indeed.'

*No evidence, no corroboration, no point. It'll never stick with the CPS.* But she could see by the D.S.'s face that there were things that might: the death of Jack and Peter Vale for a start off, and then abandoning a baby. Frankie saw her future, what was left of it, being mapped out on that paper pad on the desk. She saw endless questions and charge sheets and solicitors. It was the future she'd always feared.

They looked at each other.

'I see. Right.' The D.S. picked up her tea in its plastic cup.

'Can I go home now please?' Frankie gazed into those insipid eyes.

'I don't see why not. We'll definitely want to talk to you again so don't think of going anywhere, will you?' Frankie looked down at her tea. The liquid surface shimmered with tension, shaking as though there might be an earthquake just waiting to happen.

## *Chapter Thirty-One*

The exhaustion hits her like a tidal wave.

*Home.*

Sanctuary.

Away from all of this.

Away from Martin and police and questions and chaos.

She needs to find Vanessa, find Chloe and start again, start clean.

*Alex*. Alex would help.

In spite of everything, all the lies and the deception, Alex would lay down his life for her if she asked him to; she knows that. She'd married him because, on some fundamental level, Alex was the kind of man she could trust with her life.

And Chloe's.

The journey home is a blank. The miles tick by under the wheels, the hedges flicker past in the blue gauzy light, the signs say one thing and then another.

The Truth.

*What is the truth?* Does she even know what that is? The thing that's been buried for fifteen years? *Martin… Chloe… Charlotte… She has no idea what the truth is anymore.*

The roads become more familiar, the streets she knows come upon her one after the other. This is her truth; this is her reality. These houses, these fences, these stones are what a real life and real relationships are built from, not a fantasy from years ago.

This. Is. Her. Truth.

Swinging into the drive, she knows before she even looks up that he will have seen her. Alex will be waiting for her in the same place he's waited for her for fifteen years – and she realises it's so lovely to come home.

She gets out of the car and breathes in the sweet morning air. This is what being free smells like: fresh and clean and full of promise. She goes to close the door, but then sees the photograph caught between the seat and the floor mat. Bending down to retrieve it, she hurriedly pushes it into her bag. If she shows it to the police now, then what? What does it prove? Nothing in isolation. One dubious photograph of a boy looking into a camera lens. It would go nowhere but into D.S. Markham's bin.

Alex opens the door to greet her. He pulls her into his arms, squeezing the life out of her.

'Thank god. Thank god…' he murmurs over and over. 'I thought… I thought… Oh Christ, it's not important, you're here with me now. Nothing else matters. You're here, you're here…'

She lets him hold the weight of her, feeling as though she would love to let go right now and give up: let her legs collapse beneath her and be carried away. The door slams behind with a definite click and the sound is like music.

*Shut the world out; shut everything out.*

'Hey, hey… No, don't cry! No, Frankie! Come on, come on. Come and sit down.' He pats her arm, her cheek, checking her over. 'Where have you been? Are you hurt? What's happened to you?'

She pushes the hair out of her eyes. 'I'm going to have to get out of all these clothes. They're ruined,' she sniffs and starts weeping again. 'They just need throwing away.' She can't get her words out.

'You're fine, you're okay…' he soothes. 'Look, let's not talk about anything right now. I'll get a black plastic sack or something and bring it up to you. Go and shower, I'll fix you something to eat. Are you hungry? Thirsty? No? Just go on up then. I'll sort everything.'

She hiccoughs a sob and scrubs at her face with the back of her hand.

'I'm in a mess, Alex.' She sways with tiredness, but has a desperate need to say this one thing. 'I'm not seventeen anymore, I'm a grown woman, I need to get a grip of my life, get a grip of this marriage and stop behaving like a bloody kid.' She looks up at him through swollen, painful eyes. 'Everything I've done to you… The hiding, the lies…' She sobs again. 'I want a second chance. I know I don't deserve one.' She bites her lip. 'I'm *so* sorry for what I've put you through. I can't imagine why you're still with me.'

'Because I've always loved you and I always will.' He goes to pull her to him but then pauses and sniffs. 'But maybe not before you've showered,' he grins. 'We've both got a lot to be sorry for, and we both need to put it behind us. I've told you; I'll sort everything out, don't *worry* so much.' He gives her a little shake. 'Now get in that bathroom!'

Somehow, she manages to get up the stairs and peels off all her clothes, leaving them on the side of the basin and switching on the shower. She steps into the water, the heat of it tingling her scalp and face as she pools shampoo into her palm and begins to scrub at the matted grease coating her hair.

She is aware of the door opening through the steam and the rustle of a plastic bag. The rustling stops.

'Frankie.' His voice sounds odd.

'Yes. I'm going to tell you everything, Alex. All of it.'

'I don't mean that. I meant what I said earlier. I love you. You know that, don't you? I have always loved you and I always will.'

'Yes. I know you do and I'm incredibly grateful.' She begins to wash her body, over and over as though there can never be enough soap to make her feel really clean again.

'I know you feel bad, and guilty about what's gone on between us.'

Squeezing her eyes tight, she tries to shut out the pain and the trauma of what's happened. Pulling her fingers through her hair she lets it snag until it almost aches.

'Tonight, Alex… Tonight something terrible happened. I really don't want to talk about it, but I have to.' The images come back to her, bloody and horrible, but she knows she has to relive them. Her body starts to tremble. She sees his outline wavering on the other side of the glass; she just needs a bit of time to process the horror. She tries again.

'Someone died… Two people died. I—' She goes to say more but the words choke her.

Alex is still faltering on the other side of the misted screen. She's not sure he's heard her properly.

'There's so much that's gone wrong and so much to put right. We just need a plan.' He sounds so definite. Her hand shakes as she turns off the shower. It's instantly quiet and she tries to find it in her to utter the words again.

'Did you hear what I just told you? Martin's been detained and taken in for questioning. I've been in a police station, Alex, I need to tell you, I've been involved in—'

'Wouldn't it be better if we just drew a line in the sand?' He reaches back and grabs the towels from the rail, shunting the shower door open and passing them to her. 'We should start again, Frankie, just like I said before, leave this place, go away, start a new life where no one knows us.'

She pulls one of the towels around her. She's aware of the birds outside, a mad dawn chorus. Her eyes feel as though they're full of grit and sand.

'Alex.'

'You need to get dressed. We can't stay here. We need to hurry.'

She watches him as he shakes open the plastic bag and begins pushing her clothes inside. The stink of petrol and smoke is making her feel sick. She looks at the side of his face as he works. His lips are pushed forward in concentration, his brow slightly furrowed. A note of alarm begins to flutter inside her ribs.

'Alex?'

He pauses and looks round at her.

'Did you hear what I just said?'

'Yes.'

'Aren't you shocked?'

'What is there to say?'

'Is everything okay?'

She knows it's not, but she doesn't know how or why. There's just something seriously, seriously not right.

'We're free now, aren't we?' He turns to face her, smiling. 'It's all over… all that stuff is dealt with. Gone.'

'Alex.' His face is not the face she knows. His eyes are not his eyes. 'What are you talking about?'

It's like she's seeing him for the first time in years. The shock is almost physical.

'It was supposed to be so simple.'

'What was?' She tightens the grip on the towel.

'It was just supposed to frighten you.'

Her mouth goes to form the words again, but can't. She doesn't know what he's saying. It's making no sense. Frighten her? What is he talking about?

'The notes. The phone calls at night. The figure in the alleyway… All those things that were happening.'

She's still not getting it. She stares at him.

'You were testing me…? Was that it? To see if I would tell you? You were testing me because you thought I was having an affair?'

He doesn't answer. He goes back to tying up the sack.

'I always knew about Martin, you see. I always knew from the moment I touched you at that party, that I loved you.' His face flinches as though he's been stung. 'And that you would never love me in return. Not really.'

He looks at her face and nearly laughs; it's a bitter sound.

'You don't even remember me being there, do you?'

His words swim in the air towards her. *Alex is the stalker? The notes, the flowers, the being followed – it was all him?*

'Please don't say you remember me.' He holds up a hand. 'I know that you don't. You don't feel about me the way you feel about Martin. You never have. You were in the garden, crying… Crying over a man that was treating you like shit, but you couldn't see it. He'd done that to you, given you drugs and booze and then dumped you…

What kind of man *does* that to a beautiful girl?' He presses his lips together as if to blink away the memory. 'All the time I was talking to you – trying to help you, I knew you hadn't even seen me. All you were doing was desperately staring into the space that he'd left as though he might magically come back.'

It's as though she's in some alternate reality. Everything around her looks ordinary and normal and okay, and yet everything is as far from okay as it can possibly be.

'And I know – and have always known – that's the way it is. That moment: your eyes searching somewhere past me; that's the way it's always been between us. You wouldn't believe all the things I've had to do, Frankie,' he chuckles sadly, 'to move into your sightline. All I ever wanted was to have you look at me the way you looked at him that night. Your gaze was like a searchlight in the darkness. I've spent years trying to be picked out by it, to bathe in its warmth, but I've always been relegated to the shadows. You've always shown me kindness and regard and respect, but never love, Frankie. Not that deep, grinding, passionate love I saw on your face that night.'

His agony is palpable; there's such a terrible, terrible yearning.

'I kept thinking as the years passed: is this is the year she'll forget him? Will she move on and stop thinking about him? But it never happened.'

'Alex—'

There's a sense of unravelling; a spooling out of reality – or what she thought was reality – stretching and lengthening in front of her.

'Every time his parole date got closer, I could see what was going to happen. He was going to be let out and once he came out…'

She feels her face collapsing.

'Oh yes, I knew all about his parole dates and when they were. I knew everything, you see. Oh, I've put your clean clothes over there.' He gestures towards the chair as though this is a normal conversation.

'I knew that once he was out, you'd be like magnets for each other.' His smile winces. 'It was inevitable. I couldn't stop it... You need to get dressed, Frankie. We do need to get a move on.'

She has a feeling that she's just an automaton. Her body is functioning, but her brain has gone into survival mode: *Put clothes on, get your shoes on, get out of here. It doesn't matter how you do it. Stay calm. Stay focussed.*

'I couldn't prevent it. I knew that. I thought about it long and hard, and I came to the conclusion that if I couldn't stop it from happening then I'd just have to find a way to control it... And by the way, don't worry, I've packed us a picnic for later and I know you're exhausted but you'll be able to sleep in the car.'

*This is a dream*, her brain tells her. *You are imagining all this, none of this is real.*

She pulls on her jeans. The action is so familiar. The impossible incongruous ordinariness of the action jars.

'There was no way I could have him getting out on parole and walking the streets. I knew he'd try to find you. Something had to happen, and that something was Peter Vale. Only that didn't work out either. This is what happens when you delegate work,' he chuckles. 'No one ever does the job as well as you would do it yourself.'

'You knew that Peter Vale attacked Martin?' she hears herself saying.

Alex frowns as though she's just asked something stupidly obvious.

'Of course!' He checks his watch. 'This is taking longer than I'd planned. Have you got enough layers on there, do you think?' He catches her shoulder and turns her round to look at the back of her hoodie, pulling it down to neaten it. 'You're so beautiful, you know that?' He kisses her temple. His saliva is cold on her skin. 'We need to wrap up warm where we're going. Come on.'

Her head feels like glue; her feet wade across the floor as though she's walking through deep snow. *He knew Peter. How did he know Peter?*

He goes ahead of her out of the bathroom and down the stairs. She sees the rectangle of the front door with the arch of the skylight over the top. Just through that thin pane of glass is the outside world where she will be free; she will escape. There are people out there, people who will help. She suddenly realises she doesn't have her phone.

'By the way, I've got your phone here If you're looking for it.' Alex doesn't look round. 'It was in your jacket pocket. You don't want me throwing that away, do you?' He chuckles and opens the door to the kitchen. A wall of heat hits her. The Rayburn is going at full pelt. There's a bag of what looks like rags on the floor next to it. Alex goes over and opens the bottom fire door. There's an instant crackle and a pall of smoke. He dumps the sack, and crouches to pull something out. It's a shirt with blood on it. Frankie takes a step back as he feeds it into the licking flames and shuts the door.

'Your clothes can just go straight in the bin. Won't be a sec.'

She watches him walk to the back door and across the patio and she immediately runs into the hallway, desperately yanking at the front door catch but it won't give. A tiny cry freezes at the back of her throat as she tries again but she can see the metal deadlocks are holding it fast. She spins round. *No, this can't be happening… No…*

'You got everything you need?' Alex's voice calls out from the kitchen. 'I'll just put this last lot on the Rayburn and we'll be away. Don't fret.'

She stands, dumbly. *As soon as he opens that front door. The minute she thinks she can make a run for it…*

'Right… Here we go.' He appears with his coat on and a large wicker picnic basket slung over one shoulder. The bizarre incongruity of this whole situation leaves her breathless.

'It's still really early. You've got everything, have you? Jacket? Bag? I told you to wrap up warm.' He tuts. 'I don't suppose we'll catch much traffic. What do you think?'

'No.'

Her eyes are darting everywhere. His hands, the keys, the lock, the madness of a picnic basket. His fingers shake out the set of keys from his pocket and he unlocks the deadbolts and then the main lock. The door opens a little. She can smell the early morning air. It's out there. All she has to do is—

Alex pauses, holding on to the door edge.

'I want us to start again, Frankie. I want us to be a family: you and me and Chloe. Now there's just us. Everything else has been taken care of, so we can, can't we? The three of us.'

His face is open and pleading. She sees it all there: his love for her, how much he wants this. He's almost begging. A sudden thump of realisation stops her heart, dead.

'How do you know her name?'

'What?'

'How do you know Chloe's name? I never told you. I never said. I only told you I had a daughter... How do you know it, Alex? Who told you?'

'Jack.' He smiles.

'Jack?' She can't take it in.

'I was with Jack at the party that night.' He takes a deep breath. 'That's how I know everything.'

Her head feels like it might explode. *She sees Jack with his white buzz-cut hair coming down those stairs that night and tries to picture the boy with him.*

'—But no, I actually met Chloe and introduced myself.'

A creeping stone of terror forms a hard ball in her gut. 'You did what?'

'Last night when Peter Vale was trying to smuggle her away. I couldn't allow that to happen, Frankie. I know how much she means to you. Don't worry,' he puts his hand reassuringly on her arm and gives it a little squeeze, 'she's safe. Totally safe and comfortable. That's where we're going now – it was going to be a surprise but—'

He gestures for her to go through the door. She almost stumbles off the step as a great wave of panic and confusion threatens to engulf her. She'd like to cry out – to scream and yell and holler for the whole world to come and rescue her.

'Oh sweet Jesus, Alex... What have you done? What have you done?'

'Peter shouldn't have tried to stop me.' He escorts her across to his SUV, opening the door and helping her inside. 'He was going to take her away. You must understand that, Frankie. He was going to take her away from you just like the first time. He was going to meet Vanessa somewhere. "No, no, no," I said to him, "you're not allowed to do that. Her mother, her *real* mother needs her now.'" He pulls the safety belt around for her and leans across to clip it in. He smells of something odd: like sweat and fear and something chemical.

All she can think about is Chloe.

'Promise me she's safe, Alex… *Promise* me!' She grabs his arm.

'I promise you.' He runs round to the driver's side and slides in. 'Come on, if you don't believe me, you can see for yourself.' He grins at her and starts the engine. It's just starting to rain, and the headlights pick out the fine filaments of water as they slant through the beams.

'You're taking me to her, you promise? You're really taking me to her?'

'I said don't fret, Frankie. Of course I am. But first we have to make sure that everything is safe and neat and right, so we're going to the police station to tell them what you know about Peter Vale's death.' He begins to reverse off the drive.

'What?'

'You don't know much. Hardly anything in fact.' He smiles across at her. 'But you're going to tell them what Martin told you… About how he confessed to killing Peter Vale. After all, Peter attacked him once, didn't he? It would be perfectly plausible that Martin would want revenge – but I'll leave that bit of the story up to you to make up.' He pats her reassuringly on the knee.

Her head is swimming. She knows she'll wake up soon and this will all have been just a nightmare.

The early morning sky darkens suddenly as he pulls onto the road and the wipers begin to squeal.

'Where is she?'

'So you'll do that?'

She turns her head to look at him. A stranger is sitting in the driver's seat. She has no idea who her husband is.

'You'll do that?'

'Yes.'

'You'll do that, knowing that Martin Jarvis will get recalled and stay in prison for the rest of his life?'

'Yes.'

'And that he'll die in there. You will never, ever see him again?'

She knows it's a test.

'Yes,' she says. 'Yes, yes, yes. I'll do all of it and more. Whatever keeps Chloe safe.'

'I knew you'd agree.' He begins to laugh, his face opens into a wide grin. 'Hey… Do you want to know what's really funny about this, Frankie? Do you want to know what's making me feel so happy? This is the first time in the whole of our marriage where I really think you're seeing me. Do you realise that? For the first time, you're really listening.'

The car picks up speed and he's still chuckling.

'Can you imagine how that feels? It feels *amazing*, Frankie! This is how it's going to be from now on. This is how—'

There's a sudden *bang!* across the windscreen and the car slews violently to the left. Frankie hits her head on the side window as Alex grapples with the wheel. The wing hits the bank and they skid awkwardly, juddering to a halt.

'What the hell was that?' Alex undoes his seatbelt and goes to get out, but the rear door is yanked open and there's a flurry of wild matted hair, and rain, and fury as Vanessa launches into the back seat.

'You fucking bitch!' Frankie feels her head being violently pulled back until her scalp burns and stings. Her eyes flicker and widen with fear as there's the sudden cool hardness of a blade against her throat.

'Where is she? Where the fuck is she? I'll kill you!' The knife presses harder. 'I'll fucking kill you! *Tell me!*' she screams.

The only thing that she hears from her own throat is a tiny, strangulated cry. Her eyes flit to Alex who is pressed back against the door, his hands aloft at the sight of an unleashed, untamed animal.

'I said – *Tell me!*' Her spittle peppers her cheek. Frankie feels the knife bite. A tiny trickle of what she thinks must be blood runs down her neck as her heartbeat drums furiously in her ears.

'Peter didn't turn up!' Vanessa hisses. 'They didn't come. I can't get hold of him and I can't get hold of Jack. This is your doing… It has to be you. Where *are* they?'

Frankie feels her breath stop. *She doesn't know. Vanessa doesn't know.* She swallows hard. She can't bring herself to tell her.

'I-I don't know where Chloe is,' she stammers. 'I don't know, Vanessa… Really, truly, I don't know…' Her eyes bat over to Alex and Vanessa snaps round.

'Oh this is the husband then, is it?' Vanessa's eyes are crazed with desperation and fear. The knife flits from Frankie's throat and wavers in the air, its tip pointing at her and then at Alex. 'You know where she is, do you?'

'No! No, I don't!' Alex's hands are raised in surrender. 'Yes, I'm her husband Alex, but I don't know anything! I'm only just finding things out, just like you are. I've begged her to go to the police and she's agreed, haven't you, Frankie? That's what we've said, isn't it? You'll go to the police?'

Frankie feels her eyes widening.

'The *police*? What have you *done*?' screams Vanessa. The car echoes with the force of it. '*What the fuck have you done?*'

'Vanessa, I haven't—'

'She knows where Chloe is, though, don't you, Frankie?' Alex blurts. 'You took her, didn't you? You knew it was wrong, but you took her because you were desperate. Isn't that the way it was? Isn't that right? You might as well tell Vanessa the truth… Don't let her suffer…'

There's a thin sheen of perspiration glistening across his forehead. He glances at the knife tip and then at Frankie.

'Martin Jarvis is being questioned by the police about what happened to Peter,' he says suddenly. 'He… he's…'

'Peter? What do you mean "what happened to Peter"? What are you talking about?'

'Martin… He…'

Vanessa's grip on the handle of the knife gets tighter. 'What's he done?'

Alex shakes his head slowly as Vanessa begins to choke on her sobs.

'I don't believe you. You're lying.' The knife blade swings back and forth between them. Frankie cowers back.

'That bastard Martin. This is you. This is all your doing!' Vanessa is out of control. 'Where is Chloe? What have you done with her?' The blade tip presses to Frankie's throat.

'I haven't, Vanessa! I haven't!'

'She'll tell you. We'll go there!' Alex babbles. 'Won't we, Frankie? But I need to start the ignition, okay? I need to get you to her.'

The blade relaxes a little. Vanessa's hand is trembling so much she can barely keep hold of it. 'Okay, Drive then. Drive!'

Alex turns the engine over and the car bursts into life. The rain is beating down on the roof and the windshield is fogged with their breath. He rubs his sleeve across it. Frankie touches her neck; there's blood on her fingers. Vanessa is weeping now; a high-pitched keening sound, more animal than human.

'Which way?' Alex looks across at Frankie as they get to a roundabout. She stares back at him, open-mouthed. 'This exit?' He gestures to the left and she nods, quickly. The road lays out in front of them, bare of traffic. It's a desolate road heading towards the Welsh border. She has no idea where they're heading. Vanessa doesn't seem to notice. She's rocking a little in and out of her sightline, backwards and forwards. The noise emanating from her now is a guttural whimpering. It's a terrible sound. More than pitiful.

'My girl, my girl,' she whispers over and over. 'What have they done to you?'

Frankie closes her eyes; she can't listen.

Vanessa suddenly lurches forward into the side of Frankie's face. 'If you've hurt her, I'll kill you, you know that don't you? You know that,' she mumbles. 'I lost my beautiful Charlotte and I'm not losing Chloe too. I won't survive it. I can't survive another… Peter… My Peter… I'm all she's got now… *Me*… Do you hear that?' Her breath is hot on Frankie's cheek. 'She'll be so scared if I'm not there. She's scared of the dark, just like Charlotte was. She needs me. She hates the dark. That's when the nightmares come. She has nightmares… things whispering her name—'

Frankie's eyes snap wide. Something falls away inside her. She glances at the handbag at her feet where the corner of the photograph shows the side of Jack's face.

'What's that?' The knife moves down and points. 'That's Jack. That's Jack!' The tip of the knife trembles. 'Why would you have…?'

Vanessa dips to reach for it. The knife tip wavers as her eyes and brain process what's in front of her: the shape of her naked daughter on the bed, the protective curl of the bedcover, the smile on Jack's face as he looks into the camera…

'Jack…' says Vanessa. But there's a moment where they both see something else.

A gasp leaves Vanessa's lips. Frankie stares down.

She hadn't noticed it before.

Over Jack's shoulder is a mirror. Jack isn't smiling into the camera on the wall. It's the wrong wall. Jack is smiling into the lens held by the person taking the photograph; their image is caught in the reflection.

It's Alex.

Alex's eyes don't leave the road.

'You said you were at the party that night,' Frankie says slowly. 'You were with Jack, weren't you? That's what you said.'

Alex looks grimly straight ahead. There's the drone of the engine, the hiss and swish of the tyres, the shriek of rubber wipers against the screen. There's the sound of Vanessa's breath slipping in and out of her lungs as though she's drowning.

'I want. I want…' She can't get her words out. 'I want to know what this photograph means.'

Alex doesn't twitch a muscle. Nothing.

The blade moves to a centimetre above his eye. 'If you don't tell me, this blade is going into your brain.'

It flashes closer to his upper lid.

His mouth opens a little and he licks his lips.

'Start speaking *Alex*.' she sneers. 'I'll give you to the count of—'

'It was a game,' he says suddenly. 'Jack told me it was a game. We were kids really, not adults – you have to understand that.' He wets his lips again. 'Charlotte wanted to be a model, that's what she said. So we started taking photographs, you know, proper photographs, like we'd seen them do on TV. She wanted to send them off to people. We encouraged her… Jack encouraged her… And then the encouraging became more than that… It was more like forcing… He went too far. We went too far.'

Frankie can't look at Vanessa. Her whole body is on fire. She can't hear this. *No Alex. No Alex…*

'Then Jack saw her with Martin at that party. He knew she was upset and thought she'd been telling him what we'd done. Jack confronted her. He said some things to her that night… Awful things. Things that you shouldn't say… She ran off. Jack went after her and then saw her talking to Martin. He followed them down to Martin's boat. I had gone down to the canal after Frankie, but I couldn't find her. Jack saw me. He called me. He'd got Charlotte on the deck; she was in a bad way. I tried to calm things down, but Charlotte wasn't having any of it. She started screaming, saying she would go to the police, that she'd tell everyone what we'd made her do—'

He stops abruptly, taking a breath. Frankie stares out of the window. The road runs smoothly out in front, but she's not seeing it. All that's in front of her is the film-reel of that night: a flick-book cartoon, appalling image after appalling image.

'I saw Charlotte had hurt her head. She kept trying to get up. I tried to help her, but all the time I'd got Jack in my ear… He was going on and on and on about how if she told people, we'd be dead; we'd go to prison. She had evidence, my father would be finished as an MP – the shame of it all – but I said I wasn't going to listen to him, how could I? And then Charlotte lost her balance somehow – I don't know how it happened – and suddenly she was in the water. She was still holding my arm.' A little choke escapes from the back of his throat.

'I tried to pull her out, but I had Jack there, fighting me and fighting – and every time I grabbed her I could feel her getting weaker, until…' The choke becomes a strangled sob. 'I tried to save her! I tried. I really tried!'

'You picked up her hairband,' Frankie hears her voice saying. 'And Jack picked up the necklace. You tidied up between you.'

'We were kids, and we were scared!' Alex's eyes flash round at her, blood-shot and desperate.

'You both *raped* her. You both *murdered* her.'

Vanessa's voice is almost a whisper. Frankie barely hears the words. For one tiny instant her eyes meet Alex's but something else happens.

There's an immediate sensation of heightened reality – a strange light and buzzing in the air that tells her that something terrible is about to unfold. She doesn't see the knife blade move, only a clean brilliant red line lighting up on his neck. The wheel drags and there's a sudden swerve, weaving them into the far lane and a lorry – its headlights on full beam, the horn blaring, the roar of it bearing down on them.

The brilliant white light shows up the dark spatter of blood across the windscreen as Frankie finds her hands reaching out to grope for the wheel. Somewhere she registers the odd feel of it at the wrong angle, the speed, the bellowing thunder of the engine, as she heaves the weight in her hands in the opposite direction, feeling them slip and give.

There's a moment's silence. Then everything begins to slide. The lorry booms past in a claxon wail as they slew wildly into a lay-by – no brakes, no control – and her eyes take in what's right in front of her before her brain can process what's about to happen.

A roadwork sign bears down on them, broken and twisted, its arm-like poles bent: reaching forward. She sees it before she hears it: the splintering crack of glass as the metal smashes through the windshield, buffeting them backwards and spinning them round in an uncontrollable shrieking of tyres and crumpling metal. There's a jaw-slamming judder as the car spins out of control, a whirling merry-go-round of muted colours whizzing past, as a valley: a wide expanse of green, plunging from the side of a bridge, tips dizzyingly towards her—

And then the world goes black.

# *Chapter Thirty-Two*

She remembers some things.

The sensation of someone holding her, rocking her on their lap, their arms around her. She can hear the knit and creak of the mattress as they move gently to and fro.

*Knit. Creak.*

'*Shh*' someone's saying, 'it's okay, you're safe. You can go back to sleep now.'

She can hear the quiet hiss of a water tank filling somewhere and the steady *thrub-thrub* of their heart.

'Hear that, how strong it is?'

She nods into the warmth against her cheek.

'That means I'm never going to leave you.'

She opens her eyes.

For the next few seconds, nothing makes sense. She wonders if this could be heaven.

There are birds twittering somewhere. She can see an expanse of rolling hills and a watery pre-dawn sun that's just flickering on the horizon.

*There was some kind of childhood dream. She knows someone loved her, but she can't remember who.*

Martin's face comes back to her. She remembers his warmth. It was real and solid, and she yearns—

*Crack!*

Her eyes snap open and her body goes rigid. There's no Martin and no dream.

Slowly, she turns her head. The windscreen has gone. There's only a watery carbon sky out there and a cold breeze. Vanessa is lying between the front seats, her head twisted against the dashboard, her cheek and eye socket crushed into a bloody mass, but her mouth is trembling.

'Vanessa,' she croaks, her voice barely a whisper. 'Vanessa… Vanessa… can you—?'

There's an alarming shunt and the world teeters forward.

Frankie's head shoots back and she stares outward into sky. Sky, and nothing but sky. Early morning birds fly in a 'v' shape in the far distance.

She blinks. *What happened? What the hell happened?*

There's a soft squealing of metal against metal. She allows her eyes to track sideways.

Alex.

Only it's not Alex.

There's a space where Alex used to be.

The wind is blowing softly. Spatters of rain begin to patter onto the seat and onto the steering wheel, now buckled and bent. The bonnet is rucked up like an unmade bed. There's a mound of metal on the bonnet, dark, and spread out in the half-light, that appears to be moving. Her eyes close and open again, a dull webbed blur sends the world splintering into weird light. Through the fog, great girders of wires span through the sky in a geometric arch; she guesses they must be on some kind of bridge. Out there, to her right and left are acres of green: trees, bushes, miles and miles of it, and somewhere way below her is the sound of running water.

Nothing moves. Only the mound of metal on the bonnet flaps a little in the breeze. But then it groans. Everything freezes: the sky, her spine, time.

There's a creaking, shifting sound and her eyes flicker warily.

The mound starts to shift and it dawns on her that it isn't metal.

It's Alex.

She doesn't know if she says his name out loud or if it's in her head.

'Frankie?' His voice out there is only just discernible. He coughs a little and tries again. 'Frankie?'

'I'm here,' she says as loudly as she dares. The juddering in her arms and legs won't stop. 'I'm here. I'm okay.'

She has no idea if this is true. She gives her toes the instruction to move – they oblige. And then her fingers, her hands—

There's a sudden jolt and a slither. She grits her teeth and closes her eyes.

*This is it. This is it. This is where it's all over.*

If she stays completely still, if she doesn't move even an inch… She lets herself breathe and allows herself a tiny glimpse towards him.

*No, Alex! No! Don't do that!*

Her heart begins to stutter with shock – *Stop! Stop!*

The car slithers a little, its nose dipping into mid-air. Every movement threatens the delicate balance.

Her heart in in her throat as his weight rocks the car: juddering and shaking the frame from side to side as he tries to crawl his way back. One bloodied hand is extended, the fingernails broken and grimed with red. There's a hissing sound coming from the caved-in hole that was once his mouth.

She suddenly realises what he's saying.

'*Pleeaasssse*,' he hisses. '*Pleeaasssse*.'

The hand inches towards her. She could grab it. She could.

Gingerly, oh so carefully, she forces her elbow to lift and straighten. She will have to reach forward soon. She will have to alter her weight to—

She can feel the slight shift beneath her. Her breath catches. If she moves suddenly…

'Frankie,' he says.

His wrist is there: so close. If she were able to bend, slowly, slowly, and breathe out…

The tips of her fingers extend through the shattered windscreen and touch skin. It's cool, like marble. His cold palm slides under hers and she closes her hand and wills a grip of iron into it. *Don't let go. Just don't let go—*

'Frankie—'

Her eyes come up to lock onto his.

He's staring straight at her.

'All you have to do is hold on,' she says. 'That's all. I've got you, Alex, I've got you.'

His gaze locks onto hers. It's pleading, she can see that. She can only imagine what's down there in that drop – the rocks, the stones, the water; she can only imagine the fall, the moments of knowing, absolutely, what the end will be…

There's a muffled moan behind her. She looks down at Vanessa. Her breathing is laboured now: hard and rasping. The moan comes again. It's not Vanessa.

Something begins to dawn. She looks again at Alex. His eyes have gone from pleading to terrified.

The cries get a little louder. There's a thump from the boot.

'Chloe's in the car.'

It's not a question, it's a realisation. Alex's face begins to change.

'She hit her head,' he pants. His tongue slithers over bloodied lips. 'She wasn't supposed to… I was going to talk to her, persuade her…'

She can feel the ache in her fingers, the thrumming drive of pain in her shoulder socket.

'You hurt my daughter. You hurt my child.'

'I didn't mean to, Frankie. I did it all for you. I've done everything for you. You have to believe that – I wanted to put right what I did. I wanted to give you back the thing you lost.'

She can feel the muscles in his hand loosening; he's getting weaker. She tightens her own. There's a bang and a grating sound somewhere beneath her feet as though metal is warping. A siren wail in the distance whines through the air. Behind her, she can hear her daughter sobbing quietly. She's in the darkness all alone, too scared to cry out. Her heart begins to bleed with anguish.

'Frankie.'

She looks up into Alex's pain-filled eyes.

'Let me go,' he whispers.

'No… I can't…' The crack and buckle of hinge and joint gets louder. 'No, Alex, no—'

But he opens his hand: his fingers spanning wide. It's more difficult for her to keep a hold.

'Alex, please don't do this.'

'Save your daughter and save yourself,' he whispers again. 'I'm sorry, Frankie.'

The hand twists. His arm and face are there one second, and then suddenly they're gone.

There's a moment.

*Dear Jesus*. The wailing of the sirens gets louder. All around her, birds are beginning to gather on the bridge wires, their chatter filling the air, drowning out the sobs that rasp in her throat.

'Chloe?' she calls out, choking through her tears. There's silence. 'Chloe?'

Somewhere deep inside the boot, she can hear her crying urgently now.

She gathers herself. She has to be strong; she's all Chloe's got right now.

'Chloe. This is Frankie… I'm the one who—'

The car starts to rock. There's a squeal from the boot. She braces her feet either side of the footwell with a great shuddering intake of breath, ramming herself back in the seat, praying that her weight is enough. The rocking stops.

'Chloe,' she says steadily. 'Can you hear me? I'm Frankie. I'm the one who—' She is going to say 'saved you', but realises there are so many other things she's done. She takes a big, deep, breath.

'I'm telling you Chloe, that whatever happens, I'm right here with you.'

There's no sound from the back.

'Chloe?'

Does she imagine it, or is there a tiny shift?

'Can you hear me?'

A tiny, tiny muffled voice comes from behind her. 'Yes, I can hear you.'

'Are you hurt?' She closes her eyes. The horror of Alex's face swims back at her. She immediately shuts it out.

'Only my head: just a little bit.'

There's a sickening creak and a sudden pitch forwards and Chloe starts to scream. The sky tilts alarmingly, wavering with a sudden view of tree-tops and rushing water as the car begins to see-saw. Frankie clutches at the seat, whispering prayers, begging, pleading.

'I'm scared,' Chloe whimpers. 'Please do something, Frankie.'

Vanessa moans pitifully.

'Okay, okay…' She looks round. 'Okay… I've got this. I'm going to come and get you, right? You stay still, now Chloe, yes? You stay completely still.'

Gingerly, her fingers feeling for even the minutest movement, she reaches around for the safety belt. The catch clicks open and very gently, she lets it go. Her body resists even shifting an inch. She glances back. She has no idea what she should do. This feels like immediate suicide.

Vanessa is sprawled between the seats; there's no way round her. The blood bubbles from between her lips and her breathing rattles.

The car slithers with a jolt and there's the sound of stones falling. Chloe yelps in fear but Frankie speaks over her.

'Listen to me Chloe. Just listen, yeah?' she soothes. 'I'm going to tell you something now, and I want you to be the bravest you've ever been, right? Can you hear me?'

'Yes—' There's a whisper.

'Your mum is with me. She's okay, but she's banged her head.' She closes her eyes. *Where the hell are the emergency services?*

There's a whimper from the back.

'No, no, she's going to be fine. The emergency people are on their way, and she's going to be absolutely fine, can you hear me, Chloe?'

She has a terrible sudden thought that the sirens weren't for them... Her eyes widen. Maybe no one even knows they're here...

One eye pivots to where Vanessa's broken face lies crumpled against the dash. *Please let that not be true*, she begs whatever gods might be listening. Chloe is weeping harder now. *She's only a kid, just a kid who wants her mum*. The sound goes on and on.

'Chloe... Chloe,' she soothes, but at the same time a sudden, fierce instinct kicks in: an urgent and absolute drive. 'You keep listening to me, right?' If it's literally the very last thing she does, she's going to hold her daughter.

Slipping her hand around the side of the passenger seat, she feels for the seat release lever, and then, by the tiniest degrees, she begins to tip the seat back until it's lying flat.

'Can you hear me, Chloe? Yeah?... I want you to do something and it's very important.' She begins to squirm her shoulders up towards the headrest, until she feels it dig into her spine.

There's a hushed, frightened snivelling.

'I want you to look all around, and I want you to tell me if you can feel any loops or catches or anything like that. I want to be able to get to you, you see, and I think the seat might drop forward if we can find the way to release it. Could you look for me? Could you do that?'

There's a rustling sound and Frankie can hear Chloe moving her hand across the rear of the seat.

'There's a tab thing... Like, material stuff.'

'Yes!' Frankie breaths out. 'That's what I was hoping for. Can you pull it?'

There's a plucking sound and scratch of fabric and then a sudden *pock!* as the seat jerks forward. There, in the darkness, two round eyes blink up at her from the gloom.

Shielding Chloe from the sight of Vanessa, Frankie uses all her strength, easing herself onto her side and extending an arm until her fingers reach through the gap. There's a sudden warmth as she feels skin touching hers, then there's palm against palm, heat against heat, as she pulls herself over the back seat and into the gap, closer and closer until their foreheads are almost touching. There's the sound of a helicopter overhead.

'I've got you, I've got you,' she whispers, seeing a tiny smile of relief flicker across Chloe's face. 'Your mum's here, I'm here, we're all okay. Won't be long now, they'll come and get us soon, you just—'

The car begins to slide.

She can feel the dig and pinch of Chloe's fingernails in the flesh of her arm as she grips tighter. There's a bumping squeal, the clatter of stones and shale falling away as the undercarriage begins to grind – a deafening grating shudder that runs through her neck and down her spine. She can taste blood in her mouth.

She begins to gabble, shouting louder and louder. 'Chloe, Chloe, I'm here with you – I'm here… I know you're scared, but you don't have to be because I've got you now, right? I've got you.'

Tears threaten to overwhelm her. 'You're *not* alone,' she whispers fiercely. 'I'm not leaving you.'

There's a booming sound and a sudden bang that shakes their whole world – she knows this is it. She puts her face close to Chloe's to block everything out and squeezes her eyes tight shut. An almighty judder starts up that shakes and convulses them to the core. She knows they can't hold on. She knows this is the moment where—

The car jerks.

A gust of wind whistles and a sudden brilliance blooms all around as the whole back of the car opens in a great yawn of stark lights and people calling and radios jabbering.

'We've got you. We've got you,' a woman's voice says. She hears the rustle of uniforms as hands touch her face.

'Can you tell me your name?' she says. 'Mine's Clare, and we're going to get you out of here. You just need to hold on.'

She opens her eyes, hearing the *whop-whop-whop* of a helicopter and the roar of an engine. Great lobster claw hooks have clanked into place all around the bumper, holding them fast. She looks up. There is Chloe, her daughter, next to her. Her hand is still clasped tightly in hers. She doesn't think she can let go – ever. She looks up at Clare. 'I'm Frankie. There's a woman injured in the front,' she shouts over the din.

'Yep, don't you worry, we've got her, Frankie,' Clare smiles. 'You're all going to be fine.'

Chloe's saying something, but Frankie can barely hear her. She pushes her hair back out of her face.

'…me,' she makes out.

'Sorry?' She brings the fingers up to her mouth and kisses them.

'I said, thank you for coming to find me.'

Her heart and mind and gut all melt; she might dissolve at any minute.

'I wasn't ever going to leave you. I promised you that a long time ago.' She tries to stop her voice from breaking. 'I broke my promise once, but I'll never do it again.'

And then the tears come.

# *Chapter Thirty-Three*

There are a bunch of kids playing with a Frisbee. Their shouts and screams echo through the park. Frankie sits watching the sparrows gathering around her feet; they are tiny little engines of need. They never give up.

*It was this park. It could have been this bench.*

It would be weird if it was. She looks to her right and left. It could have been that one, or that. She remembers crying. She remembers a man perching at the other end, nervous to sit too close, and asking if she was okay.

Alex.

His goodness and his badness in equal amounts.

Then she remembers Jack.

Laughing as they played video games together on the settee. Jack finding her a place to stay and smuggling out baby things.

His kindness and his cruelty: half and half.

She thinks of Charlotte. She imagines her final moments; her jaw tightening at the thought of what she went through. A young girl with two men she should have been able to trust. How she would have begged and suffered, clawing at Alex's arms, desperately fighting for those last few moments of life. How those men thought they could do with her as they pleased.

She closes her eyes, sickened. She had been there that night; she heard her, she saw her, but did nothing to help.

She's no better than them, really. All she could do was run away. She's been running away all her life.

But she's not going to run now.

The bench shakes a little as someone sits down.

'Hello, you,' a voice says.

She turns to look at Martin. She's not sure now if he's handsome or ugly. It doesn't matter; his eyes are the same eyes she got lost in, all those years ago.

'Thank you for contacting me.' He sounds a little formal and unsure.

'I heard they'd let you out.'

'Thank you for everything you did for me, Frankie. I can't imagine what you went through with Alex.' He looks at the ground, his fingers fumbling awkwardly. 'I'm so sorry.'

She twitches a painful shrug.

'But are you managing okay?'

'I'm getting there.' She flickers a tiny smile.

'I tried ringing to let you know about my release, but when you didn't answer, I tried your work.'

'Ah. That.' She raises a sardonic eyebrow. 'It's fair to say I'm officially on sick leave, or annual leave… Or, possibly, the precursor-to-being-sacked leave. I don't think I'll be allowed to work with kids anymore, do you?' She smiles grimly. 'But only time will tell.'

'And Vanessa?'

She goes to answer but her phone pings and she dips into her pocket.

'Speak of the devil, she says she'll be here in five.'

'And she's definitely okay with this?' He rubs the palms of his hands together. They stutter back and forth.

Frankie puts her own on top and he stops.

She looks at him. 'Even from her hospital bed she was asking to speak to the police. She wanted to tell them everything she'd done. We have no idea what's going to happen, but I'll stand up for her, whatever it is.'

Martin stares down at her hands and shakes his head slowly. 'She's incredibly brave.'

'She's got guts, that's for sure.' Frankie nods. 'I went to see her a lot while she was recovering in hospital. She's received a lot of help. She feels so guilty over what Charlotte went through; she thinks she allowed it to happen. She's apologised to me: she hates herself – then there's you...' She shakes her head.

'But Frankie, no one could have known about Jack and Alex, could they? That's not down to Vanessa. They stayed away from each other all those years and I was never supposed to come out of prison. If Jack's plan had come off and I'd died, no one would have ever been any the wiser.'

Frankie blinks sadly. 'Do you think my relationship with Alex was calculated too?' She looks away to where the kids are shouting and laughing. 'Was I just another person who had to be managed and that was the best way of doing it?'

'I think, in the beginning, Alex was manipulated by Jack just like everyone else, but I believe Alex truly loved you, Frankie. I think he was a man who was haunted by what he'd done. I think it drove him insane.' He glances up. 'Is this them?'

Two figures are walking slowly down the path. One is leaning a little on the other; their arms are linked.

'Get ready to be delighted,' Frankie raises a hand, smiling. 'Chloe is a gorgeous girl.'

Martin swallows nervously.

'There's no need to be apprehensive. I've talked to them. You'll see.'

Reaching up and around her neck, she unhooks the necklace and gathers it up. Martin watches her. 'The memories don't disturb you, then?'

Frankie smiles. 'It was given with love from Vanessa to Charlotte, and it was given with love from Vanessa to me. Someone broke it for a little while, that's all, and now it's fixed again.'

'Is that like us, do you think?' he smiles.

'Everything is possible.' She gives him a look.

'What are you going to do with it?' He stares down at her palm.

'I'm going to give it to Chloe,' she smiles. 'If she'll have it.'

The figures draw closer. The younger one waves.

'Hell, she looks like you,' he whispers.

'But she has your eyes.'

'Our daughter,' he sighs as though he can't quite believe it.

They both stand, silently, listening to Chloe's excited chattering. She's not sure what his sigh is about: sadness maybe? Regret? There's no point in either; there's only the present and the future.

'Yes, I used to think of people like that: who they belong to, who they're related to.' She sees the sunlight catching in Chloe's hair. 'But now I think it's much bigger than that: it's about who loves us. That's what makes people ours.'

'I suppose it is.'

She touches the necklace. 'There's only one person that Chloe needs to belong to.'

'Who's that?' Martin goes to take her hand and she lets him.

'To herself.'

# *A letter from Elena*

Thank you so much for choosing to read *Keep My Secrets*. It was a story that came to me unexpectedly, and not at all the story I planned to write!

It started out as being a psychological thriller about a woman who was being stalked – but I hadn't worked out why that should be happening, and I didn't know who this mysterious woman was. Then, one night, I was driving home in the dark when a car zoomed up behind me: too close and too fast. In that instant, Frankie came to me; a woman being chased by shadows but also being haunted by the darkness of her past life.

This notion of how we reinvent ourselves, fascinates me. People fascinate me. I think we all re-make ourselves over the years, until the person we present to people today is quite different from the person we presented to the world, say, ten or twenty years ago. But what would happen if our old life and our new life collided? Are there events from our past lives that we'd really prefer to forget?

Hence, we all keep bits of ourselves secret, and it's those well-hidden gems that makes the work of a writer so intriguing.

If you have any thoughts about this book, I would love to hear them via a retailer review, or contact me via Facebook or Twitter.

www.facebook.com/elenawilkesthrillers
www.twitter.com/elenathrillers

Acknowledgments

I owe a huge debt of gratitude to Keshini Naidoo at Hera Books for supporting and encouraging me to write this book in the first place. There's also a massive thank you to Jennie for her eagle-eyed editing. I have no idea where she finds the patience to sort through the inevitable bloopers when the 'what-happened-when-to-who-and-why?' goes awry. What a woman!

But of course, I have to say thank you to Amy Beashel, Ko Porteous, and Susie-Sue Bassett, who are my support and mainstay through this mad writing journey, and indeed, through life. Love you loads.